HEAVEN'S THUNDER

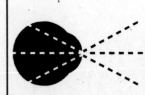

This Large Print Book carries the
Seal of Approval of N.A.V.H.

HEAVEN'S THUNDER

A COLORADO SAGA

MARY ELLEN DENNIS

THORNDIKE PRESS

A part of Gale, Cengage Learning

GALE
CENGAGE Learning®

Detroit • New York • San Francisco • New Haven, Conn • Waterville, Maine • London

GALE
CENGAGE Learning·

LIBRARY OF CONGRESS CATALOGING-IN-PUBLICATION DATA

Dennis, Mary Ellen.
  Heaven's thunder : a Colorado saga / by Mary Ellen Dennis.
    p. cm. — (Thorndike Press large print historical fiction)
  ISBN-13: 978-1-4104-4196-6 (hardcover)
  ISBN-10: 1-4104-4196-2 (hardcover)
    1. Colorado—History—1876–1950—Fiction. 2. Large type books. I. Title.
  PS3554.I368H43 2011b
  813'.54—dc22   2011028081

Published in 2011 by arrangement with Tekno Books.

Printed in the United States of America
1 2 3 4 5 6 7 15 14 13 12 11

This saga is dedicated to librarians, in particular the staff of the Penrose Library in Colorado Springs. I did every bit of my research the old-fashioned way. I read books.

ACKNOWLEDGMENTS

Edward Gibbons once said: "I was never less alone than while by myself," words of wisdom for an author who spends a great deal of time with only his or her characters to provide companionship. However, I maintain that few authors can write a book alone. I certainly can't.

Therefore, I'd like to thank the following for their incredible generosity: Alice Duncan, Lillian Stewart Carl, Annette Mahon, Mary Jo Putney, Sherry-Anne Jacobs, Terey Ramin, Garda Parker, Mary Ellen Johnson, Fran Baker and Lynn Whitacre.

The framework of my story has been constructed from many sources, but three books were exceptionally helpful in specialized areas: *Newport in the Rockies* by Marshall Sprague, 1961; *Out of the Depths* by Barron B. Beshoar, 1942; and *The Negro Cowboys* by Philip Durham, 1983.

I could never have written *Heaven's Thun-*

der without the encouragement — and input — from my best friend, Gordon Aalborg.

The strong-neck'd steed,
being tied unto a tree,
Breaketh his rein,
and to her straight goes he.
Imperiously he leaps,
he neighs, he bounds,
And now his woven girths
he breaks asunder;
The bearing earth with
his hard hoof he wounds,
Whose hollow womb
resounds like heaven's thunder;
The iron bit he crusheth
'tween his teeth,
Controlling what he
was controlled with.
— William Shakespeare, *Venus and Adonis*

ONE

Colorado: 1893

"She were named for a cow."

Seventeen-year-old Bertha Smith gazed at the paying gent who filled her rocking chair. "You're funning me, Per'fessor."

"No, I ain't," he said. "A cow wandered 'cross our crick an' took one hell of a spill."

"Poor critter." Clothed in chemise and patched petticoat, Bertha perched on the edge of her mattress. Left-handed, she clutched a wooden egg in her right hand. A crib girl didn't have to darn socks, or even listen good, but the miners forked out extra for those knacks.

"Yep, that damnfool cow broke her leg. A rancher seen the cow fall. Guess what he called the crick, Blueberry?"

She stared with her large eyes whose color had led to her nickname. "Reckon you'll have to tell me, sir."

"He called it *Cripple* Crick."

11

Bertha rose, stretched, and handed Per'fessor a bottle of beer. He stuffed a small pouch filled with gold chips down the front of her bodice. The pouch felt warm against her breasts, and the gold handily recompensed her for the half hour atop her mattress, even though she'd have to scrub the sheet beneath her quilt, and she hated laundering almost as much as she hated sewing.

Per'fessor tilted the brown bottle, gulped and swallowed. Bertha thought his neck looked like a turkey's. He wiped his mouth on his sleeve and said, "There was this cowpuncher, Bobby Womack. Bobby named the place where your crib now sets, called it Poverty Gulch. Then he found him some gold. Know what happened next?"

"Tell me." Bertha returned to her former position and again plied her needle.

"Bobby sold his claim for five hundred dollars, a spit in the bucket."

"Why'd Bobby do that?"

"He were drunk an' folks funned him for braggin' 'bout gold. Nobody believed him."

Bertha looked down at her wooden egg, pictured a chicken coop, heard Geordie's voice: *Had me a dream what told me to leave. I held a shiny nugget in my hand. Gold, big as one of them hen eggs.*

"You promised you'd come back," she whispered.

"Did you say something, girl?"

"No, sir."

"You look like you seen a ghost."

"I, uh, spied a spider creepy-crawling 'cross the floor," she fibbed. "Big hairy critter."

"I'll stomp it for ya. Nope, better not. My foot'll get gooey." Per'fessor's brow puckered. "Where was I?"

"Bobby sold his claim cheap," she said, sewing faster, trying to expunge the image of a gooey spider.

"Yep. The whiskey made him dumber'n that ol' cow what broke her leg. Womack sold his claim to Julias Myers and Horace Bennett." Per'fessor paused to glub-glub his beer. "That's why our streets're called Myers an' Bennett. Guess what happened next?"

"Ouch!" Bertha pricked her finger and dropped the egg.

"I'll tell ya." Per'fessor slanted a glance toward his boots, which slumped like dozing sentries against the shanty's front door. "Don't stop sewin'. My toes're as cold as a privy seat in wintertime. Them Denver gents went an' named the *town* Cripple Crick. She were named for a cow. What d'ya think of that?"

"I think you tell a good story, sir."

Per'fessor stood, strutted like a rooster. "It ain't that I can story good," he said with a snaggletoothed grin. "You listen good."

I want you to listen good, said the voice in her head. *I'm traveling to Colorado to find me some gold.*

Bertha handed her guest his mended sock, replaced the egg in the bottom of her leather-thong chest, and swallowed a sigh. The first time she'd heard the Cripple Creek tale, she'd thought: *poor cow.* But after she'd heard it over and over, poor cow had begat poor Bertha.

Oh, she realized full well what it meant to be crippled, Bertha did, because her own left foot turned sideways. Her pelvis jutted, her spine curved, and she could foretell bad weather 'cause she hurt real bad whenever rain or snow threatened.

Apart from her foot, she was pretty, even though she believed pretty was as pretty does and what she did wasn't pretty. Yet men seemed to favor her breasts — unless tightly fettered, they jiggled when she walked — and she'd been told her rounded hips and "wasp waist" were the fashion.

Some said her eyes looked like a cloudless

summer sky. A poetic youth claimed her eyes looked like "the trim on the plates and saucers in the dining room of the Continental Hotel." But Geordie put it best. He said her eyes were the color of the wild blueberries that grew in the deepest woods, and he'd called her Berry.

Bertha closed her eyes. Per'fessor had left for the Buckhorn saloon on Myers Avenue, but his crippled-cow account had brought back hissy whispers from her past. Memories of a room above a Denver saloon haunted her. Over and over she heard the sound of breaking glass. Over and over she saw an ugly giant — and the wrathful face of her brother.

"Berry, gather your things together," Geordie had said. "We're leaving."

She had heard those very same words a few months before, when the sound of breaking glass had been the cackle of chickens.

Behind her closed eyelids, Bertha pictured the West Kansas farm and her pa, looking like Moses on the Mount, his staff a hoe.

Her mother lived inside a picture frame.

Bertha had been born on July fourth, 1876. It was Centennial Day, but nobody on the farm cared about the American

Revolution a hundred years prior to that windy Kansas afternoon except ten-year-old Geordie. He lit homemade firecrackers to honor Bertha and the United States of America, shortly after Jubilation Smith cut the umbilical cord, said, "Shit, it's a girl," and returned to his plowing.

Following the difficult labor and delivery, Bertha's mama rose from her soiled bedding, cooked dinner for her husband, christened her daughter with tepid water from the well, changed the bloody bed linen, curled up again on the mattress, and died as the sun rose the next morning.

Bertha was fed and clothed, but she had a feeling Pa wished she were a mule. Or a tick on a mule. Or a sunspot on a tick on a mule.

In 1887, the preacher's wife told Bertha about something called Christmas. So she tied her only hair ribbon to a clump of pigweed, found her dead mama's handkerchief, and sewed Baby Jesus. Then she laughed and cried when Geordie gave her a baby turkey. She named it Noah. For several months she brushed its wing bar and crooned hymns. But the name turned out to be prophetic. Noah died in a thunderstorm. Geordie said Noah was trampled by the other dithered fowl. Pa said the turkey swallered too much rain and drowned.

16

Geordie plucked feathers, Pa chomped Noah's drumstick, Bertha threw up inside the privy, and that was the end of Christmas.

A month after Bertha had silently celebrated her fifteenth birthday, on a dusty August afternoon, she stood outside the coop. She flung feed like rainy grain, reaching from the gathered apron that covered her dress.

Bertha owned two dresses: gingham for summer and gray serge for winter. Her body had developed rich curves and the cotton fabric stretched across her bosom. She had inherited her mama's black skirt and white high-necked blouse with lace trim, but those were freshly washed and ironed for church.

"Come to say good-bye," said Geordie.

"Here, chick. Chick, chick, chick."

"I'm twenty-five, sissy, and I ain't hardly been off this place. Don't you be shutting your ears like Pa's stubborn mule. I'm traveling to Colorado to find me some gold."

Bertha drew circles in the dirt with her bare toes.

"I promise I'll come back. When I'm rich with gold, I'll bring you jewels. Blue stones the color of your eyes and red doodads plucked from the color of a setting sun and white sparkly gems that look like nighttime stars."

"Here, chick. Chick, chick, chick."

"Please give me your blessing."

"Gotta feed these here chicks then serve up dinner. I baked buttermilk biscuits."

"Had a dream what told me to leave. I held a shiny nugget in my hand. Gold, big as one of them hen eggs. In my dream, a voice said 'Time to git, George Smith.' "

Her lips quivered as she said, "False prophets will come to you in sheep's clothing, Geordie, but inside they are wolves. Did a false prophet come in the night? Did he wear sheep's wool?"

"Taught you reading and writing from the Bible and now you throw sheep and wolves in my face." He reached out and wiped away her tears. "Aw, Berry."

"Biscuits're fluffy and there's ham. I cut the fat off. You don't hanker to eat fat. Heard you say it's like chewing a piggy's wet shirt collar."

"All right, you can tag along."

Her eyes lit up like candle flames, but her full lips still quivered. "If Pa catches us, he'll whup me good. It pleasures Pa to pull down my drawers and belt my be-hind. I saw his face once and it made me all goose-bumpy, so I told the preacher, but the preacher says Pa's in the right 'cause he's my pa."

"That preacher don't know his ass from

his . . . sermon. Why ain't you told me 'bout Pa?"

She cringed at his angry tone. "I done something wrong, Geordie?"

"Lord, no!" He took a deep breath. "Berry, gather your things together. We're leaving."

Hand and hand, brother and sister walked away from the farm. It took them seven weeks to trudge the almost four hundred miles to Denver, stopping along the way to work for their food, repairing a fence here, whitewashing a house there. At night they huddled out in the open. Sometimes they were given the hospitality of a barn or hayloft. Days were soft and yellow, and Geordie said the air smelled like sun-dried clothes, but nights were touched with autumn's chill.

When they reached Denver, Geordie found employment working for a man named Tiny who owned a saloon.

"A merry heart makes a cheerful countenance," Geordie told Bertha the second night, after he had swept the sawdust-strewn barroom floor, emptied spittoons, washed down privies, and hauled drunk gents to their horses.

"Your countenance ain't so cheery," she said, thinking how her brother was aging

19

faster than the rose-patterned wallpaper that bedecked their walls. The roses had once been pink but now they looked like Noah's denuded skin before he got cooked.

"This ain't what I dreamed," Geordie confessed a week later, entering the closet-sized room they shared and sitting on the edge of their bed.

"It ain't so bad." Steamy fingers seemed to reach out and pinch Bertha's plump cheeks as she scrubbed at her gingham dress, pushing it against the side of the wash tub. Geordie's other shirt soaked in the same tub.

"You never leave this here room, 'cept to use the privy and lug water upstairs. You ain't even said a howdy to the others. You bake Tiny's bread in the dead of night and spend the day reading Mama's Bible."

"There's a flower growing, right there in the woody walk." Bertha waved her dripping hands outside their one small window. "Come look at my flower, Geordie. It's got no sunshine, nor water, but it's growing just the same. I've seen it nod howdy."

He joined her at the window. "That ain't no flower, Berry. That there's a weed."

After two weeks Geordie considered moving on. He had planned to stay the winter, but Berry didn't belong amidst the drunks and whores. She was like that weed stuck between the planks of the sidewalk, trying to grow without water or sunshine.

Inside the saloon it was hard to tell day from night. Geordie sang "I'm Captain Jinks of the Horse Marines" as he tossed a chunk of pyrite from one hand to the other. He knew the nugget had no value — the miners called it fool's gold — but he kept it as a talisman.

Tiny sopped up the last of a dozen fried eggs with a loaf of Berry's fresh-baked bread. "Dora left for the gold fields this morning and we're short some girls," he said. "Can your wife serve or sing?"

"She ain't my wife." Geordie stared at his boss. Tiny's beard encircled a neck the size of a tree trunk and he was seven feet tall in his boots. Even sitting, his stomach spread like a wagon wheel. "She's my sister."

"Well, fancy that." Tiny's eyes looked like shoe buttons. His nose flared at the base and tufts of hair, like pieces of tumbleweed, grew from his nostrils. His ears were so big they looked like the flaps on a knapsack, and his hands could heft twelve steins. "Can she serve or sing?"

"She can sing." The saloon had a raised platform behind a tinkling piano, which gave the performing girls some protection

21

from drunk customers. And if his sister earned enough coins, they could leave for the gold fields that much sooner.

Bertha was horrified. "Sing in front of all them men? I can't."

"Sure you can, Weed. They ain't listening for your voice. Just move around and smile. Bartender told me 'bout some lady named Little Egypt. She twists her belly" — he demonstrated — "and folks call her dance the coochie-coochie."

"Maybe I can dance coochie-coochie, Geordie, but I ain't never sung nothing 'cept hymns. And don't call me Weed!"

"The piano player gave me words writ on paper. All you gotta do is learn 'em proper. You can wear Dora's dress. It's right here. Ain't it purty? Red and yella. As yella as your hair."

Bertha's face lit up like sunshine after a storm. "My hair ain't yella, it's black."

"Why, 'tis holy truth. Black as the preacher's carriage. Hard to tell in this dark room."

"Must I sing, Geordie?"

"Yep. When you're real good, the men throw coins. Do try. Please?"

Dora's dress was loose at the hips and waist, but it strained the seams on top so that Bertha's breasts threatened to rise and overflow like loaves of bread cooked with too much yeast. The red-and-yellow skirt swirled above her knees, gathering into a bustle where exaggerated daisy petals flopped backwards. Black net stockings sheathed her legs.

Tiny had decided she'd sing in the afternoon for practice then join the other performers at the highly touted nighttime show.

Her twisted foot and curved spine made her graceless but the customers didn't seem to mind, drawn to her bodice as she lifted her arms toward heaven and wrung her hands. "Human hearts and looks deceive me," she sang.

Watching from the back of the room, Geordie grinned. His little weed of a sister wriggled her flounce-covered bottom like a friendly sparrow at a birdbath. She sang her hymn to the tune of "After The Ball," and despite her bouncing breasts and husky voice, her innocent joy stilled the men's usual obscenities. Everybody stared beyond the smoking stage lanterns, and even the gamblers soon forgot their games.

"This here," said Bertha, rotating her tummy in ever widening circles, "is called the coochie-coochie."

A man yelled, "Seen Little Egypt hootchy-kootchy in Chicago. Swear this here young

23

'un's better."

A shower of coins, like heavy chicken feed, rained upon the platform boards. Bertha merrily limped and pranced about the stage. The lusty crowd roared its approval. When the applause died down, she collected her coins, left the stage, ascended the stairs and entered her room. Struggling to get free from her tight bodice, she managed to wriggle the material down to her waist.

"That was fine, dearie." Tiny stepped out from the room's corner.

It was late afternoon, the sun still shining, but with only one wee window for light the room stayed gloomy, so Bertha hadn't seen Tiny before. With a gasp, she grabbed a blanket and held it against her breasts.

Tiny licked his lips and pushed her gently but firmly onto the bed.

He looks like Goliath, she thought, sitting up. "What are you doing, Mr. Tiny?"

"You pleasure me good and I let you keep all your wages."

"Geordie didn't say . . . I didn't know . . ." Rising, she scooped her coins from the top of the bureau and thrust her hand toward Tiny.

He groped at his trouser buttons. "I don't want your coins, girl. I want you."

"But I don't want you."

24

His eyes squinted like a bag of nails. He twisted her wrist above the bureau until she dropped the coins. Then he pushed her, this time roughly, onto the bed.

She screamed.

"Touch her and I'll kill you!" Geordie stood just inside the doorway. "Berry, gather your things together. We're leaving."

"No, you ain't." Tiny's voice was a guttural growl. "I thought her your wife so she's been living here outta the goodness of my heart. Now I mean to git paid."

"I've been working for both of us and you know it!"

"Git outta here, boy!"

Geordie looked around for a weapon. He dug in his pocket until he encountered his lucky nugget, then threw the small piece of rock at Tiny.

Instead of being felled, the giant simply ran his thumb across the scratch on his forehead. With an ugly grimace, he picked Geordie up by the shoulders and hurled him against the wall. Geordie crumpled like a concertina, bleeding from a gash in his scalp. A bright trickle of blood dripped from his nose and mouth and formed a crimson puddle.

Scrambling across the room on her knees, Bertha tugged at her brother's shirt. "Geordie, open your eyes and say something. You can call my purty flower a weed. You can call *me* Weed."

Tiny yanked at a scalloped mirror attached to the scarred bureau. He held the glass above Geordie's slack lips. "Shite, he ain't breathing."

"Geordie, move your fingers and wave howdy."

"Bejesus, you idiot, he's dead!"

"He can't be dead. He promised —"

"Shut up!" Tiny flung the mirror at an opposite wall, where it shattered with an explosive sound.

Bertha crawled backwards. Splinters of glass tore her black net stockings, leaving small gashes in her knees. Unaware of the pain, her fingers closed around a jagged shard the size of a long comb. Standing, arms flailing, she attacked Tiny.

"Stopitbitch!" The howl emerged as one word.

"You killed my brother, I'll kill you back!"

Tiny pushed her away, changed his mind, and stepped toward her. His boot caught in Geordie's legs. Teetering back and forth, he fell rump-ward, landing with a thud that shook the floorboards. He tried to rise, but his hands slipped on a patch of Geordie's blood.

Bertha carved a smile across Tiny's throat, then deepened the smile with another swipe of her shard.

Tiny sputtered, gurgled, lay motionless, his neck sliced like a Christmas turkey.

Bertha placed two of her coins on Geordie's eyes. Tiny stared toward the ceiling, sightless, but Bertha chose to leave his eyes open, unprotected.

"I'll feed the chicks and cook piggy meat," she cried, shoving her few pieces of clothing into the carpetbag satchel that held her mother's ruby earbobs and Bible. Reflexively, she added her brother's money pouch and the coins from her performance.

I forgot to bury Geordie, she thought, dropping her satchel and turning round and round in small circles. Spying her brother's lucky nugget, she scooped it up, fell to her knees, and dug at the floorboards.

A woman's high-pitched laughter sounded from the hallway. Bertha ceased her frantic motions, thinking how she had to get away fast. She had killed a man. They would kill her back. In her head, she heard Geordie's voice: *Run, Berry!*

She replaced her ruined stockings with cotton stockings. She tried to reattach her dance dress bodice, but couldn't close it without help, so she thrust her feet inside

27

her shoes and slipped her gingham gown over her head. Ignoring the back buttons, she fled.

After descending the staircase, she awkwardly rebounded off tables and chairs. Somebody yelled, "Coochie, girl!" Others joined in. "Coochie-coochie, coochie-coochie."

Pasting a smile on her face, Bertha rotated her tummy. At the same time, she maneuvered toward the entrance. Then she curtsied and limped through the swinging front doors.

Run, Berry!

Her feet lurched over the planked sidewalk, her left leg pivoting in an arc. Rounding the corner, she halted, unable to take another step. Her legs crinked, her sides stitched, her bosom heaved, and she couldn't seem to get enough air.

"I'm snuffed out, Geordie," she whimpered.

As she stared at the ground, she felt a warm breath on her back where the dress material hung open. Dropping her satchel, she crumpled to her knees and began to pray.

A deep voice said, "I ain't the devil, child."

She heard two words — devil child. She scrambled to her feet, made an about-face, and stared at the man clothed in a red plaid shirt, blue denim overalls, and a floppy brown hat that matched the color of his curly beard. Next to the man stood a grayish-brown animal whose fuzzy ears pitched forward as if it favored Bertha's psalm. The critter brayed, pushed its nose toward her, and this time its warm breath misted her gingham bodice.

"Why, it's a mule," she gasped.

"Clementine ain't no mule," said the man. "A mule's the get of a female horse and a male ass, and it can't make babies. Clem's a burro."

The man kept talking, but Bertha didn't hear him. She pictured a room filled with Tiny, and her hand closed around an invisible shard of mirror.

The burro hee-hawed.

That sound, so different from Tiny's growl, cleared the shadowy saloon images from her head. Opening her fingers, she stared at the blood stains. "Might there be someplace close by where I can wash my hands, sir?"

The man pointed toward a trough. She limped over to it and plunged her hands beneath the water's scummy top layer.

"Dry 'em off on Clementine, child."

Bertha stroked the burro's neck. "She sure

29

did scare me."

"Not half as bad as you scared us, rounding that corner like you was being blown by a kite-wind. You never even seen me and him come after you."

"Him? Clementine's a girl's name, ain't it?"

"Yep. M'wife named him for a mining song. Clementine don't mind none, long as he's got food and kindness. Names don't matter."

"Why'd you call me a devil child?"

"Huh?" The man scratched behind his ear with one hand, behind Clementine's ear with the other. Then his face brightened. "I said I weren't the devil, child, though m'wife might disagree. I do beg your pardon for Clem. He's never seen a gal's nekkid back and thought it might be fun to snuffle skin."

She felt sudden heat bake her cheeks as she reached behind her back for her gown's open buttons. The man offered to help. She flinched but forced herself to stand still. The man stopped at her waistband, unable to fasten the last few buttons.

"Lordy," she exclaimed. "I disremembered to take my dance dress off. Geordie'd say I put caterpillar skin atop butterfly wings."

Wriggling the dance costume free from

beneath her gingham skirt, she kicked it
away. It heaped on the walk, yella as Geordie's lucky nugget, red as Tiny's blood. She
waited for the bearded man to ask questions and tensed her tired body to run, praying her crimpy foot would support the attempt, but the man scooped up the dress
and stuffed it inside his knapsack.

"Why'd you do that, sir?"

"No use letting good cloth go to waste.
I'll hand it over to m'wife."

"Won't she wonder where you got it?"

"Yep. Keep her on her toes, it will, and
she can use the scraps to stitch fairy-tale
britches for our young 'uns."

"What's a fairy tale?"

"A once-upon-a-time story that ends
happy. Ain't you heard fairy tales?" When
she shook her head, he said, "Who's Geordie?"

"My brother which art in heaven."

The man looked like he was still fretting
over fairy tales. "Where's your ma and pa?"

"Never had me no ma."

"And your pa?"

"Pa favored my cooking and my be-hind.
Geordie said I done nothing wrong."

The late-afternoon sun was in the man's
eyes, so she couldn't read his face. He
hoisted her atop Clementine, already loaded

with pots and pans, rolled blankets, and double knapsacks.

"What are you do-doing?" she sputtered.

"I want to leave before darkness falls, and it's falling quick, like the curtain on a bad stage play."

"You gonna give me to your wife along with the dress?"

He laughed. The sound started in his boots, rose to his chest, and boomed through the air like thunder. "Not hardly, child."

What should I do, Geordie? Does this laughing man mean to harm me? She pictured the long walk to Denver and knew that, even without her lame foot, a return journey would be impossible, so she wove her fingers through Clementine's shaggy mane. "What's your name, sir, if you don't mind my asking?"

"I don't mind. It's John Templeton but friends call me Whiskey Johnnie. I'm headed for a mining town, Cripple Creek, where I pan for gold."

"You drink lots of whiskey?"

"Can't touch a drop. That's why folks call me Whiskey Johnnie."

"Don't believe I figure that."

"People seem to favor the opposite. Makes the truth more fun, somehow. Long time ago I lived in Texas, where layin' it on thick comes natural. In them days I'd get so drunk they'd say I couldn't hit the ground with my hat in three throws. In them days they called me John. Didn't add the whiskey part till I couldn't drink no more. What's your name, child?"

"You said names don't matter."

"True, but I gotta call you something."

"Call me Berry."

"Hang on, young Berry. Giddyap, Clementine."

Two

Texas: 1893

White-hooded figures crouched, waiting for three blasts from a penny whistle.

Ned Lytton crouched, too. He was supposed to be praying, but he kept thinking about that line in his father's last letter: *Men with clenched fists cannot shake hands.*

A series of amens pierced the stagnant air. Ned clenched his fists.

"Look up at the sky, Lytton," said Richard Reed. "It's inspirin'."

"What's inspiring?" Ned watched his friend undulate like a hooded Cobra. "The sky?"

"No, the clouds. See how they form white men on white horses? It's an omen."

WE MUST KEEP THIS A WHITE MAN'S COUNTRY decreed a pamphlet inside Ned's shirt pocket. From the open window of the one-room schoolhouse, he could hear children singing, "A-B-C-D-E-

F-Gee . . . H-I-J-K . . ."

K-K-K. Ku Klux Klan. A nucleus banded
together at Ned's university. For his initia-
tion, he had been blindfolded, led over
obstacles placed inside a musty cellar, finally
brought before Richard, the Grand Cyclops.
After answering nonsensical questions, his
blindfold had been stripped away. He faced
a large mirror. On his head were donkey
ears. Klansmen had burst into laughter.
Ned had laughed too, aware that the rites
were patterned after the Klan's original
ceremonies. He'd been sworn to secrecy
about the club and the identity of his
companions. He had joined because he
thirsted for adventure, excitement, and
some rollicking good fun.

Now he and eight others knelt behind a
grove of western yellow pine trees, anticipating Richard's signal. Twenty knees mashed
pink and violet phlox while the gurgling
rush from a nearby stream mingled with the
sound of droning insects. Close to the
stream, crushing clumps of wild plum, lay a
huge wooden cross.

Through raggedy eyeholes, he watched
Richard clamber up. Ned followed, his legs
all pins and needles.

Children emerged from the schoolhouse.

Richard's hand crept beneath his hood,

and Ned heard the penny whistle's triple blast. Three Klansmen hefted the cross. Drawing revolvers from bootstraps, others shot toward the sky.

The happy cadence of youthful voices abruptly ceased. One elderly man, white, dashed through the doorway, into the school yard. A beautiful colored woman practically breathed down his neck. "Run, children!" she shouted.

"Fetch help, Lily Ann!" Above a full beard, the schoolmaster's nostrils flared and his eyes burned with a feverish glow. In his fist he clutched a wooden ruler.

"But I want to stay, help you fight."

"You'll never be a teacher if you're dead."

Petticoats swirled as she followed the children.

Ned resisted the urge to chase her down. Chocolate candy would taste mighty fine after his sparse breakfast of corn pone and grits. His hood restricted vision so he yanked it off. He didn't give a damn if a crackbrained schoolmaster described black hair, blue eyes and a cleft chin to the sheriff. Tonight he'd leave Texas and return to his Denver home.

The cross had been erected, doused with kerosene and lit. Several Klansmen entered the schoolhouse. Ned heard the sound of splintering wood.

Richard was dodging blows from the schoolmaster's ruler, and Ned recalled the well-placed clouts delivered by his father's gnarled walking cane. As Ned considered joining forces with his friend, the sound of splintering wood became the angry buzz of hornets.

Shit, Ned thought, *that ain't bees.*

Children had returned with their parents. Men and women raced down the trail, holding aloft sticks, shovels, hoes and brooms.

Ned's companions turned tail. The blazing cross cast flame-licked shadows across their hooded gowns as they scattered in all directions, looking like the vanes on a pinwheel. Ned was no coward, of course, but those colored men and women looked indestructible.

Sweat poured down his face as he stomped his way through the woods toward his horse. He experienced a momentary gut-wrench, fearing his father, the honorable Edward Lytton, would be livid at his only son's expulsion from the university. The chancellor had expressed dissatisfaction at young Mr. Lytton's lack of attendance and failing grades. Ned had told the chancellor to stick his university where the sun don't shine. If he had licked the chancellor's boots, he might have been given a second chance, but Ned wasn't one to lick boots. The honorable Edward wasn't one to lick boots, either, and yet Father would never endorse the Ku Klux Klan. Father had Jewish and Catholic business associates. Father was good friends with Congressman George Henry White, an ex-slave from North Carolina.

Directing his gaze toward Richard Reed's portentous clouds, Ned realized that his thirst for rollicking good fun had become a goal — a *purpose*. Despite his father's imminent censure, Ned would disseminate the Klan's doctrine throughout Colorado.

But first he wanted to dig up some gold.

THREE

Outside Denver, Whiskey Johnnie made camp by the side of the trail. Bertha was so tired, she slid from the burro's back and fell to the ground. She tried to rise but her head felt twisty, like a Kansas tornado she'd once seen. Geordie'd said the tornado's swirls were rings of smoke from a giant's corncob pipe.

"Bed down on the blanket," Whiskey Johnnie said, "and I'll sing you a lullaby."

"What's that?"

"A cradlesong."

"You're funning me. Cradles can't sing."

Hours later, she tugged at Johnnie's shirt. "Geordie," she whimpered, "you can call me Weed. You can say my hair's yella."

"Hush, Berry," Johnnie said. "Go back to sleep."

She pressed her head against his chest like a broody hen nestled into its own feathers. "Geordie had him a dream. He saw a nugget big as an egg, but it was only fool's gold."

"Sleep, child. There's peace of soul with the dark."

Staring up at the sky, Bertha heard her brother's words: *I'll bring you white sparkly gems that look like nighttime stars.*

But the sky was as black as her hair. Black as the preacher's carriage. Black.

The warm west wind swirled tinted leaves from tree branches, and the wild sarsaparilla stems nodded hopefully toward a sky that ranged from the deepest blue to the lightest green. On their second day of travel, Whiskey Johnnie halted early, set up camp near a stream, tethered Clementine, and fished for speckled trout.

Tummy full of trout, Bertha sat close to the fire and plaited her hair, preparing for sleep. "Won't your wife wonder where you're at, Johnnie?"

"M'wife'll be mad as a bull tangled in a clothesline, but I brung her gifts from Denver — shoes, thread, store-bought soap and the like."

"Am I to live with you?"

"Not hardly. M'wife's got a heart as big as the rest of her, but she ain't too fond of me right now. She didn't want me to gally'vant off to Denver, said she'd be gone when I got back. Don't figure she'll truly leave, but I can't gift her a pretty gal along with the soap and thread."

"I ain't purty."

"Texans would say you was pretty as a red heifer in a flower bed."

"I ain't purty," she repeated, "but I've got me some coins."

"Keep your coins, Berry."

"What'll I do when we get there, Johnnie?"

He added kindling to the fire. "I seen you running like a sheep culled from the herd for supper, so I acted quick and didn't think that far ahead."

"How do other girls earn their keep?" She watched him poke at the fire with a forked stick. "Ain't there no other girls?"

"There's gals. Some are wives, like mine. Others . . . give relief."

"Like a physic for the belly ache?"

His booming laugh seemed to set the moon spinning. "Guess you could call it medicine. In Cripple Creek there's what's called parlor houses and crib houses. Whores live there. They pleasure a feller for wages."

"I could be one of them whores if I learned their ways, Johnnie. Won't you teach me how to pleasure a feller?"

41

He lowered his head and pushed at the fire until his stick broke in half.

"You gotta teach me, Johnnie. If you don't, I'll starve with my goodness. There's only whores and wives in your town, and I ain't wed. The Bible says sluggards should consider the ways of the ant and be wise."

"Whores ain't ants. And you was born wise."

"No, sir. Geordie once said how the owl's wise to fly through the night and hooty-hoot his song. I can hooty-hoot a song but I can't fly through the night. Wish I could."

Johnnie led her away from the fire and lowered her to her blanket. "There's as many crib and parlor girls as fleas on a pup in summer," he said. "But sometimes, Berry, if a gal pleases a feller, he'll up and marry her. Maybe you can find a gentleman to wed."

"A gentleman." She yawned and closed her eyes. "Won't you learn me how to pleasure a gentleman?"

Why not? thought Johnnie. *Physic for the belly ache!* He swallowed his chuckle.

"Wish I had the coins to keep her safe, Lord," he said softly. "Too bad I ain't struck my gold vein, but that's up to you, Lord, though I do wish you'd hurry."

He hunkered by the fire. "Let's dicker,

Lord. You help me get the child settled and I'll leave her be."

Thunder rumbled. Johnnie looked up and grinned. "One more thing, Lord. If m'wife's waiting for me in Cripple Creek, I'll never gally'vant to Denver again. Amen."

FOUR

Cripple Creek lay in the first range of the Rocky Mountains, twenty miles west of Colorado Springs and eighty miles south and a little west of Denver. Volcanoes had piled up the hills. Sudden valleys were marked by scrub trees and, in season, a wealth of wildflowers. Beneath the ground, a lusty devil dwelled, his penis erect. Sometimes he ejaculated gold.

When Whiskey Johnnie and Bertha arrived, they were greeted by "Amazing Grace." Several members of the Salvation Army stood outside Nolan's Saloon.

Johnnie led Clementine down the crowded street, toward the bricked front of Johnson's Department Store. "Set, Berry," he said. "See that there gal with her geegaws? Soon you'll be shopping at Johnson's. Don't move. I'll be quicker'n a jackrabbit."

Bertha watched him head toward some distant shacks. Then she bent forward,

44

rested her face against Clementine's furred neck and closed her eyes.

"I'm scared, Geordie," she said, and in her head heard his reply: *Open your eyes, Berry. This ain't Denver. See how the mountains try to touch God's feet? You're safe now.*

"I might be safe, Geordie, but I'm plumb scared."

You was scared to sing and look how good you done.

"Whiskey Johnnie says there's whores here, so I gotta learn me a whore's ways and find me a gentleman to wed."

Loving with a feller on the outside don't make you bad inside.

"Should I love with a feller on the outside, Geordie?"

Ignoring the sound of horse hooves, squeaky carriage wheels, and the Salvation Army's tambourines, she listened for his answer. If he said no, she'd starve with her goodness. But all she heard was the plop of Clementine's fresh dung.

"Geordie, don't leave me!"

A hand clasped her shoulder. She opened her eyes and sat up straight.

"We been lucky, Berry," Johnnie said. "Leo the Lion owns them Poverty Gulch cribs and one's empty 'cause a whore married sudden-like."

"Did she wed her a gentleman?"

"Could be." He cleared his throat. "I need your sack of coins to pay the rent, young 'un. Giddyap, Clementine."

The flimsy shanty fronted Myers Avenue. It sagged, but there were no gaps in the planked walls, and the peaked roof — with its black stovepipe poking out — didn't look like it would leak too bad. And the window panes were real glass, not paper.

Johnnie led her inside. "The gal what lived here left furniture and pretties. See? You got sheets, towels and a pillow."

Bertha strolled around the small room, touching, in turn, the bed, hand-hewn rocker, wood and leather-thong trunk, and a frilly window curtain. Outside, she leaned against the door, waving until Clementine's whisked tail disappeared from view. Then she walked forward, made an about-face, and studied her new home. Her crib stood between MINTA and BELLE. She looked up and down the street, moving her lips slowly the way Geordie had taught her, reading the other printed names.

The shacks seemed so tiny, pitted against the saw-toothed mountain range. Bertha felt a surge of pride. *Her* mountains. Reaching for God's feet.

A tiger salamander slithered across Bertha's boot toe. She watched mottled spots, slimy skin and long tail turn the corner as the salamander headed toward a sad, scabbed, yella-sprigged dogwood tree. Then she dipped a brush into some red paint she'd found, and, on tiptoe, printed the name BERRY above her doorway. The letters looked almost the same size. Geordie would say "Good job, Weed."

He'd like her pretty flowers, too, especially the white petals with green-streaked lips that formed hoods over clumps of twisty stems.

"Them there flowers are called ladies' tresses."

The woman who spoke had reddish ringlets, each wrapped with a scrap of colorful rag. Walking toward Bertha, she smiled. Her freckled nose crinkled and her eyes tilted at the corners. Her body was lush, her curves barely concealed by a kimono.

Clean from a quick wash, Bertha had changed into her church blouse and skirt. She cocked her head as she stared into the warm brown eyes of the whore next door.

"My name's Minta," said the woman.

47

"My name's Berry."

"I know. Your letters are so new, they shine."

"They ain't printed good?"

Minta laughed.

Bertha looked around for Clementine before she realized the braying chuckle came from the red-haired woman.

"Your letters are fine," said Minta. "The girl who lived here before couldn't write a stitch."

"If she couldn't write, how'd she wed her a gentleman?"

"She didn't. She wed a miner, old as Methuselah, with a wooden leg. Where do you hail from, sweetie?"

"Nowhere." The bright autumn sun danced behind a cloud-capped mountain, and Bertha shivered with a sudden chill.

"Don't matter where you're from. We're all running away, me and Carmen and Belle, playing hide-and-seek from something or somebody."

"You can't play hidey-seek from God."

"True." Unknotting a dark blue scrap from her curls, Minta tied the cloth around both of Bertha's braids so they swung as one. "There. The bow's colored like your eyes. Blue Berry. We'll get the miners to bring you doodads. I'll teach you how to

48

ask and make it sound like it's their idea. Of course, they'd have to go some to beat them pretty bobs at your ears."

"Them bobs were my mama's. She died on the day I was born, and my brother said they rightly belonged to me. I didn't steal them."

"Never thought you did. Poor thing, no mama." Minta spread her arms wide.

Catching her breath on a sob, Bertha buried her face against Minta's bosom and basked in the warmth of the first female embrace she'd ever received.

Bertha soon became known as Blue Berry, then Blueberry.

Inside her shack a feller could rock in her chair, drink beer, and talk about his woes. Sometimes she even darned his socks. She never rushed her gents in and out. She listened to their stories and lies like they were the truth. And except for Minta, she earned more wages than the other crib girls.

When they had no callers, Minta would brew tea. "It's what them fancy ladies drink," she'd say, lifting her freckled nose and sniffing at the air inside her shack, which in wintertime always smelled of singed wood and cinnamon.

Berry would limp a dance across the floor

behind her friend. Placing her finger beneath her own nose, tilting it upwards, she'd shout, "I'm a lady too!"

After their lady-strut, they'd collapse onto the bed, kick off their shoes, wriggle their toes toward the warmth of the small cookstove, and nibble Minta's sticky oatmeal cookies. Then they'd sing, "You are lost and gone forever . . ."

On the eve of her seventeenth birthday, Berry fell in love. With a gentleman.

Thunder drummed the sky and a smattering of raindrops snapped against the leaves.

Berry shut the window. Glancing toward the cookstove, her mouth watered. The pie on top was for tomorrow's birthday party, but one small bite of the lemon filling —

Lightning flashed. Startled, Berry's gaze shifted to the window and she caught a glimpse of a shadowy figure, skulking outside like some damnfool Peeping Tom. Yanking open the door, her scathing words died unborn.

Before her stood an honest-to-goodness gentleman. On his finger he wore a ring set with a twisted nugget. His left earlobe sported a gold hoop. While most other miners had beards, this handsome lad was clean shaven. Tall and slim, his shirt and trousers were blotched by raindrops. As lightning cleaved the sky again, Berry could see that his eyes were as blue as a Jay's feathers.

His boots crushed her wildflower garden. His whiskey bottle hovered above a mouse-eared chickweed as he bowed and said, "My name's Nugget Ned. You must be Mary."

"Mary?"

"You're not the Irish lass they talked about at the Buckhorn saloon?"

"No." Berry's heart skipped a disappointed beat. "Irish Mary bides two cribs down. Ain't you seen the printed letters above my door?"

Ignoring the drizzle, he squinted upwards. "Hard to read letters when your mind's muddled with whiskey, Mary."

"Blueberry!"

He grinned and spit rain. "Believe Per'fessor mentioned you. White skin and black hair. Cream and pepper. I had a hankering for Irish stew but home cooking will suffice."

"Home cooking? There's a lemon pie atop my stove. I baked it for my birthday." She waited for him to say happy birthday but he didn't. "Why don't you set while the pie cools?"

"I prefer my cuisine hot." Loosening Berry's bodice, Nugget Ned tasted her firm breasts.

"Come inside, sir," she gasped.

He dropped his whiskey bottle and staggered through the shanty's entrance. Tripping over the rocker, he pitched forward, caught the table's edge with his fingertips, slid to the floor.

"The bed's over there, Mr. Nugget." Berry tried to lift him but he was too big, so she stripped off his wet shirt, placed a pillow 'neath his dark hair, and covered him with the quilt. Then she blew out all candles except one, curled up in her rocker, and nibbled at a piece of pie. *I'll set here till he wakes,* she thought.

Hours later her eyes felt heavy and the empty pie plate fell from her lap to the floor.

When she awoke the next morning, her candle had guttered, pie crumbs had attracted ants, and Nugget Ned was gone.

"Please, God, bring my gentleman back," she prayed.

Nugget Ned Lytton was twenty-two. He had been booted from his Denver home after a series of escapades culminating in the pregnancy of the daughter of his father's business associate. Ned had refused to marry her. Funded by a small trust fund, he planned to dig for gold.

He confessed all this to Berry during his second visit. "When I'm rich, I'll tell Father to go to the devil. Father said I'd never amount to anything. Father said I'd crawl back to Denver. Father said I'd kneel at his feet and beg forgiveness. I'll kneel at his grave first, Blueberry."

"I prayed you'd come back and God heard my prayers," she said.

He scowled. "Prayers don't signify. How about a song?"

She folded her hands upon her naked bosom and began to sing "Oh Promise Me."

"No! Don't sing of love! Sing a song for fun."

"I can sing some lines I learn't from a piana-playin' man, but I don't like to recollect the saloon where I learnt them."

"Make me laugh, damn you," he said.

His fingers pinched the tender flesh above her elbows. *He's a gentleman,* she thought, *and they act different from other fellers. He don't mean to hurt me.*

"Ben Battle was a soldier bold and used to war's alarm," she sang, her voice blurred by tears. "But a cannon-ball took off his legs, so he laid down his arms."

Ned burst out laughing. Releasing her, he fell upon the bed. "Come lay down in my arms, Blueberry. Let's see if you can love as good as you sing."

"I can love good," she said, and set about to prove it. "I can love good," she repeated, delighted by his shouts of pleasure.

Ned Lytton cussed like a gentleman.

"Ma! Ma! Where's my Pa? Gone to the White House. Ha! Ha! Ha! Why ain't you laughing, Blueberry?"

"I don't care for that ditty, Ned. It's terrible cruel."

"Grover Cleveland admits he bedded Maria Halpin. She had a son, and Cleveland assumed responsibility."

"But he didn't marry her. President Cleveland ain't no gentleman."

"He won the election just the same. I bet my father didn't cast his ballot for Cleveland. Father agrees with you." Laughing, Ned searched through Berry's leather-thong chest for a clean pair of socks.

"Are you funning me, Ned?"

"No, I'm *funning* Father. It amused me to think that a whore and a capitalist hold the same viewpoint."

"It's been a full month since we met, but I still can't reckon half your words. What's a cap-pill-list?"

"A person of great wealth and prominence. A nabob."

"Is that like an earbob?"

Ned eyed her ruby earrings. "In a way. Your earbobs must be worth plenty. You could sell them, invest the profits, and soon you'd be a capitalist."

"I'd never sell my mama's bobs," she gasped. Clothed in a cotton shimmy, she clutched a piece of Queen Dolly soft gingerbread. Minta said Dolly Madison dreamed up the recipe during President Jefferson's administration — molasses, beef drippings, flour, ground ginger, cinnamon, and powdered sugar. "What's the lady's name, Ned?"

"Maria Halpin."

"I meant the rich lady you told me of during your second visit. The one who's with child. Her you wronged."

"I didn't wrong her. She wronged me. Her name's Johanna." Unbuttoning his trousers, Ned slid onto the rocking chair. "Fetch my whiskey, girl."

"Johanna." Berry tasted the name as Ned snapped his fingers impatiently. "Please don't drink, honey. You ain't been drunk for days and you get nasty —"

"Fetch it! Now!"

She rose from the bed and fetched the bottle. Kneeling by the rocker, she left a trail of nibbled kisses across his thighs. If she kept her mouth busy, maybe she'd keep from asking another hurtful question.

"What's Johanna look like, Ned?"

"Have you ever seen a Chinese dog with beady eyes and lots of hair?"

"Did you kiss Johanna?"

"How could I kiss a lady who has a mustache when I don't?"

"Why'd you love with her?"

"Why do I *love* with you?"

"Did you give Johanna coins?"

"Of course not." His eyes narrowed. "Why all the questions? Do you want me to pay for your love?"

"Oh, no! We lay for joy, not coins. I didn't sucker you like Johanna did. When you find your gold we'll be wed good and proper."

"That's right." He pushed her face toward his open trousers.

She resisted. "Why'd you love with Johanna?"

"It seemed the thing to do at the time."

"Did Johanna hooty-hoot for your pleasure?"

"No, Blueberry, she squeaked a mouse song."

"Where'd it happen?"

"It was during a party given by my father, the honorable Edward Lytton. Johanna lured me into my father's study."

Berry watched Ned drink, then rock back and forth, his eyes half-shut. Still on her knees, she scurried across the floor to avoid the rocker's motion.

"My father's study," Ned repeated, "where he used to beat me with his cane. 'Listen to me, son,' Father would say. 'Dig a pit and you'll fall into it.' The night of the party I was somewhat the worse for drink, and Johanna stood there with her skirts up, her back against my father's bookcase. Dickens' *Great Expectations.* Do you get the irony, Blueberry? You don't know what the hell I'm talking about, do you? Dickens could be the man in the moon, you ignorant —"

"Eat some gingerbread. Don't drink no more, honey. It makes you talk nasty."

Ned tilted the bottle, finished its contents, threw it against the wall. Berry shuddered at the sound of breaking glass.

"Sing to me, Blueberry. First, help me to bed."

She supported his heavy body, limping the short distance. Then she undressed him, lay beside him, and cradled his face against her bosom.

"My mother sang lullabies," Ned murmured drunkenly. "She died when I was twelve. Her name was Dolly. My father built her a big house in Colorado Springs, but she left for France and never came back. She said she loved me but she lied. Love me, Blueberry."

Dimly, she wondered why he never made love to *her*.

Minta wiped a freckled forearm across her brow, trying to halt the rivulets of perspiration that streaked down her face. With disgust, she watched her friend Blueberry carefully scrub a pile of Nugget Ned's trousers, shirts and socks. Blueberry staggered to her feet, limped behind some prickly bushes, and Minta heard the sound of retching.

"Must have been something I et." Sinking to her knees again, Berry thrust her fist inside a sock and waved it around like a hand puppet. "Ned brung green apples and purple grapes last night," she said, as if the gift of fruit was a string of green and purple pearls.

"You don't have no other callers, Blueberry, and you won't take coins from Nugget Ned. That ain't smart."

"I ain't wise like an owl, Min, but I ain't stupid like that cow that broke her leg crossing this here crick. That cow was ill-starred, while I'm lucky to find me a gentleman."

"Nugget Ned ain't no gentleman."

"Irish Mary told me of the wee folk who live in a faraway city called Dublin. They leave pots of gold at the rainbow's foot. Ned's my pot of gold."

"Pooh! That Irish Mary's fibbing. Ain't no wee folks. Gold's found by digging. A pot's for soup and stew. Aw, don't turn away. You're my friend and I don't want to see you hurt."

"When he finds his gold, Ned's gonna buy me pretty gowns and a fancy house. I'm to be a lady like we've played. And it's Ned who's been hurt by his pa."

"The rich don't hurt that bad, and don't hump your shoulders like a dang camel!"

"Don't you know that it's easier for a camel to go through the eye of a needle than for a rich man to enter the kingdom of God? I'll tell that straightway to Ned's pa when we meet up."

Minta slapped a chemise against the rocks.

"Ned says we're gonna have babies."

Minta stopped slapping. "Nugget Ned said he was wanting babies?"

"He says he loves to lay with me and that means babies, don't it?"

"Not always. Mercy! Are you with child?"

"Don't know for certain."

"Go see Mab."

"I can't stomach Mab's touch. And she walks like she's shat her drawers."

"Have you told Nugget Ned?"

"No, but he'll be pleasured when I do. Ned says he loves me."

"I love poking you," said Ned, rocking back and forth. His clean trousers and Berry's gown lay in a heap by the door. Her long hair covered a goodly portion of his body as she straddled his lap, her head against his chest.

"Don't talk dirty," she said, raising her face.

He grinned. "I purely enjoy the act of copulation."

"What's copulation?"

"Poking."

"We can't do this no more when I'm a lady. A lady loves from the bed, in the dark, with her drawers and nightie on."

"I'd love to present you to my father. I might do that even if my gold doesn't pan out. Father has a weak heart and I'm his only heir. I'll take you to Denver, knock on his door, and introduce you as Mrs. Edward Lytton the Third. While he's floored from my kick in the teeth —"

"You aim to kick him in the teeth?"

"That's just a turn of phrase, you idiot. It

means a surprise."

She opened her eyes wide, trying to keep the tears from falling. "Don't talk nasty, Ned."

"We don't have to talk at all. Let's poke."

"Not if you spit that dirty word."

"Are you defying me?"

"No, but I'll boot you out if you ain't respectful."

He tilted her chin with his finger and stared into her eyes. "Would you care to join me in coitus, Miss Blueberry?"

"That's better," she said, although she had the feeling coitus meant the same thing. But she didn't want to fight, not while Ned sucked her breast and pushed at the floor with his boot heels. He rocked the chair, faster and faster, until she didn't care if he called it copulation, coitus, or poking.

"I love you," she cried.

"I'm coming," he hollered.

Ned had thrown his hat in the air, digging where it fell. He had heard about others who staked claims that way. Eventually, he unearthed a vein of bright yellow-brown chips. Without assaying his find, he used the last of his trust fund to host a celebration party. He invited the most expensive parlor house girls and gave Berry a red dress. Its décolletage scooped to her breasts.

Minta twisted Berry's hair into swirls on top of her head. Curly tendrils escaped and wisped around her mama's ruby earrings.

"Have you told Nugget Ned about the baby, Blueberry?"

"No. I wanted to be sure. I'll tell him tonight, after the party."

Ned impatiently fastened the gown's small back buttons while Berry tried to pull up her bodice. "This ain't a ladylike gown," she said. "If I bend, it shows my teats."

"But your *teats* are so *purty,*" he mocked, sipping from a bottle of whiskey. Suddenly, he clutched his stomach and gagged.

"Are you sick, Ned? Fevered? Minta told me Old Jeb up and died of the fever."

"No, not fever. Whiskey. Happy. I'll hand a sack of gold over to my friend, Richard Reed. Did I tell you 'bout the Ku Klux Klan?" Thrusting both thumbs inside his ears, he waggled his fingers. "I wore donkey ears."

"Donkey ears? Whatever for?"

"Can't tell. Secret. Go smear some paint on your lips, sweetheart. I want everyone to see your mouth."

Berry felt like purring. Ned had called her sweetheart for the very first time.

■ ■ ■ ■

As soon as Berry entered the saloon, Ned hoisted her atop a crude wooden stage, joined her there, and whistled through his fingers for attention.

"I've brought the entertainment," he announced. "This here is Blueberry Smith. Some of you know her from Poverty Gulch. But you don't know she was once a Denver dance hall girl."

"That's a secret," she gasped.

He leaned closer and she smelled whiskey on his breath. "You'll sing for my friends, Blueberry, or suffer the consequences."

"How can you do this to me? I'm your lady."

"If you don't sing, I'll never marry you."

"If I sing, do you promise we'll be wed good and proper?"

"Sure, sweetheart, you have my oath on it."

Tearfully, she stepped to the front of the stage, clasped her fingers together until they formed a tight knot, and began to sing "Clementine." Through the cigar smoke, she saw Ned plunge his hand down the bodice of a woman in a yella gown. The woman shrieked with drunken laughter as she pulled Ned toward the staircase that led to the bedrooms on the second floor.

As Berry sang, the crowd pressed closer and she could have sworn she heard *coochie-coochie.* "I have need of the privy," she cried, her cheeks hot.

The men passed her over their heads until she arrived at the back of the room. When her feet hit the floor, she fled. "I told Minta I wasn't stupid like that crippled cow," she murmured, limping toward her crib. "But we're the same, that cow and me."

Ned's overflowing vein turned out to be chips of iron and sulfur pyrite — fool's gold. A week after his celebration party, he pounded at Berry's door.

"Go 'way," she said. "You ain't no gentleman to treat me so nasty at your shindig. I prayed you were fevered like Old Jeb. A shame God didn't answer my prayers, you runty toad. I've told all the girls how small-sized you are. They don't call you Nugget Ned no more. They call you Runty Ned."

"Blueberry, please open the door."

"You done me one favor. I've been practicing my talk and manners so's I can work at a different trade. I ain't gonna lay with men and I'll sing no more bawdy songs for the asking."

"I only came to tell you that I'm leaving Cripple Creek."

"Good riddance."

"I thought we'd be wed before I go."

She opened the door a crack. "Truly?"

"I swear. Preacher should be here first thing tomorrow morning. Please let me in."

"I'll let you in tomorrow morning."

"I'm leaving after we say our vows, so I'd like to spend my last night with you. I plan to travel through the mountains with Preacher as my guide. After we're wed, I'll sell your ruby earrings. A wife wouldn't deny her husband a stake and I must leave soon." He clenched his fists. "Everybody's *laughing* at me."

"Can't you file a new claim near the crick, I mean creek?"

"There's too many digging. Why should I dig when there's gold for the asking farther north?"

"It ain't that easy up in the mountains, and winter's coming." She opened the door.

He entered, pressed his face against the hollow of her neck. "You don't understand. All I need do is kneel. Bow down and ask."

"You'll pray to God?"

"Yes, I'll ask *God.* I tried, Blueberry, but my pit was full of fool's gold."

She felt his tears. Ned weeping? Lost in

65

wonder, she maneuvered their bodies toward the bed.

Early the next morning Preacher entered the crib. "Afore God, Nugget Ned Lytton an' Blueberry Smith are now wed," he said, making the sign of the cross with his gnarled finger.

Preacher waited outside while Ned shed his clothes and hers. She didn't feel him remove her earbobs because his tongue wickedly circled her inner ear, sending shivers up and down her spine, and when they lay upon the quilt, she used all her skills to make him hoot a song.

"I'll miss you, sweetheart," he said afterwards, and she heard the God's honest truth in his voice.

"When you come back," she said, "I'll have a kick in the teeth for you."

"A what?"

"A surprise."

"I'll be back soon," he said. "You have my oath on it."

Throughout the following weeks, Berry sat in her rocker and dreamed about how she would soon be a rich lady. It snowed every day. She figured the drifts prevented Ned's return, and used the last of her coins to pay three months' rent on her crib house.

She nibbled whatever food she could scrounge from trash bins of scraps behind the cafés. One night she fought with a mangy mongrel over a small carcass. Throwing rocks at the snarling dog, she recalled her brother hurling his nugget at Tiny.

I'll name the babe George Edward, she thought, kissing Ned's nugget ring, twined with thread to fit her finger.

She hadn't told anybody about her marriage, not even Minta. Ned had asked her to keep it a secret until he came home. He owed money, he said, and didn't want his wife hounded by creditors.

His wife. Mrs. Edward Lytton. Berry didn't mind the hush-hush ploy because God knew.

You can't play hidey-seek from God.

"Per'fessor just come from Denver," Minta told Berry one afternoon. "He says Nugget Ned's there, living high on the hog."

Berry stroked her bloated belly. "Per'fessor's mistaken. He saw someone who looks like my Ned."

Preacher returned for Christmas, his emaciated body blue with cold. Several tattered shirts and jackets hugged his thin frame. With his beak of a nose, he looked like a vulture and folks whispered that

Preacher had picked the bones of dead prospectors for his sustenance.

Some citizens recollected the Packer Party of 1847, when only Packer had returned alive. At his trial, the judge had supposedly said, "Goddamn you, Alferd Packer! There was only six Democrats in Hinsdale County and you et four of them!"

"I don't believe it's true what they say about Preacher eating folks," Berry told Minta. "He's a man of God."

"No, he ain't. They named him Preacher 'cause he sinned so awful in his youth."

In her head, Berry heard Whiskey Johnnie's words: "People seem to favor the reverse."

Ned believed him a man of God. That's good enough for me and George Edward.

She waylaid Preacher as he walked down the icy street. "Why didn't Nugget Ned come back with you?"

"He never gone with me." Preacher chuckled through decaying teeth stumps. "Why would Nugget Ned travel with a preacher man?"

"To look for gold."

"I ain't looked for gold. I brung the word of God to them sinners with their yella idols. 'Repent,' I said." He eyed her swollen belly, five months full. "Repent, child!"

"For what?"

Spring arrived, but Berry in the throes of labor couldn't appreciate colorful buds dotting the mountains while lush green brought the hope of new beginnings.

The delivery took two days. Crib girls worked in shifts. The midwife refused to help until money was advanced. Minta insisted that Mab scrub her hands, including long filthy fingernails, before payment. *Mab's body looks like bread dough dropped in dirt,* Minta thought with disgust.

Placing a knife beneath the mattress to "cut the pain in half," Mab sat by the cookstove and swilled from bottles of beer.

Late afternoon arrived and the scent of cooked food drifted down the row like a thin shadow. Mab rooted in her garden for turnips and plucked the feathers from a slaughtered chicken, which she then fried for her supper. The red painted name BERRY shone in the glow of sunset as Mab reentered the crib and thrust her grimy fingers into Berry.

"The babe's turned wrong," she said, opening another bottle of beer.

At dawn, Whiskey Johnnie kicked the door open. He soothed Berry through the last of the difficult delivery and cut the cord with his hunting knife.

The baby mewed piteously.

Berry opened her eyes and saw crib girls. They all floated through the room like ghosts.

Am I dead? If I'm dead, where's Geordie and Noah?

About to shut her eyes again, Berry heard a sneeze then a loud wail. "George Edward," she whispered.

Minta leaned closer. "What did you say, love?"

"Baby."

"She's perfect, Blueberry."

"I birthed a girl? Let me see her."

"She's right here."

"Dark." Berry thrashed her head from side to side. "Ned . . ."

"He's on his way." Minta choked back a sob.

"No. I was a fool to believe. Johnnie says there's peace of soul in the dark. I ain't feared to sleep. It's just . . . my poor baby . . . no mama."

Irish Mary knelt by the bed. "What do you want to name your wee girlie, Blueberry?"

Behind her closed eyelids, Berry saw Geordie toss his lucky nugget from hand to hand.

No, Geordie, no. It's not real gold, it's . . .
"Fool's gold," she whispered.

FIVE

A dozen or so miles from Poverty Gulch lay the town of Divide, Colorado. Its population of one hundred included a postmistress and a drugstore proprietor, but no census had ever recorded the swarthy outlaw who rode through the sleepy village just before dawn.

The sound of hoofbeats did not rouse the drugstore proprietor, who had spent the evening at Cripple Creek's Butte Opera House Saloon. He had been returned to Divide in the back of a buckboard, whereupon his wife had carried him inside. A stampede wouldn't have disturbed the druggist's slumber, nor his wife's, for she had donned earmuffs to drown out his drunken snores.

The postmistress peered through her window. Not a blessed thing interrupted the peaceful symmetry of the desolate, unpaved street. The railway station, saloon, hotel and livery were all eerily silent, and yet the postmistress could have sworn she'd heard a steady clip-clop, like the echo of an Indian tom-tom.

Cherokee Bill reined in his black stallion on the crest of a hill. Silhouetted against a predawn, slate-colored sky, he was tall and graceful, with dark wavy hair falling to his shoulders. Except for a slight flare to his nostrils and a dusky tinge to his skin, his features were more white than Indian, yet he proudly clothed himself in doeskin and spiked a cocky feather in the band of his black Stetson.

His fingers gripped the pommel of a silver-mounted saddle, his hand only inches away from his holstered Peacemaker .45 and the long Winchester rifle that rested beneath his thigh. Leather saddlebags held the result of a recent express-office robbery. A partner on that successful endeavor had told Bill about a wealthy Divide rancher, John Mc-Donald, but Bill would wait until tonight to survey the landowner's vast acreage. Tonight there would be a full moon.

"Gracias, Dios," he said. Cherokee Bill never forgot to thank God, or the people he robbed and killed. Placing a blanket on the hard ground, he decided to take forty winks,

one wink for each twenty-dollar banknote stashed inside his saddlebags.

He was awakened several hours later by the warning whistle of his stallion. Instantly alert, Bill peered through the brush at a field below. The field unfolded as far as the eye could see, finally merging into a panorama of jagged mountains. He focused on two distant figures, a man and a woman. Both rode golden palominos.

"I don't know how I let you talk me into this, Dimity." John McDonald bent sideways to check the cinch on his saddle. "Reckon I should be rounding up strays, rather than straying round the ranch."

"You promised, John. You said the first warm May afternoon we'd picnic. Now it's June, and you're growling like an old bear."

McDonald smiled at his young wife. Her green riding habit was designed to enhance her narrow waist and flat stomach. Too flat. Her monthly flux had commenced ten days ago. What was the use of running the largest ranch in the area if he had no heirs? Was Dimity, at age sixteen, too young to conceive?

Poppycock. John had friends with wives just as young who'd already spawned children. Dimity didn't seem to enjoy the act,

74

spreading her legs at his request but not quite hiding her sigh of resignation. Granted, she was well-bred, but his Cripple Creek parlor house girls feigned twice as much joy at his touch.

Dimity stayed abed until noon then moped about the house like a mare off its feed. She should be happy. She had few responsibilities. Rosita and Tonna cleaned and cooked while she read books — romantic applesauce. How could he compete with knights in shining armor? Or altruistic outlaws? How could he compete with Romeo, a pantywaist of the first order, who had poisoned himself for love? Dimity's loud boohoos had nearly triggered a stampede.

Perhaps this picnic frippery would raise her spirits. A fine lunch, with lots of wine, and she might be more receptive to his advances.

Was he too old?

Poppycock! At age fifty-one he had reached his prime. Prime, like the bellowing bulls that thrust their horns toward God's rump. McDonald chuckled at the irreverent image and nudged his palomino toward a distant copse of shade trees. The pastoral scene felt peaceful, and yet he held his shoulders straight, stiff, as though he wore a tight tunic and crossed sabers.

John McDonald had been a soldier in Lieutenant Colonel George Armstrong Custer's company during the war, and had hooked up with an ex-slave named Black Percival, a roustabout in the same company. Percy had a "feeling in his bones" that Custer would suffer an ignoble end, so after the war McDonald bought land in Texas and began to build his first ranch.

By the spring of 1866, he and Percy had good crops and a fine herd of cattle. Seven years later, they decided to pull up stakes and head for Colorado. McDonald sold the ranch, added two thousand head to his herd, and began his cattle drive down the route of the old Butterfield overland stage, planning to turn north at the Pecos River and proceed toward New Mexico. He had learned that the value of the Texas Longhorn increased with each mile it was driven north; a steer worth seven dollars and twenty cents in Texas was worth eighteen dollars and forty cents in Colorado. The cost of getting a steer to market varied with distance, but it could be driven to the northern range for two dollars, and after a few months on free grass, it tripled in value.

From the drive's start they had problems. The herd contained both steers and cows.

Steers traveled faster than cows, and cows were further delayed by calving. Calves couldn't keep up at all. On short trail drives there'd be a calf wagon. McDonald planned a long drive, so the calves had to be killed and their mothers prodded along with the rest of the herd. At night the cows had to be hobbled to prevent them from going back to look for their missing calves.

"Don't reckon I favor killing babies, Mac," Percy said, watching a hobbled cow bawl at the top of her lungs.

"I don't either, but I figure we've got near eighty miles of wasteland to the Pecos River. By the time we get there, the herd'll be loco with thirst and we'll lose hundreds with the stampeding for water."

"It's not the same, Mac. At the Pecos it's not us doing the killing. Mebbe if we pace the critters, tie some calves to our saddles —"

"How many drives you been on, son?"

"Son? You're only ten years older'n me, and a different color to boot. You know damn well I ain't been on no drives."

"We can't bind the critters to our saddles. We'll need all our wits to keep the herd away from poisoned alkali water trapped in potholes. So far we've driven the dogies nice and easy, but when thirst hits . . ." Mc-

Donald shrugged.

"Reckon that's true." Percy untied his bandanna and wiped the sweat from his brow. "But I've a feeling in my bones the calf killings are gonna haunt us."

They drove as far as the headwaters of the Middle Concho without further difficulty, then began to travel through miles of desolation. At first McDonald, Percy, and the hired hands tried to pace the restless herd. But the thirsty animals wouldn't bed down; it was easier to keep going. They lost about three hundred head when the cattle smelled water and stampeded at the river.

Upon reaching Fort Sumner, they discovered a ready market and sold half their herd to general contractors. The government was desperate for beef to feed the nearly starving Navajo Indians who had been crowded into a new reservation.

Restless, with money burning holes in their pockets, McDonald and Percy continued on to Colorado. Discovery of gold in the Rocky Mountains had opened a new cattle market. The mines created a demand far greater than the local supply. After selecting several head for breeding purposes, they sold the last of their herd. Whereupon McDonald established a new ranch in Divide, found a Denver bride, and settled down to launch an empire.

Poor Jane. Quiet, shadowy Jane. After three stillborn babies, she had died birthing the fourth, also stillborn. Percy never said the words out loud, but McDonald knew he remembered the slaughtered calves.

Percy's wife Tonna had miscarried twice.

McDonald had no quarrel with a vengeful God, but he reckoned the debt had been resolved, the road to redemption paved with four tiny headstones. Jane had died. He had married Dimity, who was ripe as a mare in season. Why couldn't she conceive?

"Jesus, Joseph and Mary!"

"What's wrong?" McDonald was startled from his ruminations by the fear in Dimity's voice. He had been staring at the mountains. Now he turned toward his wife — and saw the Winchester rifle pointed at his chest.

Holding John and Dimity at gunpoint, a desperado mounted on a huge black stallion stole their picnic basket, along with Dimity's golden mare.

"Cherokee Bill thanks you kindly, ma'am," he said.

As he tipped his hat and galloped away, Dimity stamped her small booted foot. Furious beyond words, she gestured toward John's sheathed rifle.

"No, my dear." McDonald removed his

79

Stetson and ran gloved fingers through his silver hair. "I'd rather be a live husband than a dead hero."

"If I had a gun, he'd be stretched out at our feet, shot through the heart."

Dismounting, McDonald grasped his wife by the elbows and stared into her pale-blue eyes. "Do you know who that was?"

"A greasy Indian who had the nerve to steal my mare. And our lunch. Fried chicken and homemade biscuits and fresh strawberry preserves. Two bottles of wine and oatmeal cook—"

"You're right, Dimity. Cherokee Bill's Injun. He's also Mexican, Negro and half white, and he's one mean son of a bitch."

"John!" Shaking off her husband's grip, she covered her ears. "No need to cuss."

"At age fourteen, Cherokee Bill killed his brother-in-law."

She lowered her hands. "Why'd he do that?"

"Hellfire, Dimity, I don't know. After the first killing, he became a skilled, consummate outlaw. He's robbed banks and trains. There's a reward for his capture, dead or alive. I've seen the posters."

"Jesus, Joseph and Mary!" Color stained her pale cheeks. "Would you have kept your gun by your side if that horrible outlaw had taken *me?*"

"No. I'd have fought if *you* were threatened." McDonald stifled a sigh. A few short years ago, arrogance and pride would have overruled sensibility. But pride had given way to prudence. Arrogance had become practical wisdom. What was the use of risking his life, perhaps losing his life, when he needed a son and heir?

In an effort to console Dimity, he patted her shoulder. "Come, ride with me atop Riesgoso. We can still have our picnic."

"The outlaw stole our food!"

McDonald mounted, swung her up into the saddle, spurred his palomino toward the trees.

"No," she protested. "I am not in the mood."

You are never in the mood, he thought, circling her waist, pressing her rump closer to the bulge in his trousers. He had promised himself that today he'd plant a seed, and he wouldn't allow a mere desperado to thwart him.

Dimity tensed. "Turn back, John. Cherokee Bill might be nearby."

"Leading a stolen horse? That's a hanging offense. He's far away."

"Then why do I feel his eyes watching us? Oh, I feel faint."

As Dimity slumped against him, Mc-
Donald tightened his arm, but there was no
passion in his grip. *She's young and she's
had a bad scare,* he justified, swallowing his
frustration. With his free hand, he reined
Riesgoso, turned him eastward, and again
spurred the stallion's flanks. Like a bat out
of hell, Riesgoso galloped toward the ranch.

The pillow felt lumpy.

Dimity shifted her head. She wondered
how many geese had sacrificed their feathers for the mattress beneath her body. She
believed in sacrifice. Yes, self-sacrifice was a
divine virtue. Didn't she let her husband
paw her night after night for the purpose of
conception?

And hadn't she faced that horrible outlaw
without flinching? She should be decorated
with a medal for valor, only her badge of
honor would be in the form of an emerald
broach, and the outlaw, captured by the law,
handcuffed, repentant, should be forced to
pin the broach on her gown, above her
breast. How could he pin the broach if he
was handcuffed? He'd be inefficient. He'd
be heavy-handed —

He might accidentally touch her breast.

"I wouldn't flinch if he touched my
breast," she told her pillow.

Less than an hour ago, John had carried her into the house. Tonna had bathed her body with a cool cloth, and helped her change into a diaphanous robe. Now the Navajo servant was preparing clear broth and strawberry muffins.

Thank God she'd bamboozled John with her bogus swoon. She ran her hand over her flat stomach. Eventually she'd have to fill it. John wanted sons. He didn't care if her pretty breasts sagged like the udders on one of his smelly cows.

She knew the act of making love was unpleasant. Hadn't her mother told her so? Tonna had made up some Indian story about feeling the rush of a waterfall, but the closest Dimity had come to waterfalls was the sweat that poured from her husband's body.

And yet she'd felt moisture accrue between her thighs when she stared up at that horrible outlaw. Why had she wanted to remove his feathered hat and run her fingers through his long hair? Why had she wanted to place her lips upon his clean-shaven face? Why had she wanted to caress his doeskin breeches? And why, for the slightest instant, no longer than a heartbeat, had she wanted him to pull the trigger on the rifle aimed toward her husband's chest?

She quickly crossed herself then stared at the diptych atop her chest of drawers. The pair of painted panels, hinged together, showed Jesus in one scene and a winged man-angel in the other. The face on the man-angel looked like . . . Cherokee Bill.

Rising from the bed, she walked closer.

Silly goose! The man in her diptych had a beard. His hair was short. He wore an ankle-length gown. He held a long staff with a cross on top.

As she stared, the staff became a rifle. She mentally shaved the beard and clothed the body in doeskin. There! Her outlaw! The eyes and mouth were the same. How could she have made those disparaging remarks? Greasy Indian and such? Cherokee Bill was God's angel. He probably robbed people for a good reason, just like brave Robin Hood.

She pictured Bill atop her bed, his dark skin pressed against her white sheets, his dark head pressed against her white bosom. With a gasp, she tore her gaze away from the bed and walked toward the window. Her cheeks felt scorched and her legs felt weak. Crossing herself again, her fingers lightly teased her breasts.

Late afternoon sunshine shone through the window's glass, then splintered like a prism across Dimity's translucent robe, outlining her swollen nipples, the darkened suggestion between her thighs, and her fluttering fingers.

Through his spyglass, Cherokee Bill stared at the gal behind the window.

He had a weakness for yellow-haired women and — what the hell was she doing? Her fingers had moved from her breasts to her — *Jesus de Christo!*

Bill fell back upon the straw with a muffled groan as he tried to control his reaction. He had made it safely through the yard, circling the cackling geese, hiding in shadows. He had entered the barn and climbed the loft ladder. The ranch throbbed with the sound of stomping boots. Now his one-eyed snake throbbed, too.

He was plumb loco to have attempted this stunt in broad daylight, but he wanted to see the woman again. She had glowered at him with anger, but he'd read something in her eyes, a signal that made any danger worth his effort. He couldn't be wrong. He had never been wrong before. So he'd wait until midnight, climb the trellis, enter her bedroom through a window, and steal her away from her husband.

Bill sneezed. Shit, he was getting careless.

Women would be the death of him. Brushing the scratchy hay from his face, he knelt alongside the loft's square opening. He had a sixth sense and could smell danger, but right now all he smelled was polished leather and fresh dung. He heard the horses snorting, their hooves striking the stalls. All else was silent. Silence had never betrayed anyone.

The most difficult part would be getting out with the woman. He couldn't climb down the wall while holding her, especially if she put up any kind of resistance. Bill lifted the spyglass to his eye again.

McDonald's house was a rambling two-story structure of whitewashed wood with a front porch. Bill could situate its living room and kitchen by the chimneys. He had been inside similar homes many times. The first floor would include a parlor and dining room. The bedrooms would be upstairs.

Tonight, under cover of darkness, he would carry sweet Yellow Hair down the staircase, through the kitchen, out the back door. If discovered, he'd drop her and reach for his gun. His horse was tethered a mile away, hidden by a copse of scrubby brush.

Bill only hoped the fried chicken he'd stolen would appease any dogs.

■ ■ ■ ■

Dimity couldn't sleep. Hunger gnawed at her tummy. Having continued to feign illness, she had refused supper.

John had joined her around nine o'clock. He had fumbled at her nightie, but she had moaned his attempts away. Jesus, Joseph and Mary, how could she endure his body with its grizzled chest hair, his breath scented with Tonna's fried onions? Her husband's muscles were still hard from years of ranching, but he smelled *old*.

She had accepted John's marriage proposal because her parents disapproved — they said he was too old. From the way he talked, she had envisioned a fine plantation with scores of servants, so she added a dozen gowns to her trousseau. Now her pretty gowns hung inside a cedar-scented wardrobe, their folds settling into permanent creases of disuse. She had imagined herself a member of Denver society. She had pictured an enormous ballroom with musicians playing violins while she and John led the first waltz. How could she have been so wrong? Denver was *miles* from Divide.

The closest town was Cripple Creek. John had once hitched up the buckboard and driven her there for a shopping expedition. Walking down Bennett Avenue, she'd bumped into a beautiful woman who wore an expensive gown and a darling bonnet. Dimity had introduced herself, then *gushed* about her marriage and the ranch; had practically invited the woman to tea. Later John said her new friend was Pearl de Vere, Madam of the Old Homestead parlor house and a "denizen of the Tenderloin."

Oh, how that Pearl person must have laughed. Dimity still blushed at the memory.

So far, their biggest party had been the wedding for her Indian maid, Tonna. There had been guitar music and wild, disorderly dancing. No violins. No waltzes. The bride and groom had shared sliced testicles, cut from a steer that roasted over a deep pit. *Testicles!* She couldn't even say that awful word out loud.

John had promised to take her to Denver. But just like the picnic, he had postponed the trip numerous times. Too much snow. Spring run-off. Steers rounded up and branded. Cows birthing. Horses birthing. John waiting for his young wife to birth, too. Dimity shuddered.

At sixteen her life was over. Soon she'd look like the fat housemaid Rosita, whose face bore a striking resemblance to John's wrinkled hound Starr, named for Belle Starr. Dimity scowled. Belle Starr — thief, rustler, concubine of criminals.

Belting her robe, Dimity tiptoed from the bedroom. She glanced over her shoulder. John slept on his back, snoring.

She walked down the silent hallway and scowled as she gazed into the room that would be the nursery. A rocking horse had been carved by Black Percy. Shelves held picture books and dolls from Dimity's own childhood. Schoolbooks included a Latin primer. She recalled a quote by an old dead man named Homer. It was her tutor's favorite. He had used it over and over until she had memorized it. *Eheu fugaces labuntur anni.* Alas, the fleeting years slip by.

"Damn!" Dimity covered her ears, even though she herself had uttered the cuss word.

She descended the staircase, taking care not to step on the board that creaked, and entered the parlor.

Starr and her mate, Blue Duck, growled.

"Hush!" Dimity wanted to kick the hounds but they shifted positions and went back to sleep, snoring like their master upstairs.

Moonlight shone through the window, illuminating the decanters on the sideboard.

Without further hesitation, Dimity poured herself a tumbler-full of ruby wine. She drank, wrinkled her nose at the taste, then drank some more.

Strolling toward the window, she admired the full moon.

Soon the moon would sliver, carved thin like a birthday cake.

Soon she'd be seventeen, eighteen, nineteen, thirty.

As the moon grew round again, so would her belly when it was overburdened with child. Full moon, full belly, full moon, full belly — she really ought to pay the kitchen a visit. All that wine on an empty stomach was making her dizzy and warm.

She dabbed at the perspiration between her breasts with the hem of her robe. She returned to the sideboard and replenished her glass. Staggering toward a blue velvet settee, she sat in an unladylike position, her breasts thrust forward, her legs spread. She gulped down the wine, sighed, closed her eyes. Rather than Romeo or Sir Galahad or brave Robin, she conjured up an image of Cherokee Bill. She pictured him bare but for a loincloth, and allowed the familiar ache to move from her legs to her breasts as she envisioned his hands stroking.

Starr and Blue Duck growled.

"Quiet!" Dimity admonished, and the trained dogs obeyed her harsh command.

Opening her eyes, she saw a figure standing just inside the arched entranceway. Diluted moonlight revealed doeskin breeches and a feathered hat. Dimity smiled. Her images had never been so real before. Why didn't he walk over to the settee and kneel, as Robin Hood often did?

She placed her empty glass on a small table, lurched upright, opened her arms wide.

"Had a devil of a time finding you, Yellow Hair," said the apparition, his teeth white in his sun-bronzed face. "I thought for certain your husband would wake and then a step squealed like a stuck pig."

"Oh, my brave outlaw, kneel and be knighted."

"*Sí*, the night will hide us. Let me carry you into the night." Walking forward, Cherokee Bill sniffed and grinned. "Damned if you don't smell like a boozy whore."

With a gasp, Dimity placed her hands over her ears. Damned? Whore? Her heroes never cussed. This apparition was real. Opening her mouth to scream, she felt the outlaw's hand cover her face.

She struggled wildly but merely lost her slippers. One slipper landed near Blue

Duck, who gathered it in with his paw and began gnawing its sole. Why didn't Blue Duck bark? Because she had told him to be quiet!

"Settle down, pretty owl." Still holding his hand across her face, Cherokee Bill circled her waist with his other arm, lifted her easily off her feet, and walked backwards toward the front door.

Dimity's stomach rebelled. She tasted sour wine and swallowed. Tears blurred her vision.

She was on the verge of vomiting into Cherokee Bill's hand when he swept her up into his arms, pried her lips apart with his tongue, and kissed her — drawing all the breath from her body. Then he carried her outside, into the night, and for the first time in her life, Dimity fainted.

The mattress bounced, the bed swerved, and Dimity's lashes fluttered.

John smells like fried chicken, she thought, huddling closer to her husband.

"I'm hungry," she said, her eyes still shut.

At her words, the jouncy motion stopped. She felt John lean sideways. A bottle's goosey neck clinked against her teeth. Opening her mouth like a baby bird, she swallowed warm wine.

"Feel better, pretty owl?"

"Yes, thank you. I was thirsty."

"I've a powerful thirst, too," John said. "But not for wine. Let me get rid of this bottle."

He leaned sideways again, and she felt the mattress bounce again.

"Whoa," he said.

"Whoa," she agreed with a giggle.

John's voice sounded different, but Dimity didn't dwell on that for too long. Because his hand was beneath her robe, inside her bodice. He palmed her breast, his thumb lightly stroking her nipple. Blindly, she caught his wrist and guided his hand lower, until it found the throb between her legs.

"*Jesus de Christo!* I never met me a woman so hot she'd make love atop a horse."

Dimity opened her eyes. She wasn't in bed next to John. She slumped across the front of Cherokee Bill's saddle. His arm rested against her stomach while his fingers —

"Leave me alone, you fiend!"

"Hold still. You're making my black dance."

Frightened, she obeyed. Cherokee Bill changed her position so that she faced him on the saddle, her legs dangling. The hard leather hurt her bottom, and the saddle horn pressed against her lower back. The wine still heated her belly but her bare toes were chilled. That and that alone took the edge off her fear.

"Put me down!" she screamed.

"This was *your* idea."

"Put me down, you mangy cur!"

"Yes, ma'am." He placed her feet upon the pebbly ground and nudged his stallion with his heels.

"Wait! Don't ride away. Where am I?"

"On the crest of a hill, above the field where we first met. Cherokee Bill thanks you kindly for your company, ma'am."

"No, wait. You can't just leave me." Dimity clutched at the outlaw's boot, but felt her hands slide as the moon spun and the ground began to rise.

"Hold on, pretty owl. Don't you be swooning again. Cherokee Bill was only funning." He hefted her up, and once again she felt his arms settle around her. "Admire the idea of making love atop my horse. Don't know why I ain't figured it before."

"Are you going to kill me?"

"Kill you?"

"Shoot me with your gun?"

"Guess you could put it that way," he teased, his voice tender. "Aw, you're scared.

Don't be scared. Cherokee Bill won't hurt you."

He took off his gun belt and slung it, buckled, over the saddle horn. Unfastening his trousers, he placed his hands beneath her buttocks and pulled her forward so that she straddled his lap.

She felt his rock-hard bulge between her thighs. "Please don't."

"I won't," he murmured against her mouth.

"You must understand, I cannot do this."

"Cherokee Bill understands."

Removing her robe, he buried his face against her breasts. At the same time, he tore her nightgown's thin material down the length of her back. As she tried to squirm free from him, her robe and gown fell to the trail.

She pushed his face away. "I can't. Not on top of your horse. He'll buck."

"I'll buck. My black's been trained to stay put. Many a time he's stood for hours without moving more than a hoof and tail."

Tempted to capitulate, Dimity remembered. "Inside the house you called me a boozy whore."

"Did I?"

"Yes!"

"Then I must have meant it. Cherokee

Bill never says anything he doesn't mean."

"Oh!" She stiffened her fingers into claws and reached for his face.

He captured her wrists with one hand. His other hand helped her inch forward until she had impaled herself on his erection.

His horse remained motionless. The moon tilted and the stars blurred. Dimity tensed, then lost all control, sinking backwards toward the stallion's mane.

Cherokee Bill pulled her away from the holsters and horn. His tongue licked the strained arch of her throat. She began to cry and felt his tongue tipple her tears as fast as they fell. What a tender gesture. He might be an outlaw but he had the soul of a Romeo. The thought sent her into an ecstasy so powerful, her body convulsed with it. "Oh . . . oh . . . Romeo . . ."

Bill grasped her buttocks with both hands and increased the rhythm of his thrusts. He thought he heard her say *romadizo,* but he must have heard wrong. Why would anyone, even a woman, say "cold in the head" during her most violent spasm?

At long last the fire died out, but not before he had pumped his own hot offering into her body.

Draped in Bill's shirt, Dimity nestled her head against his furred chest. "May we do it again?" she asked.

"No. My black's stood still long enough."

"You don't want me?"

He tweaked her nose. "I want you."

Dimity smiled, satisfied. Because Cherokee Bill, by his own admission, never said anything he didn't mean.

Six

John McDonald belched behind his linen napkin as he watched Dimity fill his breakfast plate with a second helping of eggs and biscuits.

She looked different. Softer. Although barely past sunrise, she had bathed and insisted that she, not Tonna, serve his breakfast. She even moved differently, swinging her rump under her long skirt as she walked from the dining room's sideboard to the mahogany table.

Could this new attitude have anything to do with the appearance of yesterday's outlaw? Upon recovering from her illness, had his young wife understood the importance of a husband's protection?

The swish of her starched petticoats was music to his ears. She seemed unaware of her provocative motion. It was as if she had gone to sleep a girl and awakened a woman. When she bent forward to pour his coffee, he inhaled the scent she had applied above the opening of her white blouse. Rather than a braided bun, her hair hung loose. It rippled like a field of wheat and smelled like lemons. He circled her waist, moved lower, caressed the curve of her buttocks.

"Be careful, darling," she said. "The coffee's hot."

Darling? She'd never called him darling before. Now she was looking at him, her eyes wide. "Guess what, John?"

He arched an eyebrow.

"My mare came back," she said.

"Sandpiper came back?"

"Yes. And headed straight for the barn."

"You've been outside?" Dumbfounded by both these revelations, McDonald negligently sipped his coffee and burned the roof of his mouth.

"Tonna brought me fresh eggs and told me. Then I had to see for myself, and there she was, looking none the worse for wear."

"I wonder why Cherokee Bill let her go."

"You said horse stealing was a hanging offense. Perhaps he had second thoughts."

"Perhaps."

"After breakfast I shall curry Sandpiper and take a *long* ride."

"No, Dimity. Cherokee Bill might be hiding nearby."

"You said he was far away."

"Only if he had your mare." McDonald tossed the napkin over his plate. "I'll round up Percy and a few hands and we'll search the hills. You must remain inside the house."

Her face crumpled and her eyes filled with tears. "Soon I shall be with child and I won't be able to ride."

True, thought McDonald. Jane never left the house during her confinement, endlessly sighing and sewing. A cedar chest held dozens of finely stitched baby shirts.

Was Dimity pregnant? That could be another reason for the startling change in her disposition. It had only been eleven days since she had been visited by her monthly courses, but he had claimed his husbandly rights on two occasions. Could pregnancy affect a woman so quickly? He didn't know. He couldn't remember when Jane had not been pregnant. He resolved to humor Dimity's every whim.

"Very well, my dear, you may ride. Take Tonna with you. Make sure she's well armed, stay close to the house, and don't let Sandpiper stumble."

"I shall be prudent, darling, I promise."

McDonald saw his young wife smile and realized she was ripe for bedding. Perhaps tonight she'd even let him take off her damnfool nightgown.

"Tonna, you must swear to God."

"I do not believe in your god."

Lowering her pale lashes, Dimity gazed at the beads plaited throughout the ebony strands of her servant's long braids. "You don't understand."

"Yes, I do."

"No, you don't. Cherokee Bill said he'd stay until the next new moon. That's a full month. Suppose John and Black Percy find Bill's hiding place? I must warn him."

"I will keep your secret and ride with you since I do not want my husband ambushed. Even Cherokee Bill cannot point two weapons at the same time if he is bedding you."

"Bedding me? In the daytime?" Dimity shivered and, for the first time, saw Tonna smile.

"You are so young, Dimity McDonald."

"Pooh! You're only three years older than I." She chewed her bottom lip. "We planned to meet tonight. Bill promised he'd wait by the first pasture."

"No. You must not do this. Your husband —"

"Snores till cocks crow."

"Suppose John McDonald wakes to use the privy and discovers you are gone?"

"He didn't last night. Last night I rode to Bill's campsite and we made love, wrapped inside his blankets. I rode Sandpiper home, just before sunrise, cloaked in Bill's shirt. Nobody saw me. I washed away all trace of our love, pinned his shirt to the clothesline, and cooked John's breakfast. Today I must warn Bill and return his shirt. Tonight —"

"There must be no tonight. You play with fire."

"I play with water. You were right about waterfalls. Is there an Indian potion to make John sleep? Something I can hide in his drink?"

"Ask your own Indian!"

"Please?"

"I have herbs in my garden, Dimity, but many that cure can also kill."

"Surely there's a plant for harmless sleep. Remember what I told you about Romeo and Juliet?"

"Cherokee Bill is no Romeo."

"Yes, he is. He dried my tears with his tongue. Mr. Shakespeare didn't write that, but he would have if he'd thought of it." Dimity sighed. "All right, I'll find another way. But don't expect me to give up my outlaw. There was a full moon last night, and Bill promised he'd stay until the next full moon. That's a *long* time."

102

"A month seems endless when you are sixteen, Dimity."

"A month is forever, Tonna."

Cherokee Bill grinned. "You brought a friend to share our fun, pretty owl?"

"I brought my servant to stand guard. My husband and some of his hands are looking for you. It was a mistake to return on my mare."

"It would have been far more dangerous for me to hand you over to your husband," Bill said, crushing her against his chest.

"Are you mad? Let me go." She pulled away from his rough embrace then reconsidered. His thick dark pelt felt so comfortable, not the least bit scratchy.

About to catapult into his arms again, she heard him say, "Cherokee Bill thanks you kindly for his shirt and the warning, ma'am."

"Yes, well, I . . ."

"Was there something else?"

"No. Yes. Do you have food?"

"Cookies and wine. Are you hungry again?"

Her cheeks burned. "I'll bring chicken and biscuits tonight."

"Cherokee Bill looks forward to his supper."

Dimity stamped her foot. "Where are your blankets?"

He gestured toward the trees. "Do you have need of a blanket, pretty owl?"

Bill was laughing at her, damn his soul! She swayed forward, only half faking her swoon.

He swept her up into his arms and carried her through leafy shadows. She disrobed and watched him remove his guns, boots and trousers. She feigned reluctance when he pried her legs apart. After he'd penetrated, she ran her nails down his back, drawing blood.

"Jesus de Christo," he swore. "Sheathe your claws!"

"Sheathe your sword."

"Wildcat!"

"Angel."

Shifting in her chair, Dimity glanced at John from beneath her pale lashes. "It's too early to be certain, darling, but I believe I am with child."

"I'm very pleased, my dear."

"Did Jane know so soon?"

"To tell the truth, Dimity, I don't recall a time when Jane was not with child." Seated in his comfortable armchair, McDonald sipped his drink. Dimity had brought him a second glass of hot cider, garnished with a stick of cinnamon, an odd beverage for a summer night, but tasty.

The living-room windows were open and yet he felt so hot. There was no blaze in the fireplace but he saw blue sparks. His eyes were filled with blue sparks.

"John!"

"Yes?"

"I was telling you I've been feeling poorly, especially at night."

"I'm sorry, Dimity." Now his tongue felt thick and fuzzy. And he had sharp belly pains.

"Perhaps Rosita can prepare one of the guest rooms. I need my own bed. My health is so delicate. Papa used to say I'd faint at the puff of a breeze. John darling, are you all right?"

"A touch of indigestion. Your stew was tasty but I ate too much."

"I prepared it the way you like it. Onions and mushrooms and basil and chili peppers and — John, what's wrong?" Alarmed, Dimity watched his glass of cider fall from his hand as he clutched his belly. Rising, she placed her fingers across his brow. "You have a fever! Here I've been prattling on and on about my small malady while you are truly ill."

"Not ill, tired. We rode all day. No trace of Cherokee Bill."

"Let me help you upstairs."

"Fetch Percy."

"I'll help you, John. I'm your wife."

"I don't want you to see — oh, God!"

McDonald tried to rise from his chair, but the forward motion made him sick to his stomach.

He heard Dimity scream, heard footsteps, heard Dimity say, "Can you carry him to the bedroom, Black Percy? Tonna, find the laudanum. I believe there's also some chamomile on the medicine shelf. Why are you just standing there? Fetch Rosita and tell her to boil water."

Dogging Black Percy's footsteps, Dimity entered the bedroom. She loosened John's clothes, bathed his body, helped him don a clean nightshirt. Murmuring endearments, she piled hot-water bottles across his chest and fussed with his blankets. When his stomach rebelled yet again, she held a basin underneath his chin. And she carefully measured the opium tincture that brought him blessed sleep.

McDonald was surprised to find that he enjoyed his illness. Dimity bathed his body and never flinched at his nakedness or his instinctive arousal. She fed him, blowing on the broth to cool it, lifting the spoon to his mouth. Once she even sipped from the spoon, filling her mouth, and leaned over to deliver the broth, along with a wet kiss. Amused, he watched her reaction — a becoming blush, a lowering of her pale lashes.

"You must think me wanton, John."

"Do it again, Dimity."

She did, feeding him broth and kisses until his erection poked up through the bed sheets like the blunted horn on one of his lusty stud bulls.

He had another recurrence of the first night's stomach pains. Again, Dimity nursed him capably as his belly cramped and he spewed violently into the blasted basin. Again, he gratefully swallowed the opium tincture. When he awoke the next morning, Dimity had dark smudges beneath her eyes. Her body slumped with fatigue, and he insisted, despite her protestations, that she leave the sickroom.

When his strange ailment finally came to an end, Dimity convinced him that he needed more bed rest. Between great gulping sobs, she said, "If anything happened to you, I would *die.*"

He had married Dimity because she was young and fertile. Now he found himself falling in love. So he indulged himself, staying abed many days after the pain was gone.

Dimity stamped her foot. Where was Bill?

A full moon shone down upon a carpet of dandelions, and she thought about weaving the flowers through her braids.

Where was Bill?

She had a surprise for her outlaw.

Escaping undetected from a healthy John was difficult, and she couldn't chance another stew. In fact, she had tolerated her husband's clumsy advances three times during the past week. Their brief lovemaking induced natural sleep. She occupied the guest bedroom, but if this went on much longer, she'd be caught and Bill would be shot or hanged.

Where was he?

She ached to tell Bill her scheme. Her riding habit's pockets were stuffed with the banknotes she'd found in John's office. A carpetbag held her favorite books and all her jewelry, including the emerald necklace John had given her last week. She had admired the necklace during their honeymoon, and John had sent Percy all the way to Denver to buy it for her.

"*Gracias,* husband," she murmured.

Bill could kidnap her. They would ride for

Mexico City and sell her jewels; the emerald was worth a small fortune. Then they'd purchase a ranch and make love night and day, without hiding. John would divorce her, of course, but the scandal wouldn't touch her in Mexico.

There was a second surprise, as well. The fib she'd told John had become reality. She'd never been late with her monthly courses, her breasts hurt, and this morning she had vomited her breakfast. She welcomed the inconvenience. Tonna said a woman's figure rounded after birthing. Bill would like that. He said he fancied a gal with plump curves.

Oh, how she fancied her angel. Love was pure, so God would forgive her lies and the finely chopped toadstools. She had not killed John, merely caused him discomfort. Toward the end he'd enjoyed his illness, so that made her deceit less sinful.

She paced back and forth alongside the pasture fence. She had tied Sandpiper's reins to a fence post, planning to ride away with Bill as soon as he acknowledged her scheme. He had always been early, eager to greet his *buha nocturna* — his pretty owl — but it was well past their meeting time. Soon the first burst of dawn would color the sky. Soon the full moon would sink beyond the horizon.

Where was he?

Tears washed the blue from her eyes as she remembered his words: "Cherokee Bill never says anything he doesn't mean." She remembered telling Tonna that Bill had promised he'd stay until the next full moon. She remembered telling Tonna a month was forever.

It wasn't.

Cherokee Bill was gone and she carried an outlaw's child inside her body. A child tainted with an outlaw's blood.

Her gaze touched upon her carpetbag. Tonight she'd toss her books into the fireplace and burn what her husband called "romantic applesauce."

SEVEN

A pinecone crackled. It sounded like the distant pop of a pistol. John McDonald quailed. According to the newspaper, he was lucky to be alive!

From his chair he squinted at Dimity. She sat in her chair, facing the fireplace. On the floor between them was the hide of a cow, but it might as well have been a whole herd. Ignoring his presence, she embroidered a religious motto, her needle rising and falling in a mesmerizing rhythm of continuity.

She was only two months from her birthing date and didn't like to be stared at, so he reread the newspaper, which gave a summary of Cherokee Bill's capture.

The outlaw had been apprehended inside the home of a woman. The newspaper didn't mention the woman's name, or what she and Bill had been doing at the time, but McDonald could well imagine since the article gleefully hinted that Bill's trousers were missing. Knocked unconscious by the woman's cousin, Bill was transported to Fort Smith, Arkansas, and tried before Judge Roy Parker. Accused of many crimes, Bill had been convicted for the murder of one unarmed man in a post-office robbery.

McDonald focused on his wife again. "Do you remember the outlaw who held us at gunpoint and stole your mare?"

Startled, Dimity dropped her embroidery hoops, shut her eyes, and sagged against her chair's cushion.

Damn me for a fool, thought McDonald. *Now I've gone and done it. She's frightened out of her wits.*

Rising, he hastened to Dimity's side but stopped short at the sight of her uplifted hands and splayed fingers.

"Don't," she said. "I cannot tolerate the touch of a man."

"I'm not a man, I'm your husband," McDonald blurted. Her pale-blue eyes narrowed, and he flinched, anticipating a scathing reply.

"I vaguely recall an outlaw who stole our picnic lunch," she said. "Is there something about him in your newspaper?"

"Never mind, my dear, it's not important." McDonald stifled a sigh of relief as he scurried back to his chair.

112

Dimity retrieved her tapestry and sat straight, her small feet planted together. "Read the story, John."

"I don't want to upset you, Dimity."

"Do I look upset? Read the story."

A woman with child must be indulged, thought McDonald. How many times had he sent his ranch hands to Denver or Cripple Creek when Dimity pleaded for out-of-season fruits and vegetables? Usually she flung the food at the nearest wall and demanded some new dish. The hands were ready to wring her neck.

She had burned her diptych then perversely decorated the master bedroom with a variety of gilded crosses and religious pictures, ordered from catalogues. Holding his wife beneath the bedcovers, McDonald sometimes felt the pain of Christ's crucifixion settle upon his own limbs. Dimity would tease him to a peak of desire then turn away, hugging her belly. Last night she said his fingers made her skin burn and she'd rather be stung by red ants than endure his touch.

"Is the outlaw dead, John?"

"Huh?"

"Have you lost your hearing as well as your eyesight?"

"I haven't lost my eyesight." McDonald brought the newspaper closer to his face.

He had recently purchased a pair of spectacles but vainly refused to wear them in front of Dimity. "It says here that Bill staged a prison break. He had a gun smuggled in and when the head jailer refused to unlock his cell door, Bill shot him. Then, with no hope of escape, Bill emptied his gun at the other guards. Now he awaits a new trial on those killings."

"A new trial? Whatever for?"

McDonald shrugged. "Waste of time, if you ask me. You can only hang a man once."

"I hope they hang him twice."

"What did you say? I couldn't hear you."

"I said I crave testicles, like the ones we served at Tonna's wedding."

McDonald leapt to his feet. If he slaughtered a steer and roasted it through the night, Dimity could have balls for breakfast.

Bundled in blankets and furs, Dimity shifted on the wagon's hard seat.

Next to Dimity sat the driver, handling the reins attached to four mules as if the leather straps were long-stemmed roses with razor-sharp thorns. A hardened trail hand, he wanted to bawl like a lost calf. Mac's wife, her belly swollen with child, wouldn't stop yammering.

"God will punish you for your cruelty,"

she said. "Stop bouncing this wagon, you horrible man. John, come here!"

McDonald reined in his horse. Dimity was due to give birth in one month, and they were trying to reach her parents' home in Abilene, Texas.

She had tenaciously refused to give birth on the ranch. "Jane lost four," she had cried. "The ranch is cursed and I shall die if I stay here."

He had suggested Cripple Creek or Denver, but she had insisted that the hooded figure of Death had knocked on her bedroom door and only her mother could defy Death.

Not normally a superstitious man, McDonald recalled the trail drive and the killing of the calves. If Dimity believed Death was knocking, he had to get her off the ranch.

It was March sixteenth. He had planned to leave earlier, but a February blizzard had made travel impossible.

"John, get over here right now!"

"What is it, dearest?"

"This nasty man is making the wagon bounce. When will we arrive at Papa's house?"

"Soon. Perhaps a few more days." McDonald glanced at the sky. He didn't like the look of the swirling clouds and could practically smell snow. Damn! If he turned back, Dimity would die from pure stubbornness. If he forged ahead, they would all freeze or be buried alive in an avalanche.

"I want to see my mama," Dimity whimpered. "I want him."

Him? God?

"Where is he?"

Death, not God, thought McDonald. She had seen Death knocking. Was this going to be Jane all over again? He signaled the driver to halt, dismounted, scooped Dimity into his arms, and carried her toward the back of the canvas-covered wagon.

Even as the first snowflakes began to fall, he could feel his wife's heat and touch the wetness that soaked her skirts. "Tonna," he called, trying to temper his voice with calm authority. "I believe Dimity's time is at hand."

"No, John," she protested, "that cannot be true."

"Don't squirm so, dearest. Save your strength."

"Please, John, I shall hold it in. I cannot have this baby on the trail."

There are no doors on the trail, McDonald thought. No doors for Death to knock on.

"Hush, my dear," he said. "You're fevered."

"Don't tell me to hush. You have no right. It's not *your* baby."

"I know," he soothed. "A man is helpless in these situations. I wish I could share your pain, dearest. I wish I could have our baby for you."

After he had settled Dimity inside the wagon, McDonald looked up again. Not yet evening, the sky was gray-white, the same color as the weathered boards on his house. Why had God whitewashed the sky with snow?

McDonald signaled his driver to tether the mules, shouted for Percy to collect wood, unsaddled his horse, scooped up some kindling, and began to build a fire.

The wagon's canvas top protected the two women from the harsh elements. Tonna had neatly stacked the interior with blankets, furs, and cured steer hides. She had even included a soft patchwork quilt.

"I'm cold, Tonna," Dimity moaned. "I want to go home."

"It is too late for that now."

"Why are you angry at me?"

"Because your foolishness has placed us all in danger, especially your baby."

"I don't want this baby."

"You have no choice. If your husband had known your time was so close at hand, he would not have left the ranch."

"Why are you taking off my clothes?"

"Your skirt and petticoats are wet."

"Yes. He makes me wet."

"Hush, Dimity. Do you want me to brush your hair while we wait?"

"He loves my hair. He calls me Yellow Hair."

"Do not talk of one who no longer exists."

"I dreamed I saw Cherokee Bill on a wooden platform. He laughed. A man in a black hooded robe placed a noose around Bill's neck. The man took off his hood and raised his face, only it wasn't a face. It was a skull with bones, like you'd see on the ranch when a cow is lost and found many months later, only it was human. Cherokee Bill laughed at Death."

"Then death is waiting for your outlaw, Dimity, not you or your child."

"Cherokee Bill's child."

"You do not know this. It could be the child of John McDonald."

"No, Tonna. The child is Bill's. That's why he laughed at Death."

"Lower your voice. Do you want your

husband to hear?"

Outside the wagon, John McDonald heard the agitated bray of a mule. Prodding the fire with a severed birch branch, he said, "The water's near boiled, Percy, but we need more wood. I'll fetch some."

"Take a gun, Mac. I could almost swear I glimpsed a mountain lion."

As if to prove his words true, the mules strained against their tethers.

McDonald grabbed his rifle and walked into the forest. He halted at the foot of a small rise, where the trees had thinned. Atop the rise, he saw a cougar perched upon a jutting boulder. Four, perhaps five feet long, its tawny coat was sharply etched against the sky. McDonald's breath caught in his throat.

The cougar stared, unblinking.

McDonald raised his rifle and sighted; it would be an easy shot.

The cougar remained motionless.

McDonald felt snow soak the collar of his sheepskin jacket. Why couldn't he pull the trigger? Why didn't the cougar pounce? McDonald's eyes watered. With his head tilted toward the cat, snow blurred his vision, so he brushed the back of his gloved hand across his eyes and adjusted his Stetson's brim.

When he looked again, the cougar had vanished.

McDonald lowered his rifle. He was inexplicably happy, positive Death wouldn't arrive. Not for Dimity. Not for his child. Nothing would die tonight.

Hours passed. John and Percy heated blankets and passed them to Tonna. The wagon's interior smelled like damp wool, and the small space became thick with the smoke from two lanterns.

Dimity thrashed from side to side. Perspiration streamed down her face. "Where is he? Why won't he come?"

"Hush!"

"I meant the baby, Tonna."

"He will come when ready."

"I shall die and go to hell for my sins. Do you think Bill waits for me there?"

"I do not believe in hell."

"*Jesus de Christo,* I am going to die!"

"Your child, not death, has arrived. Spread your legs, Dimity."

"You sound like *him,* Tonna."

John McDonald heard the piercing cry of an infant.

Tonna climbed out of the wagon. "You have a son," she said. "He is lusty and fine."

"Dimity?"

"She, too, has cheated death this night."

"Thank God." He hugged Tonna. "Percy, did you hear?"

"Yep. Guess I've got myself another Mc-Donald to teach the ways of ranching, Mac."

"You damned tenderfoot! Who taught who? There's whiskey in my saddlebag. We must drink to my son. Then we'll catch some shut-eye, hitch up the mules, and head back to the ranch."

"What about Abilene?"

"Texas be damned, begging your pardon, Tonna. Dimity has already fooled Death."

After they had finished the whiskey, Percy staggered to the wagon and peeked inside. Making an about-face, he said, "You know what, Mac? Your son was born on the trail between Colorado and Abilene, Texas."

"Damned if that ain't true, my friend. Damned if Dimity didn't birth him like an Indian squaw, begging your pardon, Tonna. Should we call him Little Mac? John Mc-Donald Junior's his name, but it's too big a handle."

"Why not call him Cat? Colorado, Abilene, Texas. C-a-t."

McDonald felt a grin split his face. "Did I tell you 'bout the cougar, Percy? I didn't shoot him and now I know why. My son'll

121

be called Cat."

Inside the wagon, Dimity overheard and decided she wouldn't quibble. If she had her way, the child would be called Satan, but Cat would do. With a shudder, she buried her memories of a voice shouting, "*Jesus de Christo,* wildcat! Sheathe your claws!"

By the third day, Dimity had resigned herself to the wagon's discomfort. Soon she'd be home, safe inside her warm bedroom with its gilded crosses and pictures of her Lord.

"You shall have a long rest, dearest," John had said. "Then we'll journey to Denver where you may buy new gowns and jewels, anything your heart desires."

"No, John. I've been lax of late in the running of our household, but I shall remedy that when we arrive home. And I want to give you another child right away. Another son."

Now Dimity glanced through the wagon opening, between the tied-back flaps. She saw snow, white as an outlaw's evil smile, and heard Tonna call her name.

"What do you want, Tonna?"

"Your son is hungry."

"He is always hungry. Very well, I ache

with milk. Put him to my breast."

Dimity gazed down at Cat. He appeared to have light eyes, a thin tapered nose, raven-colored hair, and a dusky complexion. So had *he* looked as a babe, John had said.

God works in mysterious ways, she thought. *Jane's four babies perished while this son of an outlaw thrives. John must never suspect Cat isn't his, so I shall foster the little bastard. But not even God can make me love him.*

EIGHT

Denver, Colorado

While John McDonald and Black Percy commemorated Cat's first birthday with a bottle of corn whiskey, and Dimity thanked God for a second son, Ned Lytton paced up and down the hallway of his father's Denver home.

Much to Ned's relief, his wife's screams were somewhat muted by the bedroom's thick wooden door. *My son is coming,* he thought, wishing Johanna would suffer in silence. Even muffled, her caterwauling was grating to the ears.

The door opened and Ned caught a glimpse of the tableau inside. Although barely past noon, several lamps and a dozen bayberry-scented candles had been lit. Logs smoldered in the fireplace, drenching the room with a smoky haze, marinating Johanna, who lay on the four-poster, her bloated belly covered by a sheet.

Dr. Bronstein entered the hallway and closed the bedroom door behind him. "This birth is more difficult than the first one," he said.

"The baby's not in any danger, is he?"

"Not at the moment, but your wife —"

"Is of little consequence. If it comes to a choice between Mrs. Lytton and my son, you must save my son. Do you understand?"

Before the doctor could respond, a servant ran down the hall, skidding to a stop when she spied the men.

"What is it, Annie?" Ned drew his gaze away from the doctor's flushed face.

"Master Reed, sir. He's in the music room. I told him Mrs. Johanna was havin' her baby, but he said —"

"I can well imagine what he said. Offer Master Reed refreshments and tell him I shall be down directly."

"Yes, sir." Annie curtsied and fled.

Ned draped one arm across Bronstein's plump shoulders. "I have every confidence in your skill. When I hold my son, I shall double your fee."

"That isn't necessary."

"Look, I know how much you doctors like money."

Ervin Bronstein translated "doctors like money" into *Yidden hobn lieb gelt* — Jews like money. Frightened, he reentered the bedroom. Suppose he lost both Johanna and the baby? Edward had requested his services. Edward was an old, trusted friend, but Ned hated Jews.

Bronstein wiped his wet face with a clean towel then checked Johanna's pulse. Poor lady. Ned Lytton was a *putz*.

Johanna's screams faded as Ned strolled down the hallway. He looked into the nursery, cluttered with toys and picture books, even though his daughter Kate was only thirteen months old. Nanny perched on a cushioned rocker, underneath a gilded cage. A silent canary perched inside the cage.

Kate lay on her side, her sturdy body clothed in a yellow sack-like garment. At the tap-tap of her father's boots, she tried to thrust her head between the crib posts. She had spiky black hair, and the clef in the chin was no larger than the crease in a linen napkin.

Should he take her from the crib? Toss her in the air? Nanny wouldn't approve. Nanny said Kate cried when he stopped playing with her, which made Ned feel soupy inside. A shame Kate wasn't a boy. Yet if his firstborn had to be female, Katherine Johanna Lytton would do just fine.

Ned put his thumbs in his ears and waggled his fingers. "Hee-haw, Katie."

He waited for her delighted gurgle then continued down the hallway and stairs until he heard the Steinway. Rachmaninoff.

His father's music room had large leaded bay windows overlooking a landscape of Colorado blue-barked willow, gray poplar, white birch, dark-green firs and red dogwood. A roaring blaze in the fireplace negated the snowy scene outside the window. A tall man straddled the piano stool, his fingers suspended above the keyboard. Spying Ned, he began to play "Daisy Bell."

"Hello, Richard." Ned reached into his father's humidor and retrieved a Cuban cigar. "What brings you to Colorado? And what's happening with the Klan?"

"Shut up! Walls have ears."

"I only meant —"

"You know I'm not allowed to discuss details."

Ned felt his face flush. To hide his discomfort, he clipped the cigar, struck a match on the heel of his boot, and puffed the cigar until its fat tip glowed.

Richard swiveled his stool, spat into his hands, and palmed untidy strands of silver-blond hair away from his eyes.

"Don't stop playing," Ned said. "I sure do

admire that song. The best thing about a bicycle is that it allows a woman to shorten her skirts and show her ankles."

"You never change, Lytton. Your wife's upstairs birthin' your second child while you fret 'bout the length of a woman's skirt."

"I fret 'bout what's underneath the skirt. Did Annie offer you food and drink?"

"Annie?"

"The servant you discomfited with your remarks about childbirth."

"There's no time." Rising, Richard walked toward the window. "I must leave soon."

"But you just got here. I thought we'd celebrate the birth of my son."

"Is it safe to talk?" Richard turned and stared at a portrait of Ned's grandfather, as if the benevolent face might carry tales.

"Absolutely. The servants' quarters are at the other end of the hall. So's the kitchen."

"Have you read about the new Jim Crow Car Law?"

"Of course." *Some mumbo-jumbo about Louisiana and a separate-equal doctrine.*

"The Supreme Court'll declare the law legal this spring," Richard said. "How does your father feel about the Cuban revolt against Spain?"

"Sympathetic. Father has interests in the

Cuban sugar industry. Why do you ask?"

"We're tryin' to raise money to help Spain."

"What do you want me to do?"

"Lie low. If Edward has interests in Cuba, he's no good to us. Have you been makin' peace with him?"

"I've been licking his bootstraps," Ned replied bitterly, "but I miss the Klan."

"So do I. Listen, Lytton, everyone believed the Klan defeated back in the eighties. Do you realize that the men who once owned the most land and slaves now control local government? They pick U.S. Senators and —"

"I know all that!" Ned scowled. He might be fuzzy about Jim Crow laws and the Cuban thingamajig, but he knew nigras once ran the Republican Party. And he knew Northern industrialists and bankers and Southern white aristocrats were now Republican partners together.

"Did you know we don't have to wear hoods anymore? For the last few years we've arranged up to three hangings a week, defendin' white womanhood. The South's governors and ministers justify our goals. A white North don't care 'bout Southern nigras. The Klan'll rise again and we'll be there, ready to take control, and I'll be

Grand Dragon of Texas."

"Grand what?"

"Dragon. Klan leader of the state, appointed by our Imperial Wizard."

"Then I'll be Colorado's Grand Dragon."

"No, Ned. You'll be a Kleagle, a recruiter. For now, your most important task is to keep Edward happy. I don't mean to lack compassion, but you said your father has an impaired heart. Think what we can do when you inherit his fortune. By the way, is he home?"

Ned shook his head. "Edward's squeamish. He'd arranged a business meeting before Johanna let loose with her second scream."

"Then I believe I will indulge."

"Would you like wine? Whiskey?"

"No. I've tempered my consumption of spirits. Does your father employ any colored servants?"

"One laundress, sweet as molasses."

"Make the arrangements."

Edward Lytton waited at a private table, early for his appointment with artist-agent Sydney Alexander. "Sandy" had convinced Edward that paintings were a safe investment. Edward had no quarrel with safe investments, especially when he could enjoy the beauty of his purchases.

As he surveyed the restaurant, he smiled at the framed photographs of railroad cars. Those smoky monsters were responsible for his wealth and prominence.

Edward had been born in Philadelphia, the son of prosperous Quakers. While still in short pants, he had accompanied his father out west to decide where the Pennsylvania Railroad should expand. Fort Sumter fell, postponing that decision. Edward's father defended the Union and died in battle, inadvertently severing his son's ties to Quaker tenets.

At age seventeen, Edward secured employment constructing the Kansas Pacific Railroad west from Kansas City. In August 1870, the Kansas Pacific met the Denver Pacific.

Edward envisioned a railroad north and south, built from Denver to Texas, fed en route by future east–west railroads. If a three-foot narrow-gauge track was built, it would allow for sharp curves and access through the steep Rocky Mountains, and it would be cheaper to construct than a line with tracks four feet, eight and a half inches apart.

He wasn't the only man with that vision. In fact, he was too late. William Palmer, another Philadelphian, had already approached influential friends, offering them railroad bonds. Palmer planned to raise capital for a line through two Mexican land grants, the Sangre de Cristo and the Beaubien-Miranda. Palmer's proposed railroad would quadruple the value of those remote areas along the Colorado–New Mexico border.

Edward sold everything he owned, including property from his deceased father. Then he borrowed all he could and went into the real-estate business.

During a trip back east, he met Dorothy Currigan. Seventeen-year-old "Dolly" was beautiful, passive and pliable. Her father had made a few unfortunate investments and was anxious to pool his remaining assets in Edward's venture.

After accepting Edward's marriage proposal, passive, pliable Dolly developed a stubborn streak. She didn't want to leave New York, and she repeatedly postponed the wedding. "Female trouble," she'd say with a sigh, though her damned female trouble didn't hinder her appetite for fine dining, nor her attendance at the opera.

William Palmer was engaged to an Eastern woman too — Queen Mellon of Flushing, Long Island. Just like Dolly, Miss Mellon had doubts about living in Colorado. Together, Lytton and Palmer searched for sites on which to construct suitable homes for their future brides.

Riding atop Palmer's Concord coach, Edward admired Pikes Peak and toured the cathedral park of violent reds called Garden of the Gods.

"I planned to have a town every ten miles along the railroad," Palmer said. "Why don't I build a special one at Pikes Peak for well-to-do people, on the order of Newport or Saratoga? That would solve our mutual problem."

Palmer built his estate near Garden of the Gods and called it Glen Eyrie, after the eagle's nest on top of the gray entrance rock. Lytton's entrance had an eagle's nest, too, and he called his home Aguila del Oro, Spanish for eagle of gold.

Dolly's father had a long talk with his recalcitrant daughter. The wedding date was set. Following a honeymoon in London, Edward and Dolly journeyed to their new home.

Dolly hated it. Edward saw the mountains as majestic, Dolly thought them hovering shadows. She found Aguila del Oro sinister. And the area was infested with rattlesnakes.

Edward allowed Dolly to visit New York

often. His daughter, Elizabeth, was born there exactly nine months after the honeymoon. His son, Edward Gaylord, was born in Colorado Springs one year later. The delivery wasn't difficult but Dolly kept screaming, "The snakes will get me, they'll get my babies, they'll sting us all."

"Snakes don't sting, they bite," Edward soothed.

Seven years later, Dolly left for London, taking Elizabeth but relinquishing Ned, the heir.

Still abroad, Dolly died of acute appendicitis. Edward moved to Denver. Aguila del Oro remained vacant.

Today, Edward was content. Wealthy beyond his wildest dreams, he had never remarried. Elizabeth taught school in New York. Ned and his family shared Edward's Denver mansion.

Unfortunately, Ned drank too much and had no aptitude for business. He was weak, just like Dolly, yet he was doing his best to produce a Lytton dynasty. After the birth of Kate, he had immediately planted a new seed. Maybe this one would be a boy — another Edward.

Dr. Bronstein found Ned inside the music room, straddling a piano stool. On the floor lay an empty bottle of whiskey.

One look at Bronstein's face and Ned lurched to his feet. "What's wrong?"

"Nothing's wrong. You have a new daughter, Mr. Lytton." Frightened by the expression on Ned's face, Ervin took a few steps backwards. *Cossack,* he thought. *Putz!*

"My father will handle your fee. Get the hell out of here!"

Bronstein pulled some Jew trick and changed my son into a girl, Ned thought.

"I'll name her Dorothy after my dear departed mother," he told the portrait on the wall, the first Edward. "That should please Father."

Retrieving the whiskey bottle, Ned threw it against the fireplace grate.

As the glass shattered, he recalled the little lame crib whore, Blueberry. He'd never met another woman so eager to please. All the same, he'd stayed away from Cripple Creek. Blueberry might insist they were "wed good and proper."

Besides, he owed the chit a pair of ruby earrings.

NINE

When Blueberry Smith rode into Cripple Creek on Whiskey Johnnie's burro Clementine, tents dotted the hills and ravines. Had Blueberry lived, she would have seen Bennett Avenue, Third Street and Meyers Avenue become flourishing business districts. She might have moved her lips carefully, the way her brother Geordie had taught her, and read the Cripple Creek Business Directory, which listed eight hundred enterprises. Among them were twenty-six saloons, forty-two real-estate offices, and thirty-six law offices.

The directory didn't list parlor houses.

Or gambling establishments.

Or dance halls.

Or the cribs.

In Poverty Gulch, sunlight streamed through a window, shining down upon a cradle. Fools Gold was asleep, her inky lashes hiding her dark-blue eyes. Her cheeks were flushed and her mouth formed a secret smile. One hand clasped a rattle half filled with uncooked pinto beans.

Outside, the painted name over the door read MINTA. Following Blueberry's death and burial in the Mt. Pisgah cemetery, Minta had moved her own belongings into Blueberry's crib. Sometimes, when the wind whistled at the windows, she could hear her friend's laughter.

Today, seated on Blueberry's rocker, Minta said, "Sorry I baked them gingerbread men. It's too hot for baking. Ain't it hot for April, Belle?"

"April?"

"April twenty-fifth, Fools Gold's birth date."

"What then became of Christmas, Min?"

Minta hid a sigh. Last Hallow's Eve her neighbor had been hit in the face with a hatchet and now she had trouble recollecting things.

"Christmas went bye-bye, Belle. Here, have a gingerbread man."

"Sure cooked them purty." Belle sat forward in her cane-backed chair and reached for the cookie.

"I planned to bake a birthday cake, but Fools Gold loves my gingerbread men. She seems to admire all men, and her not even out of nappies."

"Fools Gold?" Belle shook her head and hair bobs flew. Blonde strands tumbled forward, shading button eyes and a nose that resembled Mr. Edison's light bulb.

"My poppet."

Belle shook her head again, until her eyes were freed from the bristle-like veil. "What's a poppet, Min? A muffin?"

"A muffin's a *popover.*" Minta retrieved a comb from her trunk and began to neaten Belle's hair. "Jasmine the Brit taught me poppet. It means a baby that looks like a doll."

"What'cha' want a baby for?"

"The least I can do is raise Blueberry's bairn. It's no hindrance. I love the child."

"Blueberry knew the risk. She didn't count days nor spit in no frog's mouth."

"Blueberry was my sister, Belle."

"She was? I thought her name was, uh . . ."

"Smith. Blueberry Smith. But she acted more sisterly than my own kin."

"I got a sister. She lives in, uh . . ."

"Chicago."

Belle stared at the cradle. "It's easy now 'cause the peewee sleeps. What's gonna happen when she's growed?"

"I'll send her to a twiggy school in Denver."

"She's gonna learn trees?"

"Jasmine the Brit taught me that word, too. It means choice." Belle's hatchet-scarred brow still puckered so Minta added, "Fancy."

Belle's brow unpuckered. "It takes lots of coins to fancy-school a peewee. You're addled, Min."

"Well, if that ain't the pot calling the kettle black!" Minta took a deep breath. "Sorry, Belle, sometimes the devil puts words into my mouth and I say them before I think."

Belle squinted down into the cradle. "That there's a purty peewee."

"Her papa's a rich gent and someday Fools Gold'll look Nugget Ned straight in the eye and tell him how he wronged Blueberry, the two-faced bastard!"

"The bastard has two faces?"

"It's just an expression, Belle."

"What if you have peewees of your own, Min?"

"Can't have no bairn of my own."

"Why not?"

"It's a long story."

"Oh, I love stories. When're you meeting up with Otto?"

"Soon. Have another gingerbread while I

get dressed."

Minta shrugged off her kimono and reached for a corset. "Once upon a time" — she smiled at Belle's rapt expression — "I lived on a dairy farm in Wisconsin. At sixteen I wed the feller who lived on the farm next to me."

"You was wed? Oh, that's nice. How come you ain't lived happy ever after?"

"My husband Rolf was clearing a new acre when a tree fell on him." Minta adjusted her corset over the chemise then sidled closer to Belle so she could pull the strings. "I tried to free his body out from under the tree, lost my bairn, and the doc said I couldn't have no more. Albert wanted to wed me anyways."

"What's an Albert?"

"Not what. Who. Albert was Rolf's brother. I loved him so. Was him I always wanted to marry. When Rolf passed, Albert said we'd get hitched, but his folks talked him out of wedding his brother's barren widow, so I packed up and left for Minneap'lis. Found me some work with a lady who sewed clothes. Dang corset!" Minta buckjumped like a grasshopper. "Wish Otto'd come here so's I wouldn't have to wear this dangfool contraption."

She stepped into an altered crimson gown

140

that had once been Nugget Ned's gift to Blueberry. "Anyways, I sewed night and day and folks swore my stitches outdid anything from Paris France. Then I met the Soiled Doves."

"Birdies?"

"Whores. They were young, clean, and wanted me to do the finishing work on their pretties. Why sew, I thought to myself, when I could earn more coins on my back and not ruin my eyes in the bargain? So I joined the profession. I plied my trade in Minnesota and the Dakotas, working west, but men kept talking 'bout Colorado. They said it was a rich land with free-spending miners and millionaires. They said the streets were paved with gold."

"The streets're paved with mud, Min."

"I got to Denver first, but the dance hall girls at the Alcatraz Theater were making fifty cents a night and the crib girls did worse. I sewed some pretties quick, for coins, took the Denver and Rio Grande to Colorado Springs, then changed to the Short Line. When I finally set foot in Cripple Creek, guess who I saw?"

"Toot, toot, all aboard. I like trains, Min."

"I saw Albert. He'd come to pan for gold. We would have wed but he caught the fever." Minta sighed. "Albert was my own

141

true love."

"Ain't Otto your own true love?"

"I love him well enough, but Otto ain't the marrying kind and he don't care none for Fools Gold. That's why I'm meeting up with him at the Central."

"I'll watch your peewee real good whilst you're gone." Uncertainty clouded Belle's eyes. "It's hot for Christmas, ain't it?"

Minta swallowed a groan. Could she trust Belle? The woman's senses were muddled but she could *hear* a cry, couldn't she?

Damn Otto Floto!

"There'll be a hot time in the old town tonight." Otto Floto couldn't carry a tune in a bucket, but he felt like whooping and hollering just the same. He had stopped at the Mint Saloon for a few beers. Now he strolled east along the sunny north side of Bennett Avenue, past the flimsy fronts of the Gold Dollar Saloon, the Okay Shaving and Bath House, and the New York Chop House.

Across the street was Johnson's Department Store, looking out of place among the other ramshackle structures. Johnson's had been brick-built while most of the adjoining stores were made of green lumber cut from nearby government land during Cripple

Creek's first bonanza of '92 and '93. The lumber had dried and the buildings were in a bad state of dilapidation.

Otto turned at Bennett and Third and walked past Lampman's Undertaking Parlor and the Milk and Mush House to Meyers Avenue. On the south side of Meyers was the Butte Opera House, which Otto managed for H.B. Levie. Farther along the north side of the street were parlor houses and one-story cribs. Weaving his fingers through his oiled hair, Otto thought of Minta.

The red-haired gal with her bright brown eyes was Otto's favorite. Lord, could she give a man sugar! But she refused to leave her crib unless he paid for her keep.

Otto had been told he was a looker, and he had to agree. His reflection in the plate-glass window of the Bucket of Blood gambling hall showed a trimmed handlebar mustache with waxed ends, a straight nose, and dark eyes beneath slanted brows.

It wasn't fair of Minta, expecting him to hurt others with his neglect; there was plenty of him to go around. And if she didn't tend Blueberry's bastard, they could spend more time together.

As Otto continued strolling, his boots left immense footprints in the dirt. His hands and fingers were big, too. H.B. Levie hired bartenders with big thumbs because most miners paid for their drinks with a pinch of gold dust. Otto oiled his hair so that, when he pinched, the gold would stick better, and his black strands shone with bright yellow streaks.

He crossed the intersection of Meyers and Third to the Central Dance Hall, climbed stairs to the second floor, and entered a room with a bed, washstand, table and three chairs. Atop the table, atop a kerosene stove, simmered a pot of squirrel stew.

Clothed in a frilly chemise and corset, Minta greeted him with a smile then stretched out her plump arms. "Loosen my corset strings if you please, darlin'."

Otto's large fingers fumbled at the knots. Over Minta's shoulder, he watched her breasts spring free. Her red hair swirled to her waist and smelled of gingerbread. He could hardly unbutton his trousers fast enough.

When they'd finished, Minta rose from the bed, washed between her legs, slipped into her chemise and corset, and asked Otto to tie the strings.

"What's your hurry, Min? We ain't even et and I don't have to be over at the Butte till sundown. Come back to bed and give me more sugar."

"No, darlin'. I left my bairn with Belle, and Belle's so addled she might wander clear away. Fools Gold could be crying for the want of a bottle."

"I could be crying for the want of a tit."

"We just done that."

"You love Blueberry's babe better than me."

"I love her different. Pull the strings, please."

Otto rose, stretched, walked behind Minta, reached into her chemise, and fondled her breasts.

She leaned back, enjoying his touch. Then, with a regretful sigh, she swatted his hands away.

He grasped her shoulders. "Are you saying you won't lay with me again 'cause Blueberry's bastard waits at home?"

"Don't call her a bastard. She's a love child."

"I suppose your crib's a love palace."

"No, it ain't. I said I'd move if you paid the bills."

"Why should I pay when I can jackscrew you for free?"

"Oh! You bastard!"

"What did you say?"

"I said you're the bastard, not Fools Gold."

His eyes narrowed. "Who told you I wasn't true born?"

"Nobody, Otto." Suddenly fearful, she said, "Maybe I do have time for more sugar."

He folded his arms across his chest. "Don't you have to go home, Min? Maybe your babe's shat her nappies. Maybe Belle's shat her drawers."

"Why're you talkin' so nasty? I said I'd stay."

"I don't want no used goods."

"Oh! You bastard! I never want to see you again!" Minta had an awful feeling the devil had just put the wrong words in her mouth but she didn't care.

"Before you leave, Min, tell me who said I wasn't true born."

"Everybody says it. The dance hall girls sing 'there'll be a hot time with the *bastard* tonight.' "

"Who said it first?" he roared.

"Don't look at me like that, Otto. Nobody said nothin'. I made it up."

Growling low in his throat, he grasped her shoulders again, shaking so hard her head snapped back and forth. Then he cuffed her face with the back of his hand.

Minta reeled across the room and crashed into the table. The kerosene stove tottered and fell. Flames snaked along the dry wooden floorboards and licked at the window's tasseled drapes. Her swollen mouth tried to form words. With a moan, she grasped the edge of the table. Her fingers slid through spilled squirrel stew and she fell to the floor.

Otto knuckled his eyes free from smoke, saw that half the room was ablaze, threw on his clothes, and stepped into his boots. "C'mon, Min," he urged. "We got to git."

"Can't move. Hurt."

He hefted her to her feet, circled her waist, and swore a blue streak at the loose corset that impeded his grip.

Blinded by smoke, Otto somehow managed to find the door. Once outside, he released Minta's waist and she pitched forward. "They'll blame me for this," he muttered, before he merged into the crowd.

A young miner carried Minta across the street and lowered her to the walk. "Can you stand by yourself, ma'am?"

She nodded, swayed, retched.

He pressed his hand against her forehead. "Choke it up, sweetheart. There, that's better." He placed his shirt across her shoulders.

Bells clanged as horse-drawn fire engines raced up and down the roadway. A bucket brigade hauled water. Minta's young miner tipped his cap, returned to his place in line, and reached for a bucket. She didn't even know his name.

Structures on the north caught like boxes of lit matchsticks. Minta saw other scantily clad women rush into the street, their arms filled with gowns and jewelry. The street throbbed with the sound of men, women and cats. Where did all the cats come from? Outnumbered, the dogs fled from the cats.

The brigade watered down saloons and parlor houses, but the conflagration continued until it reached Poverty Gulch. Minta sprinted toward home. "My baby's inside!" she screamed. Hands restrained her forward motion. With a strangled cry, she watched her shanty collapse. She saw crib girls huddled around something in the street. Belle? Fools Gold? Minta pushed aside Jasmine the Brit and Leo the Lion. As she looked down, her breath caught in her throat.

Whiskey Johnnie lay on his back. His tattered clothes stuck wetly to his bloodied body. Near him stood Clementine, his hooves dancing in an agitated rhythm, his teeth stretched in a grimaced bray.

"Johnnie was stirrin' his stumps, tryin' to reach your crib," said Irish Mary. Her hair, brows and lashes had been singed and she smelled like a wet fur collar. "Fire engine cut 'im down. Preacher's fetchin' the doc."

Minta fell to her knees as Johnnie opened his eyes. His face was pitted an angry red from flying cinders. Blood stained his matted beard. "Berry," he managed. "Lost calf. Never should have brung her."

"Blueberry sleeps," said Minta. "She's at peace."

"Tell Fools Gold 'bout Nugget Ned."

"I will, I swear."

"Guess I'll gally'vant off to heaven now." Johnnie shut his eyes.

After kissing his lifeless lips, Minta staggered to her feet. Heartbroken, she wandered toward the pond where water was stored for the miners' sluice boxes.

She blinked, rubbed her eyes, and sloshed through ankle-high water. "Fools Gold!" she shouted, laughing and crying at the same time. "Fools Gold, you're alive!"

With a vacant smile, Belle thrust the soot-covered child into Minta's arms. Then she added a lockbox and a handful of gingerbread cookies.

A few days later, revolvers signaled a new fire, started this time by a hotel grease spill. Firemen answered the call, but Cripple

Creek's reservoirs held nothing but mud; all the water had been used for the first blaze.

Boilers in the Palace Hotel exploded.

Seventy pounds of dynamite at the Harder Grocery exploded.

The remaining saloons, parlor houses and cribs caught like dry kindling.

Afterwards, the Creek's citizens gazed at the smoldering debris, gave a collective sigh, squared their shoulders, and began rebuilding with brick. The first structures they erected were saloons, dance halls, and parlor houses.

"Me and Fools Gold ain't gonna live in no crib," Minta told Belle. "Even if Leo the Lion's busy heaping up wood like some dangfool beaver."

"Beaver?"

"A beaver's got a tail and teeth that can build a crib, but me and Fool's Gold —"

"Fool's Gold?" Belle wiped her bulbous nose with the edge of her sleeve. She and Minta stood on Meyers, watching the activity.

"My poppet saved from the fire, and God bless you."

"Fire?" Belle's scarred brow puckered.

"The fire that burned our cribs. That's why we've been sleeping in a tent. Phew! The smell! Charlene Johnson never bathes.

Here's your letter and train ticket."

"Tell me again what my letter says."

"It's from your sister who lives in Chicago. She wants you to bide with her there."

"My sister, uh . . ."

"Sarah." Minta felt her eyes mist. "You must give over your ticket to that man in blue when he calls all aboard."

"Toot, toot, all aboard. I like trains. Where'd I get the ticket, Min?"

"You saved my lockbox. It had all my banknotes and coins and Blueberry's nugget ring inside, the one I slipped from her finger before burial. I don't know what became of her mama's earbobs. Anyways, there was little I could do in return for your kindness except wire Sarah and pay for your passage to Chicago."

"What if I get mislaid?"

Minta bit her lip to keep from laughing. "You won't get lost. I've hired a girl to ride with you. She should be here any minute."

"Who's gonna watch the peewee while you meet up with Otto?"

"Otto's left town and good riddance."

"You gonna live happy ever after, Min?"

"Yes, Belle. I aim to get me a position in one of them new-built parlor houses."

"They won't let you bide with no peewee. Should I take her with me?"

151

"I'll never be parted from Fools Gold again, but I thank you for the offer."

"What'cha' gonna do with her?"

"I heard that Madam Robin Redbreast lost her own little girl to the cholera."

"Oh, the poor dear lady. Who's Robin Redbreast?"

"She's the madam over at Little Heaven. If I pay above my share, she might let me keep Fools Gold. That last fire reached so high, flames tickled God's feet. I'll wager God's still laughing, so I've got to hurry and talk to Madam Robin before God's good humor changes back to wrath."

"Never reckoned God was ticklish, Min."

"Everybody's ticklish, Belle. That's why God conjured up whores."

TEN

Minta gazed with delight at Little Heaven.

The two-story house was square, built with red-orange bricks. Gray paint trimmed windows, doors, and the roofline. Shrubbery surrounded gardens that already sported bright blooms. At the back of the house, a covered walkway led to the privies and servants' quarters.

Drawing a deep breath, Minta entered the front door.

The first floor included two parlors, a dining room and a kitchen. The bedrooms were upstairs. Minta walked into the main parlor and twirled around, holding Fools Gold at arm's length. "Can you believe your eyes, poppet? Look at that lamb's wool wallpaper. Look at all them shelves with what's called a petticoat mirror on the bottom. Look at them plush chairs and that horsehair fainting couch."

She placed Fools Gold on the floor in

front of the petticoat mirror. The child made faces at her own image while Minta walked toward a gateleg table. On top was a Victrola. Its funnel-shaped speaker pointed smack-dab toward a Beckwith Palace grand piano of French burled walnut.

"Madam says a man dark as chocolate plays music at night." Minta skipped her fingers across the keyboard.

Fools Gold crawled toward the sound.

"Don't let her get stepped on," warned a woman who stood framed by the doorway.

"Yes, Madam. I mean, no, Madam." Minta scooped Fools Gold up off the floor.

"Mama Min, Mama Min, gy-ee Frogold."

"She wants me to give her more music," Minta said.

"Let me help you get settled, dear. Then your wee girlie can play."

"I don't have much, Madam, just my lockbox and some clothes from Colorado Springs."

"Bless the church folk from Colorado Springs," Robin said. "They can donate their rags and feel so damn virtuous, all at the same time."

Eyes downcast, Minta said, "I don't go to church no more."

"A Christian's not a Christian just because

he goes to church, any more than a man's a calf 'cause he drinks milk."

"My sister would lock horns with you over that, Madam. She lives on Papa's dairy farm, at least she did. I've got some old letters inside my lockbox, but they stopped coming after Minneap'lis. She doesn't know I joined the profession."

Minta followed Robin Redbreast up the stairs, thinking how aptly named was this short, stout woman with her crest of dark hair, her brown eyes, and her pointy nose. Robin even clothed herself in red gowns and black capes.

"There are seven bedrooms. One's mine." Robin gestured toward a paneled door with a window inset. "That there's the viewing room where guests can choose their Angel of the evening. My girls are called Angels."

"How'd you come to name your house Little Heaven, Madam?"

"I picked out my blue velvet portieres from a shop damaged by the fire. Got them real reasonable. The gents who papered my walls and tacked my carpets seen my portieres, blue as the sky, and they wanted to paint stars on the ceiling. I was going to call my house Robin's Roost, but the first to knock on my door said the inside looked like heaven."

"I like Heaven better than Roost, Madam."

"There are five other Angels." Robin's foot touched upon the second-floor landing. "Dee, come meet Minta. Deeee!"

"Hold your horses, Madam, I'm coming."

"Horsies?" Fools Gold glanced left and right.

"Hush, poppet, and stop squirming." Shifting the child to her left arm, Minta shook the hand of a woman whose blonde hair swung down past her knees.

Fools Gold reached for Dee's long strands. "Gold," she said. "Gy-ee Fro-gold."

"She wants you to give her your hair," Minta explained.

"What a sweet little girl. Fro-gold?"

"Her name's Fools Gold but she has trouble saying it."

"Can't blame her. That's too big a handle. If you don't mind, I'll call her Flo."

The bedroom after Dee's belonged to a Chinese woman whose face topped a long ivory neck. She had a shingle of pure ebony hair and sat in front of a dressing table, her slanted black eyes staring at her mirrored reflection.

"That there Angel's called Swan. She keeps to herself." With an apologetic shrug, Robin knocked at the next door.

The woman who answered wore a transparent robe, ruffled at the bodice and hem. Minta had an immediate impression of a fluffy kitten until the girl raised large onyx eyes, set in a face the color of creamed coffee.

"This here's Minta and her daughter Flo," said Robin. "How are you feeling today, Cassandra?"

"Ca va bien, Madame."

"Have you had your chamomile and poppy oil?"

"Oui, Madame."

"If you require a purge, ask Hummingbird Lou to prepare some ginseng root."

"Oui, Madame. Merci, Madame." The girl smiled at Minta, curtsied, coughed, and closed her door.

"Consumption," said Robin. "Cassandra came to us from Louisiana. Our mountain air should cure her. My other two Angels, Maryanne and Maryjane, are twins. They occupy separate bedrooms unless a gent pays for both at the same time. I believe they're shopping on Bennett."

"Wheee, mam," said Fools Gold. "Maresee, mam."

"Flo reminds me of my little girl, though mine never tried to talk French." Robin's eyes misted and she honked into a lacy handkerchief. "After you're settled, bring the child to Hummingbird Lou's room, just outside the kitchen door. Lou's our cook. You do understand that Flo cannot sleep in your bedroom."

Minta nodded. "Thank you for your goodness, Madam Robin. You won't be sorry. I'll work real hard."

"Hush, my dear. It's me who should be thanking you. Already the word has spread that my house has got itself a brand new, freckle-faced Angel."

Reaching inside her skirt pocket, Minta pulled out a bottle. "I've been using White Lily Face Wash."

"No need. We'll negotiate your fee by the freckle."

"If that's true, your gents won't be able to afford my services."

"They'll pay." Robin opened the door to a small bedroom. "This is yours, Minta. Welcome to Little Heaven."

"Lil hef'n," Fools Gold said. "Mare-see, mam." Vastly pleased with herself, she added, "Horsie."

"Did you hear that, Madam? Fools Gold, I mean *Flo,* loves horses, and when Cassandra said mare-see . . . oh my!"

Minta's braying laugh wafted through an open window, startling the rancher who strolled toward the parlor house.

John McDonald glanced up at Little Heaven's second story. He had left his horse at the livery, planning to spend a few hours with Dee. But maybe he'd stay the whole night. After all, he didn't hear much womanly laughter on the ranch. Dimity hardly ever smiled, and she had taken to wearing a hair shirt. For penance, she said.

ELEVEN

By the year 1902, Little Heaven had acquired electric lights and a telephone. Its parlors were warmed by furnace grates but the bedrooms still relied on coal stoves.

Since it was summer, Mama Min's stove squatted, unlit, looking like a headless black widow spider with red rust markings on the underside and four legs too fat and lazy to spin webs.

Perhaps a magic spider would spin her some new cobwebby clothes, light and airy, thought Flo. After all, she'd read about a magic elf who cobbled shoes.

Flo sat on the floor. Her undershirt, attached to pantalets, had been sewn from a bed sheet. The fabric was threadbare, but much more comfortable than her brown wool dress, crumpled in the corner next to the spider-stove. Her toes were dirty and she played with her favorite toy, her dead mama's nugget ring. "There'll be a hot time, a hot time, oh, a hot time in the old town tonight," she sang softly. "I better put this, oh put this, oh, put this here nugget a-way."

She stood up and tiptoed toward the jewelry box on top of the vanity. Her fingers brushed against a crystal perfume bottle. It teetered and fell with a loud *thunk.*

"Spit!" Flo dropped her dead mama's ring into the jewelry box, sat on the floor, and turned her face toward the spool bed. Hidden beneath pink velvet cherubs slept Mama Min.

At the end of the bed were a painted chamber pot and a funny bottle called a pig, which, when filled with hot water, kept Mama Min's feet warm. To the right was a folding screen with scary painted dragons. A beaded corset bag hung from a nail, and a frilly petticoat had been flung over the screen.

Against the wall was a mirrored vanity. On top were bottles and tins of store-bought remedies: White Lily Face Wash, Dr. Worden's Female Pills, English Lavender Smelling Salts and La Dore's Powder de Ritz. Next to the powder were a curling iron and the jewelry box.

Flo loved the jewelry box. When you turned its thin handle, no longer than Flo's pinkie, music sounded and a tiny ballerina twirled. But Flo hated the vanity mirror, which showed how fat and ugly she was.

Mama Min oft talked about Flo's dead mama, Blueberry, who was slender with a pretty smile and big sad eyes.

Nugget Ned Lytton was a looker, too.

Thinking 'bout her father made Flo redhot. When grown, she'd ride her horse into Nugget Ned's house and shoot him between his lickspittle eyes.

The pink cherub coverlet shifted. Sleepy brown eyes appeared, then a freckled nose, then a mouth smeared with lip paint.

Mama Min's so pretty, thought Flo. *Too bad she ain't my real mama. I was born with Nugget Ned's black hair and Blueberry's eyes, but then God forgot what he was doing and finished me up wrong.*

Flo understood how God could forget since it happened to her all the time. She'd be sweeping the floor when she'd think of a story and she'd start dusting furniture before she finished the sweeping. Hummingbird Lou said Flo's head was in the clouds.

God lived in the clouds. He had forgotten she was Nugget Ned and Blueberry's little girl and given her someone else's too-plump body.

"What's that powerful smell, child?"

Oh, spit! "I'm sorry, Mama Min. I spilt your scent. But I didn't break the bottle. See? Should I fetch Gingerbread? She can clean it up with her tongue."

"I don't believe your cat will take kindly to French perfume. Leastwise, it covers up Snuffy's smell."

"I like Mr. Snuffy's smell."

"You do? Snuffy smells like them stogies he smokes. Open the window, Flo. Snuffy puffs them dang cigars 'cause he thinks it's *de rigueur* for a newly rich man."

"De . . . rig . . ."

"You'll learn that word when you're grown. Madam Robin expects her Angels to talk with important gents, so I've had to pick up my education right here at Little Heaven. You'll learn lots of twiggy words when you get schooled in Denver. Fools Gold Smith! You're still in your shimmy! Why ain't you clothed?"

"Why ain't you?"

"Never mind me. I'm not eight years old. Snuffy left with the rooster's crow. Before he took off, he insisted I give him some sugar, and the sun not even high enough to witness his fun. Men!" Minta's gaze darted around the room, coming to rest on the crumpled brown wool. "What's your dress

163

doing there on the floor? Hatching eggs?"

"I don't like that dress. It's hot and ugly. I'd rather wear your petticoat." Flo walked toward the hinged screen, yanked the under-garment down, and slid it over her head until the waistband fell just below her chin. Bending slightly, thrusting her rump back-wards, she sauntered across the room.

Minta's braying laugh interrupted the serious performance. "Put your dress on, child, then go outside and let the breeze blow away some of that spilled scent."

"Can I wear your petticoat?"

"A lady doesn't show her undergarments in broad daylight."

"You do."

"Get dressed or I'll spank your be-hind."

"Spit!"

"Don't use that nasty word."

"Sorry." Flo donned the shapeless wool. Then she tugged black stockings up her legs and buttoned her shoes. "Is Fanny still in jail?"

"Yes."

"I heard Dee say she carved her gentle-man up good. He had six marks on his body made from a razor, and Fanny peeled the skin off one of his fingers with her teeth. Dee said he had tooth marks on his nose, too. Why'd Fanny do that?"

"Never you mind."

"Did the gent hurt Fanny? Did he want *soixante-neuf* and not pay?"

"Don't use that word!"

"Why? It ain't spit."

"You'll eat soap for breakfast, that's why."

"I've already had my breakfast." With an impish smile, Flo raced from the room.

Minta belted her robe and walked toward the open window. It would take all day to clear out the perfume stench. *I should have punished the child for her clumsiness.* Flo had to be more careful. Suppose she knocked over Madam Robin's perfume bottle?

Flo's pudgy homeliness made her thin-skinned but she rarely cried. Instead, she hid her tears with a bravado worthy of Wilbur and Orville Wright. Last night Snuffy said the Wright brothers had tested their second full-scale glider. It crashed, of course. Only men were foolish enough to believe they could fly.

Wilbur and Orville reminded Minta of Irish Mary's rainbow pots filled with gold. Blueberry had believed Mary and look what happened. Blueberry's daughter would have to learn that birds flew, not people.

Minta shook her red curls. She should have scolded stronger for the crumpled dress, too, yet she really couldn't blame the child. The dress *was* hot and ugly. But she'd put off sewing another since Flo grew so fast.

Too fast. Men admired plump ladies, but Flo, only eight, weighed a hundred pounds. At this rate, by age sixteen she'd weigh double.

Minta tried to curb Flo's appetite but Hummingbird Lou thwarted every attempt. The heavy cook shared leftovers and desserts with Flo, stuffing the child like she'd stuff breakfast sausages.

While Madam Robin wasn't mean-natured, she did insist that Flo empty chamber pots, and Flo said a piece of candy helped ease the stink.

Early in an evening, Flo entertained. Her voice was grown, said Washman, the colored piano player. Last night she'd sung a new tune about someone named Bill Bailey, and Minta had been reminded of Blueberry. *Ned Lytton, won't you please come home, you two-faced bastard!*

Flo slept on a pallet inside the kitchen. At cock's crow she lit the black enameled steel range and prepared coffee.

"It's easy," she had once bragged. "I stand on a chair, fill a big pot with boiled water and roasted mocha grounds, add the white of an egg, or a few shavings of isinglass, or a dried bit of fish skin. Ten minutes later the coffee's ready. Hummingbird Lou lets me do it while she starts the all-day roasts. She says I cook coffee best."

Minta would be willing to wager all she owned that Ned Lytton's other children didn't rise with the sun. Their little hands weren't red and chapped from washing clothes. Nugget Ned's other children hadn't watched the free-for-all in the street after a drunk miner stole a bulldog puppy from the crib girl, Brown Mollie, and gave it over to Little Heaven's Maryanne. The police had arrived, tied Mollie up, and hauled her off to jail in a dray wagon.

Ned Lytton's other children didn't have to witness Cassandra coughing her life away, nor did they shoot craps with mean-tempered Fanny, hired after Cassandra's funeral. No, sir. Nugget Ned's other children didn't "cook coffee."

Minta heaved a deep sigh. Every morning Flo would hand out hot steaming mugs, and gents would give her gold dust and coins. Minta turned the dust over to Robin, receiving coins in exchange. She didn't trust banks, so she hid her money inside one of her pillows. Soon that money would go toward schooling Flo in Denver. If Minta had one breath left in her body, Flo would never spread her legs for a miner's pleasure.

Only last week a parlor girl down the row had died from morphine. Three small bottles and two hypodermic syringes had been found on her vanity table, right next to a tin of Dr. Hammond's Nerve and Brain Tablets.

Yes, Flo must escape, but freedom required money. Minta made a goodly amount from the wealthy customers at Little Heaven, however most went to Madam Robin, who paid monthly fees for doctors' visits, certifications of cleanliness, and legal fines since prostitution was illegal in Colorado.

Material for the gowns Minta wore every evening cost dear. She earned extra by stitching gowns for the other Angels, yet there wasn't much left at month's end. With a sigh, she gazed out the window. In the distance, dark-rimmed clouds were interrupted by flashes of lightning. Flo had maybe an hour to play before it rained. Right now the sun shone fierce.

Minta reached for a bonbon from a box of chocolates. She chewed gingerly, ignoring the pain from a sore tooth.

Earlier, Flo had eaten slabs of Hummingbird Lou's fresh-baked bread. The colored cook had also served apple quince, pungent cheese, almond custard, and a mug of Flo's own coffee, diluted with milk and sugar. Although it was past noon, Flo wasn't hungry. But just to be safe, she had filled her dress pocket with peanut brittle.

As she descended the staircase, she heard the piano. On tiptoe, she entered the parlor and saw Swan's body draped over the piano, her fingers running up and down the keys. Swan wore a soiled silk nightie. One strap had fallen, showing her *nipple.* Swan's black hair hung in its neat curtain, but her eyes looked funny.

On top of the piano lay a crumpled newspaper, so Flo knew Bobby had paid Swan a call. Bobby brought the paper. Swan would give him a playing card — a Jack of Spades or a Ten of Clubs — and a dollar to keep for himself. Then the newsboy would run lickety-split to a drugstore, show the card, and return with Swan's order.

Flo wished she could be a runner but they only used boys, which wasn't fair. Someday she'd cut her hair or hide it under a cap. She'd pretend to be a boy and get dollars like Bobby. But she couldn't tell her secret plan to Mama Min, who hated drugs.

"Morphine can kill you," Mama Min had once said. "If I catch you touching a package, even in fun, I'll spank you good."

Flo stared at the piano. *Swan's medicined herself on morphine again and there's throw-up on the floor.* Wait till Madam Robin saw Swan's *nipple.* A lady didn't show her *nipple* in broad daylight. *There's gonna be a hullabaloo.*

Hullabaloo was one of Flo's favorite words. Maryjane said grown-ups used it in the sixteenth century to hush children but Flo liked it just the same.

She stepped outside and walked one block north to Bennett Avenue. Gusty wind whipped her hair into her eyes, but her dress felt hot and sticky. Strolling past a bookstore, she retraced her steps, pressed her nose against the window, and sniffed. Except for Mr. Welty's livery stable, Flo's favorite smell was book. She loved to turn the pages and see the printed letters become people or animals. Her favorite books were *Mrs. Wiggs of the Cabbage Patch* and *The Wonderful Wizard of Oz.* She adored Dorothy, who had killed a witch, though not on purpose.

After Flo killed Nugget Ned — *on purpose* — she'd escape in the Wizard's hot-air balloon, riding high above Pikes Peak.

She darted inside the National Hotel's

lobby. The hotel had been built of brick after the Cripple Creek fires. "Scoot, little girl," the doorman scolded. "You ain't allowed in here." Flo hesitated, stuck out her tongue, dashed outside.

She skipped along the walk then stopped to stare at a window arrangement. Melting sugar oozed around strawberries and fresh-cut flowers. She didn't know why the display gave her the shivers, but it did.

It looks like a pretty picture, she thought. *No, I'm addled.* Pictures were set in frames, like the naked lady hanging above Madam Robin's fireplace. Pictures were painted by Jack Gottlieb.

Flo smiled. Jack could be found in the hills with his funny piece of furniture that looked like the letter A. Jack said it was called an easel. Sometimes he let the children play with his paints and brushes.

Turning away from the window, Flo walked over to a buckboard and scratched the fuzzy muzzles of two golden horses.

"Ain't you 'fraid they might bite your fingers off?"

Flo stared up at the buckboard's seat. "Not hardly, boy. Horses like me. Mr. Welty says I talk their language. I love all animals. I've a cat and her name's Gingerbread and she's gonna have babies."

"Kittens ain't special."

Flo stared into green eyes. The boy's hair was the same color as hers and he looked to be the same age, too.

"We got kittens on our ranch," he continued, "and Starr had new pups, even though she's near nine years old, and my mama's horse had a colt, and I once saw a cow birth a two-headed calf . . ." He paused for breath.

"A two-headed calf? You're fibbing, boy!"

"Mama fainted when she heard. Then she prayed. Mama said the calf was a free-ache of nature and brung by the devil. It died. What's your name?"

"Fools Gold Smith."

"Now who's fibbing? Nobody's named that."

Flo fisted her fingers. "Don't you call me no liar, boy. You come down off that wagon and take them words back or you'll be puking up teeth."

"I can't leave the wagon. Papa said to stay put or he'd belt my bottom good, and he'll be out from the store any minute. We ate lunch at the National Hotel. You ever been in there? My papa's buying flowers for my mama 'cause she's sick. Her belly got big. Then last night she screamed and screamed and a doctor rode to the ranch and this morning Papa looked sad, so I guess my new baby brother died, just like that two-headed calf. Come sit next to me, if you ain't scared."

"Spit! I ain't scared of nothing."

"Guess I can reckon why. You're big enough to fight back."

Flo hesitated, her foot on the wagon spokes. Was this boy being nasty, funning her size like her schoolmates? No. He'd sounded mannerly, almost prideful.

Seated, she said, "A lady who lives at my house grew her belly, but she had a carriage and nobody was sad 'cause the baby was only a *seed*. Her name's Dee and she's got yella hair like mine."

"Your hair ain't yellow, it's black."

"The good witch told Dorothy if she wished hard —"

"You can't wish for yellow hair."

"When I'm grown, I'm gonna wed me a gentleman. I'll wear pretty gowns and eat bonbons, and my hair will be *yella*. Want some brittle?"

"Sure. I like your hair, and you smell good, like store-bought scent. My name's John McDonald but folks call me Cat. Papa says I was named for two states, one city, and a cougar."

"If I had my druthers, I'd call me Horse."

Reaching into her pocket, Flo pulled out a piece of peanut brittle. Snippets of brown wool stuck to its glazed surface. She licked it clean and handed Cat the laundered sweet.

"Who's your new friend, son?" A man smiled, his eyes crinkling at the corners.

"Papa, this here's Fools Gold."

"Pleased to meet you, Miss Gold." He tipped the brim of his Stetson, separated a snapdragon from his bouquet, handed the flower over, and lifted Flo to the ground.

Squinting up, she stared at Cat's papa. "I've seen you at Little Heaven. You're Dee's gent."

"What were *you* doing at Little Heaven?"

"I'm Minta's girl and I cook coffee."

"Can Fools Gold come home with us, Papa?"

"No, son, that's out of the question."

"Why?"

"Your mama needs peace and quiet."

"We can play outside. I'll dig up the two-headed —"

"I said no!"

Flo watched Cat's papa toss the flowers into the buckboard, climb up next to Cat, and kick at the brake with his boot.

He kicked awful hard, she thought, but dismissed Cat and Cat's papa from her mind when she heard new hoofbeats.

Clattering down Bennett was a white stallion with a yella-haired lady on top. "Oh, how beautiful," whispered Flo, for once meaning the lady, not the horse.

Skidding to a halt near Flo, the stallion nickered. "I'll be hanged," said the lady. "He's never done that before. What's your name, little sorceress?"

"Fools Gold Smith."

"I'm Sally Marylander."

Flo leaned forward to kiss the stallion's velvety neck. Her nose met one of Sally's boots and she stepped back, surprised. "You're riding funny, ma'am. You've got both legs flung, one on each side."

"That's right. Don't cotton to sidesaddle. Why should I squeeze my legs together when men have the comfort of spreading theirs? Would you like to ride with Sally, child?"

"Oh, my goodness! I ain't been atop nothin' 'cept Whiskey Johnnie's burro, but he's dead."

"The burro's dead?"

"No. Whiskey Johnnie. Mama Min talks 'bout him lots. Clementine's alive but he's old and swayback. Can I really ride your horse?"

Sally smiled, kicked one stirrup free,

hooked her booted foot over the saddle horn, and extended her hand.

Flo dropped her snapdragon and tucked her skirt hem into the neck of her dress. She found the stirrup, grasped Sally's fingers, and swung herself up behind the saddle. A seam in her pantalets split its stitches. Spit!

"Stay very still, child," Sally warned. "My stallion's got a wild nature and it looks as if it's about to storm."

At her words, thunder sounded and a bolt of lightning cleaved the sky. Stretching out his long legs, Sally's stallion galloped to the end of Bennett and swerved onto the path circumventing Mt. Pisgah cemetery. Flo leaned sideways into the wind, tears of delight steaming down her face.

Sally sawed on the reins, and the stallion's speed lessened.

Flo slid to the ground in front of the fruit and flower shop.

"You weren't scared a bit," said Sally. "I don't think you even know what the word means. Pull your skirt down, child. I hope we meet again. I'll bet people say you're a big girl but you've got good bones. I'd like to see how you look when you're all grown up. You'd better scoot for home now, get out of the rain."

"Rain?" Flo looked down at the muddy street. Then she whirled about and sprinted toward Little Heaven.

Quivering with excitement, she entered Minta's bedroom.

"Mercy! What's scared you so?" Mama Min stood before her vanity mirror, crimping her hair with the curling iron. The ballerina atop the jewelry box turned round and round while sounds of a lullaby soothed its eternal pirouette. The room still smelled of spilled scent. Despite the rain, Mama Min had left a portion of the window open. Blue velvet drapes swayed in mild profusion.

"I told Cat I wasn't scared of nothin'. The lady said I didn't know what scared means."

"What lady?"

"A pretty lady on a big horse." With her fingertips, Flo pushed wet tangled curls away from her eyes. "I rode the horse."

"Oh, you did, did you?" Minta walked over to an Italian straddle chair and bent forward. "Tie my strings, please. We're to be extra busy this evening since Fanny's in jail and Madam dismissed Swan." Minta clutched at her mouth. "Open my trunk and find my bottle of Vin Vitae, Flo. Dang tooth! It hurts real bad, but I don't cotton to see the barber and have him yank."

"Will Dee's gent be here tonight?"

"Which gent?"

Flo thought hard. Cat . . . *McDonald*.

"Mr. McDonald," she said.

"What a mind you've got for recollecting. John McDonald usually joins us after you're asleep 'cause he rides all the way from Divide. Dee says his wife wears a stinky hair shirt and prays all the time. Not that I've got anything against honest prayer, Flo. Your sweet mama oft quoted the good book. But I believe a willing body can melt the chill from a man's bones better than a psalm."

Flo placed the wine-of-life bottle on top of the vanity and pulled Mama Min's corset strings tight. "The lady said I had good bones. I rode through the rain. The lady was pretty. The horse went fast."

"That's enough, Flo. Imagination's nice but fibbing's nasty." Mama Min tied the ribbons on her petticoat and reached for an orange taffeta gown with flounced sleeves.

"I did ride. The lady had yella hair and sat a white horse funny and said her name was Sally."

"Sally Marylander?"

"Uh-huh. Do you know her?"

"We've never met but I've heard Sally rides like a man. She gives us well-bred ladies a bad reputation, galloping through

178

the streets with her skirts flying. I've heard she's a Socialite."

"What's that?"

"Upper-class and snooty."

"Like Mr. Snuffy?"

"No. Socialite men are more educated than our Snuffy. Richer, too. They throw parties at the drop of a hat. Your papa could have been a Socialite if he'd stuck around. Sally's been courted by Socialite men. Heard she chose a confectioner who owns land near here." Minta powdered her nose and dusted Flo's face with the puff. "She's even got a grave blasted out of the granite on Mt. Pisgah."

"A grave? Oh, spit! Is Miss Sally gonna die?"

"The grave's for her white stallion when he passes. Can you believe your ears, Flo? Most folks can't afford markers. Your mama's grave's got nothing but a piece of weathered wood from an old buckboard."

Flo had a sudden image of a buckboard. Perched on top was a green-eyed boy.

I'll be like Miss Sally when I'm grown. I'll have yella hair and ride with my legs spread. Just see if I don't, Cat McDonald!

Huddled beneath blankets, surrounded by sacks of flour and sugar, cured ham and dried fruit, Cat McDonald crouched quietly.

"You hidin', boy?" Cookie crawled inside the wagon. "I'd hate to be in your boots, Cat McDonald. Your daddy's madder than a bangtailed mustang. He's airin' his lungs all through the house, cussin' up a storm."

Cat sneezed and watched the old man throw aside the blankets. "Howdy, Cookie."

"Don't howdy me, boy. Stomped the ranch far and wide 'fore I reckoned my wagon."

Grabbing Cat by one ear, Cookie marched him across the yard, through the open door, down the hallway, into the dining room.

Papa paced from table to sideboard. Sipping from a cup of tea, Mama sat in her usual straight-backed chair. Six-year-old Lucas stuffed his mouth with Tonna's biscuits. Five-year-old Daniel stared wide-eyed at Cat and Cookie. Dimity-Jane, just turned four, tried to control her tears.

"He was hidin' inside the cook wagon, Mac," Cookie said and left the room.

Cat's ear felt hot like fire. He wanted to dip his head in cold water. Instead, he watched Papa unbuckle then unfurl a leather belt.

Rising from her chair, Mama dabbed at her lips with a linen napkin. A large silver crucifix on the end of a chain swung across the top buttons of her black dress.

"A beating won't help," Mama said to Papa. "The boy was born bad."

"At least he was born."

"Do you blame me for our latest loss? How dare you! The ranch is cursed."

"Lucas, Daniel and Dimity-Jane were all born on my accursed ranch."

"That's because God rewarded my prayers."

"Did you not pray for the other dead babies?"

"You know I did, but the ranch is bedeviled by a spirit who grows older and stronger."

"Your devil spirit has blessed us with fat steers and a herd of palominos that rival any in the territory, and four children." McDonald directed his gaze toward Cat. "Why'd you hide in the cook wagon, son?"

"I wanted to go with you on the drive, Papa."

"You're too young for a long cattle drive. Didn't I say 'no' when you begged to come along?"

"Yes, Papa."

"You disobeyed."

"Yes, Papa."

"How long were you planning to hide? The trail hands leave tomorrow at daybreak.

Didn't you think your mother would discover your absence?"

"No, Papa."

"Are you ready for your whupping?"

"Yes, Papa."

"You're wasting time, John," said Dimity. "Words don't hurt. Wield the belt."

"The woodshed, son."

"Yes, Papa." Cat turned to leave.

"Wait!" Dimity raised her hand. "I want to witness Cat's punishment, John."

"If you insist, my dear. Please send the other children from the room."

"Why? They have done no wrong, and Lucas hasn't finished his breakfast. I want you to hit Cat seven times, one for each year since his birth."

"Cat's insubordination wasn't all that serious, Dimity. He didn't lie or steal."

"He disobeyed, John. That's the same as telling a lie. Watch your papa, children, and learn what happens when evil conquers a person's soul."

McDonald sighed. "Bend over the sideboard, Cat."

"Tell him to remove his trousers, John."

"No, Dimity. In the woodshed he could lower his pants, but not in our dining room. You can't have it both ways."

"Very well. You may commence."

McDonald hesitated.

"What are you waiting for, John? Are you too old? Is your arm too weak? Must I wield the strap myself?"

McDonald stared at his wife. If Dimity had one prevailing sin, it was her temper. He lashed three times.

"Look at your papa, children. *Eheu fugaces labuntur anni.* 'Alas, the fleeting years slip by.' Papa is like that old stallion we sent to pasture. His days of use were over. He couldn't even be put to stud."

"Dimity, control yourself!"

"Give me the strap, and I, a mere woman, will show you how to mete out punishment."

This time, anger at her words nearly obscured McDonald's vision. Yet his belt landed with accuracy on Cat's bottom.

From the corner of his eye, Cat saw Mama rub the cross at her bosom.

Staring squinty-eyed at Papa, Lucas sucked a whole sausage into his mouth.

Daniel hid his eyes with his hands.

Dimity-Jane leapt to her feet, sobbing so hard she could barely stand.

"At least your aim is true," Mama said. "I'm pleased to see that one part of your body does not tire in its task."

"I will be obeyed, I will have respect!"

183

Papa shouted. "Do you hear me, Cat? Do you hear me, Dimity?"

Cat felt the pain — like a hundred bees stinging, pausing then stinging again. He smelled the food on the sideboard, so close to his nose. Bread soaking in milk and cinnamon. Curdled eggs. A rash of bacon. Even though he wanted to sink to the floor, his fingers stubbornly clung to the edge of the sideboard.

Dimity-Jane hurled herself across the room, shielding him with her own body, glaring at her father without fear. "Hit me, Papa," she hollered. "I told Cat to hide."

"Did not," Cat mumbled.

"Hit me, Papa." Tears puddled beneath Dimity-Jane's amber eyes, and her taffy-colored curls shook with the force of her plea.

Cat sneaked a peek at his papa, who just stood there, his arm in the air.

"Why do you stop?" Mama beat at her bosom with her fists. "You must whip away Cat's evil, John. The boy will never repent if you tire."

"The boy is seven years old." Dropping the belt, Papa wiped his hands alongside his trousers. "Dimity-Jane, go upstairs and take your brothers with you."

"I haven't finished breakfast, Papa," Lucas whined.

"Do you want my strap to find your backside, son?"

"Children, obey your papa, and forget Mama's words about that silly old stallion. Evil makes Mama angry. Did you see how strong Papa looked? God gave him strength."

Cat heard Papa whisper "God forgive me" as he pried Cat's fingers from the sideboard and carried him toward the kitchen.

Black Percy spent most of his time working with livestock, so he purely loved the smell of soap. Sniffing like a hound, he walked through the yard toward the kitchen. Then he hoisted a flour barrel onto Tonna's wash bench. The upper half of the barrel had been sawed through and three holes on each side served as finger handles. "I caulked the cracks and filled her with water to swell the staves." Percy's voice was akin to a hound's, deep-toned and sonorous. "Good a rinse tub as you'll find anywhere 'cept heaven."

"It will be handy for next wash day," said Tonna.

"You're done already?"

"All that's left is one collar and the ticking." She pointed toward the line, where newly washed articles were clothes-pinned

in the progression of their cleansing —
whites, coarse towels, flannels and woolies,
calicoes. Grasping the lace collar, she
rubbed it between her soapy fingers and
held it out. "Would you hang this, please?"

"That's a woman's task."

"And you are a *man* who cannot see the
forest for the trees."

"I see the forest but I look the other way."

"Maybe I should wash your eyes and pin
them up to dry, alongside the handkerchiefs
and nightcaps." She looked toward the
strawberry patch where Cat lay on his belly.
"It is fortunate Cat wore trousers. I have
drawn the poison from his welts, but he will
not sit his pony for some time to come."

"He was wrong to disobey Mac's orders."
Percy cupped his mouth with his hands.
"Come here, boy."

Rising, Cat walked painfully toward the
wash bench.

Percy knelt on one knee. "Do you understand why your daddy whupped you?"

Cat nodded. "Mama don't like me."

"No, Cat, it's because you hid inside
Cookie's wagon. I heard your daddy say you
couldn't go on the drive."

"Papa says Lucas shouldn't eat so much
and he don't stop and he don't get
whupped. Mama would faint if Luke got

whupped."

Percy placed a callused palm across Cat's forehead. "He's fevered, Tonna."

"Bring him to the kitchen. There's calf's-foot broth simmering and I've prepared sage, burnet and sorrel."

"Is Tonna riled, Black Percy?"

"Yep. But not at you, boy."

Once again, Percy sniffed with delight. The kitchen smelled like the yard. On the floor set a barrel of grease and potash, with rain water added for the making of coarse soap. Draped over the table was the ticking of a feather bed, turned inside-out. Tonna had spread melted bar soap and bee's wax in a thin layer, and this mixture held the feathers securely until the next wash.

Handing Cat the sorrel draught, Tonna watched him drink. Then she sank down onto a chair and pulled him into her lap.

Percy walked over to the stove and poured from a large enamel pot. "This here coffee is Tonna's best recipe, Cat, better than calf's-foot soup. She takes a pound of Arbuckles' brand, adds water to wet it down, boils it for two hours, and throws in a horseshoe. If the shoe sinks, it ain't ready."

Trying to smile, Cat pressed his hot face against Tonna's shoulder.

"Cat McDonald," she crooned, "your mother is the mountain lion who runs free and your father is the Chinook wind. One starry night the wind swept down from the sky and mated with the lion. You are the result. Every time you feel the Chinook wind, know that your father whispers words of comfort. Do you understand?"

Cat nodded.

"Today you must obey orders. But your spirit is your own, and your spirit cannot be tamed. You must stand tall as the oak, my Cat, but sometimes you must bend like the willow —"

"He's asleep, Tonna."

"Good. Sleep is the best medicine. Are you *man* enough, my husband, to bring the clean clothes inside? I must press Dimity's fine calicoes, ginghams and muslins. How I wish I could hot-press the hatred from her heart."

TWELVE

During the next three years, Percy showed Cat how to handle the wild broncs, the shabby range horses called broomtails, and the treacherous mustangs. He taught Cat how to hang off the side of his horse like the Comanche did in battle.

Cat learned how to braid ropes and halters from horsehair. He became adapt at throwing and tying a steer so that the hot branding iron could singe hide into the letters JMD, his father's registered brand.

And he picked up the language of the hardened hands, drawing reprimands from his father and face slaps from Dimity.

One day Percy cornered him at the corral. "Listen, boy, a cowhand ain't picking any grapes in the Lord's vineyard, but neither is he trying to bust any Commandments with his cussin'. It just sits on his tongue as easy as a horsefly ridin' a mule's ear. Your dad-

dy's the boss and he don't cuss for pleasure."

"Why do I get the same feeling cussing as
I do drinking Tonna's Arbuckles'?"

"You're growin', boy. That's how come a
cuss and coffee taste the same. But cussin'
is wasted if it ain't done right. Always
remember not to use all your kindling to
get a fire started. When you feel the urge to
air your paunch, open up your mouth and
let a song come out."

"Singing's for birds and ladies!"

"Listen to the hands round the campfire,
then tell me again that singing's for ladies.
Stop your cussin', Cat, and I'll learn you
the guitar."

Soon Cat rode the range, strumming and
singing at the top of his lungs.

"Cat has a voice fit to rival the angels," said
John McDonald, staring at the new diptych
atop his wife's bureau. "He gets it from you,
my dear. When you sing hymns the angels
turn green with envy."

"Please do not blaspheme."

"Are you pregnant?" he asked bluntly,
surprised by her reaction to his compliment.

"How could I be with child when you
spend every night in Cripple Creek?"

"That can be easily remedied." With a

smile, he reached for her nightgown's ribbons.

She slapped his hand away.

He turned on his heels and walked toward the door. "I'll see you at breakfast," he called over his shoulder.

Truth be told, he preferred Hummingbird Lou's apple quince and Flo's coffee, but Dimity demanded his presence at what she called "the family collation." Family *mastication* was more the case, McDonald thought, picturing his gluttonous son Lucas.

Dimity's "devil spirit" continued to bless the ranch, and John McDonald acquired expert wranglers so talented that, when competing in local rodeo contests, they invariably won all the prizes. The JMD boasted the number-one broncobuster and calf roper.

Black Percy was top bulldogger. He'd jump from his saddle onto the head of a racing steer, grab a horn in each hand, and twist until the steer's nose came up. Grabbing the steer's upper lip with his teeth, he'd throw his arms in the air to show he wasn't holding anymore, then fall to one side, dragging the steer along with him until it went down.

It was bulldogging the way bulldogs did it.

Will Rogers visited the ranch and spent an afternoon with Cat, teaching him how to twirl a riata.

On Will Rogers's recommendation, Black Percy was hired by the Colonel Zack Mulhall Wild West Show to perform his bulldogging trick during Mulhall's Madison Square Garden engagement.

Confronting the McDonalds inside the parlor, Percy asked that Cat accompany him. "The boy can take care of my horse and equipment, Mac, and it'll be good for him to see new places and meet others."

"New York is a city of sin," Dimity protested, "full of painted women."

"There's no more painted women in New York than in Cripple Creek," said McDonald.

"Lucas —"

"Won't curry or feed the horses. Lucas can only feed himself. Why do you hate our eldest son so?"

"I don't hate him, John. How can a mother hate her own flesh and blood?"

"Then why do you malign Cat at every opportunity?"

Her pale-blue eyes flashed with anger. "How can you ask? Cat disobeys and he's always ready with a cuss. And he . . ."

"He what, my dear?"

"He nearly brought Death knocking. I could have died with his birth."

"But you didn't. Why do you always babble about bad blood and the devil when you talk about Cat?"

She frowned, deepening the two lines between her nose and mouth. "I refuse to discuss this in front of a servant."

"Percy isn't a servant." McDonald turned toward his friend. "I beg your pardon, Mr. Percival."

"How dare you apologize for me?" Taking small measured steps, Dimity walked from the room, and soon McDonald heard the slam of a door.

"I forgot about her temper," he said ruefully.

"It don't signify, Mac. The only thing that matters is your son. He's a fine boy."

A few days later Black Percy and Cat left for New York City.

Cat stared through the slats of a gate leading to the chutes. He had groomed Percy's horse, Snowball, a cream-colored gelding too light to be considered palomino. From a distance Snowball looked very white, given that his rider was clothed in black from boots to hat.

Snowball's mane and tail had been braided with red ribbons, and his saddle gleamed from careful polishing. Now Cat watched the horse dip his foreleg in the semblance of a bow while Percy raised his Stetson, saluting the audience.

A cowboy opened a chute and prodded a steer through. The steer eyed Percy and tossed his head, flinging clumps of mucus toward the arena fence.

Then all hell broke loose.

Percy's steer lumbered across the arena and jumped a gate, knocking off the top boards, landing in the grandstand. Atop Snowball, Percy jumped the same gate, intent on bulldogging the steer.

Trapped at the other end of the arena, Cat shouldered his way through spectators and ran toward the fracas.

Will Rogers cut across the middle of the main ring, riding at a fast canter.

Amid the screaming audience, Percy rode the steer down and leapt upon its back. A riderless Snowball jumped the fence and returned to the chutes.

Will Rogers cleared the gate. Using his spinning rope, he picked up the steer's heels and dragged the frightened animal, with Percy on top, down the stairs.

Avoiding hooves, Cat added his own wiry strength and helped pull the steer from the stands by its tail.

Later, Will Rogers was asked by newspaper reporters why he wouldn't let the steer stay in the grandstand.

"He didn't have a ticket," Rogers drawled.

Sunset bathed the ranch. Cat thought the landscape looked like the inside of the kaleidoscope he had once pressed against his eye. Loose bits of colored glass had shifted in endless variety, and this evening the setting sun was doing the same thing with its descent through the mountains. Leaning against the corral, Cat said, "There was no talk."

Percy said, "How come?"

"Didn't need talk. Bandits tie up the telegraph man and jump the train. They stop the engine and rob the mail car and ride away. A pretty lady unties the telegraph man and he tells the cowboys and they ride after the bandits. They all meet in a field and shoot each other. The guns have smoke coming out from their barrels. One bandit shot at the people watching. A lady swooned and some men yelled, but I wasn't scared. Well, maybe a little."

"You were scared of a picture?"

"The man who shot looked real."

"Guess the next time we travel to New York City, I'll have to watch your moving pictures," said Percy, setting a cloth-covered plate atop the mounting block.

"You said how you didn't want to pay five cents for what you can see for free."

Percy waved a howdy to John McDonald, who was strolling toward them. "Cat here was tellin' me 'bout his visit to a Nickelodeon, Mac. He watched a moving picture called *The Great Train Robbery.*"

"Don't tell your mama, son. She wouldn't cotton to the waste of money on a New York theater show."

"It wasn't a theater show, Papa. The actors weren't alive. Well, I guess they were, but they had their pictures took by a camera and they moved. They even chased each other on horses but some didn't ride good."

McDonald chuckled. "Your moving pictures will never last, Cat. Folks'll tire of paying good money for what they can read about in newspapers and books."

"Yes, Papa."

"What did you learn from your trip, aside from your Nickelodeon?"

"The first night of the rodeo, when Percy's steer jumped the stands, Colonel Zack said half his tickets weren't sold. On the second night there was a line out into the street with folks waiting to buy tickets."

"Why do you think that happened?"

"I suppose folks like to watch others put themselves at risk. Too bad Percy's bulldogging went off without a hitch. Still, crowds seemed to cotton to the danger of his face so close to the horns."

"Speaking of danger." Percy uncovered the plate and handed Cat a slice of blueberry pie. "I hefted this from Tonna's window. Careful. It's still hot."

"Like Tonna's gonna be when she sees her pie's been stolen?" McDonald elbow-nudged Percy.

"I can always kiss her into a better humor, Mac."

Cat said, "Is it kissing that makes a girl smile?"

"It sure helps." Percy grinned.

"There's somebody I'd like to kiss."

"Get on! Could you be noticin' Rosita's young 'un already, and you only ten?"

Cat swallowed the last bite of pie and licked his fingers. "No, it ain't her. It's another."

"Who's caught your heart, boy?"

Percy and Papa had the look of grown-ups waiting for a child to say something stupid. Cat tried to think up an answer.

Inspiration struck. "I'd hanker to kiss the pretty lady in the moving picture."

Percy winked. "Maybe you and me should visit a Nickelodeon, Mac."

Cat gazed toward the mountains. *I want to kiss a girl I met a long time ago and will probably never see again. She had a mane of black hair down her back, and her eyes were as blue as the berries in Tonna's pie. I'd sure hanker to kiss her and make her smile. She said she lived at Little Heaven, a squirrelly name for a house. The girl had a funny name, too.*

THIRTEEN

"Fools Gold Smith, get dressed!" said Minta.

"I am dressed. It's you who's wearing a chemise." Flo stood before the vanity, watching the jewelry-box ballerina twirl.

"Run down to Hummingbird Lou's room and change into that gown I stitched up last month for Madam Robin's Fourth of July shindig."

"Why?"

"Snuffy bought tickets for the bullfights."

"Bullfights?"

"Don't stand there all agog. Nobody'd guess you watched the parade down Bennett yesterday."

"Sally Marylander's white stallion led the parade, but a strange man rode him."

"Joe Wolfe. He's the owner of the Joe Wolfe Grand National Spanish Bullfight Company, the first company to ever give a show here in the United States. Did you see who waved from their carriages? They looked the same as on their posters. The great matador, José Marrero, and his wife, *Señora* Marrero, 'the only lady bullfighter in the world.' Then came the bandilleros and picadors."

"How do you know the names? Pick-a-doors and such?"

"Snuffy mentioned them. Now scoot, child."

"I'm not a child. I'm ten." Flo turned to see Madam Robin knock and enter.

"You ready, Min?" Robin wrinkled her beaky nose. "Snuffy's carriage is waiting by the door, and the dear man is smelling up the front parlor with his stogies."

"Is Mr. Snuffy to go with us, Madam?"

"No. We'll leave him off at Johnson's." Robin winked. "Perhaps our Min will have herself a new negligee this very evening. Make haste, Min."

"A moment, Madam. I have to button my bodice, and Flo's about to change clothes lickety-split."

"That's a beautiful gown, Min."

"Thank you, Madam. I sewed it myself. The pattern came all the way from Paris, France."

"Better make sure the bulls don't see you. They cotton to the color red."

"So do I, Madam. God gave me red hair on purpose." Minta smoothed the folds in her scarlet gown and added a string of pink pearls.

"Why do I have to wear white, Mama Min? God didn't give me white hair."

"Not another word, child. If you're not ready in five minutes, we'll leave without you."

Flo's glossy dark curls bounced from her swift scurry through the doorway.

"They say Joe Wolfe hit a snag." Robin dabbed scent behind her ears. "He was to bring ten Cazaderia bulls with him from Mexico, but the bulls were refused entry at the Texas border. After yesterday's parade, Wolfe sent Alonzo Welty in search of Colorado bulls. I heard he begged them off Whart Pigg and John McDonald, then boxed them at McDonald's ranch for their trip to Gillette."

"That ain't no snag, Madam. Bulls is bulls."

By mid-morning, the road out of Cripple Creek was clogged with people heading for Joe Wolfe's *Corrida de Toros.*

Minta sighed with relief when Robin's carriage reached Gillette's broad valley, resting four thousand feet below the Pikes Peak summit. Surrounding the amphitheater's main entrance were rows of gambling and saloon concessions.

"I could set up a tent with my Angels and make a fortune," said Robin, descending from the carriage. "After the excitement of the bull killings, men would flock —" She paused when Minta shook her head and pointed at Flo.

But Flo was too absorbed by the sight of Sally Marylander, astride her white stallion, to hear Robin's words.

"May I say hello to Miss Sally, Madam?"

Robin nodded. "There's Fishbait," she said, mopping her face with her handkerchief. "He's one of Denver's bunko kings, Min. We'll wait for our Flo in the shade of his tent, and maybe he'll make us the offer of an iced drink."

"Don't you be getting yourself lost or your dress dirty," Minta snapped.

Flo grasped the hem of her ruffled skirt and ran toward the white stallion. Sally had seemed so close, but now people blocked Flo's path, and her vision as well. Estimating the distance, she lowered her head and butted at bystanders. Most moved out of her way, but one didn't. The top of Flo's head met resistance. She rebounded backwards and fell, landing on her rump.

"You looked like a billy goat," said a tall, dark-haired, green-eyed boy. "Ain't hurt, are you?"

"You're nowhere big enough to hurt me."

"Grab my hand, Fools Gold."

Ignoring his offer, she rose and brushed the dust from her dress. She glanced about, but Sally and the white stallion had disappeared.

"Spit," she said. Then, "How'd you know my name, boy?"

"We've met."

"When did we meet?"

"I'm surprised you don't remember."

"Better answer me or you'll be —"

"Puking up teeth? We met three years ago. Papa drove his buckboard to Cripple —"

"Cat McDonald!"

"Howdy, Fools Gold."

"What are you doing here?"

"Same as you. I came to see the fights. They're using Papa's bulls."

"You fibbed last time we met and now you're doing it again. Them bulls hail from Mexico. I read it on the posters."

"Black Percy says the United States government wouldn't allow Mexican bulls to cross the border. And I didn't tell lies when last we met. It was you who said you'd grow your hair yellow."

Flo felt her cheeks bake. "Who's Black Percy?"

"My papa's friend and my friend, too."

"Is he black of soul or skin?"

"Skin. Percy dogs bulls and takes me with him to New York when he rodeos." Cat retrieved a leather pouch and a piece of crumpled paper from his pocket. He smoothed the small square of paper and spilled some tobacco on top, but most landed near his boots.

"What are you doing, Mr. McDonald?"

"Rolling a cigarette. Papa's hands taught me how."

"Snuffy smokes cigars."

"Who's Snuffy?"

In an uncanny mimic of Cat's voice, Flo said, "Mama Min's friend and my friend, too."

"When I visited New York last November, I saw myself another motion picture show. Hang it!" Cat dropped the paper and tobacco, pocketed the pouch, and brushed his hands alongside his trousers.

"What's a motion picture show?"

"Ain't you heard 'bout moving pictures? You sit in the dark and watch scenes flash onto a big screen."

"When I'm rich I'll buy me a motion picture show."

"You don't buy them, Fools Gold. You pay to watch."

"Then others will pay to watch me."

"Black Percy and me saw a live play. It was called *Sunday* and starred a lady named Ethel Barrymore."

"Ethel." Flo tasted the name. "I think I'll name my new puppy Ethel. Brown Mollie raises bulldogs and she gave one to me 'cause I read her some stories when she was laid up with a stomach ailment. Mollie can't read. Can you read?"

"Sure. I've been reading books since I was two years old." Cat inwardly cursed himself. She wouldn't believe that. Why hadn't he said five years old? "I've got some coins, Fools Gold. Can I buy you a lemonade?"

"I'm not allowed to accept gifts from gentlemen."

"Are you still living at Little Heaven?"

"Yes."

"That's where ladies of the half-world live, ain't it?"

"No! That's where Angels live."

"What's the difference between what I said and Angels?"

"Angels don't accept lemonade from nasty, *ugly* boys."

"No, they earn coins from bedding men. Papa's hands call it 'saucing the clam.' "

"Oh! You take them words back, Cat Mc-Donald!"

Cat saw tears mist her dark-blue eyes. "Sorry, Fools Gold. Guess I went and lit all my kindling to start a fire."

"When I'm older I'll pleasure men, too."

"No, you won't."

"Yes, I will, and they'll buy me negligees from Johnson's Department Store . . . and motion picture shows."

"No, you won't," Cat repeated, wondering why her angry words hurt so bad. "When you're older you'll marry me."

"Never!"

For a moment he just stood there. Fools Gold was prettier by far than the skinny ladies in the moving pictures he'd seen. Leaning forward, he planted a kiss on her quivering lips.

"You villain!" Fools Gold stamped her foot. Then she twirled in a blur of lace petticoats, sprinting toward the concessions.

Percy's wrong, Cat thought. *Kissing don't always make a girl smile.*

Flo found Minta and Robin, whereupon they joined the three thousand other spectators inside the amphitheater.

"There's Joe Wolfe," said Robin, pointing toward a specially raised box where Wolfe stood at attention. He wore a black sombrero and a green velvet suit dotted with silver buttons. Next to him stood a flute player from Cripple Creek's Butte Opera House.

"Bullfights always have a bugler," Minta told Flo. "*Señor* Wolfe couldn't find one, so he hired that there flute man."

The show was called to order with a spirited passage. Matador Marrero, his wife, two banderillos and *Los Picadores* lined up in the bull pit. Wolfe threw the matador an iron peg, the signal to begin.

The banderillos plunged darts into the neck of the first bull while the audience stamped their feet and cheered.

"I don't like this here bullfight," Flo said, but her voice was lost amidst the crowd's noisy adulation.

The picadors aimed lances, and the amateur bull soon reached a state of professional anger.

Matador Marrero, clothed in black and gold, strutted to the center of the ring. He stood motionless, watching the bellowing animal. When the bull charged, the matador didn't move away. Instead, he passed the bull around him with a scarlet cape.

After several charges, Joe Wolfe blew his silver whistle.

Matador Marrero received his rapier from a picador.

Flo stood with the rest of the audience.

"No!" she screamed. "Stop him!"

The bull, very weak, made his last charge.

"Somebody stop him!"

Marrero thrust his rapier from above to the heart, and the bull keeled over, dead.

Flo scrambled across toes until she reached the narrow aisle. Covering her ears to drown out the sound of stamping feet, she pitched forward.

An arm captured her waist and halted her plunge.

"Fools Gold, it's me, Cat McDonald."

"Make them stop, Cat."

"It's over. My papa's bull is dead. Are you gonna throw up? It's okay if you do. I puked when one of Papa's palominos got lost and picked by buzzards."

"Buzzards," she echoed.

"Yep. I found him before he was bones. The birds had pecked out his eyes."

"Eyes, oooh . . ."

"Untie my bandanna, Fools Gold. You can puke into that."

"No. Dizzy."

"Percy, help me!" Cat shouted.

Flo felt large hands lift her as if she weighed nothing, and she nestled against a shirt that smelled of soap chips.

"They killed the bull for no good reason," she said, staring down at Minta.

"No good reason? He was attacking the matador."

"But they stuck him with knives. If not, he would have trotted back to his pen."

"The bull wanted to kill the matador, Flo. Didn't you see those sharp horns? I know you love animals, darlin', but a bull's just a dumb beastie. He's got no soul."

From Black Percy's arms, Flo cried, "It's the men who have no souls."

FOURTEEN

"Have you seen our Flo, Madam?" Minta shivered, even though the kitchen was warm as toast.

"Goose walk 'cross your grave, Min?"

"No, Madam. I recollected Blueberry, that's all. Tomorrow will be the fourteenth year since her passing."

"Flo's getting dressed in your room." Robin pulled the cork from a champagne bottle. "Wait till she sees her birthday present. Think she'll faint?"

"Not hardly. She didn't faint when she had that awful cough and the doc spread hot oil, turpentine, and leeches all over her chest. Dangfool worms sucked worse than vampires."

"Vamp-what?"

"Pires. Critters in a story Flo recited. Vampires are dead, but at night they suck the blood from sleeping folks. You should see Flo act out the story."

"Min, dear, I'm not sure it's a good idea to let a thirteen-year-old girl read tales 'bout dead —"

"Fourteen tomorrow, Madam. Hard to believe she's growing so fast."

"Remember when you first came to Little Heaven and our Flo preened at herself in the petticoat mirror? Why'd you shiver so, Min? Goose walk 'cross your grave this time?"

"No, Madam. When you spoke of preening in the mirror, I recollected Swan."

"It was a fine funeral, Min. All the menfolk passed the collection plate so's Swan could be buried inside a silk-lined coffin."

Minta retied the sash on her black kimono, dividing the petals of several red roses at her waist. "The men who paid the most were the ones who killed Swan, Madam."

"Morphine and strychnine killed Swan."

"And she bought her drugs from them who paid the most for her funeral. I want a fine funeral, but my body's to be sent to my sister afterwards. I want to be buried in Wisconsin and — mercy! Why are we talking death on the eve of my girl's birthday?"

"Death's a part of life, Min."

"Death is death. I wonder what became of Otto Floto. It's been thirteen years since the fires." She heaved a deep sigh. "Where does the time go?"

"Time's been good to you," said Robin, appraising Minta's abundant red hair and bright brown eyes. Missing teeth marred the perfection of her face, but when she smiled with her mouth shut, she could charm Old Scratch.

Robin admitted to thirty-nine, shaving her age by a dozen years. Her once slender form was now an hourglass, her face wrinkles hidden by rice powder, and her hair — frizzed so often that most strands had broken off or fallen out — was always covered by an elaborate wig. Every morning she swallowed spoonfuls of Dr. Barker's Blood Builder and Brown's Cure for Female Weakness. Despite her age, Robin could still entertain a gent — when she was in the mood.

She had begun as a Denver crib girl, then shared a house with three other girls. After many offers of marriage, she chose a physician, but he oft spent his nights making house calls, so she left Denver with a visiting steamboat captain. The captain staked her to a new start in St. Louis, where her parlor house was a great success. After a few years, Robin sold the house and returned to Denver to collect on an insurance policy from her deceased husband, whose house calls had resulted in a fatal case of syphilis.

Robin invested her money in railroad bonds, but lost it all by June 1894, when no fewer than one hundred and ninety-four railroads went belly-up.

During her years in Missouri, a man on the police force had fallen in love with her and he took frequent trips to visit "friends" in Denver. One evening he told Robin about a prominent Denver citizen. It was rumored that the millionaire killed his first wife in order to marry another woman, but there was no proof. Robin's policeman proposed he concoct some story about Robin witnessing the deed. Together, they successfully blackmailed the millionaire, who then hanged himself. Robin found herself with child, but her daughter died of the cholera. After the Cripple Creek fires, she built Little Heaven. However, her policeman had recently retired and she'd soon be joining him in St. Louis.

Minta would become Little Heaven's new madam.

Blinking away the past, Robin admired Flo's birthday cake. The butter had lain in rose leaves, and the eggs had been delivered straight from a henhouse. A gill of wine, warmed cream, nutmeg and currants had been added, and fine sugar sifted across the top. Fifteen candles waited to be lit, one to grow on.

"Do you remember everything I've told you about the running of Little Heaven, Min?"

"Even if I didn't, I've been here long enough to notice with my own two eyes." Minta placed her empty glass on top of the table, next to *Three Weeks* by English author Elinor Glyn. The book had been banned in Boston because of its description of an illicit affair. Following the ban, it sold fifty thousand copies in three weeks.

Seeing as how Robin wanted the rules explained, Minta said, "The charge for a quick date is five dollars. Fifteen to thirty dollars for spending the night, more if *soixante-neuf* is desired. The madam's share is half the set fee."

"Good. Go on."

"Beer's one dollar, a split of champagne five. Angels get their share of tips on drinks and music."

Robin poured more champagne. Then she reached for a stack of papers next to the birthday cake. "Have you seen this two-week grocery bill for Worcestershire sauce, rum candles, steaks, roasts and chickens? Eighty-one dollars. The dairy bill's forty-three. No good madam stints."

"I won't tighten the purse strings." Minta's finger crossed her heart.

"Here's a bill for wine, whiskey and beer. Three hundred and ten dollars. But most of my profits are in the meals and drinking. A gent can spend two hundred dollars for the weekend, and that don't always include an Angel."

"Yes, Madam."

"I've written the fees inside a ledger, but —"

"The men's names have to be kept secret, though some like John McDonald and Samuel Peiffer don't care. Rowdy gents must be led from the house quietly, and Angels must be treated like babies. They can get moody and suicide on laudanum or morphine, as Swan did."

"Laudanum's more the way. You can buy quarts at any pharmacy. Look out for Suzy. She takes it lots."

"Suzy takes it for her monthly courses. Frenchy's been charging clothes on Bennett again, and she's way behind with her payments. Dee's drinking too much."

"Dee's getting on in years. She's plumb scared."

"Do you want me to talk to her?"

"Yes. Might as well slip you into my place easy-like. I'll be retiring next Christmas."

"Beth's been mooning over John Mc-Donald. She believes his flattering talk and thinks he'd leave that pious wife for love of her. By the by, McDonald telephoned. He'll be here tonight, and he's bringing his oldest boy for a first visit. Near the same age as Flo, I suspect. Who should gratify him, Madam? I'd do it myself, but I'll be pleasuring Samuel Peiffer."

"Give over young McDonald to Dee. The boy needs an experienced Angel. Damned if I ain't fuzzed from this here champagne."

"Me, too. When I get to heaven I'll sip wine all day long. I plan to set up shop in heaven and become one of God's angels." Braying her laugh, Minta left the kitchen, climbed the stairs, and inched open her bedroom door.

Blueberry would be so proud, she thought. Flo was mannered and sweet. She spoke some French and Mex, she sewed like a danged tailor, and she'd done real good in school.

Recently she'd taken to eating less and she'd slimmed down some. Her face was round like Blueberry's, but the cleft chin was Nugget Ned's. Her eyes were her mama's, so blue that in shadows they looked like purple pansy flowers.

Flo walked and talked like a lady, but she

bit her nails, so Blueberry's nugget ring stayed inside the jewelry box until the child broke herself of that nasty habit.

When parlor chores were finished, Flo could be found at the livery, where she groomed and fed the horses, lugged heavy pails of water to the troughs, and pitched hay into the stalls. As a reward for her labors, Alonzo Welty let her ride the horses and she had become an expert equestrian, able to control the wildest steed. With a sniff, Minta shook her head. Although obedient in all other respects, Flo insisted on riding astraddle like Sally Marylander.

"How do I look, Mama Min?" Flo sauntered across the room.

Minta remembered the morning near seven years ago when Flo had spilled scent and modeled a petticoat. This evening, her petticoats were safely hidden by the skirts of a blue satin gown with oyster-white eyelet lace at the bodice and sleeves. Her dress was mid-calf in length, meeting high kid boots.

"You look very pretty, child, but you have an odor."

"I bathed. Then I had to change the wood shavings in Alice and Teddy's cage, and Spinach went and hid under the stove, and

Ethel Barrymore messed on the kitchen floor."

"What were Spinach and Ethel doing in the kitchen? I've told you over and over that your pets belong outside."

"I had to bandage Ethel's hurt paw or she'd have barked all night. Spinach wriggled inside when I wasn't looking."

Minta grimaced. "A green garter snake for a pet! Honestly, Flo."

"President Roosevelt's son has a garter snake, only he named it Emily for a skinny aunt."

"And you named your rabbits Teddy and Alice for the Roosevelts. You must let your animals go, darlin'. There's too many. Dogs, cats, squirrels, rabbits, and now a snake."

"I'll let some go when their wounds are healed. The Roosevelts have the pets I do. Also guinea pigs, a black bear, a parrot, ponies and a kangaroo. They live inside the White House."

"It ain't gonna stay white if the Roosevelts' pets mess like yours do. Next thing I know you'll be draggin' some dang kangaroo through our parlor. Phew! Why don't you dab some of my scent behind your ears to lessen Ethel's smell?"

"No need. I've got my own perfume. Mr. Peiffer gave me a big bottle."

"He did? Whatever for?"

"My birthday. He thought I was only twelve but I set him straight. Soon I'll be slim like Sally Marylander. She said I had good bones."

Shrugging off her kimono, Minta swayed toward the straddle chair. "Tie my corset strings tighter, Flo. I've got to fit my new red gown and I sewed the waist at twenty-three inches. Should have made it twenty-five. I look like . . . what's the name of your pregnant pussycat?"

"Mrs. Wiggs. You're giddy, Mama Min. Have you been into the champagne?"

"Madam Robin poured a taste to celebrate your cake bein' baked, that's all."

"May I drink champagne tonight?" Flo knotted the corset strings with nimble fingers.

"Yes. One glass at midnight to toast your birthday. Now, get on with you. I've set Suzy the task of greeting guests at the door, but it's your party."

"I don't like Suzy."

"Why?"

"For one thing, she says she's from St. Louis. I mentioned places Madam Robin told me about and Suzy looked plumb addled. No, more like scared. I can't believe she ever lived there. I think Suzy fibs."

■ ■ ■ ■

During her interview with Madam Robin, Sarah Dusseldorf said she had traveled straight to Colorado from a parlor house in St. Louis. Her fiancé had died, she said. She bawled her head off, and Robin didn't question her new Angel very closely. If she had, she would have discovered that Sarah had never set foot in Missouri.

In truth, Sarah had fled Denver, changing her hair color from blonde to brown and her name from Sarah to Suzy. She didn't intend to remain long at Little Heaven. It would be a respite to get her bearings and recover from her duel with Madam Rebecca Silverheels. Madam Becky had been jealous because Sarah was bedding Cortez Wilson, a foot racer Becky considered her gent. Outside the city limits, in Denver Park, Becky and Sarah shot at each other. They both missed, but during the drunken brawl that followed, a well-placed kick had left Sarah with a broken nose.

Sarah heard that Becky considered the episode unfinished and was loading her gun anew. Customers stayed away, former friends shunned Sarah, and she decided to disappear. She didn't really believe Becky would trail her to Cripple Creek, or that Cort would press charges over the money Sarah stole from him, but it was better to be safe than sorry.

She liked the name Suzy. She liked Little Heaven, too. Madam Robin was old and easy to fool. Her apparent successor could be a problem, but tonight Minta was muddled from champagne. Still, it never hurt to butter the bread.

"Your daughter's sure a pretty little thing, Miss Minta," lisped Suzy, hoping her words sounded heartfelt. Flo was pudgy on the bottom, flat as flapjacks on top. Her eyes and mouth were too big. Beautiful hair, though. Hair was important.

Paying Suzy no heed, Minta sat on a long horsehair sofa in the middle of the room and watched Flo. Right now Flo talked to the piano player, Abraham Washington, called Washman. Next to Flo and Washman stood John McDonald's son, lofty as his father and handsome to boot.

There'd been decor changes since Minta had entered Little Heaven's parlor thirteen years ago. The Victrola still pointed toward the piano, and the petticoat mirror still reflected hemlines, but Robin had added tufted banquettes and a dozen potted ferns. Artist Jack Gottlieb had wiped out the painted stars on the ceiling and created a colorful fresco, where naked satyrs chased hedonistic nudes around the crystal chandelier.

Drawing her gaze away from the satyrs' exaggerated penises, Minta gulped down her champagne and focused on Suzy, seated next to her.

"It's easy to see where Flo inherited her beauty," Suzy lisped. "I mean, with you as her mother and all."

Minta hiccupped and stared toward the piano again. Flo was drinking from a bottle of Coca-Cola and casting sheep's eyes at the McDonald boy. Where the hell was Dee?

"When do you think she'll be ready?" Suzy said.

"Ready for what? Have you seen Dee?"

"No, ma'am. Ready to become an Angel."

"What in blue blazes you talkin' 'bout?"

"Your daughter."

"Flo an Angel? Never!"

"She'd make you a fortune, Miss Minta. She's a virgin, ain't she?"

"Shut up, Suzy! Flo's a child. Where's Dee? Dang, my head's fuzzed with bubbles."

"Only one cure for a fuzzed head. I'll fetch another glass."

"Cure for champagne's champagne? That's a new one."

222

"Champagne's not hard whiskey, Miss Minta. It's a ladies' drink."

"She was always a lady, even when she played at being one. Now she's lost and gone forever."

"Who?"

"Blueberry. Do you think she's finally found her rainbow?" Minta heaved a deep sigh. "People fly now, you know."

"That's right, ma'am. Wait here while I fetch the champagne."

Nothing sadder than a drunk whore, thought Suzy. She herself had vowed never to touch another drop. Apart from her fractured nose, four teeth had been broken during the Denver Park brawl, two directly in front.

Because of that fight, she had lost some of her beauty but not all. Her body, clothed tonight in amethyst silk, was first-rate, and she knew how to use it. Her hair was beautiful and she used that too.

Although she considered the brown color duller than her natural blonde, Suzy arranged her shiny strands in an elaborate coiffure, the heavy masses skewered with dozens of hairpins. During an evening she'd take out the pins one by one, letting rich waves fall over her breasts to her waist. The gent who selected her for his partner had the privilege of removing the remaining hairpins while she knelt at his feet, her face between his legs. By the time her hair hung loose, her gent was usually wild with lust.

Her nest egg was growing by leaps and bounds and so was her reputation.

For her own credo, Suzy had adapted what she called "The Eight Pees." Plan purposefully. Prepare perfectly. Proceed positively. Pursue persistently.

After all, no farmer ever plowed a field by turning it over in his mind.

As she watched Suzy stroll toward the iced champagne, Flo tried to dismiss the woman's unsettling presence and concentrate on having a good time. The parlor furniture gleamed and even the ceiling nymphs seemed to be sharing her fun.

Everyone had told her how pretty she looked. They were fibbing, of course, but she liked hearing it.

Good bones, she reminded herself. *Miss Sally said someday I'd have good bones.*

Cat McDonald had good bones. He had removed his black silk tie and celluloid collar and rolled up the sleeves of his white shirt. His arms, face, and the part of his chest that showed were sun-kissed. She remembered the kiss Cat had given her at the Gillette bullfights. If he kissed her tonight, she'd kiss him back.

Whistling down the rim of her Coca-Cola bottle, she heard a satisfying hum. Then she raised her eyes to meet Cat's lazy grin.

"If I had my guitar," he said, "we could join up with the piano player. I'd strum and you could blow into your bottle. They'd call us the Little Heaven Congeries."

"What's a con-jur-ee?"

"A collection of things. Horse, steer and goat, or Tinker, Evers and Chance."

"Tinker Evers and what?"

"Chance. Ain't you heard of Joe Tinker, Johnny Evers, and Frank Chance?"

Flo pictured the pages in her history book. She had a good memory but the names didn't sound familiar. "Are you teasing me, Cat McDonald?"

"No. They play baseball for the Chicago Cubs. Last year they met the Detroit Tigers in the World Series. Evers and Chance kept the Tigers from scoring by throwing the ball like a bullet shot from a gun. Tinker to Evers to Chance."

Flo felt her cheeks flush. She hadn't known what the word con-jur-ee meant and Cat had just shown superior knowledge about a stupid game called baseball, even if she did admire the animal names, Cubs and Tigers.

Making a silent pledge to learn more about baseball, placing her empty bottle on the table next to the Victrola, she said, "Never expected to find you here at Little Heaven."

"Never expected to find you entertaining in Little Heaven's front parlor, Fools Gold."

"Spit! It's my birthday. This party's for me."

"And when the party's over?"

"I'll bed down in the kitchen. And you?"

"I'll bed down with a lady named Dee. Understand she's got long yellow hair. Sure do admire yellow hair." Cat laughed, his teeth very white in his sun-darkened face. "I'd rather bed down with you, Fools Gold."

"I sleep alone!"

"Glad to hear it. Didn't know it was your party, but I'm prepared." From his trouser pocket, Cat retrieved sharp white bones threaded with string. "Happy birthday, honey."

Flo had begun to close her eyes for his kiss. Now she opened them wide. "What's that?"

"A present. Snake bones."

"I have a snake named Spinach because she's green. Thank you for the gift, Mr. Mc-

Donald, but I don't cotton to dead animals."

"Snakes are reptiles. These bones belonged to a rattler who snuck up on me and my horse, El Dorado. I killed the snake with one shot."

Flo felt her eyes widen even more. "You have your own horse?"

"Yep. Dorado's a palomino. I got him for *my* birthday." Cat thrust the bones into Flo's hands. "Take this and use it as a necklace."

"I told you, I don't cotton to dead animals."

"*Reptiles,* honey."

Flo saw red. If Cat had spanked her behind, it wouldn't have hurt worse than her injured pride. First con-jur-ees, then baseball, then his snickery remark about yellow hair, now reptiles. Spit!

"Don't call me honey, you bye-blow cad," she said, watching Dee sidle up next to Cat.

"Here you are, young gent," Dee cooed. "Minta's giving me the eye 'cause I ain't doin' my job proper."

Cat grinned but his eyes looked like chips of green ice, and Flo wished she hadn't called him a bye-blow cad.

He slung one muscled arm across Dee's shoulder. "Let's go, *honey.*"

Turning on her heel, Flo marched into

the kitchen. She tossed the bone necklace toward the far corner then washed her hands at the sink pump.

You're a snake, Cat McDonald!

Minta accepted a new glass of champagne from Suzy. Why didn't Flo like the woman? Even if Suzy wasn't so eager to please, she brought Little Heaven a tidy profit. Soon that profit would be Minta's.

Dang, her corset felt as tight as a reluctant virgin's hidey-hole. What had Suzy said before? Something 'bout how Flo was a virgin and she'd make a fortune.

Minta stood, swaying slightly. "I've got other plans for my girlie," she said.

"Other plans, ma'am?"

"I'm sending Flo to Denver." Downing her drink, Minta blew the bubbles out through her nose, into a lace handkerchief. "I'm gonna find a nice family to board her an' she'll 'tend a good school, learn twiggy things jus' like I told Belle. I've been savin' my money since Flo was little. She's gonna be a true lady an' no one's gonna' split her head with a hatchet."

"The child is lucky to have a mama like you, ma'am." *Time I plowed my field.* "How much money you got saved, Miss Minta?"

"Enough."

"Two, maybe three hundred?"

"Silly Suzy. Three hundred wouldn't clothe an' feed her good. Got myself lots more, all in gold."

"Here, drink my glass of champagne, Miss Minta. I ain't touched it."

"No. My dress'll get too tight."

"Such a pretty gown. Red becomes you with your hair and all."

"Why're you saying that? Red clashes something awful with my hair, but I purely enjoy wearing it."

"I only meant that you look pretty in whatever gown you choose," Suzy said quickly.

"I sewed Flo's dress myself. Better than anything from Paris, France."

"I wonder if you hid it good."

"Flo's birthday present?"

"No, ma'am. The gold you saved for her schooling. Is it at the bank?"

"I don't trust banks. Banks're run by men. Where's your gent, Suzy?"

"He's coming through the door right now, along with your Mr. Peiffer. Did you hide the gold in your bedroom?"

"Samuel, yoo-hoo, here I am." Minta waved her handkerchief. "Flo's getting ready to sing. Help me over to the piano, you handsome devil."

Suzy almost snorted through her crooked nose. Handsome devil? Samuel Peiffer barely reached Minta's bosom. Why did he bed her? Beth said Samuel admired the young girls. Beth was sixteen and swore she could pleasure Samuel if she didn't entertain John McDonald steady. Suzy watched Samuel preen like a bantam rooster. True, he barely reached Minta's breasts, but he took advantage of that fact by slurping at her bodice, looking for all the world like a baby sucking a sugar teat.

"After Flo's party you can play," Minta admonished. "I'd rather play now, Samuel, 'cause you got me all hot, but if you wait I'll add *soixante-neuf* and not charge extra."

Suzy could have sworn Peiffer tried to hide his disgust with a satisfied smirk. Smoothing the folds in her purple gown, she sauntered forward to greet her own guest.

So Minta had lots of money and didn't believe in banks. A shame Peiffer had entered the parlor when he did. Another glass of champagne and Minta might have told where her gold was hid. Still, sometimes it paid to hold your tongue. Suzy didn't want Minta distrustful.

Yes, a good whore should learn two things about her tongue. When to hold it and when to use it.

"Curfew shall not ring tonight." Flo held the last note as long as she dared. With her eyes closed in sorrowful ecstasy, she heard sobs from the Angels. Flo had sung about Bessie, whose lover was doomed to die with curfew's knell, at least a dozen times. The response was always the same. When she sang about Bessie's climb to the church tower and her swing twixt heaven and hell, suspended on the bell to keep it silent, her listeners always wept.

Had Cat McDonald wept?

There he stood, leaning against the wall, holding a bottle of Coca-Cola in his hand, grinning down at Dee. He hadn't even watched her performance, the snake.

Good bones, what a laugh. Dee was old but slender. If Flo climbed a church tower and swung on a bell, the rope would break and her lover would die at curfew's knell.

She turned her face toward Washman. "Please play 'The Bird on Nellie's Hat.' "

"You said the notes're too high, Miss Flo."

"True, but I feel like screaming. I read where some singers shatter glass with their high notes. Let's bust us some green Coca-Cola glass."

When she had finished, Flo curtsied.

That's the best I've ever sung. So there, Cat McDonald! I didn't shatter glass, but I reached the high notes just fine.

Minta smothered Flo inside a hug. "Blueberry would be so proud. You sing like her, only better."

"Don't cry."

"I can't help it. Your new song's so pretty." Minta swiped at her tears with the back of her hand. "Mercy! Do you plan to cut your cake or should we feed it to your pets?"

"Mercy! You're still giddy from champagne. Where's Madam Robin?"

"She had some business with Alonzo Welty. Here she comes now. Never mind the cake." Minta looked down at the small man standing by her side. "Thank you kindly for the use of your puff tie, Samuel. Here, bind this over your eyes, child."

Blindfolded, Flo was led outside. She felt the dark tie loosened and stared with disbelief.

Hitched to a post was a dappled gray mare, an enormous red bow tied round her neck.

"Mine?" Flo glanced left and right at all the smiling faces. Even Beth stood within the circle of John McDonald's arms, grinning as if she'd just swallowed a bowl of sweet cream.

"Alonzo Welty found her," said Robin. "The Angels and me bought her legal. Alonzo's letting her stay at the livery, no charge."

"Thank you. Oh, thank you. Does she have a name, Madam?"

"Alonzo didn't say."

"I'll call her Dumas, because I just finished reading *The Complete Works of Alexandre Dumas.* The book's written by a man, but if Whiskey Johnnie could name his boy burro Clementine, I can call my mare Dumas. May I ride her?"

"Now?" Minta stroked Flo's glossy curls. "Astride? We didn't bother buying a sidesaddle since the leather would crack with disuse."

"Mr. McDonald will tether your mare out back, won't you, John, dear?" Robin placed her arm across Flo's shoulders and led her toward Little Heaven's entrance. "Tomorrow you can ride Doo-ma over to Welty's. It's after midnight, Flo, so we must cut your cake. Don't forget to blow out the candles and make a wish."

"Mr. McDonald is tethering my wish."

"Make another. It can't hurt."

I wish Nugget Ned Lytton would fall down dead, thought Flo, entering the parlor and watching Hummingbird Lou place the cake

233

on top of the piano. Looking down at the candles, Flo pursed her lips and changed her mind. *I wish Cat McDonald would kiss my mouth the same way he sucks that Coca-Cola bottle.*

"I can't drink more champagne. My head's just now beginning to clear," said Minta. "Bring me a cup of tea, Suzy. Water's boiling on the stove."

"Yes, ma'am, right away."

The kitchen was empty. Reaching into her bodice, Suzy retrieved the packet of laudanum she had taken from her room during Flo's performance. She stirred the laudanum into the tea, and added five spoonfuls of sugar. Minta had a sweet tooth. Minta had lots of money, all in gold, and she didn't trust banks. Which meant the gold was hid somewhere inside her room.

The laudanum would take care of Minta, but what about Samuel Peiffer? Suzy couldn't drug his drink. She would have to think of something else quick, while they still celebrated the young girl's birthday. *Young girl!* How old was Flo? Twelve? Thirteen? Hard to tell.

Beth said Peiffer liked young girls. Beth was a vainglorious brat, full of herself, but she had the instincts of an alley cat.

If Beth was right, Suzy could get rid of Peiffer and add to her nest egg, all at the same time. *Plan purposefully. Prepare perfectly. Proceed positively. Pursue persistently.*

Suzy laughed, startling a green snake that slithered underneath the warm cookstove.

Samuel Peiffer missed being a dwarf by fifteen inches. Despite his earlier shenanigans with Minta, he preferred his lovers flat-chested and young, the younger the better.

He had slunk out of Boston after repeatedly raping the eleven-year-old daughter of a financier. Nobody could pin the deed on Samuel, but the somewhat dim-witted child kept babbling "Sam, Sam, the baker's man," and the financier had threatened castration.

Samuel stared across the room at Minta's girl. Her pink tongue licked, capturing cake crumbs. What a beauty! Let others admire the voluptuous nudes cavorting on the ceiling above his head. He fancied plump thighs and sparse —

"Mr. Peiffer?"

Samuel looked up at the new parlor girl, the one who'd recently arrived from St. Louis.

"Mr. Peiffer, I'm Suzy. Madam Robin brought me here to take over Little Heaven when she retires."

Samuel had heard that Minta was next in line and yet he knew Robin had once owned an establishment in St. Louis.

"It's a secret, sir." Momentarily, Suzy pressed her first finger against her lips. "Madam Robin wants me to slide into the running of our house without a hitch. I'm only telling the important guests."

"I won't breathe a word," said Samuel.

"I'm aware that Minta is your choice for this evening, but I have a transaction that might interest you. Minta doesn't know. Robin and I thought she might be angered since she wasn't consulted. You see, Minta believes she's to be the new madam, but Robin thinks her too old."

And greedy, thought Suzy. Leaning against the piano, Minta was turning her teacup upside down in her eagerness to finish every sweetened drop.

"What kind of transaction?"

"A birthday present for young Flo. It would involve a large fee, paid to me in advance. Flo's unsoiled." Noting Peiffer's scowl at the mention of recompense, Suzy said, "If that's not your cup of tea, sir, there are others who —"

"Hold on! I find myself intrigued by your covert tone." As Samuel fumbled inside his jacket, a knife fell out. He scooped it up off the floor and negligently returned it to his pocket. Fingering a wad of banknotes, he said, "Tell me more."

"As you can see, Minta's tipsy. If you care to, uh, tutor young Flo, you must help Minta to her room and make her comfortable. Then you must wait for the clock to strike three."

"Do you think the child might enjoy *soixante-neuf,* Madam Suzy?"

Sarah Dusseldorf took a few moments to savor her new title. Tempted to remove all her hairpins and toss them in the air like confetti, she merely said, "I am certain your experienced lips and tongue will bring her pleasure, Samuel dear."

After listening to Suzy's request, Robin couldn't quite hide her displeasure. The house was full-up and the girl had a bellyache from her monthly.

"So you do understand, Madam, how I wouldn't be much use to my young gentleman."

"How young, Suzy?"

"He'll be satisfied with a quick date, even though he's paid for the night. And he can brag to his friends about how Madam Robin herself —"

"Not the McDonald boy. He looks like he

can go the whole night and then some."

"Cat McDonald is with Dee, remember? Oh, God, the pain!"

"Take a spoonful of laudanum, Suzy. I'll entertain your young gent and let you keep your share to boot. You've been doing very well at Little Heaven. I'm sure Minta would agree."

FIFTEEN

The parlor clock chimed three times.

Suzy sauntered to her bedroom door, inched it open, and covered her mouth to stifle her laughter. Clutching his shoes, Samuel Peiffer strolled down the hallway. He was clothed in his expensive tweed trousers and starched white shirt, but his socks unraveled at the toes.

She waited until the small man had descended the staircase before she tiptoed across the hallway and entered Minta's room. Holy Mother of God! The poor woman slept on her back, surrounded by a swirl of petticoats and red ruffles. Even drugged, she moaned with every breath. Her corset stays hadn't been loosened. Suzy had told Samuel to make Minta comfortable. What had he been doing for two hours? Twiddling his thumbs? Diddling his drumstick?

The room was dim, the shadows menacing. Suzy tied back both drapes, and moon-light shone on a dragon-decorated screen. Tossed across the screen was a pretty, black, rose-patterned kimono. Suzy rummaged through a jewelry box, scooping necklaces and earrings from the satin-lined interior, placing the gems inside her bodice. Soft music sounded from the box, but Minta didn't stir. A nugget ring slipped from Suzy's grasp, hit the floor, and rolled away.

She opened the trunk at the foot of the bed and sifted through gowns and negligees. Hellfire! Where would Minta hide her gold if not inside her trunk? Suzy knelt and care-fully slid her arms beneath the spool bed's mattress. Pinching the ticking, she felt for any unusual lump.

"Who's there? Samuel?"

Suzy froze in place.

"Too much champagne," Minta moaned. "My belly's in a tumble. Please untie my corset. Hurry, Samuel."

Suzy crawled sideways, crab-like, until she reached the dressing table.

Minta fell back against two plump pillows.

Suzy waited then crept toward the bed again.

Minta bolted to a sitting position. "Suzy, is that you?"

"Yes, ma'am. I heard you call for help."

"I've been poisoned. Never felt so poorly. Take off my corset. No, better bring the slop jar first." Minta retched.

Suzy rose and took a few steps toward the slop jar, but stopped short. *I won't get another chance. In the morning Minta will recollect that I was kneeling by her bed, not entering her room. Tomorrow Samuel will tell Robin about my Madam masquerade and our special fee.*

"Why are you just standing there, Suzy? Fetch the jar and tell Madam Robin to send for the doc—"

"You're not poisoned, ma'am. It's the champagne and laudanum mixing in your belly like a purge."

"I didn't take laudanum. Where's Samuel?"

"He's having himself a joyful time, Miss Minta."

"What are you talking about? Leave my room at once!"

"No, ma'am. Not until you've told me where you hid your gold."

"What gold?"

"The money for your daughter's schooling. I've taken care of her education, so it's only fair you give over your gold in return."

"What did you say? Oh, God, my head and belly hurt. Go 'way, Suzy. We'll talk

241

tomorrow."

"Where's your gold hid, Miss Minta?"

"Bank."

"You said you didn't trust banks. Where's it hid?" Suzy warned herself not to lose her temper. Rage had led to her duel with Madam Becky. Suzy liked Little Heaven, and without the gold she didn't care to inflame a rhubarb.

Everybody had witnessed Minta's drunken state, so Suzy could deny visiting Minta's room. She could even disavow her transaction with Peiffer. After all, it was his word against hers. What about the jewelry? She'd plant an earring inside Hummingbird Lou's room, and swear she'd seen the colored cook lurking upstairs.

"Get out of my room!" Minta shouted.

Bitch! Giving orders as if she were Queen of the World. Furious, Suzy ran to the bed, tugged a feather pillow out from under Minta's curls and held it above her face.

"Where's your gold?"

"That money's to be spent on Flo. I'll never tell."

"You'll tell." Briefly, Suzy pressed the pillow against Minta's nose and mouth.

Restricted by her corset, Minta coughed, choked, gagged. "Leave me alone!" she cried. "Why are you doing this? I've always been good to you."

The pillow descended. Minta struggled weakly.

"Where's it hid?" Suzy held the pillow aloft.

"Don't . . . please . . . don't," Minta panted, tears streaming down her cheeks. "Pillow."

"Yes, I've got your pillow. Now it's over your face again. Ain't the feathers heavy? Feel how they clog your nose. Mercy, Miss Minta, your fingers are pulling at the air like a child waving bye-bye. Do you want to take a breath? The pillow's gone now. Tell Suzy where the gold's hid."

"Albert."

"Who?"

"Albert, I . . . can't . . . breathe. Corset's . . . too . . . tight."

"Where's the gold hid?"

"Pillow."

"Yes, ma'am, anything you say." Suzy pressed hard and watched Minta's fingers fall limply to the pink-and-white counterpane. "Where'd you hide your gold? I'll count to three —" Suzy felt all the color drain from her face as she lifted the pillow. "Miss Minta?"

No answer. Minta's eyes stared at the ceiling. Her breasts didn't rise and fall, and her lips were creased in a secret smile. Was she smiling at someone named Albert?

Maybe she's smiling because she never told me where she hid her gold. Damn my temper. I should have used a lit candle. She'd have talked before letting herself get burned. Why didn't I loosen her corset stays? Why did I use the pillow? Oh, God, pillow!

Grabbing a handful of hair, Suzy lifted the dead woman's slack head and tugged at the second pillow, the one that hadn't smothered Minta.

Wait. Got to think. Patience and planning. They'll send the law lapping at my heels if I don't plan carefully.

Samuel Peiffer's jacket lay crumpled in a heap. Suzy groped for his knife. She thumbed a tiny button to release its blade, returned to the bed, and settled the second pillow — like a shield — across Minta's chest.

Suzy slashed. Feathers flew and a heavy leather pouch fell free.

Not taking time to count her find, she continued slashing Minta's bosom through the pillow. She left Minta's face alone. Let the dumb whore smile at her Albert; it was only fair.

Suzy put the bloodied knife back in Peiffer's jacket pocket. On her way out, she grabbed Minta's pretty kimono.

After adding the kimono, jewelry and pouch to her carpetbag, Suzy tiptoed down the staircase. Vaguely, she wondered how Samuel fared with the child.

Samuel sat next to the kitchen table and stared down at Flo.

He had expected the girl to be awake, waiting, not asleep on a pallet. Moonlight spilled through the window and etched the inky lashes that swept her flushed cheeks. She lay on her side, breathing softly through parted lips, her childish body covered by a blanket.

Perhaps this was a mistake. Samuel didn't want to force himself on the girl. Rape meant banishment, and his Cripple Creek business was flourishing. He bought up the miners' assayed claims for one quarter their value then resold the land to businessmen who had the machines to blast or dig.

He shifted uneasily in his chair. He knew the men who visited Little Heaven thought Flo a sweet child. She entertained with songs, and he'd never heard one whispered word about buying her time or sharing her pallet.

Suzy had charged him a fortune for the young girl's company. Why? Because Flo

245

would soon be joining the other Angels, that's why. Peiffer was an important guest — hadn't Suzy said those very words? Samuel, an important guest, had been invited to "tutor" the girl. Invited, hell! He'd paid dearly for the privilege.

So why was he shilly-shallying?

Cat McDonald untangled his body from Dee's legs and sat up. His father's money had been wasted. The naked Angel slept, breathing heavily through her mouth.

Dee was drunk. What's more, she smelled of whiskey and sweat. Cat preferred the smell of Fools Gold. Flowery soap and a dab of scent couldn't disguise her natural perfume — dogs, horses, mashed oats and polished leather.

Why was he thinking about that child? Her hair was too wild, her eyes too big, and she looked like a boy on top. Still, she blushed prettily when he teased her.

He favored Dee, if only she hadn't been besotted with whiskey. He had supported her to the bedroom, but rather than falling asleep like a good drunk cowhand, she had smothered his body with hers, thrust her breasts into his hands, and kissed whiskey fumes down his throat. When he didn't respond, she had mumbled something about his first time. *Then* she'd slept.

First time? Not hardly. He and Rosita's oldest girl had been shedding their clothes for months. Maria was seventeen, older than Cat, but she'd been more than willing to meet up with him in the barn. After the first time, she said how she fancied a wide-awake hombre who could take a deep breath and start all over again.

Lately she'd been pulling him onto the hay every chance she got. Cat didn't mind, but he had a feeling his brother watched them through a peephole in the loft's floorboard. Lucas spied.

Dee's whiskey-kisses had left Cat with a powerful thirst. There was a well near the privies, but the kitchen was closer. And warmer!

Fools Gold slept in the kitchen. If Cat woke her, she'd be madder than a smoked hornet. What did others do when thirst hit them? Brave the April night's chill?

Soon it would be dawn. Hadn't his father said something about Fools Gold brewing coffee at cock's crow?

With a sigh, Cat lowered his head to the musty pillow.

Samuel Peiffer heard the clock strike four.

He rose from the chair. Pins and needles

247

pricked his legs and he nearly fell. Staggering forward, he stubbed his big toe on the
table leg and swore a blue streak.

Flo lifted her head. "Who's there? Is that
you, Mr. Peiffer?"

"Call me Samuel." Gingerly, he tested the
sore toe that poked through his sock.

"What time is it? Are you wanting something to drink, sir? I can fix coffee but it
will take ten minutes. If you leave and let
me get dressed, I'll start the coff—"

"Didn't Suzy talk to you, child?"

"Talk to me about what, Mr. Peiffer?"

"Your special birthday present."

"Dumas? Has she slipped her tether?"

"Your mare's fine, girl. I'm talking about
the other gift."

"Do you mean your perfume, Mr. Peiffer?
Didn't I thank you properly?"

"No. When a man gifts a pretty girl, he
expects a kiss in return."

"I'm not pretty, but thank you just the
same."

"I want a kiss, missy. I paid a fortune —"

"You did not, Mr. Peiffer." Standing
upright, Flo gathered the blanket around
her body. "I don't want to hurt your feelings, sir, but I know the price of scent. You
were either cheated or you're fibbing."

"Damn right I was cheated. Get over here

248

right now."

"You can have your perfume back."

"I don't want the perfume. I want you."

"But I don't want you." Flo took a deep breath. "You've made a mistake, Mr. Peiffer. I sleep alone."

Samuel felt sweat bead his forehead. As if he were dying, portions of his life flashed before his eyes. His sisters, all tall, laughing at his smallness. His mother locking him inside a closet when company came to call. The doctor's "stretching machine." Father, disgusted, sending his only son away to boarding school. The schoolmates and schoolmasters who taunted. Holding back his pee, his bladder nearly bursting until the water closets were deserted. His first woman, bovine, who'd just about smothered him to death. His first child partner, a prostitute. The sense of completeness, of power —

"If you don't leave, I'll scream."

Samuel circled the table and seized the girl's blanket, but she wriggled free and took off toward the back door. Dropping the blanket, he lumbered after her.

Frantic with terror, Flo tried to scream. But nothing came out except mouse squeaks. Her heart's pounding sounded louder than her cry for help. Mr. Peiffer pawed at her nightie until it tore apart. She lost her balance and fell to the floor.

Mr. Peiffer crouched on top, caught both her wrists with one hand and spread her thighs apart with his knee. She went limp.

"That's better," he said, releasing her wrists to unbutton his trousers. "You treat me nice and I'll add more to what's already been paid."

Flo clawed at Mr. Peiffer's eyes then elbowed her way backwards. Once again she tried to scream, but this time nothing came out, not even mouse squeaks. Panic had dried her spit.

Mr. Peiffer crawled on all fours. Stopping, he screeched, "Snake! Christ! A snake!"

Spinach! Thank God. The snake's unexpected appearance gave Flo a few precious moments to rise and grasp the door's handle.

She heard soft thuds and glanced over her shoulder. Mr. Peiffer was thumping Spinach against the stove. Then he flung the dead snake toward the wall.

Tears stung Flo's eyes. Kicking at the doorjamb, she felt Mr. Peiffer catch her hair, jerk her back toward the room's corner, and push her to the floor. Searching for a weapon, her fingers closed around Cat's sharp bone necklace.

Mr. Peiffer was on top again. Flo swung the bones and heard Mr. Peiffer's roar of pain. Moonlight revealed streaks of crimson streaming down his face, but he wouldn't get off her. He grabbed her wrist and shook until she dropped the bones.

Suddenly, he was gone.

Spinach lay crumpled next to the wall, looking like a green lasso. Mr. Peiffer sagged against the same wall while Cat McDonald's fists pummeled.

Mr. Peiffer's face, already bloodied from the bones, looked like a lumpy red potato.

Cat paused for breath, and Mr. Peiffer slid to the floor, unconscious.

"Fools Gold, are you all right?" Cat knelt and cradled her shoulders with his arm.

At his touch, she opened her mouth to scream but nothing came out.

"I came downstairs for a glass of water." Cat covered her with a blanket. "Do you want to cry? If you do, I'll hold you. Please *say* something, Fools Gold."

She stared at the ceiling.

"I'll find my papa, Fools Gold. Can you hear me? I'll fetch Papa. Then I'll fetch Minta."

Sixteen

Ethel Barrymore stared mournfully at Little Heaven's drape-drawn windows. Crouched behind a chokecherry shrub, Gingerbread washed her whiskers. Alice and Teddy twitched their funny bunny noses as if they smelled blood. Flo's scrappy tomcat, Zane Gray, stalked a squirrel.

Madam Robin had told Flo to wear her blue birthday dress so she'd "bedazzle Min's sister." Robin had also told Flo not to visit Minta's room, which now reeked of lye soap. But Robin wasn't home, and Minta's window faced the front yard. Flo's pets had assembled in the yard and watching them made her feel better. After all, they lived and breathed while the stillness of death hovered over Little Heaven.

Flo couldn't see Lampman's Funeral Parlor, not even from her high vantage point, but she knew Madam Robin was there, along with Mama Min's sister.

Inside Lampman's Funeral Parlor, the glass case on top of a table contained mementos from Cripple Creek citizens who had met violent deaths. The case included the lunch pail from a miner struck by lightning, the pistol of a gambler who had shot himself through the mouth, and a lock of Minta's russet hair.

Green Brussels carpet covered the floor. A fern in an iron stand gravitated toward a window. On a desk near the entrance, obituary notices had been scattered. One read in part: "Minta LaRue died early today at the Little Heaven. She was stabbed in the upper body by Samuel Peiffer. He was arrested and led away handcuffed, bleeding from face wounds. Minta's body was discovered lying on the bed fully clothed, by a patron. The name of the patron could not be learned."

Toward the back of the mortuary was the morgue.

"She's dead," Robin cried, her tear-streaked face offset by an elaborate wig. "Minta's sins won't rub off on you now."

"The stain on our family will never rub off," said a steely-eyed matron, her padded backside propped against a coffin. "It's as red as the dye on her hair."

"Minta never tinted her hair!"

"Just as she never sewed for her livelihood? You should have told me what she was before I traveled to this loathsome cow town."

"Mining town, ma'am."

"I'll take no further responsibility."

"But she's penniless," said a man in a dirty oilcloth apron. "Her money was stole the same night she died. Do you want to see your sister buried in potter's field?"

"That harlot is no sister of mine." With a snort, the gray-haired battle-ax turned to leave.

"She's not penniless," Robin said.

"What did you say?"

"Her coins and jewels were pinched by a girl named Suzy. We figure Suzy was in cahoots with Samuel Peiffer."

"I don't care to hear about —"

"Minta saved your letters in her lockbox, ma'am, but her gold was hid inside my safe," Robin fibbed.

"How much?"

"It was to be used for her daughter's education."

"Minta's barren."

"Yes, ma'am. Fools Gold was adopted."

"Fools Gold? Not even a decent Christian name."

"Minta oft said she wanted to be buried in the family graveyard, behind the dairy barn. There's enough money in my safe to pay for her funeral and send her coffin by rail."

The battle-ax waved her gloved hands in the air. "Look, I just told you —"

"There will be lots left for them who tend her grave."

"How much?"

Robin mentioned a sum. "An amount will be sent each month. My lawyer will handle the details." She retrieved a scrap of paper from her reticule. "I want these here words on Min's headstone. 'I do set my rainbow in the clouds and it shall be a token of a covenant between me and Minta.' "

"The Old Testament says a covenant between me and the earth, you dim-witted fool."

"Ain't no use spitting nasty names, ma'am. It's these here words or no fee at all."

"I'll bury my sister on the farm, but I won't be a part of her blasphemous funeral."

"Do you want to see Minta's child? She's waiting at home, all spruced up special."

"The child be damned! Good afternoon, miss."

"Madam," said Robin, wishing Samuel Peiffer had slashed the sister instead of Minta.

Or had somebody else killed Minta? Peiffer kept insisting he didn't do it. Even if he spoke true, he still deserved to hang. Rumors had surfaced about a rape scandal in Boston — an eleven-year-old child!

Robin's eyes filled with tears again. Peiffer had tried to rape Flo, but the McDonald boy had stopped him in time. Then, after finding Minta dead, John McDonald had carried Peiffer's unconscious body to her bedroom, protecting Flo's reputation.

Minta's jewels and money were missing. Peiffer swore Suzy had arranged his visit to the kitchen. They were in cahoots for sure.

The police surmised that Peiffer's wounds had been caused by Minta's nugget ring, found on the bedroom floor. The police also deduced that Minta had tried to defend herself by wielding the ring, and Suzy had pummeled Peiffer's face in an effort to keep all the stolen goods for herself. If John and Cat McDonald knew anything different, they maintained their silence.

Peiffer's bloody knife had been found in his jacket pocket, so the trial would be a mere formality. Suzy had disappeared. Flo didn't seem to remember Peiffer's attack, and she hadn't uttered one word since the night of her birthday party.

Dabbing at her swollen eyes with a soggy handkerchief, Robin turned toward the mortician and outlined her plans for Minta's funeral.

The Elks Band led the funeral procession, their red fezzes bobbing up and down in time to the music.

Flo marched, her feet avoiding ruts in the street, even though her eyes stared straight ahead at the mountains.

Robin marched on one side of Flo, Hummingbird Lou on the other, alongside the hearse, which held a lavender casket covered by red and white roses.

Dumas followed the funeral wagon. Atop her dappled back lay a cross of pink carnations, the same color as Minta's burial gown. Minta had sewed the gown herself.

Better than anything from Paris, France, thought Robin, noting with satisfaction that a crowd of miners and curious children lined the streets. Buggies and phaetons were filled with heavily veiled women from every parlor house. The sky was clear but thunder rumbled.

"I wrote to that awful sister of Min's and told her to plant red rosebushes at the grave," Robin said. "Minta sure cottoned to the color red. Them bushes will drop their petals every year like teardrops."

Flo nodded.

"Don't fret, pun'kin. Minta's money is gone, but I've got plenty to spare. It's in St. Louis, and I'll send for some right away. You'll be schooled in Denver."

Flo shook her head. The thunder sounded again, louder than the music, and she pressed her hands against her ears.

"That's what Min wanted, Flo, so I don't want to hear any argument from you."

Robin wished the girl would argue. Shout. Scream. Cry. Make any sound at all.

Three weeks after Minta's funeral, Flo entered Little Heaven's kitchen. She carried a rabbit under each arm, planning to give Alice and Teddy the carrot greens from a salad she had prepared earlier.

Madam Robin sat at the kitchen table, her head buried in her arms. Flo heard great gulping sobs. Lowering her bunnies to the floor, she raced toward the table.

Robin raised her head. Her wig was askew, her eyes rimmed pink. A crooked trail of tears coursed down her face, streaking the

258

rice powder and rouge.

"Dear God," she cried. "What am I to do? Look what arrived in today's mail." She held up a piece of cream-colored stationary. "This came from St. Louis. Listen. 'I found your name and address in my husband's desk drawer. Apparently he formed a business transaction with you. My husband died a month ago. He was in debt from gambling and the bank panic. He left five children. If you owe him money, send it quick. His last words were about me and the children.' "

Flo's eyes misted. Dropping to the floor, she rained kisses across Madam Robin's knees.

"She didn't have to add that last part, Flo. It was cruel. I didn't know he was married. We planned to cross the ocean on the *Lusitania* when I retired. I sent him my profits, every cent, except last month's, which paid for Minta's grave and funeral."

Flo fumbled inside the pocket of her white pinafore then pressed a handkerchief against Robin's palm.

"You want me to blow my nose?"

Flo nodded.

"Crying doesn't make it better? All right, stop wagging your head like that. It'll fall off." Robin sniffled. "I'm poor as Job's turkey, child, and I don't know what to do.

Why are you pointing at yourself? What can *you* do? Sell your pets?"

This time Flo reached into her pocket and retrieved the stub of a pencil. Turning Robin's letter over, she wrote: DUMAS.

"Sell your horse? Thank you, but the amount we'd get would be a drop in the bucket."

Flo wrote: ANGEL.

"What do you mean? No, don't write it again. I'll never allow you to join the profession. Minta would creep from the grave like a dang vampire and suck the blood from every gent who entered your room."

IT'S THE ONLY WAY. BETH AND JESSIE ARE GONE. FRENCHY AND SCARLET TOO.

"No!"

I WANT TO HELP.

"No!"

Flo scowled. Why was Madam Robin so stubborn? How would she pay the next grocery bill? Since Minta's funeral, Flo had returned to her old eating habits. Hummingbird Lou had stayed on without pay, but the larder was empty.

What if Lou decided to cook Alice and Teddy?

Flo licked her pencil and bent over the piece of stationary.

WHY NOT? MY MOTHER WAS A WHORE."

Robin slapped Flo's face. "Blueberry conducted herself like a lady, and she gave up the profession for your daddy."

Flo bolted. Robin scurried to the open door and watched her run toward Welty's livery. In no time, she'd leave the stables atop Dumas, her skirts flying.

At first Robin had fretted over Flo riding out alone. What if she got lost or hurt? Then the artist, Jack Gottlieb, had knocked at Little Heaven's door and told Robin that Flo came almost every day to watch him paint. He didn't mind, he said. Flo missed her mama, and he knew how it felt to pine for someone.

Flo bit the end of her thread and jabbed her needle into a pincushion. She heard Washman's piano. That meant a few gents had visited. But they wouldn't stay long when they discovered that Dee and Robin were the lone choices. Maybe one would linger with Dee if she didn't pass out early from drink. Since Minta's death, Robin had aged ten years.

Only Flo could save Little Heaven.

She had thought it over all afternoon while watching Jack Gottlieb paint, and she'd reached a firm decision. She'd become an Angel.

According to Robin, Flo had been attacked by Samuel Peiffer the night of her party. But Flo couldn't remember anything that happened after her songs and the gift of Dumas. The next thing she knew, Mama Min was dead and so was Spinach. And she couldn't talk. When she opened her mouth, nothing came out.

She had watched the police lead Mr. Peiffer from the house. "Tell them I was with you," he had yelled.

How could she tell them that? She couldn't even talk.

Leaning forward, she studied her open mouth in the mirror. She had teeth and a tongue. Her throat didn't seem to be missing any parts. It was as if someone had nipped her voice box the same way she'd nipped the greens from this morning's carrots.

Turning sideways, she studied her reflection, wishing she had a corset to slim her waist and plump up her bosom. What bosom? Shortly before her birthday party, she'd borrowed Beth's Princess Bust Developer. Beth said it was "a new scientific help to nature." But science couldn't change what nature hadn't provided.

Flo smoothed the folds in the orange taffeta she had just altered. Then she rolled her thick hair into the popular Gibson Girl style. She looked older but not old enough. Opening Mama Min's La Dore Rubyline, she rubbed pink color onto her cheeks. She fingered carmine lip rouge across her mouth, brushed a black paste mixed with water across her lashes, and added a puff of Floral Complexion Powder.

She wished she could fit Minta's heeled silver-gray oxford shoes, but her feet were too small. Her own patent-leather Colt Bucher boots would have to do.

Squaring her shoulders, she glanced around the room. Vanity. Straddle chair. Dragon screen. Spool bed. The mattress and cherub counterpane had been burned, but just like Flo's boots, the new mattress and muslin sheets would suffice.

After descending the staircase, she entered the parlor.

Washman was playing a jazzy rendition of Porter Steele's "High Society."

Dee gave Flo a startled look.

Madam Robin was nowhere to be seen, thank goodness.

A man with combed-back strands of mud-colored hair approached. He held a whiskey bottle. "My name's Jim Willy," he said, "and

I'm new to Cripple Creek. The madam didn't tell me nothin' 'bout you. I was gonna leave for better digs, but I guess I'll stick a while. You're awful young but big. I like bedding big girls."

Flo batted her lashes at the skinny gent. If she ever owned another snake, she'd name it Jim.

"Cat got your tongue, missy? Never mind." Jim's teeth made dents in his lower lip. "I prefer me a girl who knows when to keep her yap shut. Care for a drink?"

Flo considered the offer. No, she'd not add drinking to her other sins. She shook her head.

"Bought me a bottle and I've near finished half. Hope you don't mind if ol' Jim gets hisself pissed."

Flo smiled.

"Ain't you a pretty thing when you smile like that? Got me an itch to retire upstairs, but I ain't paid the madam. Where is she?"

Probably in the kitchen. When Washman finished his ragtime piece, he took off in that direction. So I'd better hurry and get this Jim upstairs, because once it's done, Robin can't say no to another time.

Flo walked quickly toward the staircase. Jim Willy followed, his odor leaving a distinctive trail. Mr. Willy didn't bathe.

"In a rush, are you?" He ran one finger along his tight linen collar and madras bow tie. "Slow down, missy, we got the whole night. Besides, I ain't paid yet. What's the charge?"

Flo held up ten fingers, put her hands behind her back then held up five fingers.

"Fifteen dollars?"

She nodded.

"Only figured to spend ten. How 'bout ten?"

Flo shook her head no. She climbed the first few steps, grasped the hem of her dress, and lifted the orange taffeta above her knees.

Mr. Willy attempted a whistle. "You sure got pretty legs. I like them boots, too. Reckon I can spend fifteen, but you better earn it." He flicked his tongue, lizard-like.

Flo climbed the stairs, entered Minta's bedroom. When Mr. Willy staggered inside, she slid a chair beneath the doorknob then reached behind her back for the buttons on her gown.

"What's your hurry, missy? I ain't drunk all my whiskey. Sure you don't want a thimbleful?"

Flo shook her head, held out her hand, and stamped her foot.

"Oh, I get it. You can't talk." Mr. Willy tilted the bottle, drank, wiped his mouth with his sleeve. "Why're you waggling your fingers like that? You want the money first?"

Flo nodded.

"Ain't sure it's worth fifteen for no dummy. I like my gals to scream."

I thought you liked ladies who keep their yaps shut.

Flo buttoned her gown and pointed at the door.

"What'll you do if I bed you for free? You can't yell for help."

Seizing the jewelry box, Flo aimed it at the mirror.

"All right. I'll pay. Show me your legs again."

She shook her head.

Mr. Willy took off his trousers, kicked them across the room, and sat on the edge of the mattress in his red union suit. "Money's in the front pocket."

Anchoring the jewelry box under her arm, Flo bent down, picked up Mr. Willy's skinny pants, and pulled fifteen dollars from his pocket. She laid the jewelry box on the vanity, wound the key, and set the money next to the box. Music sounded and the ballerina twirled.

Squeezing her eyes shut, she walked toward the bed. Mr. Willy lifted her petticoats and ran his hand up between her legs. With a gasp, Flo opened her eyes and moved away.

"What's this game? Come back here!"

Shaking her head, she retreated until her behind pressed against the vanity.

Mr. Willy stood. "If it's a game you want, a game you'll get, but you'll bend over when I catch you." He patted his backside. "Reckon my meaning?"

Her fingers closed around the jewelry box.

"Oh, no. We don't want others running to the sound of broken glass." He grabbed her wrist.

Yanking her hand free, she dropped the box.

"Pun'kin, you in there? Washman says you sashayed into the parlor, dressed in Minta's gown. I'm sorry I hit you this afternoon, but I'll spank you good if you've done what Washman says you've done. Open the door."

Mr. Willy had turned at the sound of Madam Robin's voice. Flo ran toward the door and kicked the chair away. Shouldering Robin aside, she stumbled down the stairs, fled through Little Heaven's entrance, and raced toward Welty's Livery.

By the time she had bridled Dumas and mounted from the block, rain had begun to fall.

■ ■ ■ ■

Jack Gottlieb needed more wood, but was it worth getting soaked? The woodpile was outside, next to his crude corral.

"I could use my paintings for firewood," he told Leah's heliochrome. "I have lots to spare and it might be fun to see them go up in smoke, just like my life."

He shivered. It was cold inside his two-room cabin. There was no warmth beneath the quilt that covered his cot. The hand-built table and chairs and rocker mocked him. Only his dead wife's photograph and a Disc Gramophone, with its funnel and cabinet, interrupted the stark monotony.

He had ordered the gramophone from his Sears Catalogue because Leah had loved music. Thirty dollars thrown away, money he could ill afford. Now he turned the gramophone on and sang "Sidewalks of New York," sang about the east side and west side, until he reached the last line of the chorus. He didn't want to think about the sidewalks of New York. If he did, he'd think about Leah, and he didn't want to think about Leah. But he couldn't sleep, he was chilled to the marrow, and —

His marriage to Leah Schoenbrod had

been arranged in advance, before she shipped out from Germany. The day after her arrival, they stood before a rabbi. Jack had crushed a glass beneath his heel for luck, lifted her veil, and fallen deeply, irrevocably in love.

Within three years they had two sons. He worked in the garment district. With Leah's encouragement, he painted whenever he had a free moment. Then came the tenement fire. Jack was at work. He was told how Leah stood by the open window of their sixth-floor apartment, trapped from the flames above and below; how she'd dropped both children toward the extended arms of the people on the sidewalk — the sidewalks of New York. Hopefully, smoke had blinded her, disguising the sight of two smashed bodies and skulls. Hopefully, she had died from the collapse of the building rather than searing flames.

Following the fire, he hadn't known anything for two years. Crazed with grief, he had been confined to a sanitarium in upstate New York. For therapy, he began to paint again. At first he covered his canvasses with black. Then, as he emerged from his own dark place, he added a tree, a flower, a piece of sky. He had left the Catskill Mountains for the Rockies, praying the change in scenery and altitude would expunge the past and —

Right now, he needed to expunge the cabin's chill.

He stepped outside and strode toward the woodpile. Through the pelting rain he saw the outline of a horse with no head. Had he gone stark raving mad again? No. The horse nuzzled a crumpled heap on the ground. A human heap.

Dear God, it was Flo, Minta's daughter, the parlor house child. What was she doing here?

"Never mind why she's here, you idiot. Get her inside where it's dry."

Could he carry her? She was a plump girl, and sodden clothing increased her weight. Taking a deep breath, inhaling rain, Jack slung her body over his shoulder. He prayed that her bones weren't broken and he wasn't doing more harm than good.

Kicking the door shut, he placed her on the cot. She moaned.

"Where does it hurt, Flo?" He remembered she couldn't talk, or wouldn't talk, so he ran his hands over her body, searching for broken bones.

Her mouth formed a scream. She rose from the cot, limped to the cabin's corner, and slid to the floor.

"I'm not going to harm you," he said. "But you know that, else why'd you come here?" *No broken bones, though she's wounded her leg.*

She staggered upright and stood against the wall, her blue eyes smudged with black. Rain dripped from her dirty face. Her hair, a thick mass of curls and rattails, tumbled down her back. Her orange gown was muddy. Its damp bodice clung to her heaving bosom.

Grabbing a clean towel and shirt from a wooden shelf, Jack tossed them toward her. "I've got to fetch some firewood or you'll catch your death, child."

When he returned, she had put on his shirt and folded the quilt around her lower body. She stood near the dying embers but moved away when Jack dropped his wood.

"I won't harm you," he said again. "May I bandage your leg?"

She shook her head.

"If I give you warm water and bandages, will you do it yourself?"

She nodded.

"Sit on the rocker while I fetch my supplies."

Jack settled into a chair by the table and watched her cleanse her leg efficiently, as if she tended a hurt animal. Why had she ridden to his cabin? She visited during the day, almost every day. Why had she sought him out tonight? He couldn't escort her home in this storm.

"Stretch out on the cot, Flo."

She shook her head, her expression anguished. No, frightened. She was scared to death. As if he would ever touch a child. What the hell had happened at Little Heaven?

"Then stay put in the rocker while I sit here and sketch a portrait. Is that all right? Do you trust me to leave you alone?"

She nodded, but still stared at him wide-eyed, and he was reminded of a deer he had once startled. Its reaction had been the same: large staring eyes and a body poised for flight.

He sketched with charcoal, occasionally adding more wood to the fire. The cabin grew warm and smoky. Flo rubbed her eyes. Her lashes fluttered. She slept.

After a while, Jack dropped his pad to the floor and his head to the tabletop.

When he awoke, the girl stood before him, dressed in one of his shirts and a pair of blue jeans, tied at her waist with a piece of rope. Her face was clean, her hair neatly braided. The fire in his cookstove had been lit, and steam poured from the spout of an enamel coffee pot.

"That coffee sure smells good," he said, glancing toward the window. "I had hoped the rain would stop but it looks worse. Now it's a thunderstorm."

As if to prove his words true, there was a rumbling noise. The cabin shook. Flo paled and covered her face with her hands.

Jack ached to hold and comfort her, but he didn't dare. "Are you afraid of thunder, child? Hasn't anyone ever told you that thunder is God's cough?"

She shook her head.

"I came here from New York. Outside the city are mountains called the Catskills, and people who live there say thunder is the sound of the little people bowling. Have you read the story of Rip Van Winkle? No? Rip bowled with the little people and got so tuckered he fell asleep for a hundred years. When he woke, things had changed. Wouldn't it be wonderful if we could sleep and change things?"

She nodded, walked to the window, rubbed a pane of glass with her shirt sleeve. Thunder sounded again, but this time she didn't react the same. This time she whimpered.

"What's the matter, honey?"

She yanked opened the cabin door. A blast

of wind blew rain inside. Without thinking, Jack pushed her away and shut the door. "I'm sorry," he began, then paused.

Flo whirled in circles. Strands of hair escaped from her braids and stuck to her wet face.

"What ails you, child? Stop spinning."

The girl obeyed, though she now rocked back and forth. "Dumas," she said.

"Alexandre Dumas? The author?"

"Dumas. Mare. Gone."

"Your mare's name is Dumas? She's not gone. I built a barn out back, just a few sticks nailed together, but it's got a roof. Last night I put your mare inside with my own nag."

"I thought she was dead, like Mama Min and Spinach."

Jack gently grasped her shoulders. She didn't flinch, thank God. "It's okay if you cry," he said. "We'll talk afterwards. They say time heals all wounds, but it's tears that help cleanse the hurt. Cry, child. I'll cry, too. We'll cry together."

Autumn leaves couldn't hide Little Heaven's sagging roof or the gardens overgrown with fungus. Weeds had choked out the more desirable plants, and the house itself exuded

274

an odor of defeat, not unlike rotting vegetation.

"Where is she?" Cat McDonald tried to keep his voice steady. "Where's Fools Gold, Madam?"

Robin wore a loose black dress with no corset, but it didn't really matter since her hourglass figure had shrunk to skin and bones. Blocking his entry, she said, "Flo's gone."

"Gone where?"

"Gone for good. She's found a new place."

"Another parlor house?"

With a shrug, Robin began to shut the door.

"May I come in, Madam? Please?"

"Why not?" She swung the door open.

Cat took off his Stetson and wrinkled his nose. The house smelled of vomit and grease. He followed Robin into the parlor. All the furniture was missing — couches, tables, banquettes, piano. Ceiling satyrs and nymphs were an ironic rebuke to the empty room.

"Had to sell my goods," Robin said.

"What happened?"

"I couldn't find new Angels. Them that applied were a scruffy lot. Others were scared away by Minta's murder. I'd offer you a chair, but as you can see I'm hard up for chairs."

"Please, Madam, where's Fools Gold?"

"Why're you asking?"

"I haven't been to Cripple Creek for months. Not since her party. Today my father sent me on an errand, so I thought I'd see how she's fared."

"I suppose you wanted an appointment to bed the girl."

"Bed Fools Gold? She's a child."

"Did you want to marry her?"

Marry her? Cat shook his head.

"Did you plan to tote her home to your sainted mother? A new pet for your ranch?"

"No, Madam. I just —"

"Cat McDonald, you handsome devil. Where've you been?" Dee staggered through the parlor entrance and slumped against the wall. "Tell Washman to play a tune, Madam. Would you care to dance, Cat?" She tried to curtsy, lost her balance, slid down the wall.

Cat took a few steps forward. "Can I help, Madam?"

"Nobody can help." Robin coughed into a handkerchief. "Dee's drinking rotgut. She's too sick for the cribs, so I'll tend her as long as I'm able."

"Make them go away!" Dee screamed.

"Hush, dear, you don't want young Mc-

Donald —"

"Bugs!"

Cat felt the hairs on the back of his neck prickle.

"She sees bugs sometimes," said Robin.

Dee waved her hands frantically. "Spiders! Get them off me!"

Cat walked backwards until he left the parlor. Then he whirled around and raced through the hallway, toward the front door. Once outside, he took several deep breaths.

Should he continue down the row? Should he knock on doors? Did Fools Gold entertain gents in her own bedroom now?

No, she's a child!

This morning he had decided to visit Cripple Creek and rescue Fools Gold, save her from a life of sin, just like the heroes did in his New York motion picture shows. He had planned to tell Dimity that Fools Gold was recently orphaned, the daughter of a minister. He'd devise a motion picture plot, or borrow one. Last month he'd seen *Uncle Tom's Cabin.* Uncle Tom had fallen to one knee, and Aunt Sally had bowed her head. Surely Dimity would bow her head when Cat recited the sad tale of the angel who'd carried Fool Gold's mama up to heaven. Cat would fall to one knee, just like Uncle Tom. Fools Gold was smart. She could be taught to playact and — gone, Madam Robin had said. Gone where? Another parlor house?

Cat untied Dorado's reins from the hitching post and swung into the saddle. Ignoring stirrups, nudging the palomino with his heels, he rode toward the wind. Maybe a gust would blow away his damnfool hero's mantle.

Silently, he chastised himself, for in his head he knew that motion pictures were make-believe, but in his heart he wanted to believe they were real.

SEVENTEEN

Divide: 1912

A dark-blotched, cream-colored bull snake eyed a pocket gopher. Slithering behind the McDonald barn, the snake wended its way toward a shady shadow.

Oven-like heat had overpowered instinct.

Fifteen feet above the bull snake, the barn's loft was strewn with more than hay. A horse blanket lay crumpled against one corner. Orange peels and pie crumbs decorated the open pages of a popular novel, *The Winning of Barbara Worth*. Its author fictionalized rugged heroes, adventuresome stories and moral instructions.

Cat's trousers and Maria's blouse and skirt were heaped on the straw, next to Barbara Worth. So were Cat and Maria.

Cat sucked Maria's breasts, teasing the nipples erect with his tongue, until he felt her back arch.

"Dios mío!" she cried.

He penetrated.

"*Gato . . . Gato . . . te es muerte.*"

Slowly, he withdrew then slid inside again. Maria wrapped her legs around his waist.

"*Dios mío!* Oooh . . ."

Untangling her legs, Cat rolled sideways and dabbed at his streaming brow with his shirttail.

She stared at him, her dark eyes lazy-lidded. "Why you stop, *Gato?* Maria's turn?"

"No. It's too damn hot. Be a good puss and hand me my pants."

"Poose? *Madre de Dios, Gato,* you are the poose."

"Hush!" Cat sat up. "Did you hear something?"

"I hear my heart." Pushing him down, she straddled his hips.

Cat stifled a sigh. Maria was now twenty, and her passion had not lessened in their three years of meeting at the barn.

What's more, she was a damned boomerang.

He was tired of her reaction to his touch. Press her belly and she spread her legs. Tongue a breast and she arched her back. Still, she was the ranch's only diversion, except for her sister Bridgida, who was one year younger than Cat.

Until this spring, he had considered Bridgida a child, though he admired her skill with a horse — she rode like the wind. Then, without warning, the tiny girl had washed her dirty face, braided her knee-length hair, and grown breasts.

Aroused, Cat mapped his campaign as carefully as a cavalry soldier planning an Indian raid. Fastening Dorado's reins to a fence post, he'd wait for Bridgida to ride along the trail. He'd lift her from her horse's bare back and escort her to an old willow. There, they'd talk about the ranch. He treated her like a fine lady, aping Bronco Billy and Tom Mix, his favorite motion picture heroes. With an effort, Cat kept his hands from straying toward her soft curves.

Tonna had told him about a girl's first time and the hurt it brought. If a girl was willing and loved a man with all her heart, Tonna said, the hurt was less. Cat didn't understood Tonna's reasoning — why would it hurt less if love was involved? — but he could wait. After all, he had never experienced an inexperienced girl. Not Maria. Not the parlor girls along Myers Avenue.

Cat visited Cripple Creek's tenderloin district twice a week. The girls clustered around him, draping themselves across his broad shoulders, sitting in his lap, weaving their fingers through his thick hair. He had even heard that one girl had tried to kill herself with chloroform after what the Madam called "a Cat fight with a rival."

Little Heaven was closed, its doors and windows nailed shut with boards. Two years ago, Papa had interrupted Cat's riata twirling. "Listen to this newspaper story, son. 'Mrs. Robin, for some time an inmate of Heaven, attempted to take her life with a dose of carbolic acid and is now between life and death at Sisters Hospital. Another inmate, Dee, was found dead in the same establishment. The cause of death is not known, and whether or not the woman committed suicide is a question. When found, the dead woman was in a crouched position on the floor.' "

"Did you say inmate of heaven, Papa?"

"That's what it says here. I'm sure they meant Little Heaven."

Poor Robin. Poor Dee. Poor Papa. He didn't visit Cripple Creek anymore —

"*Gato* . . . oooh," Maria moaned, rocking back and forth.

As if yanked by a pair of reins, Cat's meandering thoughts receded and he yielded to the task at hand.

"Madre wants me to wed Rodolfo," Maria said with a sigh, her needs fulfilled, at least for the moment. "Rodolfo has *mucho dinero y muchos años.*"

"Congratulations, sweetheart. You deserve an older man with lots of money."

"You do not care?"

"Of course I care."

"No. You think only of Bridgida, who will take Maria's place. You make tease, *Gato.* How can you stomach Rodolfo doing what we do?"

"It breaks my heart, *querida.*"

"Truly, *Gato?* Oh! You make tease again. *Hijo de puta!*"

"For shame, sweetheart. If Rosita could hear —"

"My mother has heard worse."

He laughed. "What happened to your pretty accent?"

"I lost my accent when I was still in nappies."

"Hush!" Cat staggered to his feet. "That's Dorado's stall!" He stumbled toward the ladder.

"*Gato,* wait! Your trousers!"

"Toss them down. Hurry!"

Cat tucked his shirt inside his jeans, pulled his belt free, and headed toward the corral. Spying his brother, he said, "What the hell do you think you're doing, Luke?"

Though he stood on the mounting block,

Lucas was only an inch taller than Cat. "I'm going for a ride," he said.

"On my horse?"

"*Maman* says the horses belong to Papa. *Maman* said I can ride any horse I want."

Cat scowled. Recently Dimity had insisted her children call her *Maman,* with the French inflection. She believed it sounded tonier. Luke used it like a religious litany.

"Not *any* horse, Luke. Dorado's mine."

"How dare you call our sainted mother a liar!"

"I didn't say she lies. All the horses belong to Papa, but Dorado was a gift and Papa put my name on his papers. That means he's legally mine."

At the sound of Cat's low voice, the palomino whinnied and pushed his nose against Cat's shirt.

Luke jumped down from the mounting block and tugged at Dorado's reins, jerking his head away from Cat. A steel bit nearly cut the stallion's mouth.

Enraged, Cat hefted his belt but hesitated when he saw Luke cower. Dropping the belt, he attacked with his fists.

The fight was short-lived. Cat felt fingers grasp his shirt at the neck and pull him backwards. "Let me loose, Percy. You don't understand."

"I don't understand how you'll hit a boy half your size who can't defend himself. Ain't you shamed?"

"He's twice as wide," Cat mumbled, cooling when he saw his brother's bloody nose.

"You'll be sorry! Wait till I tell *Maman!*" Luke wiped his nose with his sleeve, saw the blood, and pitched forward. Percy caught him. "Cat tried to kill me," Luke screeched.

Percy eased him to the ground. "It ain't that bad. Wash off at the pump and find Tonna. She'll clean the cut and give you a slice of new-baked rhubarb pie."

"I didn't try to kill him," said Cat.

Luke scrambled to his feet. His shirt had popped its buttons, and his white belly heaved like a cow about to calve. "I'm telling *Maman.* She'll have you whupped good."

Cat watched Luke duckwalk toward the house. "I didn't hardly burn one piece of kindling before you came along, Percy. Leastwise, I saved Dorado from Luke's sharp spurs." Removing the palomino's saddle and bridle, Cat opened the corral gate and slapped Dorado lightly on the haunches, prodding him inside.

"Dimity will brand your soul with her words, boy."

"Papa's fair-minded. He won't whup me."

"Mac's in Denver at the Cattleman's Association. It wouldn't surprise me if Dimity whupped you herself."

"I'm too big."

"You're too big for your britches. Bein' tall and strong and fightin' with your little brother don't make you a man."

"I'm a man, Percy. If you don't believe me, talk to Blanche over at the Bon Ton. Ask Maria."

"I don't have to ask. All the hands know 'bout that gal. Even Rosita suspects. That's why she plans to hitch Maria up with Rodolfo."

"Does Mother know?"

"Not unless somebody's told. Better hide Dorado, or Dimity will give him to Luke."

"But Papa —"

"Can't fight her. It's more peaceable to let her have her own way."

"What am I going to do?"

Percy nodded toward the tack. "Saddle Dorado. I'll tell Dimity I sent you down-range to mend fences and chase mavericks."

"I've a better idea." Cat reached into his shirt pocket, retrieved a piece of newspaper, and smoothed the folds.

Percy looked down. "The Marines have landed in Cuba to protect American interests. You plan to join the Marines, boy?"

Cat turned the newspaper over. "It says here they're making 'movies' in Canon City, near the Royal Gorge. A company called Selig Polyscope. They need cowboys who can ride and fall off a horse."

"Fall off?"

"Remember the shoot-out I saw at the nickelodeon? Plenty fell. It says here these pictures are two-reels with Tom Mix, and I'd sure like to meet Mr. Mix. That Polyscope outfit plans to be here until autumn, so I reckon I'll get me a job making movies."

The summer air was scented with Michaelmas daisies. In the far distance, junipers were scattered over canyon slopes. A redspotted toad had strayed from the junipers. The toad found a rain pool, squatted in the shallow water, and issued forth his breeding call, a high ringing trill that lasted several seconds.

It was his death knell. A blackneck garter snake struck, yellowish stripes and keeled scales flashing in the sunlight.

As the snake assailed the toad, a tasseleared squirrel scampered away, its bushy tail streaming like a banner, its paws narrowly avoiding the two figures who lay behind thick foliage.

My trousers spend more time off than on,

thought Cat. *My rump gets more sun than my face.* Lowering his mouth, he found the tiny breasts of would-be actress Ruthie Adams.

She giggled.

Damn that gurgling laughter. Cat missed Maria's Spanish litany. Ruthie was too ticklish.

Twisting her fingers in Cat's hair, she pulled his mouth away from her breasts, pressed his head between her thighs, and threw her arms in the air.

Her motion brought to mind Black Percy's bulldogging.

"Anybody see the McDonald kid?"

Ignoring the harsh male megaphonic voice, Cat worked faster with his tongue. He felt Ruthie's body shudder as her head wove back and forth on the blanket of leaves. Finally, her spasms lessened and her legs relaxed.

Cat resisted the urge to glance toward an imaginary rodeo stand and receive his printed time from the judge's card. Over Ruthie's recumbent form, he peered through the brush and made out a pair of polished boots, ending at flared jodhpur knees.

The man who had boomed into a megaphone was only a few feet away, his boots

288

firmly planted on the dirt path that circled the flowered glen.

"Sweetheart, keep quiet," Cat warned in a whisper.

"I need a towel," she whispered back. "I'm wet, and it's all your fault."

"Here, take this." Cat unknotted his neckerchief and placed it between her legs.

She grabbed his hand, directed it toward her breasts, and giggled.

"Are you plumb loco?" He covered her mouth, his thumb and first finger forming a vee so that her small turned-up nose could breathe. "DuBois will fire the both of us."

Her body jiggled with suppressed laughter, and her brown eyes teared.

"If we're dismissed, we'll never see each other again."

He felt her nod and removed his hand. Damn, he couldn't find his BVDs. On the ground, he wriggled into his trousers and stood up.

"McDonald!"

"I'm right here, Mr. DuBois. You don't have to shout."

"What are you doing here?" DuBois lowered his megaphone. "You're supposed to be getting ready for your next scene."

The bushes hid everything below Cat's shoulders. He felt Ruthie reach into the open flap of his trousers.

"McDonald, answer me!"

"I came here to think over the next scene, sir, get in the mood you might say, and I guess I fell asleep."

DuBois shook the spit from his megaphone. "Where's your bandanna?"

Damn! Local cowboys were required to wear red, yellow or blue bandannas at all times. Since the cameras could only record black and white, the audience never realized the colorful code and it was easier than learning names. Unfortunately, DuBois knew Cat's name all too well.

Ruthie pressed something damp against Cat's palm. "I have it right here, sir." Extending his arm, he showed DuBois the musky red material.

"It doesn't do much good if it's not tied round your neck. By the way, we've decided to shoot your Roman stunt tomorrow morning so you can get ready."

"Ready for what?"

"Colonel Selig wants to see you perform that bull-dodging trick."

"Bull*dogging*." Cat felt Ruthie's hand grope inside his trousers. "Stop it!"

"Can't stop it now. Selig's got a wild bull, and the fairground arena's been cleared."

"But I ain't bulldogged in months, Mr.

DuBois."

"That's not the way Lonnie Higgins and the others tell it. They say you performed your stunt recently, inside New York's Madison Square Garden."

"They heard wrong." Cat gasped. "Stop it!"

"I told you, it can't be stopped. Colonel Selig wants you at the arena as soon as you're saddled up. Better find your hat and cool off. Your face is so full of sweat, it's dripping onto your shirt."

Cat watched the small man strut down the path. When the jodhpurs had rounded the bend, Cat grasped Ruthie's wrist, pulled her hand away from his groin, and lifted her to her feet. "If you ever do that again," he said, "I'll wring your pretty neck."

"Peachy. I love threats." With a giggle, she handed him his BVDs.

"Here's another one. If you don't behave, I'll bulldog you."

"Sounds like fun."

Cat smacked her backside. "It's not fun, it's dangerous."

"I adore danger. I adore dark clouds gathering. Didn't I leave my father's house during a storm and join Selig's crew? Pa had me engaged to a schoolmaster. Can you believe that cow flop?"

291

Cat felt no pity for the schoolmaster, who was much better off without Ruthie. She had a hankering for danger all right. She'd been buzzing around the assistant director when Cat first arrived in Canon City. Leaving Claude DuBois flat, she'd staked her new claim. DuBois was furious but she didn't care.

Now Cat gazed fondly at the light-brown hair she curled in imitation of her idol, Mary Pickford. Ruthie had the boyish figure admired by movie audiences. She'd never have to bind her breasts for the cameras. In some ways she reminded him of the parlor house child, Fools Gold.

Except Ruthie Adams ain't no child, he mused, watching her step into her blue skirt and thrust her head through the square opening of a white middy-blouse.

"I picked out my last name because Adam was the first man," she'd told Cat. "I'm gonna be the best actress in the world. Number one, except for Mary Pickford, who's best of all. I'd stand naked in front of the cameras if it would make me a star."

No sir, at age nineteen Ruthie wasn't a child.

Fools Gold would be seventeen. Cat had searched for her in Cripple Creek, but she'd vanished, and it didn't pay to ponder her fate. He'd be better off finding a way out of this damnfool bulldogging stunt.

Absently, he kissed Ruthie and sent her toward the arena while he headed for the barn.

He had arrived in Canon City eight weeks ago, given a demonstration of his skills and been hired. Because of his dark hair and sun-darkened skin, he frequently played an Indian. Having learned to ride Comanche-style from Percy, Cat could hang from the back of his horse for long periods of time. Lonnie Higgins taught him how to ride like a Cossack.

Lonnie, a sixteen-year-old "extra player" in their motion picture, *Mountain Gold,* was the son of a local citizen who rented the production horses and other equipment. "Riding Cossack ain't easy," he'd said. "You've got to pass from one side of your horse to the other, underneath his belly."

"Shoot, Lon, I've dogged bulls with my teeth," Cat had boasted, then repeated his boast at the Hell's Half Acre Saloon.

It was just a matter of time before he got himself in big trouble. "Braggin' sits on your tongue as easy as a horsefly ridin' a mule's ear," Percy would have said.

Cat had never bulldogged with his teeth. Percy wouldn't let him — too risky. But was

Cat in any more danger bulldogging than performing film stunts?

There were no trick cameras on Colonel Selig's set. If a scene called for a runaway team to be halted, Cat or Lonnie would rein-whip their horses into pursuit. Sometimes they would be trapped between the frenzied team, escaping death by a hairsbreadth.

Atop Dorado or a spotted paint, Cat would ride at full gallop, mingling with the sharp-horned steers for a stampede scene, climbing a steep mountainside, jumping from a cliff into a river. And for all this, he was paid five dollars a day.

Many of the hired cowboys had sustained injuries. A few horses had broken their legs and been shot. Fearing Dorado might suffer the same fate, Cat had demanded the paint for stampede scenes and mountain stunts.

After filming wrapped, usually at sunset, Cat and Lonnie would gather with the other cowboys inside the Hell's Half Acre Saloon, where they displayed their skill at roping and marksmanship. Cat never missed the lemons arranged in a row of empty shot glasses. Hell, he could shoot the pit from a cherry.

Sometimes it was more dangerous off the set than on.

Colonel Selig used women for the saloon and street scenes. Quite a few were willing to meet Cat in secluded glens, and he finally had his first inexperienced girl. She had wept with the pain then begged for more.

Danger was Ruthie Adams. Because of Ruthie, DuBois wanted Cat fired, but "the McDonald kid" was too valuable, usually standing in for the great Tom Mix himself.

The stunt rescheduled for tomorrow morning involved Cat riding two horses Roman-style, his boots planted on each horse's back while he reined in a runaway team separated from the buckboard. At the same time, Tom Mix would chase the loose wagon, scoop Myrtle Steadman from her jouncy perch, and transfer her to the back of his horse, Tony. The scenes would be spliced so that it looked as if Mix had stopped the team before he saved Myrtle.

No, they wouldn't fire Cat, not unless they found him with Ruthie. Morality was maintained on the set. You could vamoose for a few hours, but if discovered it meant instant dismissal.

As he saddled Dorado, Cat conjured up each of Percy's dogging motions. *First you wrestle the horns, then sink your teeth, then fall to the ground with the steer. Wrestle the horns, sink your teeth —*

Maybe he should admit he lied and give a roping demonstration. He'd twirl his riata and make jokes, like Will Rogers did. What had Rogers said the last time they were together? "I tell you folks, all politics is applesauce." Cat had laughed his damnfool head off because Papa called books and movies applesauce. "Invest in inflation," Rogers had said. "It's the only thing going up." The noise from the arena was going up, too. Cat had a feeling Selig's guests wouldn't cotton to a rope demonstration, no matter how many jokes he told.

He recalled the Joe Wolfe Bullfights. Wolfe's bulls had been untrained and confused. Hopefully, that would be the situation this afternoon. Cat pictured Fools Gold at the fights, how she'd almost fainted in the aisle. "It's the men who have no souls," she'd cried.

Leading Dorado by the reins, approaching the fairgrounds, Cat saw that every bit player, every actor, the entire production team and all the locals, including Lonnie's father, Woody, were gathered at the sidelines. Many were placing bets.

"Give 'em hell, McDonald!" Lonnie shouted.

Ruthie stood next to Lonnie. She untied a bow from her Pickford curls, wended her way through the crowd, and met Cat at the arena's entrance. "My schoolmaster once told me how ladies would give knights ribbons and such," she said, handing him the red strip of satin. "That ol' bull won't stand a chance against you, Cat. Guess what Colonel Selig and Claude DuBois named him?"

"Honey, it doesn't matter what his name —"

"Titanic, after the ship that hit an iceberg last April."

"Canon City's too damn hot for icebergs."

"If you think Canon City's hot or Titanic's fierce, wait till we meet tonight."

As Cat braided Ruthie's ribbon through Dorado's mane, a thrill coursed through him. This was his chance to prove he was a hero, like Tom Mix.

He felt a grin stretch his face. His bull had been named for a ship that had floundered on its maiden voyage, and that was almost too portentous.

"Titanic's probably some runty vest-pocket cow," he told Dorado.

The palomino buck-jumped like a huge golden grasshopper, and sidestepped into the ring.

EIGHTEEN

Not a breeze stirred. Atop a high pole, an American flag drooped in desolate folds. Three shades lighter than the flag's blue bunting, the sky was cloudless, disturbed only by the spread wings of one red-tailed hawk.

Circling the arena, Cat waved toward the faceless assemblage. Sweat blurred his vision. All he could see were Stetsons, bonnets, handkerchiefs and beer bottles.

The door to the stock chute swung open.

Cat gave chase, but inadvertently overrode the bull. Dorado just missed being gored as Cat slid down the palomino's tail, pivoted, grabbed Titanic's horns, and stared into a pair of pink-rimmed eyes.

Titanic was untrained, confused, and furious. He slammed Cat's body against the arena fence while spectators scrambled for more distance. Tossing Cat left and right, up and down, Titanic tried to dislodge him.

Cat hung on. His mouth opened, gasping for breath, but any thought of sinking teeth into that saliva-smeared upper lip had taken wing with the hawk.

Eye to eye, Cat continued grasping Titanic's horns, afraid to let go, afraid he'd be impaled. His hat fell to the ground.

Titanic pawed the hat then folded to his knees, driving sharp horns into the dirt, battering Cat against the hard-packed earth.

Lord, get me out of this and I'll never brag again, Cat prayed, maneuvering his bruised body until he sat atop Titanic's sweat-lathered haunches. *I'll cut down on my gal-poking, too.*

"Amen," he said, and made an irrefutable decision. Forget dogging. He'd ride the damn bull. To hell with the crowd! To hell with Selig and DuBois!

Weaving his fingers through Titanic's short mane, Cat leaned forward. "Wouldn't you rather snoozle some pretty lady cow, amigo? Let's head for the chutes."

Titanic nodded vigorously, and Cat just missed being epauletted by clumps of nasal mucus.

He looked toward the stands. Folks were throwing beer bottles into the ring. Were they trying to be helpful? Not hardly. They'd seen Titanic tire and were goading the bull into a renewed frenzy.

Titanic bucked. Cat rotated through the air like a flipped flapjack until his backside hit the dirt. He stood up and tried to run but his legs were as shaky as a sapling in a wind storm.

Powerless, he shut his eyes. He pictured Fools Gold and remembered how he had wanted to kiss her and make her smile. Too bad he'd never get another chance. Soon Titanic's horns would pierce his heart. If those crested spikes propelled him over the fence, Cat hoped he'd land on one of the bastards who'd thrown beer bottles.

He heard a roar from the stands and opened his eyes. Tom Mix circled the ring, riding his horse Tony. The former rodeo star waved a Colorado flag in front of the disoriented bull.

Hobbling to the side of the arena, Cat felt hands lift him over the fence. Hauled to safety, he watched Titanic eye the flag's red ball, snort, paw the ground, joggle his horns, turn, wiggle his haunches like a fat fan dancer, and trot sedately toward the chutes.

Tom Mix tugged at Tony's reins.

The black horse reared up, his hooves flailing at the sky.

Mix tipped the brim of his ten-gallon hat

and galloped around the ring again, the Colorado flag streaming out behind him.

The crowd cheered.

Seated smack-dab in the middle of the stands, Mrs. Tuttle removed her straw bonnet and wigwagged it toward the ring. But her friends couldn't determine whether she was paying homage to Tom Mix or Tony.

Mrs. Tuttle was a comfortably curved widow who ran a boardinghouse for gentlemen. She had two strictly enforced rules. Her gents must keep their doors shut while changing clothes, and there were no females — except, of course, Mrs. Tuttle — allowed on the premises.

With the arrival of Selig's motion picture cowboys, Mrs. Tuttle visualized the scratchy ink on her ledger pages pulsating with profit. To that end, she had converted her sitting parlor into a bunkhouse, charging twelve dollars a month for bed and breakfast.

She'd managed to squeeze fifteen mattresses between her sofa's clawed feet, her stuffed armchairs, her molded footstools and heavy credenzas. Pewter lamps with tasseled brown shades provided a dim glow. An ornately framed painting above the fireplace depicted a ship atop choppy, green-tinged waves.

"Mr. Tuttle loved the sea," she'd tell her gents. "A shame he died up in a tree, killed by lightning during a heat storm."

Tonight Mrs. Tuttle was at the home of a friend, another widow, drinking beer and chatting about this afternoon's performance. Both women agreed that Tom Mix was magnificent but they preferred Cat McDonald's anatomy.

Inside Mrs. Tuttle's boardinghouse, the subject of her discussion was trying to find a less lumpy spot on his mattress. "Leave me be, Ruthie," he moaned. "There's not one part of my body that doesn't throb with pain."

"My body's throbbing too, Cat."

"Are you plumb loco? The men'll be returning soon from Hell's Half Acre."

"Eyewash! They'll drink and brag yet a while. You just lay there and let me —"

"No. This afternoon I promised I wouldn't . . . I swore I'd cut down on my . . . forget it. God won't hold me to my word since it was Tom Mix, not God, who saved my hide."

"Wasn't Tom peachy?"

"Don't forget who tired the bull for him, first."

"Lucky Myrtle. Tomorrow Tom'll lift her

from that buckboard seat and set her on Tony. I get all shivery thinking about it."

"You get shivery thinking about what you'll eat for dinner."

"Will you be able to perform your Roman stunt?"

"Sure." Ignoring the pain from his bruised ribs, Cat struggled to his knees and lowered his mouth to Ruthie's breasts. "Unbutton my pants, honey. My hands are bandaged."

"You don't need hands. Just keep doing what you're doing with your mouth."

"My mouth wasn't much good this afternoon. I wonder how Percy sets his teeth in the snout."

"You were so brave, Cat. Most others would have run from those horns at the very beginning." She began writhing.

"Slow down, Ruthie, and let me play toreador." He nudged her legs apart with his face and licked the inside of her thigh.

She giggled.

"Still think Tom's so peachy?"

"Your tongue, Cat, faster. Oh, I'm gonna die."

"Don't die yet, or you'll miss the best part."

"Well, well, what a pretty sight," said a familiar voice. "Colonel Selig sent me here to see if you'd be able to perform your stunt tomorrow. I'll tell him yes and no."

"DuBois!" Cat rolled over on his back.

"*Mister* DuBois, kid."

Sitting up, Cat covered Ruthie with the blanket. "This is all my fault, sir," he said. "Miss Adams came here to see how I was feeling and I pulled her down onto the mattress."

"Is that true, Miss Adams?"

"It's the truth, sir," Cat replied earnestly. "Miss Adams wanted to leave. She knows the rules. I made her stay."

"I suppose you tore her clothes off."

"Yes, sir."

"With your bandaged hands?"

"No. My teeth."

Fingering his small, clipped mustache, DuBois smiled. "Oh, I get it. You bulldogged Miss Adams."

"Yes, sir." Cat nearly groaned out loud. Eight cowboys now stood behind the assistant director, gaping at the scene inside Mrs. Tuttle's parlor.

DuBois said, "Your story's so good, I'm tempted to let you off. But you must know how Colonel Selig feels about maintaining moral standards. Cat McDonald and Ruthie Adams, you're both fired."

Cat walked down the 300-block of Main

304

Street, then entered Selig's headquarters. He was ushered into an office immediately. The director, who resembled Teddy Roosevelt, sat behind a scarred wooden desk.

Squeezing his Stetson between his bandaged hands, Cat finished his explanation. "So you see, sir, it wasn't Ruthie's fault. You can fire me, but she has no place to go."

"I've heard she has a family. Her father's a minister, I believe."

Cat blinked with surprise; he hadn't known that. "Her father would never let her return, sir. Besides, Miss Adams wants to be a movie star."

"Miss Adams will never be a movie star."

"Why not? She's beautiful and she works hard."

"Didn't she tell you about her screen test?"

"No, sir."

"We had her play a girl sending a soldier off to war, the War Between the States. It was a sad scene, very tender. The actor knelt at Ruthie's feet, his arms around her waist. The scene was supposed to end with a kiss. Do you know what happened?"

"Ruthie giggled?"

"Correct. We tried the scene three times."

"Ruthie's ticklish but laughter could be

an asset. What about comedies?"

"Claude had witnesses."

"I've explained all that, Colonel Selig. It was my fault."

"I admire you for trying to protect Miss Adams. I admired your courage yesterday, too."

"Do you mean the bulldogging? I'm sorry, sir. I could have hurt somebody bad, including my horse and Mr. Mix. It sure cured me of fibbing."

"You've never bulldogged with your teeth?"

Cat shook his head. "A friend, Black Percy, does that stunt. Percy would say that to prove my lies, I'd fight with you till hell freezes over then skate with you on the ice."

"Stubborn as well as courageous. I like those qualities in my actors."

"I'm not an actor, sir. Is there any chance . . . I mean, Ruthie Adams?"

"No chance at all, son."

"Would you allow me to buy the paint I've been riding?"

"I thought you owned a horse. A golden stallion."

"The paint would be for Ruthie. I'll let her stay at my ranch until she recovers. She was plumb scared last night. In fact, she's bawling her eyes out. If you tested her now, she wouldn't giggle."

Selig walked away from the desk and stretched out his hand. "If you ever want to work for me again, Cat McDonald, give me a call. Selig Polyscope is spreading out, severing all ties with Chicago. We'll film more in Colorado, but we'll be based in California. And the paint's yours, payment for yesterday's performance."

"But I didn't dog your bull."

Selig chuckled. "After that business with the bull, Myrtle is giving Tom the kind of looks that would melt snow from the top of your Pikes Peak. We've added more love scenes."

Stumbling from the building into bright sunshine, Cat smiled. The interview hadn't gone badly. He had money in his pocket, along with Colonel Selig's California address. Now he needed only to find Ruthie and help her pack her bags. It was a long ride to the ranch and she would insist they stop along the way so that he could change her sobs into giggles.

Halting Dorado, Cat looked over at Ruthie. Her nose and eyes were redder than his bandanna. Even her curls drooped.

"Stop bawling," he said. "You've been crying ever since we left Canon City and I can't take it anymore."

"But I'm dead, finished forever in the movies."

"That's not true, honey."

"Yes, it is. I'll never get another job, not even if I give the great Tom Mix himself sugar. My daddy tells everyone I'm dead and I'll be staying at your ranch as your mistress, not your wife."

"Do you want to marry me, Ruthie?"

"I want to be in the movies."

"You can work on the ranch as a cook."

"I can't cook."

"You talk French, don't you? You said you could."

"A little."

"I'll tell Mother you're a famous French actress."

"*Actrice,* Cat. That's the French word." Ruthie wiped her drippy nose with her sleeve.

"Mother will throw a big party for *Mademoiselle* Adams. Father will roast a steer, and we can eat its testicles."

"Cat McDonald, don't talk dirty!"

"After a while you can try movies again."

"Do you really think so?" Ruthie smiled through her tears.

"Sure." He adjusted his hat brim. "Let's make tracks. It's getting late and we're miles from Divide."

"Can't we stop? I'm tired."

"No. Even if we had time, look at the sky."

She glanced up and Cat groaned. Her nose wasn't red from crying. It was sunburned. No matter what he said, she insisted on wearing her hat like movie star Josephine West.

"What's wrong with the sky, Cat?"

"Clouds are gathering for a storm."

"Oh, no!" Reaching over her shoulders, Ruthie grasped her cowgirl hat and placed it on top of her head. "Please, Cat, can't we find a house or something? I don't want to greet your mother soaking wet. I won't look like a famous actress at all."

"If you hadn't ridden so slow —"

"Well, pardon me for living. How would *you* feel if you were going to a strange place with strange people? My daddy warned me. Yes, he did. He said I'd go straight to hell."

"My ranch ain't hell."

"It's not a movie set." Her eyes filled with tears again, and her lower lip quivered.

"Don't cry! Only yesterday you said you liked to see storm clouds gathering."

"I'm hungry."

"I've got cheese and jerky and bottles of pulque and tequila, a farewell gift from Lonnie. I think I see something in the distance, atop that rise. It looks like a deserted miner's shack. Come on, honey. We'll build a fire, eat, sleep, and head out tomorrow at dawn."

Dismounting, Cat led the horses into the gusting wind. He had removed the bandages from his hands, but his ribs throbbed. Reaching the cabin, he sent Ruthie inside while he tethered the palomino and paint.

When he entered, Ruthie stood against a wall, tears streaming down her sunburned cheeks. "I lost my hat in the wind," she said between sobs.

Their shelter had four walls, but the wood was nailed together haphazardly, leaving gaps. The entire structure was smaller than Mrs. Tuttle's parlor. A window framed the darkening sky. Rodent droppings had left a fusty odor. The rickety walls vibrated, but calculating the age of its weathered boards, Cat figured the cabin had withstood blustery storms before.

"Stop crying, Ruthie. I see a woodpile. Let's start a fire."

"I want to die."

"I'm warning you, Miss Adams, either stop that infernal sniveling or beat it!"

"Why don't you kill me and get it over with? I can't be in the movies and I lost my pretty hat. Kill me and bury me out back.

They won't discover my body for a hundred years."

Placing both hands around her neck, Cat squeezed lightly. "Are you sure you want me to kill you, sweetheart?"

Ruthie couldn't shake her head no and increase the pressure of his hold on her throat, so she stood motionless, quivering like a captured squirrel. Cat released his grip and rubbed his hands alongside his trousers.

Ruthie slid to the floor. "Don't be mad," she said.

The girl was unbelievable. She had slowed their ride with her blubbering, a storm was brewing, and Cat had a feeling her French actress role wouldn't fool Dimity one bit.

Why was he blaming Ruthie? He had grabbed the bull by the horns, so to speak, which had led to her boardinghouse visit. He had insisted Ruthie ride with him to the ranch. Why? Because he felt sorry for her? Responsible? Other cowboys would have stood in line to become her "protector."

Once before Cat had wanted to rescue a lost soul — Fools Gold. It hurt when he couldn't find the child. But Ruthie Adams was no child. Yes, she was. There she sat, huddled against the wall, trying without much success to stifle her sobs. Cat knelt and pulled her into his arms. "I'm sorry," he said. "Let's start a fire and drink some tequila. Put your arms round my neck and I'll carry you. That's a good girl. You'll feel better tomorrow morning."

By daybreak Ruthie's sobs had become giggles. They had shared the tequila. Then, while he slept, she'd drained half the pulque. A short nap hadn't sobered her.

Cat didn't know what to do. There wasn't enough food for another day and night. His body ached, aggravated by his sleep on the hard floor. And relieving himself in the bushes outside, he'd seen new clouds on the horizon. Already, a misty drizzle splotched the ground.

Inside, Ruthie was breakfasting on the remaining pulque. Cat's angry slam knocked the cabin door from its hinges. Grabbing the pulque bottle, he threw it at the wall.

As she danced to the music in her head, she swung her hips against his sore ribs.

Maybe the drizzle outside would *clear* her head.

He dressed her in a white cotton skirt and middy-blouse, fumbling for buttons.

Giggling, she pressed her breasts against his fingers.

He gartered her stockings and shoved her

feet inside her shoes, wishing he could shove the laughter back down her throat. Her hair looked like a bird's nest. A brush and comb were in her gear, lashed to Dorado, so they would have to stop away from the ranch and tidy her curls. Her Persian lamb coat was already packed. Cat maneuvered her arms through his sheepskin jacket sleeves and led her outside.

"It's raining, it's pouring," she sang, dancing round the paint, her feet splashing through puddles as if she were a fractious child. "The old man is snoring. Went to bed —"

"Ruthie, please, the sooner we get started, the sooner we'll reach the ranch."

She nodded, reached for the saddle horn, missed, swayed drunkenly.

Her face had blistered from yesterday's sunburn. Beneath his open jacket, her wet blouse stuck to her body, outlining her small breasts.

Should they ride back to the Mountain Gold set? Should he leave her in Canon City to fend for herself? That bastard DuBois would take Ruthie under his wings, or more likely his skinny flanks.

Swearing a blue streak, Cat lifted her up onto the paint.

■ ■ ■ ■

As Cat had predicted, the weather worsened and rain fell in pelting sheets. The horses could move no faster than a walk or trot. Every time they trotted, Ruthie vomited pulque. After she'd fallen from her horse three times, landing in muck, Cat shifted her to his own saddle. But Dorado couldn't make much headway with two people on his back.

Finally, the wind lessened and the rain stopped.

Dismounting, Cat led both horses. Time had no meaning. It was night. The stars were hidden by dark clouds, signaling another storm was on its way.

"I'm sick," Ruthie whined. "I smell awful. I'm hungry and thirsty."

"I know. But we have to keep moving."

"It's dark. We're lost."

"We're not lost, and I've ridden through the dark before." He shifted Ruthie onto the paint. "I'll tie you to the saddle so you can sleep. When you wake up, we'll be home, just in time for a good hot breakfast."

"I want to be a movie star," she whimpered, lowering her dirty face to the paint's mane.

314

They had reached the outskirts of the ranch when it began to rain again. By Cat's reckoning it was breakfast time, and his mouth watered at the thought of Tonna's biscuits. He felt the rain plaster his shirt to his chest. Ruthie still wore his jacket and he had lost his Stetson hours ago.

Should he dress Ruthie in clean clothes and comb her hair? Cat laughed until he coughed. She'd be soaked straight away. He dismissed the idea of stopping first at Percy and Tonna's small house. He was chilled, hungry as a spring bear, and he wanted to rest his aching body. Ruthie would have to do. Maybe Dimity would feel compassion for the poor bedraggled girl.

With the house in sight, Cat maneuvered Dorado next to the pinto. "Honey, wake up."

"Are we home?"

"Almost. Do you remember what we planned? You're *Mademoiselle* Adams, the French actress."

Ruthie tried to sit up. "Cat, the ropes!"

"I'll untie them if you're sure you can make it the rest of the way without falling."

"I can't meet your mother like this. I'm wet and smelly and filthy and —"

"The worse, the better. We want Dimity . . . my mother to feel sorry for you. All you have to do is say a few French words and eat your breakfast. Then you can sleep in my bed."

"All right, Cat, I'll be *Mademoiselle* Adams. I'm so tired of being me. I want . . ."

If she says I want to die, I'll send her back to Canon City.

Ruthie lifted her chin. "I want to make a good impression."

We must be making some impression, thought Cat.

Dimity stood at the sideboard, scrutinizing the platters. Steam escaped when she lifted a lid, and Cat could practically taste Tonna's flapjacks.

He glanced toward Ruthie. Despite her proud stance, her clothes were torn and muddy. Outside, you couldn't smell the muck on her skirt, but the heated dining room called attention to every individual scent. Her sunburned face was puffy, hiding her bright eyes. Her Pickford curls straggled down past her shoulder blades.

Valiantly, she curtsied. "*Adieu, Madame* McDonald."

"Farewell? I don't understand."

"I meant *bon*-uh-*jour.*"

"*Mademoiselle* Adams is confused," Cat said. "As you can see, she's exhausted."

"I can see she is not what she pretends to be." Dimity pressed a perfumed handkerchief against her nose. "Did you find her in Cripple Creek, Cat, at one of those houses you visit?"

"No. I was in Denver, attending a rally for the Bull Moose Party. We met through mutual friends and supped together. She's on vacation, so I invited her to the ranch. After all, Mother, *Mademoiselle* Adams is a celebrated French actress and —"

"*Mademoiselle* Adams is a French fake." Turning toward Ruthie, Dimity said, "*Le coer a ses raisons que la raison ne connait point. Cherchez la femme,* Miss Adams?"

"*Oui, Madame* McDonald."

"You agree, *mademoiselle?*"

"*Oui.* I mean, no."

"Your French is vastly improved, Mother."

"I've been taking lessons from a French cleric. He instructs me *a bon marche.*"

Cat shrugged. "I speak Spanish."

"Would you explain what I just said to *mon Chat,* Miss Adams? What's the matter? *Chat* got your tongue? My cleric instructs me a *bon marche,* at a bargain price, because I am building him a chapel on the ranch. I previously stated an old maxim, the heart has its reasons that reason knows nothing of. *Cherchez la femme* means there's sure to

317

be a woman involved."

Ruthie gasped and hid her face with her grimy hands.

"Mother, you believe in Christian charity. Surely you would not refuse Miss Adams the hospitality of a hot meal, a bath and a bed."

"I may refuse this cheap tart anything I choose." Dimity gestured toward the swinging doors that led to the kitchen. "Tonna feeds strays. When the storm quits, you will get your whore off this ranch. Do you understand?"

"Perfectly," Cat said through clenched teeth. "After breakfast Miss Adams will bathe and sleep in my bedroom while I rest inside the bunkhouse. Come, Ruthie, let's find Tonna."

Dimity laughed, a shrill triumphant sound. "When you return, I have a surprise for you, *mon Chat.* A bolt from the blue you are not expecting. One I am sure your stray, *Mademoiselle* Adams" — she sarcastically emphasized the French title — "did not expect either."

As if to underscore her words, lightning flashed and Cat flinched. Entering the kitchen, he inhaled the familiar aroma of sweet pickles — watermelon rind, sugar, cinnamon and cloves, all boiling together

318

atop the enamel stove.

On the kitchen table were two plates, heaped high with eggs, bacon and biscuits.

Tonna had clearly foreseen Dimity's reaction to Cat's homecoming, but the coffee pot was in the dining room so she'd probably gone to fetch her own thickly boiled Arbuckles'.

Ignoring his food portion, Cat placed a fork in Ruthie's hand.

"I want to die," she said.

"Eat breakfast first. I'll give Mother a chance to calm down then try again."

"You'll take care of me?"

"Of course."

"On the ride here, you said something about marriage."

"We'll talk later, after you've rested."

"Eyewash. Now that we've reached your posh ranch, you don't want me."

"Ruthie, please."

"I'll kill myself."

Kill herself? Different from her usual I want to die. Could she possibly mean it? No. Ruthie was too selfish. She wouldn't end her own life.

And yet, by playing motion picture hero again, he had toted her here to face his mother's scorn. Percy was on the mark. Dimity did possess a tongue that could brand a person's soul.

Fools Gold would have fooled his mother. Despite her background, she looked every inch the lady. Even cleaned up, Ruthie looked like a piece of frivolous thistledown. She'd been born to adorn, a pretty charm dangling from a bracelet. But she was Cat's charm now, and he'd be damned if he'd abandon her.

He knelt by her chair. "Eat your breakfast, honey. Soon you'll meet a pretty woman with long beaded braids. Her name's Tonna. I told you about Tonna. Remember?"

"She feeds strays?"

"Tonna will salve your face and show you to my bedroom. There, you'll dream about how you're going to be a first-rate movie star, like Mary Pickford."

After kissing the tip of Ruthie's sunburned nose, Cat stood and walked across the kitchen.

He had barely set foot inside the dining room when a small form almost knocked him over backwards. Leaping into his arms, she straddled his waist and clung to his shoulders. "I didn't know where you went, Cat. Percy said I shouldn't fret, and I tried to act grown-up and not cry, but I'm ever so glad you're home."

Cat tilted Dimity-Jane's chin. She was

small for thirteen, didn't hardly weigh more than Dorado's saddle. "You'd better get down, Janey," he said. "My clothes are soaked. Tonna will have to hot-press your pinafore ruffles all over again."

"I don't care." She shook her golden-brown curls. "I have lots of dresses, but I'd rather wear calzoncillos."

"Do you know what calzoncillos are?"

"Sure. Drawers."

Cat tried to keep his lips from twitching by disentangling his sister's fingers and setting her pint-size boots on the carpet. "Who taught you that word, little sweetheart?"

"Bridgida. You should see Bridgida, Cat. She's grown since you went away. She's almost as fat as Luke. Well, no one's as fat as Luke."

"Dimity-Jane, return to your seat at once!" Rising, Dimity knocked over her cup of tea. The hot liquid sprayed Luke's hand. He jerked it away, upsetting his plate of steak, oatmeal and biscuits. Daniel, seated next to Luke, waved his arm like a whisk broom and a basket of buttered toast skittered across the table, tottered on its edge, and fell into the lap of a man who wore a clerical collar.

"Mind your mother, child," the cleric said, setting the basket on the table.

"Yes, Father." Dimity-Jane's long lashes shadowed her flushed cheeks as she looked down at the carpet and worried a half-eaten biscuit with her boot.

Luke scooped up the biscuit and stuffed it into his mouth.

"*Mon Dieu,* Lucas dear," said Dimity. "Do not eat food off the floor." She swiveled her head toward Daniel. "What's the matter with *you?*"

"Luke's hot oh-oatmeal spilled on my trou-trousers and bur-burned my peenie."

Dumbfounded, Cat glanced around the table. In eight short weeks everything had changed, and not for the better.

Walking over to Daniel, he dabbed at the cereal with a linen napkin. "There you go. I've cleaned up the spill. Later I'll tell you about the spill I took in a bullring."

Daniel jumped up, gave his big brother a hug, stepped back and blushed furiously.

"Sit down, Daniel. You too, Dimity-Jane." Dimity sank onto her own chair. "I will not have our family collation disrupted by an outside influence. Lucas dear, you may refill your plate from the sideboard since your brother caused it to flip-flop."

"Cat didn't cause the flip-flop, *Maman,* you did." Dimity-Jane squirmed onto her seat. "You jumped up and —"

322

"A lady doesn't jump."

"You did, *Maman.* I saw you."

"*I* see that you need an hour on your knees. Perhaps, with prayer, you will remember your manners. For goodness sake, Cat, find a chair. Or would you like to change your dirty clothes first?"

He shrugged, coughed, poured himself a cup of coffee, and chose an empty chair close to Dimity-Jane. "Where's Father, sweetheart?"

"Sitting next to me, Cat."

"I meant Papa."

"Papa won't eat with Luke. Papa says Luke's a glutton. *Maman* said God provides food to be eaten, but Papa said Luke can eat with God, not with Papa. *Maman* said Papa was *satane.* That means damned."

"Dimity-Jane, you are excused!"

"Is that really necessary, Mother?" Cat sighed. "I apologize for being a disruption. I'm sure Janey will eat her breakfast quietly now, won't you, little sweetheart?"

"Dimity-Jane, leave the table at once. Father, please escort the child to her bedroom and pray with her."

"Of course." The cleric dabbed at the corners of his mouth with his napkin.

"I want to pray, too," said Daniel.

"Very well. What about you, Lucas dear?"

323

"I haven't eaten all my food, *Maman,* and I'm still hungry, *Maman.*"

"You may take your food into the kitchen."

"But I want to stay here."

"I will not tolerate a disobedient son." With an angry nod, she gestured toward the three retreating figures. "Do you wish to join the others in prayer?"

"No, *Maman.* I'll go so's you can talk to Cat alone."

"Wait!" Dimity looked at Cat. "Is that woman still inside my kitchen?"

"I suppose," he said, thinking how he wasn't hungry anymore. Luke's gluttony was sickening. No wonder Papa ate with Percy and the hands.

Dimity withdrew. When she returned, she said, "I have instructed Tonna to remove your stray from the house. Miss Adams can mark time with Tonna until I decide what to do with her. Lucas, please leave the room."

"Yes, *Maman.*" Luke refilled his plate and walked toward the kitchen.

Cat stretched his long legs under the table and reached for a piece of toast. "You are right as usual, Mother. I should change my wet clothes before —"

"Stay right here. This won't take long."

"I'm sorry I brought Miss Adams without

324

your permission, but she had no place to go."

"Couldn't she have returned to France?"

Too bushed to wrangle, Cat disregarded Dimity's sarcasm. "May I retire to my bedroom now, Mother? I need sleep more than food."

"It isn't your bedroom." She walked over to the sideboard, poured a cup of tea, returned to her seat. "I have decided that you shall sleep in that old cabin near the bunkhouse, with your wife. It requires some fixing up, but your wife —"

"Ruthie and I aren't married."

"Bridgida can start with lye soap. A broom should take care of any spiders. The mattress is despicable. Since I believe in *Christian charity,* I shall give Bridgida a brand new feather mattress."

"What does Bridgida have to do with anything?"

Dimity patted her neat bun of braided hair. "*Mon Dieu,* you don't know. You've been gone, chasing strays. How many strays did you rope and brand, Cat?"

"From your tone of voice, I gather Percy told Papa I was working in Canon City, not riding the range or visiting Denver. What don't I know about Bridgida?"

"She carries your child."

"That's impossible! Bridgida and I never . . . how can I put this without offending your sensibilities? Bridgida and I kissed once or twice, but that's all. If she's with child, it's not my child."

"You were born evil, Cat. You may have fooled John and the others, but with God's grace I have seen through your lies."

"Does Bridgida say the child is mine?"

"Yes."

"Then she lies."

"No, Cat. At first she said Lucas forced her, but after many hours of prayer she recanted. She wept and begged forgiveness and confessed the child was yours. She said she was afraid you might whip her with your belt or cut her with your spurs if she told the truth. She showed me bruises, which didn't surprise me."

Cat threw his toast across the room. "Luke rode Bridgida like he rides the horses. If she had bruises from a belt or cuts from a spur, they were caused by Luke."

"Liar!"

"Mother, please listen." Cat walked around the table and hunkered by Dimity's chair. "If Bridgida's wounds were new, it had to be Luke. I've been in Canon City these last eight weeks."

"That's why you rode away from the

ranch. You were afraid Bridgida might tattle."

"I left because I fought with Luke."

"Then you admit you have a temper."

"Yes! You've always babbled on and on about bad blood, but if I've inherited anything, it's your temper."

"Nonsense. See how calmly I sit here and discuss your sins."

"I have many sins, but beating a girl to make her conjoin with me isn't one of them. When did Bridgida confess?"

"Three days ago. Her wounds were still raw."

"Then it couldn't have been me. I've been in Canon City and I can prove it. Ruthie . . ." He swallowed the rest of his words at the sound of Dimity's shrill laughter.

"You defend yourself with your whore? That's priceless, Cat."

"I'm not defending myself. There's nothing to defend."

"You visited the ranch under cover of darkness. You're a coward, a sneak, just like Cherokee —" Dimity's hand shook as she lifted her teacup. "Just like an Indian."

"Why would I make the long trip back and forth, Mother? That's insane. If I wanted to bed a woman, I could easily find one who's willing. And I don't play an Indian unless I'm acting. I've been a motion picture actor these last eight weeks. I played an Indian and a hero, and I was damn good at it. Now I want to help Papa run the ranch. That's what I was born to do."

"You were born to hang from the end of a rope. You were born to get a girl with child then disappear."

Cat strove to keep his voice on an even keel. "You said Bridgida had cuts made by spurs. I don't use spurs. I don't even own spurs."

"Of course you do. I am well aware that you won silver spurs at a rodeo."

"Take a look in the barn. Luke rides with spurs. Percy will tell you that he has to salve a horse's flanks and belly after Luke rides it. Are you so blinded by your hate for me that you can't see Luke for what he really is? He's greedy and cruel and sly. His face is scabbed with the sores he picks open. You, who are so fastidious, watch him shovel food into his mouth with his fingers. Papa won't even sit at the same table —"

"Shut up!" Dimity slapped Cat's face. "How dare you slander your brother! I want you to leave the ranch today. This is no longer your home."

"Wrong, Mother. As the eldest son I shall

inherit from Papa."

Dimity rose from her chair. Biting her lower lip, she grasped the edge of the table so hard her knuckles whitened.

"Thank you for breakfast, Mother. I shall now retire to my bedroom."

"*He* always thanked people."

"Who?"

"Your father. He had a habit of thank—"

"Had?"

"Yes. Your father is dead."

"Have you lost your mind? Janey said Papa's inside the bunkhouse, eating breakfast with the hands."

"John McDonald is not your father!" Dimity shouted.

Rising, Cat grasped his mother's arms above the elbows. "What are you saying?"

"Your father was the devil!"

"Now you sound like Tonna." Cat felt relief course through him. "She says my father was the Chinook wind and my mother the mountain lion."

"John McDonald is *not* your father." Dimity shook herself free from his grasp.

"I don't believe you."

"Your father was the devil, but he came in the guise of a man. He was a murderer. He had Indian, Mexican and Negro blood running through his veins, just like you. Bad blood. His name was Cherokee Bill, and he was hanged for his evil deeds on the day you were born."

"I don't believe —"

"Yes, you do. You know I would never invent a story like that. I wouldn't have told you now, except you provoked me. Eighteen years ago, God tested my faith and I failed. I gave in to temptation, but afterwards I prayed for absolution, and God rewarded me with Lucas. Lucas was a gift to prove I had become worthy of God's grace."

Cat paced from the table to the sideboard. He remembered how at the age of seven he had nearly lost consciousness from a whupping. He wished he were seven again so that he could blot out his mother's wordy whiplash.

She stood there, fingering the huge cross she wore on a chain. Her eyes glittered, but once again she worried her lower lip with her teeth. Did she believe Cat would run to her husband with this wild tale?

Yet if Dimity spoke the truth, it would explain so many things. Cat's "bad blood." Her dislike and neglect.

Suppose he did tell Papa? She'd deny every word. Furthermore, the accusation would come from a boy who had attacked a ranch hand's daughter.

Poor Bridgida. Although she had mature curves, she was tiny, barely five feet tall. Luke would savor overpowering a smaller adversary, and a girl to boot.

"If God gave you Lucas as a gift, he was still testing you and again you've failed," Cat said. "Surely God would not commend your disregard for Luke's cruelty. Mother, he *raped* Bridgida!"

"If Bridgida were not Rosita's daughter, I would have sent her away. Instead, we shall post the bans immediately and my cleric will say the words to make you man and wife. A Catholic ceremony, Cat, binding you forever."

"I will not father Luke's child. I will not wed Bridgida."

"Yes, you will. I have talked this over with John, and he agrees. If you do not assume responsibility, John will disinherit you. Make no mistake about that, my son."

It was the first time she'd ever called him son.

As Cat entered the kitchen, the swinging door knocked Luke backwards. He'd been spying, uninterrupted, so Tonna must be inside her small house, tending Ruthie.

Ignoring Luke, Cat walked outside. He managed a few steps before his legs weakened and he slumped against the wash table.

A murderer, Dimity had said. An outlaw named Cherokee Bill. No, she wouldn't invent a story like that. Cat's father was a murdering outlaw who'd been hanged for his crimes, and Cat had his blood. He felt bitter bile lap at the back of his throat, swallowed it down, and brandished his fists at the sky, dimly aware that the storm had blown away.

"*Gato?*"

As Cat turned away from the wash table, he saw a yellow skirt and dirty toes, not quite hidden by a tree trunk.

"Did you speak *con su madre, Gato?* Are you angry?"

"No, I'm not angry. Come here."

"I would not blame you if you were," said Bridgida.

Cat watched the tiny girl approach. She wore her sister Maria's embroidered blouse. Too large at the neckline, it fell from one shoulder. Her bare feet squished through the muddy yard.

Lowering her thick dark lashes, she murmured, "I did not want to say it was you, *Gato,* but *Señora* Dimity made me stay in a room with *el padre* until I changed my story. She said I would kneel there forever, without food or water. She swore she would send my mother and my brothers and sisters from the ranch, and she would stop Maria and Rodolfo's wedding. When I fainted, she waved a feather beneath my nose, and *el padre* did not care."

"Don't cry, *querida.*"

"The day you left, Luke wanted to touch me but I wouldn't let him. He waited until I was in the barn, watering the horses. Then he . . . there was nobody there, so he pressed his hand against my mouth and pulled me up the ladder and threw me onto the straw. Luke used his belt and spurs. I spilled blood, *Gato,* from my cuts. And blood ran down my legs, from . . . from Luke's *bicho.* Luke saw the blood. It sickened him so he ran away."

Launching herself at Cat, Bridgida buried her face against his shirt.

"Hush, *querida,* hush," he crooned, stroking her back. "Don't cry. It's over."

"It is not over, *Gato.* Luke follows me everywhere and he has used his belt and spurs three times. Blood does not sicken him anymore. I wanted to tell *Señor* Mac, but I told my mother instead. It was she who went to *Señora* Dimity. Now my mother says I am a bad girl, a *puta.* I am not a *puta, Gato.*"

"No, Bridgida, you are not a *puta.*"

"I am so happy you are home," she sighed, lifting her tear-drenched face. "What should we do?"

"For the time being, stick close to Rosita and Maria. Don't let Luke find you alone."

"But I want to ride. When I ride I feel better."

"I'll take you riding, little one. Luke will never touch you again, I swear. If he tries, he'll wallow in his own *vómito* and I'll castrate his *bicho* with Tonna's dullest kitchen knife."

"So it's true, Tonna." Cat pounded his fist on Tonna's kitchen table. "The blood that runs through my body is his. Bad blood."

"There is no bad or good blood, John Mc-Donald."

"Don't call me that!"

"Quiet. You'll wake the girl. Why shouldn't I call you John McDonald? It is your name."

"It's his name, not mine."

"You talk like a child. Even if what Dimity says is true, it does not take away your name."

"Even if? You said she spoke the truth."

"I said she did not lie about Cherokee Bill."

"You play with words."

"Do a few angry words from Dimity make

you any less a man? Do they take away your name? You have not changed. You are still John McDonald, named for your father. Many years ago, on the long walk to Texas, children lost their parents. They were raised by others and became fine men and women."

"They were not the son of a murderer."

"How do you know this? Their fathers could have killed during a war raid."

"That's different."

"The blood is not bad?"

"Yes. No. I don't know. Oh, God, what am I going to do?"

"Right now you must drink sage and sorrel to help your fever, and eat some of the calf's-foot soup I prepared for your friend's awakening. You should not make a decision on an empty stomach."

"My friend. I forgot Ruthie." Cat's laugh ended in a coughing fit. "What a fine mess. Ruthie and Bridgida. Percy once said I was too big for my britches."

"You are big, Cat, but you must also be strong enough to forget your mother's hurtful words." Tonna sighed. "I shall talk to Dimity about Bridgida."

"It wouldn't help. In any case, I can't leave Bridgida here on the ranch with Luke. I swore he'd never touch her again."

"Are you planning to leave?"

"Yes. I've made my decision without your soup. I had the offer of a job from a man named Colonel Selig. I can't return to Canon City because of another man, but I can make my way to California where Selig lives." Digging inside his pocket, Cat pulled out a piece of paper. "Damn. It got wet from the rain and the ink's faded, but I think I can read the numbers."

"If you leave the ranch, Dimity has won."

"What has she won? Luke? I'll come back, but first I'll make movies. Movies are spirits inside a camera. The camera captures a horse running or a bird flying or a man fighting. Then the pictures are shown on a screen, a paper window that many people can watch together."

"A picture book that moves?"

"Yes." Retrieving a small stick from the cookstove, Cat blew out the flaming end, turned over the paper with Selig's address, and printed BILL PERCIVAL. "Reckon I'll change my name. Bill for my real father, Percival for Black Percy."

"My husband would be shamed. John Mc-Donald has treated you well and does not deserve this dishonor."

Cat scratched through the name and wrote another. Tonna glanced down and nodded. "Always remember," she said, "that I keep a pot of Arbuckles' on the stove, waiting for your return."

"That pot over there?"

She nodded again.

"By the time I return, it will be too strong to drink."

"Perhaps," she said. "But you will be too strong to care."

NINETEEN

An enormous tent housed the Cowboys' Square Dance. Steers were penned nearby, their bucolic bellows competing with the *ka-ping* of spittle hitting cuspidors, the *twang* of guitars, and the *plunk-thwack-plunk* of a bull fiddle.

Bridgida had heard similar sounds her whole life. Mesmerized, she watched grayish-brown moths court death by fluttering their wings at suspended lanterns.

She wrenched her gaze from the moths, and stared at a long wooden table, where remnants from a potluck supper scented the air with fried chicken, crushed oranges, and melted chocolate. Several dogs danced on their hind legs, trying to reach the leftover food. Bridgida smiled. The dogs looked like the dancers who twirled to the caller's chant.

"Está es una buena comida, Gato," she said.

"Eat your fill, sweetheart," he replied. "It's

the last *good* meal we'll have for a while."

"Cat, come dance with me. Bridgida don't mind, do you Bridgida?"

"No, Ruthie, I do not mind."

Cat winked at Bridgida. He had once thought her shallow as a dry-bed stream, and yet it was Bridgida who kept their small band together. She washed their clothes, cooked their meals, and tended Ruthie when the actress sickened from too much drinking.

Last week Cat had left Ruthie at the Watering Hole Saloon. Returning to their hotel room, he'd found Bridgida huddled under the bed covers, tears coursing down her cheeks. "What's wrong, *querida?*" he had asked. "Are you ill?"

"No."

"Do you miss your brothers and sisters?"

"No, *Gato.* It is just that I can never be a woman."

"You're a lovely woman. Don't you look in the mirror?"

"The mirror does not reflect what's inside. Inside, I am coward."

He lay down beside her and gathered her into his arms. "Luke?" he asked softly.

"*Sí.* Luke has made me scared to love like a woman."

Cautiously, Cat traced her full breasts

then explored her curves through her cotton nightgown. When he caressed her taut navel with his thumb, she shivered.

"I am frightened, *Gato*."

He knew he should rise from the bed. He had vowed to leave his two girls alone. What would a movie hero do in this situation? *A movie hero wouldn't be in this situation!* Suppose he was? Cat pondered a plot. His hero would be worldly wise, gentle and tender.

Could he act that role?

"Don't be scared," he said, shedding his clothes and tugging her nightgown up over her head. "I won't hurt you. You're my *pájara pequeña*."

"I wish I were a small bird, *Gato*. Birds know what to do."

"Birds fly."

Stretched out on his side, he wrapped her long braid around his neck like a noose and pressed his mouth against her mouth. She yielded slowly, her lips parting on their own volition, not from any pressure he exerted. Her breath was sugar-sweet, her kiss flavored with innocence.

He shifted positions, straddling her body, his body anchored by his knees. Placing his hand between her thighs, he caressed the soft inner skin, moving upwards. He felt her light touch, shy and curious. She stroked his hips and belly. Her fingers danced across his groin until she had him fully in the grasp of her hand.

Hard and ready, Cat slid through her fingertips and penetrated. She tensed. Sweat beaded his brow, and his temples pounded like a drum, yet he stayed inside, motionless, until he felt her relax. After what seemed an eternity, he began to thrust with a definite rhythm.

"*Gato,* I am not afraid," she had cried.

He hadn't touched her since that night, and yet he felt guilt-ridden. Bridgida was no plaything. A movie hero would have searched out the preacher straightaway.

I will not father Luke's child. I will not wed Bridgida.

Cat shook his head to nullify memories. He eyed Ruthie, who followed the caller's chant as if she were a thirsty steer on a trail drive. She was already four sheets to the wind. Cat reeled her in by her waist and she giggled.

At least she'd stopped complaining about their swift flight from the ranch. After kissing Dimity-Jane good-bye, Cat had saddled the two tired horses, collected his duds, and grudgingly accepted a money stake from Black Percy. With Ruthie mounted on the paint and Bridgida behind him atop Dorado, Cat had ridden away from his mother's words.

In Colorado Springs they rented a room at the Plaza Hotel for a dollar-fifty a night. Only then had Cat collapsed, giving in to his illness. Ruthie bawled, but Bridgida nursed him capably through his cough and fever. Upon recovering, he had thumbed through the newspaper and discovered a write-up about an annual event called the Shan Kive.

"It says here they'll build up a 'trail' consisting of various kinds of shows, a camp of one hundred Indians, and five hundred cowboys," Cat told his two girls.

"Five hundred cowboys? Eyewash!"

"It's a big show, Ruthie, bringing together rodeo stars from all over the state."

He had signed up for a few events, but still somewhat collywobbled, he didn't have much success, and Percy's stake was running low.

"Take a chew of tobacco and spit on the wall," the caller chanted. "First gent balance to the second couple. Swing the girl with the possum jaw. And don't forget your taw. Everybody, swing."

With that, the dance ended. Walking toward Bridgida, Cat reached for the whiskey flask inside his jacket pocket.

"Me, too," Ruthie said. "Thirsty."

When she returned the flask, he shook it. Empty. Where was he supposed to find money for more whiskey? If Ruthie didn't down a shot upon awakening tomorrow morning, she'd have headaches all day long. Truthfully, he no longer cared if his pretty charm found herself another protector and would gladly hand her over to one of the rodeo cowboys who envied Cat his two *concubinas*. But it was Bridgida who had caught the eye of a young bronc rider, Tom Callahan, after Cat had drunkenly confessed her circumstances.

"If you let me have her, I'll treat her good," Callahan had said during a private moment at the Watering Hole Saloon. "I travel the circuit, so there's none to know it ain't my loaf in her oven."

At age twenty, Tom's arms were corded with muscles and scarred from rodeo tumbles. His eyes were Colorado-sky-blue, his hair a bright red-orange. Which was why, he told Cat, he'd bronc-bust rather than dog the bulls.

"I'm not Bridgida's pa," Cat had said. "If she wants to go with you, I can't stop her."

"That ain't true. She won't leave unless you say so."

"Why would she want to stay? We share a

343

room at the Plaza and eat Boston Baked Beans from Burgess at two bits a quart. Damn, I need another drink."

"I aim to win the five-hundred-dollar purse for bronc-busting at the Festival of Mountain and Plain." Tom opened a new bottle of mescal. "That could be a stake for me and Bridgida. What do you say?"

"I say you're drunk. Want to wager the purse on who drains this bottle and reaches the worm first?"

"No. Will you talk to Bridgida?"

Before Cat could reply, Ruthie slid her body across his lap and placed his hand beneath her skirt, cussing in between her giggles. She had taken to cussing the way a duck takes to water.

His father's blood coursed through his veins as Cat carried her behind the saloon, pinched her mouth open with his fingers, and poured mescal down her throat until she gagged on the worm. He thought she might leave him after that, but she continued to stick, like nettles stuck in a cactus. Maybe she was the cactus rather than its nettles, tough on the outside, soft and sweet inside. Maybe she drank so much because she was so unhappy.

"Come on, Ruthie," he said. "Let's show everybody how they dance in the movies."

She said "Dizzy," and pitched forward. Cat caught her before she hit the ground. With Bridgida in his wake and Ruthie's limp body draped across his arms, he ducked his head, trying to avoid the moths that seemed drawn to his glittering green eyes.

Cat emptied his sack of groceries on the bed.

Naked as a jaybird, Ruthie sat on a cane-backed chair. "Did you buy whiskey, Cat?"

"Don't call me Cat! A black cat's bad luck, and some rodeo cowboys won't perform in a building with any cat at all."

"Pardon me all to hell, *John Chinook*. Did you buy whiskey?"

"I bought soap, tooth powder and food. Three pounds of pig's feet for two bits. Our Bridgida fancies peach butter and ginger snaps. There's also pork and beans, but at five cents, they only allowed one can to a customer. Later, you two can visit Hall and Sons Grocery and buy one can each. Then we can wait a while and do it again. That'll give us six cans. We've got the fixings for a salad — green onions, lettuce and asparagus. Our Bridgida fancies asparagus."

"I'm tired of hearing 'bout what our Bridgida fancies."

"Get dressed, Ruthie."

"Did you buy whiskey?"

"No. The groceries cost two dollars and thirty-four cents. I didn't have enough left —"

"How much was the asparagus?"

"Twelve cents." Cat nodded toward the bed. "There's some white Borax soap. Why don't you walk down the hall and try a bar?"

"I want to die."

"Take a bath first."

"I hate this stinking Indian rodeo."

"I suppose it's my fault you stink from whiskey."

"I never drank till I met you. I was an actress till you jackscrewed me inside Mrs. Tuttle's parlor and got us both fired."

"What? You couldn't wait to spread your legs and —"

"*Madre de Dios,* lower your voices." Tears streamed down Bridgida's face.

"Don't cry, *querida.* Soon we'll head for Denver and I'll win lots of money. Then we can find the Dick Stanley Wild West Show."

"Another rodeo," Ruthie wailed.

"Dick Stanley's cowboys perform a rehearsed show. If I'm not hired for my riding and roping tricks, I'll bulldog a damn steer with my teeth."

"I want to die!"

"Then go ahead and die!"

"I'll kill myself and you'll be sorry." Ruthie ran to the clothes rack, retrieved Cat's six-shooter from his holster, placed the gun's barrel inside her mouth, and cocked its hammer.

"*Gato,* stop her!"

"Hell, no, I want to see if she'll really pull the trigger."

"Are you loco?"

"Hush, Bridgida. Don't get upset. It's not good for the baby. Here, have a ginger snap."

"I knew it." Ruthie lowered her arm. "You don't care if I live or die."

Cat snatched the gun away and returned it to his holster. "Next time," he said, "check for bullets."

Crumpling to the floor, Ruthie covered her face with her hands.

Cat hunkered by her side. "Stop your bawling. That was mean, and I'm sorry. Shan Kive cowboys say Dick Stanley's on his way to California."

"California," she breathed, turning her face toward Bridgida. "That's where they make movies. That's where Mary Pickford lives."

"Get washed and dressed," said Cat, "so we can buy those special beans for five cents. After I talk to Colonel Selig, we'll eat steak every night. Denver's Festival of Mountain and Plain should change our luck. It's a big show. Tom Callahan told me about it."

"May I ride in the show, *Gato?*"

"You miss your riding, don't you, sweetheart? I wired Percy for money, so I'll buy you both new duds and maybe we'll stay at a fancy Denver hotel."

"New clothes? Peachy!"

"Does this rodeo have lady riders, *Gato?*"

"It does now. Callahan says the festival was first held in eighteen ninety-five, but they only had parades, Indian races, and a masked ball."

"Do they still have the ball?" Ruthie's eyes bugged.

"If they do, we can't go. It's for the socially prominent and rich."

"But how are they to know you're not rich? You can prove you're John McDonald's oldest boy and —"

"No!"

"Well, pardon me all to hell."

"Parades and a dance," said Bridgida. "It does not sound like it will bring prize money."

"They added a bronc-busting contest in nineteen hundred. First prize was won by a big bay mare named Peggy." Cat grinned.

"The way your baby kicks, Bridgida, we should call it Peggy. Callahan says that in nineteen-oh-three they added exhibition riding, a cowgirls' race, other money events, and a Grande Finale."

"What is that, *Gato?*"

"Most rodeos have one, Bridgida. They had a ripsnorting finale at New York's Madison Square Garden."

"Here we go again. Tell Bridgida 'bout your bulldogging, Cat. Tell her how Tom Mix saved your worthless hide."

"Don't call me Cat!"

"Bridgida calls you *Gato.* That means Cat, don't it?"

"Sure, but *Gato sounds* different. Callahan says Denver's Grande Finale has a parade and a stampede, followed by a pretend battle between cowboys, cavalry and Indians. If you're real careful, Bridgida, you can ride in the parade."

Ruthie entered their Denver hotel room, her heels clicking. She had spent her clothes money, and Bridgida's as well, on high-heeled pumps, a white silk blouse and a long red skirt. The skirt was so tight Cat could see the outline of her saucy rump.

Tossing his Stetson toward the bed, she

wriggled onto the cushion of a stuffed arm-chair.

"Don't do that!" Cat shouted.

"Do what? Your hat? But it was in my way."

"Are you plumb loco? It's bad luck to put a cowboy's hat on the bed."

"I didn't *put* it. I *threw* it. Hellfire! We can't call you Cat because cats are bad luck. We can't eat peanuts because peanuts are bad luck. You wear the same smelly clothes —"

"Only when I win."

"— and Bridgida and I have to wear the same clothes, too. Anyway, the events are over, except for the wild-bronc contest this afternoon. And the finale. Can I really ride in the parade?"

"Sure." Removing his Stetson from the bed, he placed it on the bureau. "Callahan's found a pony for Bridgida, so you can ride the paint."

"Did you win enough money to join the show that's headed for California?"

"Yes. But if I win this afternoon, we'll skip Stanley's show and travel to California by rail. The purse just hit a thousand dollars."

Cat drew a bronc named Tipperary. The

horse had never been ridden successfully before.

"Bad luck," said Tom Callahan.

"Your bronc, Old Cyclone, ain't much better."

"Bridgida says she'll wed up with me if you say the word, Chinook."

"I didn't know you wanted to *marry* her."

"We talked about it one night during Shan Kive, remember?"

"Yep, but we were both drunk."

For the first time, Cat saw Callahan's anger.

"Do you want me to pay for Bridgida? Name your price, Chinook. I'll even hand over my rodeo belt."

"It's not yours yet!"

Still fuming, Tom turned to watch the horses being prodded into their chutes.

Cat scowled. Bridgida belonged to him. Why shouldn't the son of Cherokee Bill have two *concubinas*?

Released from the restrictions of his chute, Tipperary plunged, kicked and bit at Cat's boots. As Cat desperately tried to hold on, the wild bronc snorted, twisted and whirled.

Cat smelled the dust before he landed. He heard cheers turn to gasps, just before he staggered upright and brushed off the seat of his pants.

Tom Callahan won the purse.

Ruthie and Bridgida were waiting outside the chutes. Bridgida had tears in her dark eyes. "Are you all right, *Gato?* I was so frightened, and do not tell me to name my baby Tipperary."

"I won't. I never want to hear that name again."

"It's my fault," Ruthie wailed. "I threw your hat on the bed."

"It's nobody's fault. Don't move. I'll be right back." Cat strolled over to Callahan. "Well done, amigo. I'll talk to Bridgida. If she wants to marry you, I won't say no."

"Thanks, Chinook. Here's my money belt."

"Keep the damn purse. Call it my wedding gift."

Returning to the chute gates, Cat saw that Ruthie was some fifty feet away, flirting with the peanut vender. She chewed nuts like a cow chewing its cud. Hadn't he told her it was bad luck to eat peanuts during a show? So what? Except for the finale, the show was played out.

Bridgida wore a fringed deerskin dress, and her long black braids were intertwined with colorful beads. Brusquely, Cat said, "Callahan wants to marry you."

She nodded. "Tomás spoke of marriage at the Shan Kive."

"If you want to wed Tom, it's fine with me."

"De verdad, Gato?"

"Sure. Do you think it's easy sleeping three to a room? Falling in the dirt so I can put food on the table?"

"Oh, I did not think —"

"I didn't mean that, little bird. If you don't love Callahan, we'll stick together."

"Gracias, Gato, but Tomás is good and kind and he will be papa to my baby."

Cat forced a cheerfulness he didn't feel into his voice. "Then it's settled. Let's saddle up our horses for the finale."

"My pony does not need a saddle."

The Grande Finale was delayed for thirty minutes, due to a brief but violent rainstorm that turned the arena's top layer of dust to mud. Cat wondered if Bridgida should ride in all that sticky goo, but she insisted her pony was sure-footed.

"He's mostly quarter horse," she said, "what Tomás calls a short horse. My pony is smart and can turn quickly."

"I should have said no from the start, sweetheart. You could hurt yourself. Or the baby."

"The baby sleeps inside my belly and cannot get out. My mother rode until the day I was born. Perhaps that is why I love horses so much. *Por favor, Gato?*"

Reluctantly he said yes, then watched her join the group of "Indians" while he adjusted Dorado's girth.

Circling the arena, he waved his hat toward the stands. He had been told to rope steers during the stampede. Ruthie and Bridgida were riding with the Indians. Tom Callahan was a cavalry officer, armed with the traditional sword of command.

Music sounded from the grandstand. The trick riders drew loud cheers. Cowboys twirled their riatas. Clothed in cavalry-blue tunics, several riders wielded their swords at the crowd.

Then came the Indians. Most, like Ruthie, had blankets over their saddles. Bridgida rode bareback.

Dorado's golden coat shined in the glow from a brilliant sunset as Cat spun his lasso. It had been a rip-roaring show. He'd won enough to keep them going until he located Dick Stanley. Not them. Bridgida would join Callahan tonight. Why was she in such a rush to get hooked up with that tomfool bronc-buster? Hell, she deserved some happiness. Why hadn't he bowed to Dimity's will and married the girl himself? Because of Cherokee Bill?

If Ruthie found out Cat was the son of a murderer, she'd find herself another protector, but Bridgida would soothe his soul the same way she'd nursed his sick body. She'd be sweet and gentle and wise — like Tonna.

Cat felt as if lightning had struck his noggin.

Callahan loved Bridgida, but Cat did too. He loved her in a hundred different ways. He loved her tiny body, her soft black eyes, and her dusky skin that flushed pink when she laughed. Her laughter was the music of bells.

He thought about the night he'd played "movie hero" and comforted her. He hadn't been acting. He'd never behaved so with a woman before, holding back, concerned with *her* pleasure.

You were right, Percy. Bridgida smiles when I kiss her.

With his brave little bird by his side, he could put to rest his demons. He could be the son of John McDonald, not Cherokee Bill.

Why hadn't he recognized his feelings sooner? He had taken Bridgida's sweetness for granted and now he'd lost her. Suppose he told her how he felt and let her choose? If she wanted Callahan, so be it. If not, Cat

355

would marry her tomorrow, tonight, this very minute. There had to be a minister in that vast crowd. What a grand Grande Finale — a wedding ceremony between a cowboy and an Indian!

Kicking Dorado's flanks, Cat rode away from the cowboys, toward the Indians. He ached to tell Bridgida he wanted to marry her. He couldn't wait. To hell with Callahan! To hell with the rodeo! He maneuvered Dorado against the tide of horses and riders, grinning like a lovesick fool at the surprise on their faces. The signal for battle was to be a bugle blast from the stands. Only then were the cowboys, Cavalry and Indians supposed to stage their pretend war.

Other riders broke ranks, following Cat, shooting their guns at the sky. Indians whooped and hollered and nudged their ponies into a gallop. Callahan joined Bridgida, "stabbing" several Indians along the way.

Cat urged Dorado toward Callahan and Bridgida. Ruthie had been swallowed up in the confusion. "Bridgida, I must talk to you."

"*Gato,* is this not fun?" She smiled and waved.

"I love you. Did you hear me? I love — Bridgida, watch out!"

With horror, Cat saw Callahan's horse stumble against Bridgida's pony. She tried to right her pony by tugging hard on the reins, but lost control when the pony folded to its knees.

Callahan kicked his boots free from the stirrups. He had the presence of mind to forcefully spike his sword so he'd avoid falling with it.

The sword's sharp, curved hilt stuck deep in the spongy ground.

Bridgida fell from her pony and landed on the blade's tip, impaling herself.

Cat and Ruthie caught up with Dick Stanley's Wild West Show in Arizona.

Stanley thought the young man standing before him was a kid, no more than eighteen, but staring into John Chinook's steely green eyes, Stanley decided he'd been mistaken. Chinook's eyes looked old. And when the kid who wasn't a kid smiled, his eyes didn't follow suit.

Since he had no fear of death, Stanley hired him.

Chinook said his father was Cherokee, which was another puzzlement. Although Chinook had tar-black hair, his skin sometimes turned white, as if he had a memory jogger he couldn't forget.

Stanley hired Chinook's woman to collect tickets and sell Coca-Cola. She said how she was superstitious and wouldn't hawk peanuts during a show. She cussed like a sailor, drank like a Saturday-night cowhand and giggled a lot.

Chinook said he'd never rode through a hoop of fire before but he didn't mind trying. Said he'd been taught to dog bulls with his teeth. Stanley only hoped there wouldn't be any trouble with the woman if Chinook caught fire or got gored by a bull.

John Chinook's eyes looked like they hid a sorrowful secret, but Stanley didn't care to learn what that secret was.

In truth, he didn't want to rile anyone who courted death like some damned moth drawn to some damned flame.

Twenty

Denver: 1913

Katherine Johanna Lytton had a secret. She was madly in love with Richard Reed. Oh, she realized that "Uncle Richard" was old enough to be her father. He was, in fact, her father's friend. But that didn't stop her eighteen-year-old heart from fluttering every time Richard shot the breeze. She had never kissed a man with a mustache. Would it tickle?

Her sister Dorothy, who at this very moment lay in bed with the whooping cough, said Kate was "romantically inclined."

True. Kate had been madly in love often, but she had never said "I love you" to a man. Grandfather Edward was fond of the words "American initiative." Grandfather said if you wanted something badly enough, you had to reach out and grab it. That hadn't worked very well when it came to his wife, the long dead Dolly, yet Kate thought it was worth a try. So she'd used every bit of her initiative lately, determining how she'd "grab" Richard Reed.

Should she play the coy maiden or the brazen hussy?

Eventually he'd kiss her. After all, Kate had been told over and over how beautiful she was — the image of her father when he was eighteen. Her eyes were a lighter blue, but she had Ned's coal-black hair and cleft chin. She was tall and slender, with a tiny waist and breasts that looked small. Nude, her breasts were surprisingly full.

She had never bared her breasts to Richard, or any other man, but she'd reveal every inch of her body if it meant a declaration of love.

Richard would arrive in Denver tomorrow. Tonight Kate had to suffer through a tedious party at Rosalind Tassler's house.

"Katie? Is that you? C'mere an' give your daddy some sugar."

Framed by the music room's doorway, she twirled.

"Hee-haw." Thrusting his thumbs inside his ears, Ned waggled his fingers. "You look lovely, darlin'."

"Do you really think so? Mummy was peppery when I bought another gown, but I knew you wouldn't mind."

She twirled three more times, like a ballerina, flaunting her princess dress of periwinkle-blue Liberty silk, embroidered with dark-blue flowers at the hemline and sleeves. Her hat was natty blue straw with a poof of five small egret feathers.

"Of course I don't mind." Ned reached for his cigar smoldering in an ashtray. "Damn Johanna's impertinence! Buy yourself a dozen new dresses. Where's my sugar?" He thrust his chin forward and pursed his mouth.

Daddy's drunk again, thought Kate, kissing the air close to his jowly cheeks with her freshly glossed lips.

Satisfied, Ned studied his daughter through the haze of cigar smoke. Once, a long time ago, he'd been upset because she was a female. Over the years, his displeasure had turned to pure bliss. Katie was smart as a whip, and her beauty swelled his heart with pride.

His heart didn't embrace many people. He had felt affection for the little crib girl, Blueberry. He had a reverential admiration for Richard Reed. But he truly loved his eldest daughter. Because of Kate, he planned to limit his involvement with Klan activities and learn more about his father's vast business holdings. To that end, he had successfully requested that Edward let him handle the Lytton coal mining interests, including the Colorado Fuel and Iron Company. Ned had even joined the Mine Owners Association, along with his friend Randolph Tassler.

"Buy a dozen new dresses," Ned mumbled to nobody in particular.

Kate had left the music room.

Rosalind Tassler lived on Emerson Street. Her house bristled with rusticated stone corseting, pinnacle roofs and a columnar porch.

Inside, the Tasslers' parlor clock had struck seven, but evenfall's light permeated the stained-glass windows, garishly illuminating several young men and women who played a kissing game. Kate had been chosen three times and Rosalind, a willowy blonde with sea-green eyes, had been chosen twice. Other girls glared with barely concealed envy, so Kate continued playing even though she was bored.

The parlor doors opened, a new guest entered, and Richard Reed's image crumbled into dust. How could she have believed herself in love? Uncle Richard was ancient, while this man was in his late twenties, perhaps early thirties. Rosalind's guest had captured the sun and streaked his brown hair with its rays. His eyes were a smoky-gray. His long legs were clad in corduroy. His chest strained the seams of a shabby suit jacket.

"Who's that man, Rosalind?"

"Hell and damnation! Father will be fussed. My brother probably invited him to get Father's goat."

"Who *is* he? If you don't tell, I'll never speak to you again as long as I live."

"He's a distant relative. My grandfather visited Greece and fell in love with a peasant woman. The family soon brought him to his senses, but the result of Grandfather's indiscretion was born, you might say, on the wrong side of the blanket. Grandfather's bastard Greek daughter married another Greek and gave birth to *him*. His name is Mike Loutra and he works for the United Mine Workers of America."

"Introduce me."

"I can't. I've got to find Alan. If Mike's not invited, we must call the police. He's trouble, Kate, big trouble."

Even though his mind was occupied with more important matters, Mike Loutra caught the admiring glances from the beautiful girl who wore a blue dress. The price of that dress would feed a family of miners for six months. What the hell was he doing on Emerson Street?

He had met his cousin Alan inside a Denver bookstore. Alan had laughingly issued the party invitation. Mike had impulsively accepted. He knew Alan and his father didn't get along. He knew his attendance would be an irritant. But he wanted to fill his belly with food and forget his recent setbacks.

Mike had reached the United States in 1903, and found his way to the steel mills of Steubenville, Ohio. There he loaded pig iron and scrap, but was fired for not contributing money to the straw boss. Picking up another job at a rolling mill, he stayed three years while educating himself in English and in American politics. He was a voracious reader and had the unique ability to memorize everything from statistical facts to folk tales. Securing a union card, he headed for Denver, shuddered at the underlying decadence, and turned south toward the coal mines. By 1912 he was employed by the Mine Workers of America as an organizer. The pay was three and a half dollars a day, plus expenses.

Then and only then had resolute Randolph Tassler sought him out and offered him a job. Mike refused.

He had met Alan several times in coffeehouses and bookstores. Despite, or possibly because of his father's hostility, Alan had become a labor sympathizer, and Mike planned to exploit that interest.

The beautiful girl still stared at him, boring holes through the frayed collar of his blue work shirt.

Two hours later he knew her name, and his belly was bursting. He had avidly consumed crabmeat canapés and baked ham with piccalilli sauce. His head buzzed pleasantly from the Tasslers' supply of undiluted, bottled whiskey.

Alan's companions were treating him like a curious circus attraction, but he didn't mind. At the end of his performance he'd extract payment, a donation for the miners who planned to strike. Mike would cloak his request in the guise of a charitable contribution. After all, John D. Rockefeller was known for his benevolence, even as he was known for his indifference to suffering.

Mike had heard that John Rockefeller, Jr., recipient of his wealthy father's interests in CF&I, believed that if children perished because their parents had insufficient nourishment, then one must concede that their deaths were a blessing. After all, unskilled labor was merely animated machinery, adding little value to the finished product.

Inebriated, oozing with good cheer, Alan circled Mike's shoulders with his arm. "My friends would enjoy hearing one of your folk stories, cousin." He turned toward the other guests. "Mike's been all over the country an' has learned lots of good tales. Wait till you hear the one 'bout people wantin' to change the name of Arkansas after the Civil War."

Mike grinned. "I can't tell that story in front of the ladies, cousin."

"We'll go outside on the porch."

"That's not fair!" Rosalind stamped her foot.

"I'll tell you later, sis."

Kate noted the exchange and frowned with annoyance. She wouldn't be around later to hear Alan's rendition of Mike's folk story, and even if the story was a fable, she wanted to hear Mike tell it. The whole evening had been exasperating and was rapidly becoming worse. Fat Timmy Kettle, who rarely bathed, had sweetly pinched her tender skin until she was black and blue —

And she hadn't met Mike Loutra!

She had never been so obviously ignored. Even Richard, on his rare visits, petted her and made a fuss. She strolled down the hallway and entered the water closet. Its

366

claw-foot tub was large enough to hold a small battleship. On the walls were framed displays of butterflies pinned to white cardboard. Near the sun-window were several pots filled with high-stemmed geraniums.

Kate looked into the mirror above a blue Dutch tile table. Had her appearance altered? Was that the reason for Mike Loutra's indifference? Had her complexion suddenly accumulated blemishes? Did her new dress fail to reveal her assets? She should have bought one with a lower décolletage. Hellfire! She should have worn a gown with no bodice at all.

"— a speech made in the Arkansas state legislature by a member when some unspeakable creature proposed that the name of the state be changed."

Confused, Kate whirled about, then realized that the voice she heard, Mike's voice, drifted through the open window, carried on the breath of a breeze.

"Cite the speech for us, cousin," said Alan.

"Mistah Speaker, for more than thirty minutes I've been tryin' to get your attention, but every time I've caught your eye you've squirmed like a damned dog with a flea up its ass."

Pressing a handkerchief against her

mouth, Kate stifled her laughter. Furtively, she pulled the window's curtains aside and leaned forward.

"My name is Cassius Johnson from Jackson County, Arkansas, where a man can't stick his ass out the window and shit without it gettin' riddled with bullets."

Mike, Alan, and the others huddled on the porch beneath a suspended glass lantern. *Alan will never tell Rosalind this story,* Kate thought, as Mike continued.

"I'm out of order? How can I be out of order when I can piss clear across the Mississippi River?"

"What'd he say?" Leaning against the porch railing, Timmy Kettle cupped his ear with his sausage fingers.

"He said piss across the Mississippi." Alan scowled. "Shut up and let him finish. Go on, Mike."

"Where was Andrew Jackson when the Battle of New Orleans was fit? He was right thar, suh, up to his ass in blood! And you propose to change the name of Arkansas? Never, when I can defend her!"

The porch lamp highlighted Mike's features. Kate gazed at his face, mesmerized. He had nicked himself while shaving.

"You may shit on the grave of George Washington," Mike continued, "and piss on the monument of Thomas Jefferson. You may desecrate the remains of the immortal General Robert E. Lee. You may rape the Goddess of Liberty and wipe your ass on the Stars and Stripes, and your crime, suh, will no more compare to this hellish design than the glare of a lightning bug's ass to the noonday sun. And you propose to change the name of Arkansas? Never, by God, suh, never!"

Though her stomach hurt from the effort, Kate held her laughter in check.

"You may compare the lily of the valley to the glorious sunflower. Or the sun-kissed peaks of the highest mountain to the smokin' turd of a dung hill. Or the classic strains of Mozart to the fart of a Mexican burro. You may compare the puny penis of a Peruvian prince to the ponderous bullocks of the Roman gladiators. But change the name of Arkansas? Never, by God, suh, never!"

The handkerchief didn't quite capture all of Kate's pent-up laughter. Releasing the curtains, she stepped away from the window.

"What the hell!" Alan's voice. "The water closet! Shit, the window's wide open!"

"Get everybody inside, cousin, before other *ladies* decide to eavesdrop."

"Aren't you coming?"

369

"No. I'll stay here and admire the view."
Mike waited until the men had stumbled
through the front entrance. "Are you laughing at me or with me?"

"With you." Kate poked her head out the
window. "In my whole life I've never heard
a performance like the one you just gave,
Mr. Loutra."

"I apologize if I've offended you, but it's
your own fault."

"Really! Is it my fault that the architect
decided to build a water closet at the front
of the house? Help me out, please."

"I beg your pardon?"

"Help me climb through the window." She
flung one gartered leg over the sill. "What's
the matter? Have I offended *you*, Mr.
Loutra?"

He lifted her out. Shivering at his touch,
she saw his lips twitch with the semblance
of a smile.

"Are you cold, Miss Lytton?"

"You know my name," she said, walking
toward the porch steps.

"Of course. Your father is Ned Lytton, the
not-so-humble servant of John D. Rockefeller, and a member of the Mine Owners
Association."

"And you are a member of the United
Mine Workers Union, along with John Law-

son and Mother Jones."

"Where'd you hear about Lawson and Mother Jones?"

"I'm not stupid, Mr. Loutra, and I read the newspapers. My father swears it's all a pack of lies, what Lawson and the others say about the mines. Father has copies of the Colorado Fuel and Iron magazine, *Camp and Plant.* Its photographs show neat houses and recreation rooms with billiard tables."

"Billiard tables?"

"Do you know what billiards are, Mr. Loutra?"

"Sure. I'm not stupid and I read the newspapers."

"Father's magazines describe the mining town of Sopris as a Rocky Mountain gem with lace curtains fluttering in the windows and pianos or sewing machines in the parlors."

"Bullshit, Miss Lytton. That magazine ceased publication in nineteen-oh-three and never did write about 'Wop Town,' where Italians patched together their own community out of dry-goods boxes and barrel staves. Privies were a few boards laid out across a pit with gunnysacks for doors. Before she came to Colorado, Mother Jones read that a reporter from a Pittsburgh paper asked a CF&I manager why his mines weren't correctly timbered. The manager said, 'Oh damn it, dagos are cheaper than props.' "

Mike could see that she struggled to assimilate his words. "Has your father ever seen a mining town?" he continued, wondering why he bothered. "Endless strings of coal cars wind among the piles of rock, climbing toward the company store, the mine offices, the identical company houses. Has your father ever been inside a company house? Little cubes of clapboard with cardboard partitions nailed over studs. Those rows of neat houses have no sidewalk, no decent street, no trees."

"No trees? That's intolerable."

"Shall I describe the mines, Miss Lytton? The echo-less air smothers the sounds of picks or boots while the beam of a pit lamp catches the sweating sheen of a wall. Tiny particles of coal dust fill your lungs. The air is infinitely fine and infinitely combustible. Between nineteen ten and nineteen thirteen, six hundred and eighteen Colorado coal miners lost their lives in mine accidents. By nineteen ten, the cost of mining coal in terms of men came out to a life given for every thirty-eight thousand tons. The men are paid only for the coal they mine, not for the coal they couldn't get to or the rails they lifted or the rooms they timbered."

Young as she was, shallow as she appeared, Mike could see that a shrewd intelligence darkened her eyes until they gleamed like a wall of blue coal. But she merely said, "Why are you telling me all this?"

"Because that dress you wear cost the life of a miner."

"That's so unfair. I'm not responsible for my family's wealth or who I am. Would it make any difference if I stopped buying party dresses?"

"No. I must apologize, Miss Lytton. I've had too much pure whiskey, and you happened to be handy. Let's return to the parlor. It's cold."

"Your rhetoric heats the yard. Rosalind says you come from Greece. I'd never guess. You speak English without the trace of an accent, and your words paint pictures."

Mike sat on the steps. "The miners come from everywhere in the world, Miss Lytton, lured here by the promise of instant prosperity. Did Cousin Rosalind tell you I can also speak Italian fluently?"

"Please call me Kate. I do believe I feel a bit chilled. You may stand up and put your arms around me."

He stood, shrugged off his jacket and draped it across her shoulders.

Kate smelled tobacco in the threads, a male scent, a Mike scent. "Aren't you going to kiss me?"

"What?"

"You heard me. If you've tried to frighten me away with your words, it didn't work. It's difficult to believe all you've said, but I'll make sure my father visits a company house and takes me along. And I'll kiss you if you don't kiss me first."

"Are you crazy?"

"My grandfather says if you want something badly enough, you must reach out and grab it."

"For free?"

"For fair trade. I want to kiss you. Don't you want to kiss me?"

"No."

"Because of my dress?"

"Because of your name. You'll say I'm unfair and you're not responsible for your name."

"Are you married, Mike?"

"I don't have time for courting."

"You don't have to court me. I knew how I felt the moment you entered Rosalind's parlor."

"Tomorrow I leave for Ludlow. The miners plan to strike. They'll abandon their company houses and camp on the grounds, close to the mines."

"That's tomorrow. It's still tonight."

"Whatever you're feeling now, you'll feel for someone else next week."

"No, I won't." Warmed by her confession, she placed his jacket across the railing, walked down the steps, and nudged a flower with the toe of her slipper.

He followed. "I can't figure you out, Miss Lytton. I've never met anyone like you before."

"I've never met me before, either. Very well, I shall be a proper lady and visit you in Ludlow." She paused at the sound of his laughter. "What's so *damn* funny?"

"It's so *damn* tempting. I'd have a photographer handy. Kate Lytton in the midst of a union camp. Your father would shit bullets. Sorry, didn't mean to cuss. You're very sweet, but you can't possibly understand what's involved in a strike. Do you think it's noble? Romantic? There will be a city of tents and at least a thousand people. Cold weather and mud. Lice. At best, the sanitary conditions will be inadequate, the food limited. The possibility of death —"

"You'll be there. I want to be with you. I love you."

"You don't know what you're saying."

"Yes, I do. You said you had no time for

courting. I accept that. But I won't wait three months or six to tell you how I feel. Won't you please kiss me before I throw myself into your arms and embarrass the both of us?"

"Because we feel a physical attraction for each other, that doesn't mean it's love."

"Define love."

He shook his head. "I've never been in love. I've never even talked about it. Frankly, I can't believe we're having this discussion. I'm leaving. Good-bye."

"No!" She stumbled forward, reached out and captured his upper arm.

Angry, Mike turned, the sudden motion causing her to release his arm. But his scathing words died unborn when he saw her flushed face and wounded eyes. Powerless, he kissed her.

He had meant to embrace her quickly and bolt through the night, but her lips parted and her body yielded. She smelled clean. How long had it been since he'd held a woman? He couldn't remember.

Kate ended the kiss and stared into Mike's smoky eyes. Miffed by his indifference, she had simply wanted revenge — at first. But her impulsive love declaration had been the truth.

Father would go through the roof, she

thought. *Mother would faint. I don't care. Mike leaves for Ludlow tomorrow. I have no time for flirting or secret assignations. I have no time to play the proper lady.*

God, her breasts, thought Mike. Beneath the blue gown's material, they were full and up-tilted. He didn't have time for this nonsense. He was a union man. He had come to the party tonight for the purpose of securing donations, and she had caused him to forget his mission. The union. He needed to concentrate on the union.

With a groan, he ran his fingers across her bodice, felt her nipples harden, heard her indrawn breath.

"Gazebo," she gasped. "Back of the house, hidden by trees. No, please, don't touch me there again. I've never . . . I just want to talk."

He scooped her up into his arms and carried her around the side of the house, toward the trees. Seated on the gazebo floor, she snuggled against his chest. He talked, kissed her, talked some more. He told her about his childhood in Greece, his family, his years in America.

She listened, waiting for his next kiss.

"Promise you won't come to Ludlow," he said.

"I promise, but you must promise to visit

me in Denver." Breathing softly into the hollow of his neck, she murmured, "Do you propose to abandon me to my loneliness? Never, by God, suh, never!"

Kate reached Ludlow on the twenty-third of September, 1913, in time to watch strikers and their families arrive at the tent colony. They hunched over their household goods, trying to avoid the wind-driven rain. Rented horses dragged wagons through the mud. When they came to a hill, men, women and children all got out and pushed, straining against the wheels.

Next to Kate stood Don McGregor, a reporter for the *Denver Express.*

"Prosperity," he said. "Hah! Straw bedding. A small pile of kitchen utensils. Those pots and pans are so decrepit, they'd earn the scorn of any secondhand dealer on Larimer Street. No books. Not one single article worth protecting from the rain." He studied her face. "You look familiar. Do I know you?"

I've been on the society pages of your newspaper a dozen times. "We've never met, Mr. McGregor, but I've read your articles. My name's Katherine Lyt . . . ship."

Dear God, she'd almost blurted out Katherine Lytton. She could see her father's face

378

if he read about his daughter in a Don McGregor piece.

Why had she traveled to Ludlow? Admittedly, she missed Mike Loutra, although he couldn't possibly be as wonderful as she remembered. Nobody could. Furthermore, Mike had told her *not* to come.

She was supposed to be on her way to New York, visiting her Aunt Elizabeth. Her aunt had tickets for *The Sunshine Girl,* a new Broadway musical starring the celebrated dance couple, Vernon and Irene Castle. Kate was an avid baseball fan, and Elizabeth had suggested that, during the first week of October, Kate might attend a World Series game.

"Welcome to Ludlow, Miss Lightship." McGregor arched an eyebrow. "And what, may I ask, are *you* doing here?"

He was staring at her mud-spattered harem skirt and her blue velvet coat, trimmed with ermine. Her valise was of the softest leather, and her hat was the same blue straw she had worn to Rosalind's party, although the feathers were quite ruined by the rain.

She should return to the Ludlow station, take the first train back to Denver, continue on to New York City. But first she wanted to see Mike again, visit him in this horrible place, so she could erase his image from her mind and get on with her life.

"What I'm doing here is none of your business." Leaving McGregor, Kate wended her way to the large central tent, where she found Mike doling out hot coffee to the miners as they straggled inside.

He looked tired. Yet above the dark smudges of fatigue, his gray eyes were soft with compassion. Though he stood inside the tent, his hair had captured the sun's rays. *What sun?*

"If there's enough coffee, I'd appreciate a cup," she said, dropping her valise and taking off her wet hat.

He stood motionless, coffee pot suspended.

"I realize you can't kiss me hello, Mike, but —"

"You *promised* you'd stay in Denver, Kate."

"I guess you can't trust the word of a Lytton," she teased. Then, more seriously, "I tried to tell everybody what you said about the mining towns and strikers, but they wouldn't believe me. They didn't want to believe. They'd read the coal company magazines, heard the optimistic words in the mine owners' speeches and —"

"Go home, Kate. I mean it."

"I wanted to come sooner but I caught my sister's cough. Isn't there something I can do?"

"Have you ever bandaged a wound? Have you ever cooked a meal?"

"I can learn." *I'll leave tomorrow,* she thought, *but first I'll prove that I can help.* "Where's Mother Jones?"

Mike extended his coffee pot toward the spry eighty-three-year-old woman, who wore rimless glasses, a long black skirt and a white shirtwaist. Her head bobbed up and down as she led a group in song: "The union forever, hurrah, boys, hurrah."

Mother Jones was surrounded by painted placards. One read: DO YOU HEAR THE CHILDREN GROANING, O COLORADO!

Another proclaimed: WE ARE NOT AFRAID OF YOUR GATLING GUNS, WE HAVE TO DIE ANYWAY!

A third: WE REPRESENT CF&I'S PROSPERITY SLAVES!

As Kate walked toward Mother Jones, she spied a woman with a baby at her breast. Placing her own warm coat around the nursing mother's shoulders, exchanging it for a thin shawl, Kate murmured, "Fair trade, Grandfather."

Hours later, after the rain had stopped and candles dotted the night-darkened colony like hundreds of grounded stars, Kate washed her hands and face with a sliver of soap. Then she searched for Mike.

She found him stretched out in back of a truck with four bald tires, and she snuggled her body against his. *I'll leave the day after tomorrow,* she thought. *There's still so much to do. I'll leave the day after tomorrow, or maybe the day after that.*

"Maggie Brown," Mike said. "The newspapers call her the unsinkable Molly Brown. She's in Europe, but she sent word that she plans to help." He yawned. "She'll donate food."

"If Molly Brown's willing to help, so am I."

Mike felt Kate's smile against his neck. His sweet *Americanidhes* was actually here in his arms, even though she must leave first thing tomorrow morning. *Christ Pantokrator!* She'd never survive the rigors of a tent city.

Would the miners accept her? Kate Lytton, who spent more on clothes in one month than a coal miner earned in a year?

Kate Lytton, who had never known a hungry day in her life? He'd seen her exchange her blue coat for the nursing mother's red shawl, but she had lots of coats in her closet. Or she could buy a new coat. Oil and water didn't mix. An immigrant Greek and Ned Lytton's society daughter could never blend.

Mike knew that his culture measured history by the devastating rotation of epic victory or epic defeat. He also knew that, at Ludlow, the call to arms was a silenced mine whistle, the battle uniform a patched pair of overalls, the camp standard a bucket of coal. In his war against industrial America, Mike would have to first do battle with his own conception of the past.

Could Kate Lytton do the same?

TWENTY-ONE

Kate fell in love with the children.

She had been ten when her brother, Edward Steven, was born. But the long-desired heir was frail and puny while Kate was brash and sturdy, her father's favorite. Edward Steven had no more importance in Kate's former world than one of her mother's pampered poodles.

The strikers' babies didn't have canopied cribs. They didn't have infant tubs — or even pails — for bathing. They didn't have toys. On Kate's third day in Ludlow, she spied a tiny girl seated in the mud. Gathering pebbles, the child threw them one by one into a dented saucepan, clapping her hands after each satisfying ping.

The little girl sang, "The you-yen fo-ev-vah, hoo-way, boys, hoo-way."

By the first week of October, children played hide-and-seek among the neat rows of tents with their painted numbers. When the sun came out, clotheslines sagged. Flags sprouted — Greek, Italian, American, and the two-colored banner with the stitched name LUDLOW.

And Kate remained at the colony, still vowing she'd leave "tomorrow."

The camp was laid out on the prairie beneath twin canyons, which led up cedar-covered mesas to the mines. Behind the camp was a deep arroyo, a steel bridge, a pump station, and a covered well with rickety steps leading down in stages to foul-smelling water. South of the tents was a rise called Water Tank Hill and the curving tracks of the Colorado and Southern. Then came the railroad junction of Ludlow, with its yards and switches and coal cars.

The scabs began to arrive. With others, Kate queued up at the depot to jeer them as they got off the train.

On October seventh, John Lawson and Mother Jones were addressing the camp from the back of the union automobile. One CF&I clerk and two gunmen showed up on the road west of the tents. There were shots exchanged.

Naked, Kate thought later. She had never really understood before what the word naked meant. The strikers were on an open plain, caught between railroad tracks and the mine guards who camped within the hills. Every night searchlights danced over the grounds and shined through tent roofs. Exhausted, Kate managed to sleep, but she often dreamed about bullets puncturing the canvas, and sometimes she pictured herself and the children buried alive inside a deep dark hole.

Guards rode by on their horses, and strikers heard about the drunken boasts at Baca's saloon. Kate's hands blistered as she dug cellars under tent floors or shoveled rifle pits along the dry ravine. She ignored the oozing pustules and took scant notice of her pain because Mike was there. If he wasn't always by her side, his spirit, his dedication, his belief in the cause had become her own.

"My darling *Americanidhes,*" he said one night while she scrubbed her dirty face. "Do you know how much I love you? In Greece the practice of love is smothered by impossible standards of modesty."

"Are you saying I'm immodest?" Kate ran the pitiful sliver of soap over her thin arms and beneath her breasts.

Mike grinned. "I wish I were a little bar of soap, my girl," he sang, "tied to your bath with a string. I'd slide from you slowly, and you'd catch me again, and you'd put me wherever you like."

Turning away from the basin of water, Kate flung herself at Mike's chest and tickled his ribs.

"I'd wash your sweet little body, my girl," he continued between gasps of laughter, "and foam from all my passion."

November. The Colorado National Guard arrived. They were commanded by a Denver ophthalmologist named John Chase, who had earned his spurs during the Cripple Creek strike. There was Major Pat Hamrock, coach of the state rifle team and owner of a Denver saloon, who had been part of the shameful campaign that crushed Sitting Bull. And there was Karl Linderfelt.

Linderfelt had fought in the Philippines, perfecting his soldiering techniques during a war in which the destruction of food stores and the burning of insurgent barrios had become unofficial policy. Now, in militia uniform, he faced those insolent foreigners who occupied the Ludlow tents: Wops and anarchists! He had learned, he liked to say, that you cannot go at it with kid gloves.

The occupation began as a sort of holiday. Across from the depot and a little south of the Ludlow camp, brown conical tents were planted. Soldiers dug latrines, carried water, and piled up coal.

The militia was to be an impartial force, summoned to disarm guards as well as strikers, and keep watch against the importation of scabs. The Ludlow community greeted them with loud cheers.

Outside the camp, strikers relinquished the colony's weapons. Kate counted twenty-five, maybe thirty old guns, heaped on the ground.

"Where are the rest?" John Lawson demanded.

A little boy gravely dropped a popgun on the pile.

"Damn my countrymen," Mike grumbled.

It was dark and cold. He and Kate huddled beneath blankets inside the tent they shared.

Their tent was large enough to hold a bed, dresser and mirror, a crude cookstove, a small icebox, two stools and a warped wooden table. A telephone had been installed, its wires leading to a nearby telephone pole, since Mike was in constant communication with John Lawson.

"What's wrong, darling?"

"The Greeks are married to their guns. Although they were supposed to turn them in to Lawson, they wouldn't give them up.

They don't trust me, but because I'm a Cretan *palikari*, they allow me access to their section of the camp. I swear they're forming a Balkan army. My countrymen have confused this miserable tent city with the Great Idea of Byzantine reclaimed. And your reporter friend, Don McGregor, isn't helping matters."

"He's not a friend. What's McGregor doing now?"

"Pumping up the military myth of the camp with his prose. He's creating a powder keg, Katie, a goddamn powder keg."

Three months later there was still no sign of a settlement. Winter hit hard. The ground turned slushy or slicked over with ice. Water froze in barrels. Men hunted rabbits, but the game was being pushed back deeper into the hills. Strike benefits never stretched far enough to fill thirteen hundred empty bellies, and those same bellies often growled with hunger.

Kate dreamed about steaming bowls of oatmeal, a dish she had despised as a child. Every morning, upon awakening, she found herself licking her lips and weeping softly.

Mike no longer insisted she return to Denver. He needed her. She was his strength. She had become a symbol of courage to the camp. They knew her background and it gave them hope. If Kate Lytton believed in their cause, wouldn't others from her world commit?

Standing on the platform next to Mother Jones, Kate proudly wore the thin shawl she had traded her coat for on the day of her arrival. She stood straight and tall while Mother Jones' high-pitched Irish voice rang through the meeting hall. "You will be free. Poverty and misery will be unknown. We will turn the jails into playgrounds for the children. We will build homes, not log kennels and shacks as you have them now. There will be no civilization as long as such conditions as that abound, and now you men and women will have to stand the fight."

Kate sent letters to Aunt Elizabeth and her parents. She was fine, she wrote. Perhaps a bit hungry, she hinted. Just like Molly Brown, she wanted to help the strikers' children. There was no need to try and change her mind since her actions were charitable rather than political, and the Lyttons, like the Rockefellers, had always maintained an altruistic facade. The last line was a lie, except for the altruistic facade part, which she couldn't resist adding.

Aunt Elizabeth responded with a food

donation, transported by rail. Her father sent a telegram, insisting she return home at once.

Kate's red shawl became a camp banner. She found she had an instinct for nursing. She lost count of the number of babies she had delivered. "Do you hear the children groaning, Colorado?" she'd cry, slapping the backside of a newborn.

February fourteenth. Kate took the train to Denver and arranged a secret meeting with Alan Tassler at a Market Street coffeehouse.

He almost didn't recognize her.

She had always been slender, but now her body was as thin as six o'clock. Dark bruises of exhaustion above her sharply etched cheekbones emphasized the blue of her eyes. She had cut, no, *chopped* her hair, and the uneven strands curled above her collar. She drank three cups of nutmeg-flavored coffee, and gave him a blissful smile.

Alan had meant to hand over the contributions and leave straightaway. Instead, he found himself ordering more coffee, a wedge of pungent cheese, and a loaf of fresh-baked pumpernickel.

"Your father," he said, "is in a rage."

"I expect that's true," she replied as though commenting on the weather. "I'm surprised he didn't barge into the camp and kidnap me."

"Are you serious, Katie? We've heard you're well armed, especially the Greeks. Don McGregor writes that most Greeks are veterans of the Balkan Wars, young and tough and itching for a fight. My father wouldn't step foot in Ludlow, and neither would yours. Ned wavers between damning you and insisting you were coerced."

"I volunteered freely."

"Honey, it's not too late. Ned would take you back with open arms."

"It's much too late. Mike and I were married on Christmas day." Her eyes brightened then dimmed. "The camp needs food and clothing."

"I'll take care of it."

"Thank you. Babies are starving." Her expression changed again, but this time her eyes were unfathomable, as if they hid behind a theater's scrim. "The miners' wives," she said, "used to scrub floors in the superintendents' homes so their husbands would get a good room to mine. Women would scrub, bent over like dogs, while their own floors were carpeted with coal dust."

"Maybe if you talked to your father, Katie. You've always been able to influence him."

Her lips turned up in a tight smile. "I went

to the house this morning, but Father wouldn't let me in. Dorothy said she'd gather some clothes and leave them outside, especially underwear. God, I need underwear. Cook promised she'd put together a sack of barbecued spareribs and artichokes stuffed with peas and ham. *Artichokes*, Alan, when hungry children with runny noses choke on their own phlegm." She sighed. "We need medical supplies very badly."

"I'll collect food and medicine and leave the baskets inside the gazebo."

"Thank you." She wove slender fingers through her cropped hair then smiled wistfully. "May I have another piece of bread?"

Once I believed myself in love with Katie, thought Alan, *and I suppose I still am. Hot damn! She's married to Mike. We're related. Wait till I tell Rosalind. She'll pee her drawers.*

On Thursday evening, March thirty-first, Ned Lytton lit a cigar. Then he belatedly offered one to his guest, Randolph Tassler.

"Are you aware that Alan's providing the insurgents with food and clothing, Tassler?"

"Of course. It's a small rebellion, Lytton, and can't compare to your daughter living at the camp. She even married Mike Loutra, a union leader."

"Isn't Loutra your cousin?" Ned replenished his drink from a decanter atop the music room's sideboard. "They probably had a Greek wedding ceremony. I can't believe it's legal. Loutra poisoned Katie's mind against her family, pulled the wool over her eyes. They share a tent. My daughter's a decent girl, so he had to marry her."

"Look, I didn't request this meeting to discuss Alan or Kate. I came to enlist your aid in a noble cause."

"Johanna handles our charitable contributions."

"I didn't say charity. I said noble cause. Last month Governor Ammons withdrew all but two hundred troops from the strike zone. General Chase, Pat Hamrock, and Karl Linderfelt still remain, thank God. Chase lives like a warlord, so he's loyal to management."

"He should be. He gets four hundred a month, plus one hundred seventy-five dollars per week for 'expenses.' "

Tassler relit his cigar. "Chase told the governor that his soldiers would welcome an opportunity to demonstrate their efficiency."

"Bull! I've heard the men play baseball with the strikers, and some helped shovel snow after December's blizzard."

"That was then. This is now. The 'college

boys' have completed their tour of duty and Ammons turned the strike over to local authorities."

Ned drained his drink. "I'm pleased Major Hamrock's still involved. He's experienced, fought wars for the suppression of lesser breeds. He fought at Wounded Knee and —"

"That's my point. We're in a war and we have to fight fire with fire. I've talked to the other Mine Owners Association members and they agree."

"Agree to what?"

"The formation of a new company, armed and drilled by military officials who will be subject to the orders of the county sheriff."

"Who is subject to our orders."

"Exactly. Since these selfless volunteers will draw no pay from the state, I've been authorized to tap the resources of other men in authority." Tassler reached for a crystal ashtray and snuffed out his cigar. "How much will you contribute?"

"How much do you need?"

Tassler named an amount.

Ned felt his face flush, but he attempted to hide his agitation by refilling his glass. "My funds are spread a bit thin right now. Recent business slumps and stock market panics. You know how it is. Edward's in

New York getting our business affairs in order, but I expect him back shortly. Will you stay for dinner, Randolph?"

"No. I have other appointments. With men of influence. Thank you for your time."

I can ask Johanna to dip into her trust fund, thought Ned. *If the strikers are defeated and that damn tent colony destroyed, Katie will have to come back home.*

After his initial anger, Ned found that he missed his daughter. He regretted his hasty decision during her one visit. He should have let her enter, convinced her to stay, on hands and knees if necessary. His beautiful Katie, living in a tent, consorting with immigrant scum. The battle against the union had become very personal. How could he *not* contribute to Tassler's noble cause? Furthermore, Randolph's tone of voice had been condescending. As though he, Ned Lytton, had no more importance than one of Johanna's damned poodles.

"I'll deliver the money in three days. Is that soon enough?" Ned gestured toward the sideboard. "Would you care to join me in a toast? Celebrate our victory?"

"I don't imbibe spirits, Lytton. Drink is the devil's brew."

TWENTY-TWO

The long winter finally ended. April arrived and a bright sun melted the tent colony's few remaining patches of snow. Freshly washed clothes swayed in the breeze, a chorus line of headless dancers on an outdoor stage.

Saturday, April eighteenth. John D. Rockefeller was at Pocantico Hills, perfecting his golf swing, putting and driving balls for the amusement of his grandchildren.

In Denver, Ned Lytton hosted a birthday party for his eight-year-old son, Edward Steven. There were pony rides and performing clowns and a layered cake that Cook vowed was as high and fussy as the Majestic building on Sixteenth Street.

Sunday, April nineteenth. The Ludlow Greeks celebrated Easter. Determined to have a finer holiday than the American Catholics, they put a lamb on the fire and purchased two barrels of beer. They even gave some of their women outlandishly American sports bloomers.

Garbed in his native Cretan *vrakes,* Mike basted the lamb while Kate and other newly bloomered women played a baseball game on the diamond across the road. Four militiamen arrived, one mounted on a black horse. They had rifles. Soldiers often came to watch the ball games, but they'd never brought guns before.

Trouble, thought Kate.

Her friend, Pearl Jolly, turned to the soldiers and said, "If we women would start after you with BB guns, you'd drop your rifles and run."

"Never mind, girlie," said the man on the horse. "You have your big Sunday today, and tomorrow we'll get the roast." He beckoned to the other soldiers and they left the field, heading toward their own campsite.

Kate felt her tense muscles loosen. Threats on both sides were so common. She determined to enjoy the celebration.

Following the singing and dancing, she and Mike shared a warm glass of beer in the privacy of their tent.

"As a child I stood under the dome of a Byzantine church," Mike said. "I held an unlit candle in my hand and stared at the face of Christ, painted in the dome. Soon the candles were lit, one after another. I lit mine. People lifted the empty winding-sheet above them and carried it round the church."

Kate smiled. "I once said you painted pictures with words. I hope our children will do the same."

"Children? Katie, are you —"

"No, Mike. I'm not pregnant. But if I were, it wouldn't change anything. Someday we'll buy a house with trees in the front and backyard. We'll have a Saint Bernard puppy, like Mrs. Bebout's dog. Our children will be well-fed and they'll sing 'Ring-a-Rosy' rather than 'The Union Forever.' "

"Is that *all* you want, my darling?"

"I want you to love me — now, tomorrow, forever. Aren't you going to kiss me? Or do I have to throw myself into your arms?"

Mike took off her bloomers and shed his *vrakes*. "I wish I were a little bar of soap," he sang, as Kate urged his entry, meeting his thrusts with a savage, almost tempestuous response. Behind her closed eyelids, she saw Mike's childhood vision — hundreds of lit candles. She heard the swelling anthem of resurrection and added her voice.

The next morning Mike was gone, having penciled a note about joining John Lawson in the nearby town of Trinidad. New strategies to end the never-ending strike, thought Kate.

She really should visit Denver again. Fight her way into the house. Kneel at her father's feet and — he'd never listen. Father was a member of the Ku Klux Klan, and Klan constituents wouldn't embrace the plight of immigrant strikers. They'd just as soon see the colony go up in smoke.

What about Grandfather? Although no longer religiously affiliated, his Quaker roots were planted deep. He had spent the last few months in New York but he could have returned by now.

She shrugged her body into a white dress from Dorothy's February bundle then brushed her cropped hair, which she had cut with a blunt pair of scissors. Short, it took less time to neaten and stayed a lot cleaner. "Do I look like a boy?" she'd asked Mike, after the deed was done.

"My darling," he had replied, "nothing on earth could make you look like a boy."

Just the same, her breasts had flattened to pancakes.

Since it was Monday, she decided to add her few dirty clothes to Maggie Dominiske's. Maggie washed clothes on Monday, probably had water heating atop the cookstove this very minute.

Stepping outside her tent, Kate saw Maggie standing next to Pearl Jolly and Louis Tikas. Tikas was Greek, a friend of Mike's, and one of the camp leaders.

In front of Tikas stood a soldier named Patton — *Corporal* Patton, Kate remembered — and three of the men who had witnessed yesterday's ball game.

"All right," said Patton. "We'll be back." The soldiers turned toward the militia tents.

Tikas walked away, his puttee trousers and knee-length boots retreating down the row. A pair of field glasses, strapped to his left shoulder, bounced with his hurried movements. A slouch-brimmed hat fell to the dirt but he never broke stride.

"What's happening?" Tossing her laundry back inside the tent, Kate walked toward Pearl and Maggie.

"It's crazy." Pearl wrung her hands. "An old Italian woman says her husband is being held by strikers against his will. Patton insists we release him or the soldiers will inspect our tents."

"Oh, no! It has to be an excuse to tear up the camp and search for weapons. Is that why Louis looked so nervous?"

"He's afraid he won't be able to hold his Greeks back this time. Where's Mike?"

Kate inhaled her reply with a gasp. She had noticed sudden motion on the Colorado and Southeastern railroad tracks. All down the tracks stood militiamen with rifles. *Trouble,* she thought. *I had a feeling yesterday, a sense of inevitability.*

Aloud she said, "Mike's with Lawson. Where did Louis go?" She gestured toward the tracks. "Shouldn't we find him?"

Mary Petrucci, who had joined them, said that Tikas was heading for the depot to meet with Major Pat Hamrock.

Kate heard music. A few of the Greeks were still celebrating Easter with a mandolin, flute, and some kind of violin. Shading her eyes from the sun, she walked to the front of the colony and looked toward Water Tank Hill, where soldiers were fixing breastworks around two machine guns.

The camp's background music abruptly ceased; the Greeks had seen the machine guns, too. Quickly they gathered their weapons and set out for the railroad cut east of the colony, where there was good cover in a field of weeds growing out of sand banks.

Linderfelt's soldiers on Water Tank Hill shouted to their leader, pleading for the order to fire. Tikas raced toward his tents, waving a handkerchief, screaming for his men to return. They ignored him.

Kate was watching Tikas when she heard gunshots.

Who shot first? Does it really matter?

Women and children stood in the open, exposed. Kate ran toward them. "Get inside the tents!" she screamed, when suddenly there was a tremendous explosion. Dear God! The militia had planted sticks of dynamite inside the colony. When? Last night, of course, during the Easter celebration.

The earth rumbled and shook over and over again — more dynamite, detonated from a safe distance behind the militia tents. People scattered in all directions, like pocket gophers flushed from their holes.

"The tents!" Kate yelled. "Everybody crouch down inside the tents, or hide in the pits we dug. Take whatever food and water you can carry, but hurry!"

Howling dogs added to the racket. Bullets shredded canvas and ricocheted off heavy iron stoves.

"Here, Katie, take these." Pearl handed over two armbands, each embroidered with a red cross.

Kate attached the bands around the sleeves of her white dress, but gunfire dogged her heels as she searched for the wounded.

Reaching her own tent, she found five men, very much alive, stretched out on the floor. The men included Tikas, who was telephoning Trinidad for reinforcements. "Looks like we're due to be here a while," he said, "and we haven't eaten anything since last night. Have you got the fixings for sandwiches, Katie?"

Sandwiches? During an assault by machine guns? Yet people had to eat, she supposed, happy that Louis had directed her to perform such a mundane chore in the midst of all this madness.

"I think we have some leftover lamb." She suddenly realized the tent flaps were tied back and the militia could see her reflection in the mirror. She dropped to the floor, just as gunfire pierced the tent and the mirror shattered.

Avoiding shards of broken glass, she crawled toward the tiny icebox, stood up, and made sandwiches. While delivering them to the other side of the tent, she was spotted, and again the shooting commenced.

"For God's sake, stay away!" screamed one man. "You're a hoodoo!"

"It's the white dress and red crosses, Katie," said Maggie's husband Joe. "Makes you a perfect target." He tossed her a pair of overalls and one of Mike's blue work shirts from the pile of neglected laundry. "Put these over your dress and get rid of those damn crosses."

John Lawson responded to Louis Tikas's phone message by ordering his aides to enlist every man available into a relief army. Seated inside the union's familiar red touring auto, he drove toward Ludlow. Along the way, he dropped Mike Loutra off to recruit volunteers at Suffield, six miles from Trinidad.

"Promise me you'll keep an eye on Katie," Mike pleaded. "Sometimes her stubbornness outweighs her fear."

Lawson ran into gunfire south of Ludlow, forcing a detour east and north across open prairie. He parked and proceeded on foot along the arroyo, unable to move any closer than the steel bridge where Louis Tikas waited.

"It's not good, John," said Tikas. "We can't get medical attention for the wounded. A doctor made it inside the camp and crawled to the well when told that there were badly hurt women and children hiding. Once down there with them, he was trapped by cross fire above the entrance."

"Can't we eliminate the damned machine guns?"

"Impossible. Linderfelt marched some of his men north along the tracks to the railroad depot. They hid around buildings or behind lumber piles, attacked the easterly flats, and dislodged strikers from the sand cut. That left machine guns free to rake the camp, practically unopposed. I'm worried about the women and children. Several are in the tent pits, but they can't climb out to get food or water. We tried a white flag but the soldiers ignored us, just like they ignored the red crosses on Katie Loutra and Pearl Jolly, who simply wanted to help the wounded. It's chaos, John, utter chaos."

"We're bringing reinforcements."

"So are they. Right now we outnumber them, but they have superior weapons."

"Tell the men to hold out, Louis. Tell them I've gone to notify the governor and bring a relief force. One other thing. Make sure Katie Loutra is out of harm's way. I promised Mike."

Flames and smoke took possession of the tent colony around seven.

"Move the women and children to Frank Baynes's ranch house, Katie," said Pearl Jolly, silhouetted by the waning twilight.

"That's suicidal, Pearl. The ranch is a mile away, and we have to cross open flat between the tents and the arroyo. If we go south, we'll run into machine gun fire."

"We can't stay here. We'll burn to death. I'd rather be shot then burned, wouldn't you?"

"Look!" Kate pointed at the depot, where a southbound local freight train rumbled toward the station. Its headlights showed militiamen firing across the tracks. The train halted with a screech of brakes. "This is our chance. There have to be at least thirty freight cars and they'll provide a barrier." Even as she spoke, Kate headed for the pump house and well.

From the corner of her eye, she saw a soldier running a blazing torch up a tent side. She looked to her left and gasped with horror. Mrs. Bebout's Saint Bernard loped down the path, a blazing stick of wood between his jaws. The dog's shaggy fur was singed and he was confused. Oh, God! How many times had Kate seen the children throwing sticks for the dog to retrieve?

Yearning to chase the bewildered animal, knowing she couldn't waste a precious second, Kate continued running toward the well.

Once in the arroyo, the surge of refugees

split in two, half veering toward the Black Hills, three miles away.

"I'm going back, Pearl!" Kate shouted.

"For God's sake, why?"

"Mary Petrucci and her children are missing. Cedilano Costa and Patricia Valdez —"

"Katie, wait! They could have escaped earlier."

"They all hid in Alcarita Pedregon's pit. What if they're still there? They'll suffocate from smoke. I have to go back."

As Kate reentered the colony, she noted that the shooting had become desultory, the gunfire subordinate to the crackle of flames.

Approaching Alcarita's tent, she thought she heard the sound of crying children. Dear God! Cedilano Costa was in an advanced state of pregnancy, while Patricia Valdez still breast-fed her three-month-old baby. Kate had given both tiny Petrucci girls hand-stitched cloth bunnies for Easter.

"Hey, I got me one," said a man's rough voice.

Kate felt arms encircle her waist and belly.

"Let's hang him from the telephone pole," said a second man.

Kate wrenched free and whirled around, planning to cut left and sprint for Louis's tent.

"Look out! He could have a gun!"

408

She saw the soldier swing his Springfield rifle, and raised her arm to take the blow. But the man struck with such force, the stock of his rifle snapped. Kate fell, her arm broken, her scalp gashed.

Still conscious, she heard the first voice.

"Gawd, it's a girl!"

"Let's get out of here. We don't wanna hang no girl."

"Shouldn't we see how bad she's hurt?"

"We're supposed to find Louie the Greek. Let's go!"

Kate shut her eyes. *I'll get dirty lying on the ground,* she thought. *Mummy will be mad but Daddy'll laugh and say, "Buy her a new dress, Johanna."*

No, wait. Her dress wouldn't get dirty because she wore Mike's overalls and shirt. She desperately wanted to wash away the blood that poured down her face. Despite the camp's muddy grime, she had always managed to keep herself clean for Mike.

"I wish I were a little bar of soap," she whispered. "I'd slide from you slowly and —"

Kate slid into unconsciousness.

Louis Tikas was shot in the back three times. Frank Snyder, age eleven, left the hole beneath his tent to fetch his baby sister some water. A bullet shattered his brain. The Pedregon pit was uncovered, exposing the bodies of Patricia Valdez, the pregnant Cedilano Costa, and eleven children. Mary Petrucci and Alcarita Pedregon had escaped to find help, just before Kate had been attacked outside what was now referred to as the "death pit" or "black hole."

Briefly regaining consciousness, Kate had managed to crawl away from the burning tents. When found, her broken arm was set but she stared blankly into the distance. The rifle's blow had caused a severe concussion and she was unable to walk or talk. In despair, Mike brought her to Edward Lytton, knowing she would receive superior medical attention.

When fed, she'd swallow — even oatmeal, a dish she had despised as a child.

She was told, by Ned, that Mike had died from a stray bullet, but her expression never changed. Sometimes she'd raise her arms, hands clawed, fingers splayed. In her own mind she was trying to catch an imaginary baseball. But she always missed and the ball would roll into a flaming pit and she'd hear a man atop a black horse shout, "Never mind, girlie, tomorrow we'll get the roasted baseball!"

■ ■ ■ ■

Seated on the edge of her chair, Kate stared through the music room window.

She watched the sky turn blue then black — sometimes dotted with candle-stars — then blue again. From time to time it rained. *The rain will put out the baseball,* she thought.

Had her brain projected images on a motion picture screen, it would have shown a house with trees in the front and backyard, children singing "Ring-a-Rosy," and a shaggy Saint Bernard running through the grass, a piece of scorched wood between its flaming jaws.

"She might improve if her husband paid her a visit," the doctor suggested. "There's always hope, Mr. Lytton."

"It's hopeless, Loutra," Ned told Mike over the telephone. "Thank God I have the means to make Katie comfortable. She can't even feed herself. We have a nurse with her at all times. No, you can't see her. The doctor says the sight of anyone or anything connected with Ludlow might cause irreparable damage. I'll let you know if she improves. You have my oath on it."

Ned knew his medical pretext wouldn't

keep Loutra at bay for long, so he contacted Randolph Tassler. Tassler said an assassin was out of the question, but he'd arrange for Mike to be taken into custody, charged with marijuana possession. Marijuana had been outlawed in order to combat insolent demands by Mexican workers who looked at white women; workers who also had the audacity to insist their children be educated while they harvested sugar beets.

In a voice dripping with sarcasm, Randolph Tassler said that Mike would appreciate an opportunity to join a convict chain gang — where he'd benefit from fresh air and physical labor.

Mike Loutra now spent his nights at the Colorado State Penitentiary. During the day he built roads.

Kate remained incommunicable, so Ned turned to Richard Reed, admitting a renewed interest in the Ku Klux Klan. After all, who had been responsible for Kate's illness? Immigrant Catholics and Jews. Katie was so young. Greeks and dagos had poisoned her mind against her family. Ned vowed to avenge the loss of his daughter.

But first he wanted to drink himself senseless.

TWENTY-THREE

Cripple Creek: 1914

Aspen trees, shiny with flower catkins, signified the end of winter.

Fools Gold Smith focused on a catkin. "I can't remember the lady's name," she said, shifting her gaze toward Jack Gottlieb. "It sounds like Appaloosa."

"What lady?"

"The Greek lady who changed people into statues."

"Her name was Medusa. Hold still, Flo."

"I know how her victims felt."

"Medusa was decapitated by Perseus. I know how *he* felt." Jack waved his arms, and paint from two brushes spattered the spongy ground.

"The Master Artist might not agree with your color scheme," Flo teased.

"Stop moving!"

"Please let me stretch. I've been in this same position for hours and hours."

"Don't exaggerate. You sound like one of your Vitagraph heroines."

"Do you know why movies are called movies, Jack?"

"I suppose because they move."

"Exactly. I wish I were a Vitagraph heroine. At least I wouldn't be stuck in one place like a statue."

"Ungrateful girl. I must be the only artist in the world who lets his model read a movie magazine while she poses."

"Here's an article by somebody named Henry Arthur Phillips. Three names, Jack. He must be very important. Mr. Phillips says, 'Plot material is the telltale dust of deeds that lies heavy behind the curtain of Commonplace Event.'"

"I give up. Squirm, run, hop, jump. Anyway, the light's wrong."

"The light's perfect. You're just hungry."

"No, you're hungry. You're always hungry and you're always moving. First you had to wash your hands because they were sticky from the sap of stems."

"You were the one who suggested I make a circlet for my head."

"I said primroses, not weeds."

"The weeds looked lonely."

"Lonely? They grow like weeds. After that, you had to spoil Dumas and Whistler's

Brother with the last of our sugar cubes."

"The horses looked lonely."

"You went to the cabin for something to eat three times, but who's counting? I doubt you've been posing five minutes."

"Now who's exaggerating?" After carefully placing her magazine in the crook of a tree, Flo donned Jack's bathrobe. "I've a hamper full of cheese, fruit and pasties, so I'll pull down one of those blankets strung up between the trees and we'll have ourselves a picnic."

"Picnics are for the young."

"Picnics are for everybody. And you're not old, even if your beard does show a few silver threads. Thirty-eight isn't old, Jack."

"It's twice your age, honey."

"I've got buttermilk cooling in the stream." Spreading a blanket over paint-spattered flowers, she sat, stuffed a wedge of cheese into her mouth, and reached for a meat pie.

Jack sank down onto the blanket. "You're going to get fat again."

"I don't think so. When I was ten years old I weighed the same as I do today, and I was awfully heavy."

"You were ten inches shorter."

"Eight. The cabin wall says I've grown eight inches. I wish Sally Marylander could see me now."

"Who's Sally Marylander?"

"A beautiful lady from my past. I wonder if she ever buried her horse. That would make a fine subject for one of your paintings. A ghostly white stallion galloping across the sky."

He reached for an apple. "You'd gain weight if you ate parlor house food instead of our plain fare."

"When Mary Pickford approached Biograph Studios and D.W. Griffith, he said, 'You're too little and too fat, but I think I'll give you a chance.' Maybe I should cut and curl my hair like Mary's."

"Over my dead body. If I chopped six inches off your body, ironed the cleft in your chin with a clothes press, and painted your hair yellow-ocher, you'd pass for Pickford."

"Funny you should say that about painting my hair yellow. I once told someone I'd have yellow hair when I grew up."

"Give it a chance. You're not grown up yet."

"His name was Cat McDonald and he saved me from . . ." Her blue eyes clouded over. "I never thanked him, but I couldn't speak. I think I loved him. Oh, that's silly. I was a child." She spread the bathrobe's cocoa-colored silk more evenly and tightened the bow at her waist.

Jack propped himself against a tree, beneath a canopy of leaves. "Move closer to me. I'll have to change the pigment on my canvas if the sun keeps shining down on your face. You'll look like a Negro."

"What's wrong with that? Did you ever see the Negro preacher who gave weekly harangues? He drew large crowds. When I was a little girl I stood on the corner one afternoon with some five hundred others. We all sang 'There Is Sunshine in Your Soul.'"

"Maybe I'll reproduce that scene for one of my paintings."

"Good idea," she murmured, changing positions so that her head was pillowed in his lap. "You sell your Cripple Creek scenes as fast as you finish them." She yawned. "I wonder what became of Cat McDonald. Sometimes I see his father shopping on Bennett. John McDonald's old now, and he looks so sad. I remember when he'd visit Little Heaven before . . . before . . ." She yawned again and closed her eyes.

Jack saw the mounds of her breasts rise and fall. When had she grown breasts? Only yesterday her boyish form had posed against their cabin wall or her mare's dappled flanks. He could probably trace her growth

417

by stacking his canvasses in a row and watching her figure develop. Her face, too, although that wasn't so obvious. She'd lost the startled deer expression, thank God, yet her eyes still held a hint of vulnerable sorrow.

In many ways Flo reminded him of his deceased wife. Leah's hair had been waist-length and raven-black, like Flo's, but Leah's eyes had shined sapphire blue rather than Flo's dark cobalt. Leah's mouth had possessed a full lower lip, the same as Flo's, but it hadn't led a person's gaze downwards, toward a cleft chin.

Jack recalled the morning when Flo had sobbed out her pain at the death of Minta and her green snake, Spinach. She had whimpered about a small man who'd hurt her with his hands and knees, and she'd wept until she had no tears left.

When the storm inside and outside his cabin had subsided, before Jack could escort Flo back to Little Heaven, she had pleaded to stay with him, promising to cook and clean and sleep on a pallet inside the second room, which held his completed paintings.

How could he say no? How could he relegate Flo to the scene of Minta's murder and Samuel Peiffer's brutal attack?

Now, five years had passed. Flo was the

daughter Jack would never have. Long ago, he'd understood that Leah was the only woman he'd ever love. Sometimes when his need was great, he'd visit a parlor house, but he'd throw himself under a speeding train before he'd touch Flo. She, who had never known her father, treated him with daughterly affection and a teasing camaraderie.

Jack couldn't imagine how he had existed before Flo. Her thirst for knowledge rivaled her love for riding. She had a mind like a blotter and was able to absorb long passages from Shakespeare and poets like Robert Frost. She amused Jack with silly monologues picked up from the melodrama players at Cripple Creek's Imperial Hotel. He began to use her as a model.

If she had one fault, it was her devotion to movie magazines. She was obsessed with the unhappy childhoods of Mary Pickford and Helen Holmes. While Flo posed, she read articles out loud: "How I Became a Photoplayer" or "Funny Stories That Are True by the Players Themselves."

She had never seen a movie.

The sun shone with midday brilliance when Flo blinked open her eyes. Jack dozed. Carefully lifting her head from his lap, she stretched like a cat. Then she headed for the cabin, her bare feet ignoring pebbles and twigs, her voice singing out a greeting to her pets — a raccoon called Stripes, a skunk named Stinky, and the green garter snake she'd named Jim.

Inside, she sifted through her stack of movie magazines. Some were three years old and she had memorized many of the articles. Selecting a few recent issues, she paused to gaze about the cabin. Jack could afford what he called "pretty pieces," but Flo was happy with their familiar furniture and scratchy gramophone. One addition had been Minta's dragon-decorated screen, which now separated Jack's bed from the rest of the front room.

Jack had rebuilt the roofed stalls out back then added a new structure nearby to hold his paints and canvasses. That left the cabin's second room free for Flo's use, and she filled it with a bed, bureau, and shelves to hold her books. The only items she had taken from Little Heaven were the screen, the ballerina jewelry box, Blueberry's nugget ring, and a framed rotogravure of Minta.

Last year Jack had traveled to New York City and attended something called an Armory Show. When he returned home, his excitement was palpable. "That was the first exhibition in the United States of European and American post-impressionistic art," he told Flo.

"What's post-impressionistic?"

"Colored prisms. Circles and cubes, honey, but they showed a subject. There was this painting by a French fellow, Marcel Duchamps, called *Nude Descending a Staircase*."

"I can see circles for the breasts, perhaps the belly, but cubes?" Flo had glanced down at her own body as if contemplating where cubes might fit.

"Despite the public's outrage, three hundred exhibits were sold."

"Couldn't you have bought one?"

"No. I'll have to stick to the poor man's way of collecting. Lithographs and book illustrations."

And collect he did. The cabin walls were covered with Jack's pictures and her pictures. An illustration from *Harper's Weekly*, called *A Winter's Night on Broadway* hung next to a studio portrait of Mary Pickford. George Bellows had copied his painting, *Stag at Sharkey's*, creating an inexpensive lithograph, and Jack's copy hung between magazine photographs of Charles Chaplin and William S. Hart. Illustrated title pages from Flo's books shared the wall space with

Sarah Bernhardt as *La Dame Aux Camellias*, Lillian Gish, fresh from D.W. Griffith's *The Musketeers of Pig Alley*, and Kathlyn Williams, a serial heroine.

"Hungry again?"

Startled, Flo whirled about. "No, Jack. I ran inside to fetch us more magazines."

"Us?"

"Me, then. Aren't you going to paint this afternoon?"

"No."

"What's wrong? You haven't been the same since you got back from New York."

"I guess I want to paint those newfangled pictures like that fellow Duchamps."

"We don't have a staircase." When Jack didn't acknowledge her attempt at humor, she said, "Go ahead. Paint your circles and squares."

"I would if it were a few years ago, but for the first time I'm making money. Sandy says I'd get triple for the paintings I've done of you."

"Sell the ones of me."

"I can't. Won't. They look too much like you."

"I don't understand. Is it because I'm not wearing clothes and you think I'd be shamed? Make my eyes brown and my hair yellow." She grinned. "Chop off six inches, run a clothes press —"

"Hush. I love you the way you are, and I wouldn't want your likeness hanging in some fat old man's office."

"Is it fat old men who buy your paintings?"

"I suppose. Sandy says he's sold plenty to the new wealth out in California, the ones you're always reading about. Producers and directors and actors. Your Charles Chaplin bought a painting of Dumas."

"Why didn't you tell me? May we take down the Bellows lithograph and put a sketch of Dumas next to Mr. Chaplin?"

"Do you need my permission? You'll do it anyway. Just like you keep cumulating pets."

"I let them go when their wounds heal. That reminds me. I want to pick some flowers for Brooksie's grave. She was a wonderful dog, and I miss her so much."

"If pets were worth their weight in gold, we'd be rich as Midas, and I could paint my circles and cubes."

"You said your agent sold to fat old men," she said, deciding a change of subject might be prudent. "Charles Chaplin isn't fat and he's not old."

"My canvas of Myers Avenue was bought by Edward Lytton, a rich Denver businessman. I don't know if he's fat, but he's old,

423

and Sandy says he'd pay dear for a painting of you. Sandy went and showed Lytton a charcoal sketch of you atop Dumas."

"Edward Lytton? Do they call him Ned?"

"Not that I know of. What's the matter, honey? Are you all right?"

"I'm fine. Ned is sometimes a nickname for Edward, that's all. But you said he was old. Wait a minute! You said earlier that *you* were old. How old is Edward Lytton?"

"We've never met. Sixty, maybe more. Why?"

Flo smiled to erase Jack's worried frown. She had never discussed her father with anybody. Jack believed her Minta's daughter. Everybody did. Many had figured Minta LaRue's legal name was Smith. Since Robin's demise, only Irish Mary, Jasmine the Brit, Leo the Lion, and one mortician knew the truth.

"Why don't you sell some paintings of me, Jack? That way you can paint your circles and squares?"

"I'll think about it." He placed Flo's magazines on the table. "As long as we're inside the cabin and Sandy's due this afternoon, we'll skip the posing. Sit on the rocker and hide your eyes."

"Why?"

"I have a surprise, a birthday present."

"My birthday was last month and you gave me that brand-new book of poetry."

"I wanted to give you a pretty dress but I can't reckon your size anymore. Then yesterday I went shopping for groceries —"

"And forgot the sugar."

"And forgot the sugar. But I found you the best birthday present. Sit and hide your eyes."

Curled up in the rocker, Flo covered her eyes but peeked between her fingers.

Jack ducked behind the screen. When he emerged again, he carried a newspaper.

Abandoning all pretense, she dropped her hands.

"This paper is dated May sixth," he said. "It's from Colorado Springs, and there are three gifts inside."

"Three gifts?" Doubtfully, she eyed the flat pages.

He spread the newspaper across her lap and pointed toward an illustration that depicted a woman in a feathered hat.

"The Colorado Springs Dry Goods Company," she said, puzzled. "Lace drawers are half price. Is it drawers you plan to give me?"

"I like the bird on the hat better. Choose a dress, Flo. They've got them in dimity, mull, crepe, and other sheer fabrics."

"They cost so much, all the way up to fourteen ninety-five. The thinner the material, the more they cost. I'll choose a dress from the four ninety-five group."

"Sandy's due any moment. He's bringing payment for the Myers painting, a draft signed by Edward Lytton. It should be more than enough for a dozen store-bought dresses, a hat, shoes and gloves."

She looked up into his face. "Truly, Jack? You're not funning? But that's four gifts."

"No. Only one." He turned a few pages. "Here's the second."

She glanced down at a boxed advertisement for the Princess Theatre and the words LES MISERABLES practically screamed at her from the page.

NINE REELS; THE BIGGEST SHOW ON EARTH, the advertisement continued.

General admission was twenty-five cents, but that included all the single reels of pictures that would be shown before the big show started.

Her gaze traveled to the very top of the bold announcement. THE ADVENTURES OF KATHLYN it said in large letters. Gosh, that would be Kathlyn's tenth serial story, subtitled THE WARRIOR MAID.

"We're going to the movies, Jack? Oh, my! Kathlyn Williams is my favorite actress. I must be dreaming."

"Here's another dream." He turned the page.

"Colorado Springs is to be the home of a real movie company," she read out loud. "Romaine Fielding, recognized as one of the most popular stars of the motion picture world — oh, my gosh!"

"Mr. Fielding," Jack continued, "will make a trip to the Garden of the Gods today with the view of selecting a location for an outdoor studio. He will maintain offices at the Antlers. When interviewed last night, the star said, 'Nothing will budge me from this spot until the snow begins to fly next winter.' "

"Did you know that Romaine Fielding writes and directs all his films and takes the lead in each reel?"

"I do now."

"Romaine Fielding won first prize for a popularity contest in *Motion Picture Story* magazine. Are we really going to meet him, Jack? Is that my third gift?"

"I can't promise we'll get close enough to shake his hand, but we'll try. Today's the tenth. We'll leave tomorrow. Romaine Fielding plans to stay six months, so he should be there, even if we shop for your new clothes and watch that big picture show at the Princess."

Upon reaching Colorado Springs, Jack decided they'd stay at the Antlers Hotel, a twin-towered structure whose five floors boasted bright green and white awnings at every window. A grand piazza ran across the front of the building, and ten loggias opened on to spectacular views of the park and mountains.

"Maybe we'll bump into Romaine Fielding," Jack said.

"Can we afford this?"

"We won't get suites, but two rooms are well within our budget. Breakfast is included, and we can eat lunch for a dollar at the hotel's café. Let's check in and go shopping."

Much to Flo's dismay, the new spring suit cost twenty-four fifty. But her white gloves, Colonial shoes, stockings and embroidered drawers were all half-price. Jack bought the hat depicted in the newspaper, the one with the stuffed bird on its brim. Flo didn't want to hurt his feelings but she hated the hat. The bird's glassy eyes and bright feathers looked so real, so dead.

They left their packages with the hotel doorman and stood in line in front of the Princess Theatre, both enjoying huge scoops

428

of ice cream from a paper cup.

Then they stood in line again for the second show.

"That's enough," Jack said, after they emerged from the theater. "We skipped lunch. Aren't you hungry?"

"I'll never eat again. I want to be as slender as Kathlyn Williams. I loved *Les Miserables.* I think I'll name my next horse Hugo, after Victor Hugo. Maybe I can find a used copy of the book." She sighed blissfully. "There's another movie at the Empire Theatre. I read the poster while you went looking for a water closet, and I learned what it's about. Do you want to hear?"

"Would it make any difference if I said no?"

"Battle of the Sexes," she said from memory. "Or The Single Standard for Men and Women, which is wonderfully expounded in this film, is the great conflict of modern society. It is the war of opinion over the question of the single standard of moral responsibility for men and women. This powerful and sympathetic photodrama demonstrates the utter degradation of any theory justifying the husband in conduct contrary to the marriage vow. Oh, how I wish I could have shown that poster to the girls at Little Heaven."

"Let's eat."

"Don't you want to see the battle of the sexes, Jack?"

"I'll take you to that movie when your hair turns yellow, Fools Gold!"

Flo stood by Jack's open window. "Wake up, sleepyhead. It's a beautiful day."

"How can you tell? The sun's not risen yet."

"I was afraid there'd be rain, but it's clear as can be, a perfect day to meet Romaine Fielding."

"Romaine who?"

"Don't close your eyes again. What a slugabed. Please get up. The dining room's open for breakfast."

Flo watched Jack consume every bite of his bacon, eggs, toast and grits. "You're a big old bear. You fill your belly during spring and summer, and live off the food all winter."

"Old bear? Yesterday you said I wasn't old."

"Growly bear, then. Why are you so crusty? Does it have anything to do with Romaine Fielding?"

"I guess I'm scared he'll take one look at you and star you in his next movie, and I'll lose my favorite model."

"Don't be silly." She blushed, thinking how her blush mirrored the color of her new spring suit. Like Minta, Flo adored different shades of red, and her suit was a soft pink, trimmed around the edges with bright amethyst silk, which Jack said brought out the purple in her eyes.

She had copied Kathlyn Williams by braiding her hair into a bun, then fluffing out the strands in front like a halo. Her new white gloves provided the finishing touch, hiding the nails she still bit, and Flo knew she looked nice. But nice enough to catch Romaine Fielding's eye?

"Grab your hat and let's be on our way," Jack said. "The hotel clerk told me they're not filming at Garden of the Gods. In fact, Fielding has rented the Glen Eyrie estates. He's paying a thousand dollars a month. Can you imagine?"

"Are we going to Glen Eyrie?"

"No. Today they're using a studio on North Cascade Avenue. That's just a few streets from here."

After stepping through the hotel's entrance into sunshine, Flo saw that others had the same idea. Men, women and children headed for the movie site while automobiles had to move over to the side of the road. One motorbike zigzagged down the street, and Flo heard somebody shout, "That's Romaine Fielding!"

"Hurry, Jack."

"We can't make much progress in this sea of humanity, Flo. The men are practically trampling women under their boots. This is your real battle of the sexes."

Eventually they reached North Cascade Avenue. Ropes kept spectators separated from the busy crew and actors. A stage was under construction. In one corner, furniture had been placed to represent a drawing room.

"I didn't know they filmed inside outside," Jack said.

"Most people think inside scenes are acted in real houses, but the cameraman could never get enough light to make a shadow on the film."

"Did you read that in one of your magazines?"

"Yes. Romaine Fielding said it. 'We set our scenes on the big stage and when the pictures are flashed on the screen, the audience will never know but that the interior before them is a sure-enough house.' Oh, look! There's his motorbike leaning against a tree. Mr. Fielding must be here."

"Of course he is. All we have to do is —"

"Jack! Oh, my gosh! It's him!"

"Romaine Fielding?"

"No. Cat McDonald."

TWENTY-FOUR

Cat McDonald sweated bullets. Damn sun! Or maybe Peggy Bliss, another bit player, was making him sweat. Gazing past Peggy's suggestive shoulder, Cat saw Fools Gold.

The parlor house child stood between an old lady and a man with a beard.

Child? Cat grinned. The gangly filly had become a sleek thoroughbred. Her pink skirt promised a tiny waist, slender hips and long legs. Her full breasts slanted upwards. Right now her face was all eyes, but he could still admire her dark-winged brows, fanciful nose and full lower lip. Her hair was a fluffy cloud, the color of Colorado coal dust. She wore an ugly hat.

A spectator pushed his way forward, jostling Fools Gold, and the bearded fellow placed his arm protectively around her shoulders.

Cat wondered how many "protectors" Fools Gold had satisfied during the last five years. Had she settled into a fashionable house, entertaining a different gent every night until she found one who suited her needs?

Just looking at Fools Gold brought back memories. Cripple Creek. Divide. Lazy days on the ranch. The comfort of Tonna's love and Black Percy's friendship.

He should have wed Bridgida and settled down, handed Ruthie some money and sent her to California, whupped Luke into a fear of ever touching Bridgida again. Dimity would have kept her mouth shut, and Cat could have gone on playing the part of John McDonald's son.

Because of his damnfool pride, Bridgida was dead. His fault. He had tried to die too, by joining up with Dick Stanley's Wild West Show. He had dogged bulls and ridden through hoops of fire. He had taken lots of spills, none fatal. Then came God's practical joke. *Dick Stanley* died. Rodeo star Jack Hoxie took over and the troupe played out their contracts until they reached Los Angeles — city of the angels.

For the next two years Cat worked as a bit player. He couldn't get a meeting with Colonel Selig. Telephone calls were intercepted and his letters came back unopened. He had a feeling Claude DuBois was interfering in his life again. Doors were slammed in Ruthie's face.

Jack Hoxie, now starring in films as Hartford Hoxie, managed to get Cat a tryout for his latest movie. The movie's supporting actor sometimes arrived on the set drunk. Sometimes he didn't show at all. Hoxie persuaded his director to try Cat in a difficult scene, just in case their alcoholic actor disappeared for good.

The loose script called for a drifting cowboy to ride across the desert, knock on Hoxie's door, and collapse from exhaustion. Cat didn't eat or sleep. Entering the studio, avoiding the crew and players, he wet his face and patted it with dirt, then walked briskly over the lot for three hours until his body begged for food and rest. The cameras rolled. Hoxie answered the knock and watched an exhausted Cat sway and begin to fall. Hoxie reached out for his friend. Cat was only a few inches from the ground when Hoxie caught him. "If you want to shoot a close-up of this, make it quick!" Hoxie shouted, turning Cat's nose away from the dirt. "You'll never get it again."

The alcoholic actor heard about Cat's tryout and managed to remain sober, but Cat was offered a small part in Romaine Fielding's new movie, and here he was, with

Ruthie Adams, back in Colorado where his journey had begun.

Fools Gold had seen him. Should he pretend he didn't remember her? Peggy stood there, waiting impatiently for instructions regarding tonight's rendezvous. Why stir the hornet's nest?

He walked a few steps away, turned, walked toward Fools Gold. "Hello," he said, lifting the rope so she could duck underneath. The bearded man followed. "We seem to meet in the strangest places. Would you care for a glass of lemonade?"

She smiled, remembering. "No, thank you. Cat, this is Jack Gottlieb. Jack, Cat McDonald."

"My name's John Chinook now. I changed it just before I played the rodeo circuit. Cowboys are superstitious, and cats are bad luck."

"I wondered why I never saw you in Cripple —" She paused, her cheeks apple-red. "Have you been a rodeo star these last five years?"

"Yep. I see you're doing fine, Fools Gold. You look swell."

"Thank you." She smiled again. "It's my new clothes. Jack bought them for me. We're staying at a fancy hotel, the Antlers, and I saw a movie at the Princess . . ."

She looked like a woman but talked like a child, thought Cat. Maybe it was an act. Maybe the gent who bought her clothes and paid her bills wanted her to behave that way.

It might be fun to steal her away for one night. How many *young* men would pay for her services when there was a field of flowers out there, free for the picking.

Still, Fools Gold was one of the most beautiful flowers Cat had ever seen. He'd cotton to feel those long legs twisted about his body. Surely she'd learned a few beguiling skills in five years, although Cat doubted any woman could bring him pleasure. Ruthie performed from habit. Other willing ladies provided comfort, but Cat's delight was in the pursuit, not the conquest.

"And it ended with Kathlyn in mortal danger," Flo said breathlessly. "I know she's going to escape, but I couldn't reckon how."

Cat shrugged. "They'll manage to twist the plot. I've heard some directors will even place crocodiles on the streets of California. How long are you planning to stay in Colorado Springs?"

"There's a train out early tomorrow morning," said Gottlieb. "Flo was hoping to meet Romaine Fielding. She admires his work."

"You've seen Romaine's films?"

"I've read about them in my movie magazines. Will we be reading about you soon, Cat?"

Her voice was a caress, her blue eyes full of promise. Cat wanted to stroke her smooth cheek and lick the cleft in her chin, but he'd be subtle. He couldn't afford to anger her protector and acquire yet another *concubina.*

"Why should you read about me when I'm here in person, Fools Gold? Would you consider joining me for a picnic tonight?"

"I wish I could, but we're eating in the Antlers' grand dining room. I've never tasted mutton with caper sauce. You could join *us.* Is that all right, Jack?"

"Of course, honey."

Cat turned away to hide his scowl. That hadn't been what he'd meant and she knew it, though her innocent act was rather intriguing.

He turned again, facing Gottlieb. "Would you do me a favor, sir? See that pretty brown-haired woman who is looking daggers at me? Would you tell her I'll be delayed a while?"

"Certainly. I'd like to wander about the set and see what paintings they've selected for their inside-outside walls."

"Thank you, sir." Cat led Fools Gold toward the shade of a huge willow tree. He ached to kiss her, but he'd wait for her to make the first move.

"Where are you staying, Cat?"

"At the downtown Plaza Hotel, not far from the Antlers. Do you have your own room, Fools Gold?"

"Yes."

Good. If she continued to refuse his picnic offer, maybe he could spend a few hours in her bed. Maybe they'd make love beneath the stars *and* beneath the sheets.

"Stand under the tree," he said. "It's hot. But it'll cool by evening. Couldn't you get away from your friend and ride with me? I know a place in the mountains where we'd be alone."

"I'd like to, Cat, but I can't leave Jack. His feelings would be hurt."

This time Cat hid his scowl within a cough. What kind of game was she playing? They couldn't stretch the contest since she'd be leaving tomorrow. Gottlieb seemed a decent enough chap, and easy to give the slip. Perhaps she wanted to negotiate a fee. If that was the case, she could go to the devil. Cat hadn't paid for a woman since his Cripple Creek days.

"Would a new dress change your mind?"

She smiled. "You always did like to tease, Cat."

"A new hat, too," he said, surprising himself. Why didn't he quit and let the little whore go about her business? Because he wanted her. She was the first woman he'd wanted in years.

"Spit!" she said with an impish smile. "Jack bought this hat for me. I don't like it, either. I wish the bird would come to life and fly away."

Little bird. Bridgida. Fly away. "Let's find your friend, Fools Gold," he said brusquely. "I must get back to work."

"Did you hear about Madam Robin and Dee?"

"Yes."

"Cat, don't walk so fast. Do you still have Dorado?"

"Yes."

"I've kept Dumas. I have a new snake and . . . Cat, please, I can't keep up. Cat!"

Flo leaned back on her pillow. "We only met a few times when I lived at Little Heaven, but Cat wouldn't even talk about it. Then he walked away. Did I do something wrong, Jack?"

"Chinook was afraid he'd be dismissed if he didn't get back to work. Don't fret, honey. I'm only sorry you couldn't meet Romaine Fielding."

"Don't apologize. I had a grand time watching the actors and the cameramen, even if they didn't film anything. Romaine's motorbike was missing, so he's probably at Glen Eyrie."

"Do you want to try again tomorrow?"

"No, thank you. I've had fun, but we should get back. I need to feed my pets . . . and when are you going to tell me what's in your telegram?"

"You were so upset I didn't want —"

"Bad news? What's wrong?"

"Nothing's wrong. The wire's from Sandy Alexander. He's arriving in Colorado Springs this afternoon to meet up with Edward Lytton. Sandy says Lytton wants to talk about buying more 'Jaygee' paintings, and he wants the artist to be there."

"But that's wonderful."

"I'm sure he's going to press for a canvas of you. That's why he wants 'Jaygee' there."

"Please, Jack, sell him the Jaygee painting of me atop Dumas, or the one with me and Stinky. Charge him a fortune."

"If he buys one, he'll want more."

"Good. Snore his wealth, Jack."

"*Schnorven.* You need to practice your Yiddish."

"Take advantage of his wealth. It can't hurt me, and you'll be able to paint your circles and squares. Am I to go along?"

"No. If I decide to sell, I'll tell Lytton my model's not a real person."

"I don't mind staying here." She gestured toward the bureau. "I have a new movie magazine and I found a copy of *Les Misérables* in the hotel library."

"We'll still have our grand dinner. Mutton with caper sauce and steamed citron pudding. I'd better get downstairs now, honey. I don't want Sandy knocking on your door. Lytton might be with him."

After Jack left the room, Flo opened her new magazine but couldn't concentrate. *I must have done something wrong, said something stupid.*

Cat looked the same, except older. Well, of course. He was five years older. But his leaf-green eyes looked older than that. He had been friendly at first, then cold, then angry.

She looked down at a magazine illustration of Lillian Gish. "I know what I did wrong. I never thanked Cat for saving me from Mr. Peiffer. No wonder his feelings were hurt."

Cat said he lived downtown at the Plaza Hotel, not far from the Antlers. So she'd leave Jack a note, ask the lobby clerk for directions to the Plaza, visit Cat and thank him properly.

"I hope he's there," she said to Lillian Gish. "I hope I'm not too early."

Cat was late, and Ruthie Adams wanted to cry some more, but she had no tears left. Where the hell was he?

A wire had arrived this morning from California. The alcoholic actor in Hartford Hoxie's film had gone somewhere to dry out, and the studio wanted John Chinook to play the role. The director already had Chinook's test and would film the rest upon his return.

Cat had promised to come home for lunch since he had a meeting tonight. Romaine Fielding liked to hold his meetings at night.

Ruthie had bathed, styled her hair in the ringlet curls Cat loved, clothed her body in a sheer black negligee, and the mirror said she was a knockout.

With a practiced twist of her wrist, she downed her tequila and sucked on a piece of lime.

Cat could be cruel sometimes. He said she was gorbellied, which wasn't true. She looked almost the same as she had when Cat stole her away from Tom Mix. When she told people about giving Tom Mix sugar, they laughed. She coulda had Hartford Hoxie, too. All those long nights during the rodeo and she hadn't even tried. Who'd figure Hoxie for a movie star?

She refilled her glass, drank, and sucked another wedge of lime.

Cat said he wouldn't let her near the movie set until she stopped drinking so much, but that two-bit actress Peggy Bliss was the real reason. Romaine Fielding didn't hold meetings at night. Peggy did. Cat had once joked about naming Bridgida's baby Peggy, after a horse that kicked. Bridgida had been Ruthie's best friend in the whole world. Then she went and died, sticking herself through the middle with Tom Callahan's sword.

"Poor Bridgida. Poor me." Ruthie scooped up a pair of silk drawers from the floor and dabbed at her wet eyes.

Damn, it was hot. Her negligee stuck to her skin. The woman in the store had given her the wrong size. Maybe she'd gained a few pounds, but she wasn't half as big as that new actor, Roscoe "Fatty" Arbuckle. She'd met him at a party, and he seemed real interested, even waggled his sausage fingers down the front of her dress. She couldn't remember what happened next because she drank too much bubbly. She might have vomited all over Fatty. She

445

might have been tossed, naked, into a pool. She might have —

A knock sounded.

Had Cat forgotten his key again?

She staggered across the room and opened the door.

"Is this Cat McDonald's room?" asked a dark-haired, blue-eyed girl.

"John Chinook and Ruthie Adams live here, Miss . . ."

"Smith. Fools Gold Smith. I'm from Cripple Creek and —"

"Cripple Creek? I've heard that name before. I know. Cat's mother said it. She said Cat visited *houses* there." Ruthie giggled. "Come inside. I was about to pour myself a drink. Won't you join me, Miss Smith?"

"No, thank you."

"Aw, c'mon. I'm an actress and I've *met* lots of stars, if you get my drift, and you prob'ly do, you bein' from Cripple Creek an' all." She winked. "I've *met* Fatty Arbuckle an' Tom Mix an' Hartford Hoxie. Won't you come inside? Please?"

"All right. I'll stay a few minutes. Then I really must —"

"Set an' rest your feet. I used to have pretty shoes like yours, but a bull shat on 'em between Arizona an' California. I hate it when that happens, don't you?"

"Have you known Cat long, Miss Adams?"

"Years an' years. We're gonna be married, Cat an' me, an' I've been to his ranch. His mother gave me a big party. Fools Gold is a funny name. Is it really yours? I made mine up, the Adams part. My father named me Ruth from the Bible, but I like Ruthie better. Do you live in a whorehouse, Miss Smith?"

"No. I live with a dear friend, an artist."

"I once lived with Tom Mix. Can you believe that?"

"Yes."

Ruthie scowled. Fools Gold, funny name, said yes like she didn't really mean it. She was very pretty. Cat would be home any minute and he'd take to this peachy girl like a bee to honey, like Douglas Fairbanks to Mary Pickford.

Ruthie opened the door. "Cat and me got plans, Miss Smith, so you can leave now. I'll tell him you stopped by."

"That's not necessary, Miss Adams. Cat probably wouldn't remember me. He and I *met* a long time ago."

"Remember how we figured Romaine Fielding had left for Glen Eyrie because his bike was missing?"

"Yes," Jack said. "Why?"

Flo waited until the train had chugged its way through a dark tunnel. Then she looked down at the newspaper. "It says here that John Chinook was hurled from Romaine Fielding's bike while going forty-five miles an hour. He must have borrowed the bike after we talked."

"Is he all right?"

"Of course he's all right. Doesn't a cat have nine lives?"

Jack waved his arms, and paint pelted the ground. "Stop moving, Flo!"

"What's the difference? Your circles and squares don't look like me."

"Getting your anatomy right is much more difficult to achieve with circles and squares. I should have studied up on the new Cubism before attempting it myself."

"I'm sorry, Jack. Wasn't I the one who begged you to sell me to Edward Lytton?"

"I didn't sell you. I sold my paintings of you. But you're right. I don't think I'm cut out to paint prisms. It's giving me a headache and Sandy's mad as hell. I'll prime this canvas and we'll start all over again, so you might as well read me that movie magazine piece."

"It's another story about John Chinook. It's hardly a year since we saw him, and he's made five movies and could have starred in more. Colonel Selig requested him for the lead in *The Count of Monte Cristo,* which was filmed in Colorado. Cat said no. Now he's signed a new contract. It says here that he demanded his own dressing wagon to be pulled around the set by prop boys. And he insisted on Dan Clark, Tom Mix's favorite cameraman."

"Chinook's getting mighty big for his britches."

"After his first movie with Hartford Hoxie, when all those letters came asking about the actor who swooned on Hoxie's doorstep, one magazine said John Chinook could write his own ticket."

Jack sat down next to Flo. He stared at the magazine's black-and-white photograph. *Handsome devil,* he thought. But the kid's smile didn't reach his eyes. Maybe that was Chinook's appeal.

"I can't understand why Chinook's so popular, Flo. From what you've read, all his pictures are the same."

"True. He rides into a town. A schoolmarm or saloon girl or rancher's daughter begs him to stop trouble. After he cleans up the town, in the very last reel, he kisses the girl and rides away. It's a shame movies don't talk. Cat plays the guitar and sings. At least that's what he told me."

"Talking pictures?" Jack laughed. "They'll have talking pictures when your hair turns yellow."

"I read where some ladies in Cincinnati fainted when John Chinook appeared on the screen. They had to stop the reel until the ladies recovered."

"I can't reckon why."

"One story said that Chinook's horse, Dorado, and his dog, Pistol, get as much fan mail as he does. I'd like to star in a movie with Dumas. I'll bet Dumas would get more fan letters than Dorado and Pistol put together."

"Do you really want to act, Flo? I could have Sandy put in a word with some of those film fellows who bought my paintings. Maybe even Charles Chap—"

"No! Please don't! I'd be scared to death, Jack. And what if I had to kiss the hero? I couldn't let a man kiss me, even if it was only pretend."

"Calm down, honey. I didn't mean to get you all riled. You're trembling like a leaf."

"The morning we saw Cat on Romaine Fielding's set, I thought he was going to kiss me. I would have fainted, Jack, like those ladies in Cincinnati, but not for the same reason. I would have fainted from —"

"Please, Flo, I'm sorry. I forgot. You don't have to kiss anybody."

"It would serve Cat right to have a woman faint from fear, not love."

Damn Cat McDonald, thought Jack.

Why was he blaming Cat McDonald? It was Samuel Peiffer who had caused Flo's fear. And yet she had changed since last May's confrontation with "John Chinook." Maybe they should pack up and leave Cripple Creek.

After buying "Jaygee's" paintings, Edward Lytton had talked about his granddaughters, Kate and Dorothy, both close to Flo's age. Except for school, Flo had never mixed with girls her own age. She had acquired all the social graces, but she never got a chance to use them.

And moving somewhere else might get Cat McDonald out of her head.

Jack heard the echo of Flo's voice: *I think I loved him. Oh, that's silly. I was a child.*

TWENTY-FIVE

Colorado Springs: 1914

"Marylander!" Flo listened for a cough, a sneeze, a telltale snap of twigs. "Marylander Scott, where are you?"

The child was probably outside the barn, near the corral. No matter how many times Flo scolded, Marylander always found her way to the stables.

Flo took off her straw hat and let sunshine caress her forehead. Despite a soft breeze, tortoiseshell combs held her thick chignon in place. She wore a pink blouse and loose knickerbockers that reached below her knees, discreetly covered by her magenta skirt.

It was a perfect afternoon for a stroll along the cobblestone-crusted path that circled Lorenzo Scott's estate. Flo admired verdant grass, interrupted at intervals by flower beds. Song sparrows perched on a birdbath, in harmony with horned larks and red-winged blackbirds. Leafy shade trees looked like umbrellas for Lemuel Gulliver. Clipped hedges separated the lawn from a path that led to the stables.

"Marylander, if you don't come out this very minute, I'll tell your mother you're missing and I'll be dismissed and you'll have a new teacher who's not so lax as I."

"Governess. That's what a friend of Mummy's called you."

"No, I'm a teacher." Flo tried to determine where the little girl's voice came from. "There's a difference."

"What's the difference?"

"A governess would send you to bed without supper. A teacher would have you copy a chapter from *Anne of Green Gables*."

A sturdy figure stepped out from a cluster of spruce trees. "That's not fair!"

"It's more than fair. What are you holding behind your back?"

"A bouquet. I picked it for you."

Flo burst out laughing. "A bouquet of carrots? Shame on you, Marylander, adding fibbing to your other sins. You picked your bouquet for Dumas, after I've told you over and over not to visit the horses without me."

"Why?"

"Because your daddy calls your mummy's horses equine ruffians."

Marylander skipped across the path, holding her carrots over one shoulder like a droopy orange and green parasol. Her white pinafore had a smocked yoke with gaily colored stitching. Somehow, it had remained clean while her stockings were torn and her shoes scuffed.

"I don't know what equine ruffian means. I'm only ten years old."

"Ten going on twenty-one!"

"That would make me the same age as you, so you can't tell me to copy a book chapter."

"Yes, I can. You'll have no more rides on Dumas if you disobey."

"You're mean!"

"No. Your mother's horses are mean. Your mother's favorite pastime is breaking mean horses."

"I'm sorry, Flo, honest. May I give my carrots to Dumas? Please?"

"Yes, if you promise to finish your studies. Since I've spent an hour searching for you, we don't have much time left before the dinner bell."

"Do I still have to copy a chapter from *Anne of Green Gables*?"

"Of course."

"Then I can't promise. It would be a fib 'cause it takes a long time to print a whole chapter, especially with my eyes."

Why, you little devil, thought Flo. If only Marylander's eyes were as sharp as her brain.

Amending the punishment to a page, Flo escorted her charge to the corral, whistled for Dumas, and held Marylander up to feed and pet the mare.

Later, seated comfortably inside the schoolroom, Flo watched her charge fill lined paper with big print. She was such a pretty little girl. Her silver-blonde braids were tied at their ends with red ribbons. Freckles interrupted the pale complexion; pale despite long hours spent in the sun. Hazel eyes were magnified behind the lenses of the glasses she needed to see even halfway across the room.

Following a nearly fatal case of scarlet fever, Marylander was slowly going blind.

Flo had become reacquainted with Marylander's mother, Sally Marylander Scott, outside a bakery on Tejon Street. Just like their first meeting thirteen years earlier, Flo had been admiring a window display. This time, instead of fruit and flowers, the display was an opera scene made of taffy. This time, instead of galloping down Bennett astride her white stallion, Sally had been seated inside a chauffeured automobile.

Sally's husband, Lorenzo, was the bakery's owner and candy maker. In fact, he managed a successful confectionery business that stretched across Colorado, and he'd built his wife a ranch on Turkey Creek, seventeen miles south of Colorado Springs.

Due to her declining eyesight, Marylander, their only child, had problems in school. The Scotts had decided a private tutor was the solution. "We want someone who can live on the ranch, perhaps a young woman," Sally had hinted. "Someone with infinite patience. A sense of humor wouldn't hurt, either."

Flo had eagerly volunteered. Living with the Scott family was the perfect solution to her own problems.

After Jack had abandoned his circles and squares, his success had grown phenomenally. There were many "fat old men" willing to invest in "Jaygee's" work, many galleries willing to service the profitable artist. Sandy pleaded with Jack to move to New York City, Chicago, even Denver, where large studios and art materials were more readily available. Jack compromised by buying a house and connecting studio in Colorado Springs. He admired its architecture, derived from England, featuring Tudor-inspired towers, cupolas, and gables with exposed beams.

"There's indoor plumbing," he told Flo, "so you can spend hours every morning soaking in a nice hot tub."

Soaking in a tub was one of her problems. She felt useless. She had been content to keep their small cabin clean, wash and mend clothes, cook meals, pose for Jack, and ride Dumas. Once again, Dumas was confined to a livery. Furthermore, the mare shied away from those horrible automobiles. Jack had even bought a bright red Buick Bearcat.

Flo knew she'd never wed. The thought of a man touching her in any way except friendship made her ill. Although she understood her revulsion was the end result of Samuel Peiffer's attack and Minta's murder, all mixed together, she couldn't help how she felt.

That was her second problem. Approaching spinsterhood, she lived with a handsome widower. Jack had offered to marry her and continue their abstemious relationship, but she couldn't say yes. Someday he might find another woman to love, another Leah.

Sally's offer was the answer to a prayer.

Flo had lived at Turkey Creek for nine months. In the beginning it had been difficult. Marylander was a spoiled, rebellious child, accustomed to getting her own way. She used her handicap without shame to manipulate her parents and the servants. It had taken every ounce of Flo's patience and resolve to keep from giving in to Marylander's demands.

Just like Flo, the child loved horses more than anything else in her darkening world. For once her parents stood firm. Marylander could ride the pony they'd bought her, but she must keep away from Sally's "equine ruffians."

"A pony's just a big dog," Marylander complained.

Flo knew how the child felt. Her big dog had been the burro, Clementine.

Dumas shared the barn with Sally's wild horses. Dumas was tame enough to be ridden by Marylander, yet active enough to please the little girl's sense of control. Flo used her dappled mare as a bribe, a reward, a punishment.

It worked. In fact, it worked too well. Sally and Lorenzo had enrolled Marylander in the Colorado Springs School for the Blind and Deaf. Classes would begin next September.

"But she's not blind, Sally," Flo had protested.

"The doctors say we can't stop the loss of

her sight. You've done wonders, Flo dear, but you're not trained to teach our little girl how to read and write once her vision's gone. She won't live at the school, so Lorenzo and I want you to stay on as her companion."

I always end up taking charity, Flo had thought. But it didn't pay to fret over what couldn't be changed, and, for now, Marylander could still see through the thick lenses that covered her lovely eyes.

A small hand tapped Flo's shoulder. "I finished the whole page," Marylander said. "We don't have time to ride before dinner, so would you read me a story from your movie magazine?"

"All right. There's one about Mary Pickford. She just completed a movie called *Romance of the Redwoods.*"

"No, not Mary Pickford. Would you read me that new story 'bout John Chinook?"

"Open them, Flo." Jack gestured toward a pile of gaily wrapped boxes on top of his parlor table. "The Scotts will be returning soon from St. Mary's Church. If you were Catholic, we wouldn't even have these Sunday mornings together. Aren't the Scotts planning an outing? Monument Park?"

"Yes, but I don't have to walk through Monument Park, Jack. I need only gaze at your latest painting. Redheaded finches, clownish chats, gaudy yellow orioles — oh, my! If I touched your birds, they'd fly away."

Just like you, he thought. *One touch and you shy away. I never wanted to lose you but I suppose it was inevitable. Don't all birds leave the nest?*

Jack had meant his marriage offer sincerely, yet could hardly contain his relief when Flo refused. With full maturity, she had developed an elusive, fey quality — eager, impulsive, and pure. She looked like a flower on the verge of blooming. Jack envied the man who'd unfold those lovely petals.

"Open your boxes," he urged.

"I don't understand. It's not my birthday."

"But August twelfth is Julie Penrose's birthday."

"Now I really don't understand."

"Do you know who Julie Penrose is?"

"Everybody knows about Julie. How she was widowed and decided to marry Spencer Penrose. How he packed his trunks and tried to escape her attention by sailing to Europe on the steamer *Kaiser Wilhelm der Gross.* How Julie trailed him from Pikes Peak and caught the *Kaiser Wilhelm.*" Flo smiled. "Spencer married her in London and they've lived happily ever after. My goodness, Jack, I sound like I'm telling a bedtime story to Marylander."

"Speck has bought some of my paintings and we've become friends."

"Speck?"

"Childhood nickname. Speck, or Spencer, plans to throw Julie a birthday ball at the Antlers Hotel, and I've been invited. A handful of film stars will be there. Producers and directors, too. Teddy Roosevelt was invited. He attended the grand opening of the hotel, you know. President Wilson was sent an invitation, but he might be too busy with affairs of state." Jack paused when he saw Flo's eyes spark like a blue match against black flint.

"What actors plan to attend?"

"Speck might have mentioned Mary Pickford and Douglas Fairbanks. Oh, and Lillian Gish and D.W. Griff—"

"John Chinook?"

"I'm not sure about your Cat McDonald, though I did try to find out. Socially, Chinook's not the same as Fairbanks, or even Hart and Mix. He keeps making those two-reel oaters produced by Triangle. Didn't you say that he's angered Triangle by his impossible demands?"

"Yes, but he's contracted to them and his 'oaters' are very successful. It doesn't really matter to me whether he's at the Penrose ball."

"Does it matter if *you're* there?"

"I wasn't invited."

"I'm inviting you now."

"Are you saying that I'll be in the same room with Mary Pickford, Lillian Gish and D.W. Griffith?"

"Don't forget Teddy Roosevelt."

"Who?" She blushed. "Minta would say 'Presidents is Presidents.' "

Flo stepped carefully from Jack's Bearcat and stared up at the twin-towered structure. Jack had once told her that the Antlers, originally named for the deer and elk trophies on its walls, had been built Italian Renaissance style, with silver-gray bricks and a red tile roof. The August moon shone down upon decorative iron balconies, projecting from the third floor. Two years ago she and Jack had stayed there as guests, but tonight it looked different.

I look different, too, she thought, walking through the Cascade Avenue entrance into a huge gold, ivory and red lobby. Green velvet draperies hung at the tall windows, and the floors were covered with Oriental rugs. A central staircase of Italian marble seemed suspended against a wall of stained and leaded glass. At one end of the lobby was a balcony for the hotel's permanent orchestra.

Jack's gifts included white pumps, sheer stockings, and a violet gown whose neckline dipped to Flo's bosom, then gathered underneath in a Napoleonic empire style. On each side of the bodice, circling her breasts, were clusters of seed pearls in a flower petal design. Girded layers of more seed pearls cinched her hips, ending in another intricate flower on her left side.

The gown opened to her waist in back. Embarrassed by all that bare skin, Flo had ignored fashion's dictates and worn her long hair loose. Jack said it crackled like ebony flames.

Her only makeup was lip rouge and a puff of powder, her only ornament Blueberry's nugget ring, adjusted to fit her finger by a local jeweler when she finally stopped biting her nails.

Clothed in a black tuxedo, Jack led her toward the Grand Ballroom on the second level, below the lobby. "This room can handle over six hundred people," he said. "There aren't any columns, just space. There's a completely equipped stage, so the ballroom can double as a concert hall, and a gallery can be projected from the north end. By the way, this floor also has bicycle rooms and a bowling alley. If you like, you can change into your bloomers and —"

"Hush. I must be dreaming."

"Let's find our host and wish his wife a happy birthday. Then you can meet your actors."

As if moving through a dream, Flo found herself being introduced to Mary Pickford. Two years older than Flo, tiny Mary's curls barely reached Flo's chin.

"We once had the same last name," Mary said. "Until nineteen-oh-seven my billing read Baby Gladys Smith."

"Yes, I know."

"What else do you know about me?"

"When you first met D.W. Griffith, he said you were too little and too —" Flo pressed her hands against her mouth, her cheeks burning.

"Fat?" Mary laughed. "Would you like to meet the famous, albeit tactless, Mr. Griffith?"

"Thank you, but I wouldn't know what to say."

"Let him do the talking. He loves to talk." Mary led Flo toward the tall director with his heavy-lidded eyes and high-beaked nose.

After being introduced, he kissed Flo's right hand and said, "What a unique ring, Miss Smith. The twisted nugget is small but succinct."

"My ring is a souvenir from the Cripple Creek gold rush. It's a pleasure to meet you, sir. I recently attended a showing of your early film, *The Massacre.* I liked the way you were able to display the whole face on the screen."

"Ah, the famous close-up. If you want to meet the individual responsible for my departure from convention, Miss Smith, say hello to Billy Blitzer." The director threw his arm around the shoulders of a shorter, stockier man.

Billy's face had grooves between his nose and mouth. "I told David that some of the things he wanted me to do were impossible, Miss Smith. The high angles, the switchback, which David insists we need for suspense, and —"

"They're calling it crosscutting now," Griffith said. "Right, Claude?"

A short, wiry man, with slicked-back hair and a thin mustache was the only person not clothed in formal attire. Instead, he wore a white shirt, fawn jodhpurs and polished boots. He shrugged at Griffith's question about crosscutting.

"I must apologize," Griffith said to Flo. "A young woman like yourself wouldn't be interested in a technical discussion of my films."

"You're wrong, sir. I've been reading about movies my whole life. A switchback means going back and forth between the action, doesn't it? Your massacre movie had Indians fighting, and a closer picture of the settlers fighting back." She extended her arms then brought her hands together in a four-fingered square. "We see a close-up of a child cowering. You cut to a troop of cavalry miles away. Back to the Indians and settlers, the cavalry, the Indians. It's very exciting and gives one a sense of being part of the action."

"Afterwards, we must initiate the fade-out," said Blitzer. "David wants miracles."

"Naturally, Billy. That's why you have to do what I say. I don't care what anybody else thinks about it. What do you think, Miss Smith?"

"I think you're very nice to talk about movies when you could be enjoying the party."

"I'm never bored talking about my movies, and I enjoy hearing your opinion. What do you say to that?"

Flo twisted her ring.

"Do you have an opinion I won't appreciate, Miss Smith?"

"No, sir. Yes, sir. I . . ." She took a deep breath. "I saw *Birth of a Nation* and didn't care for the Ku Klux Klan part. I had colored friends when I was a little girl and they were not at all the way your movie depicts Negroes. I'm sorry, sir, but that's how I feel. On the other hand, the scene where Mrs. Cameron visits a Federal hospital and finds her wounded son made me cry."

"Do you cry easily?"

"Only at your movies. I can't wait to see *Intolerance*."

"Could you cry on demand?"

"I doubt it. Anyway, I believe false weeping went out of style at the turn of the century, along with swooning."

"Excuse me a moment." Once again, Griffith turned toward the man in boots and jodhpurs. "Did you obtain your financial backing, Claude?"

"Yes. Edward Lytton, a businessman from Denver, agreed to finance a western serial if I film it here in Colorado. He wants to call his company Dollyscope, after his dead wife."

"Dollyscope? Sounds like Colonel Selig's Polyscope."

"I know, but Lytton's the one with money to invest. He's always admired Selig's *Adventures of Kathlyn* and Pearl White's *The Perils of Pauline*. He wants his son Ned to work with me and learn the motion picture business."

Flo felt the color drain from her face.

"Are you ill?" Mary whispered.

"I'm fine, thank you."

"You don't look fine. Claude, fetch Miss Smith a glass of wine."

"That won't be necessary. Here comes my protégé, Miss Adams, and from the way she's carrying her wine, it hasn't been touched." Snatching the girl's goblet, Claude extended it toward Flo.

I'm going to spill this on my beautiful dress, she thought, her fingers digging into the stem of the goblet. *First the mention of Ned Lytton. Now, Ruthie Adams, the girl inside Cat's hotel room. Why is she here without "John Chinook"?*

Ruthie wore a lemon-yellow gown whose décolletage plunged to the very tips of her small breasts, and she had rouged her nipples. Loss of weight made her appear younger. So did the foolish expression on her face when she stared at Mary Pickford. Obviously aware that Mary would be in attendance, Ruthie had avoided competition by arranging her curls into a pompadour. She leaned suggestively against Claude while shifting her stare to Flo. There was not the slightest flicker of recognition.

"Darling Mary," said Claude, "would you play the lead in my new serial? I'd make it worth your while."

Ruthie's face expressed instant dismay. "But Claudie, you promised —"

"Hush!" Placing his arm around Ruthie's waist, he squeezed and she giggled.

"No, thanks," said Mary. "A serial is not my cup of tea. Why don't you ask Miss Smith?"

The small man swiveled toward Flo. "We haven't been formerly introduced. I'm Claude DuBois. Until recently I worked for William Selig. I helped shoot his Tom Mix movies. Can you ride a horse, Miss Smith?"

"Yes. Why?"

"Edward Lytton wants his serial to be a western. After outlaws take over the ranch, my heroine must gallop through the countryside, searching for her missing father, finding herself in peril at the end of every reel."

"That's nice," said Flo. "Please excuse me, Miss Pickford. Miss Adams. Gentlemen. My nose needs powdering."

"Mine needs powdering, too." Mary

handed their wine glasses to Blitzer and crooked her arm through Flo's.

Flo saw Ruthie reach for Mary's other arm, drop her hand, and follow a couple of paces behind.

When the three women were out of sight, Griffith looked at Claude DuBois. "You asked Miss Smith if she could ride. Were you considering her for your serial?"

"Not really. I responded to Pickford's prodding. I prefer somebody trained in the art of acting."

"Miss Smith would photograph beautifully. What do you think, Billy?"

Blitzer squinted, as though visualizing a movie scene. "I wouldn't even waste film testing her."

"Are you serious?" DuBois fingered his mustache. "How do you know she wants to be in movies?"

Griffith grinned. "Did you see her face light up when she talked about my pictures? 'I've been reading about movies my whole life,' she said."

"But she could be employed. Or married."

"Employed, perhaps, but not married. She wore no wedding band, only that nugget ring on her right hand."

"Do you think I should offer her an acting role?"

"If you don't, I will. It might be fun developing a new motion picture star."

Griffith began expounding on his other discoveries. With relish, he described the various aspects of Princess Beloved's anatomy, coming to an abrupt halt when he spied the three women strolling toward them — Pickford, Smith and Adams.

DuBois drummed his fingernails against his jodhpurs. "We were discussing Mr. Lytton's new serial," he said. "Would you consider playing the role of my heroine, Miss Smith?"

"No, thank you. I'm not an actress."

"But Claudie," Ruthie whined, "you promised —"

"Shut up!"

Griffith winked at Blitzer. "Would you recite something for us, Miss Smith?"

"Here? Now?"

"Right here. Right now."

"There's no sound in pictures," said DuBois.

"I want to see her mouth move and read the expression in her eyes. Isn't that correct, Mary?"

" 'They always say you don't have any lines to remember, but you do have lines to remember in your head. You don't speak them, but they are in your mind. Think of your lines first, and have them register the same way they do when you're speaking.' Is *that* correct, David?"

"Very good, Mary. I don't know about Claude, but my company doesn't want actresses. We want people to think what they're doing. If you think what you're doing, the expression on your face will be right."

"I'll recite for you," Ruthie said eagerly.

"Maybe later, my dear. For now, I'd like to hear Miss Smith."

Flo glanced at each member of her small group. Ruthie sulked. Claude DuBois looked uncomfortable. Was he already regretting his offer? Mr. Griffith, Mary Pickford and Mr. Blitzer smiled expectantly. Were they secretly laughing at her? Did they consider her a Colorado souvenir, like her ring?

"What should I recite?" Flo straightened her shoulders and raised her chin.

"Anything at all," said Griffith.

She could recite Griffith's poem, *The Wild Duck*. It was a beautiful ode, full of emotion, and she had memorized every stanza. But the director might think she was trying to bowl him over. Several other poems and

472

book passages spun around in her mind. None seemed right. Then she recalled the film poster she had recited for Jack two years ago. She had repeated it often, teasing Jack mercilessly.

Opening her eyes wide, she paraphrased, "The battle of the sexes for men and women is the war of opinion over the question of the single standard of moral responsibility for men and women, the degradation of any theory justifying the husband in conduct contrary to the marriage vow." She looked directly into Ruthie's brown eyes. "It wouldn't be a single standard if the *wife* could indulge in conduct contrary to the marriage vow. Do you agree, Miss Adams?"

"I'm not sure what you just said, but I ain't married. I was engaged but I left my first fiancé when I became an actress and my second when I found Claudie again. Didn't I, Claudie?"

"Yes. Now go *find* us a waiter with a bottle of champagne and six glasses."

"That was very good," said Griffith. "I'm happy to see my instincts are still astute. Are you married, Miss Smith?"

"No, sir."

"Employed?"

"I'm a . . . governess."

"Charming. But a waste of talent and

beauty. Please tell me your first name again."

"Flo."

"Florence?"

"No, sir. Fools Gold."

"Most unusual. Stop chuckling, Claude. That's quite rude of you." Griffith clasped Flo's hand in his. "Unfortunately, big-city audiences might laugh, like DuBois here, because they wouldn't believe your pretty name real."

"Is it any more unreal than your creations?" Mary smiled. "Blanche Sweet, Bessie Love —"

"It shouldn't be hard to change, Miss Smith. I'm inspired by the seed pearls on your gown, and all we need do is add three letters to Flo. W-e-r. F-l-o-w-e-r. If you agree to star in Claude's serial, he can call it *The Foibles of Flower.*"

DuBois pulled at his mustache. "Would you play my heroine, Miss Smith?"

Flo's mind raced. Next month Marylander would attend school, and, as a charitable gesture, Flo could stay on as her companion. "When would you begin filming?" she asked.

"That depends on how quickly we draw up the contacts, hire a crew, purchase and transport our equipment. Edward Lytton wants us to film in Colorado Springs, as Romaine Fielding once did. If you have family here, you wouldn't be separated from them."

Perfect. She'd be able to stay close to Jack, Sally and Marylander. Dumas, too.

Best of all, Ned Lytton would be learning the motion picture industry. She could meet her father, only he wouldn't know she was his daughter. As Flower Smith, she could furtively study her father, perhaps initiate a revenge scheme.

What about kissing? "One more question, Mr. DuBois. Does Mr. Lytton require love scenes?"

"I have no idea. Would it make a difference?"

"Yes, sir. I wouldn't care to show that kind of . . . emotion . . . on the screen. I'm not saying there shouldn't be men in your movies, but I truly believe the audience would enjoy watching the heroine save the hero."

"Bravo!" Mary exclaimed.

"An interesting concept," Griffith said with a smile.

"Interesting," Flo agreed. "But it defies convention. A heroine saving a hero has never been shown on the screen, at least not to my knowledge. So I'm afraid I'll have to refuse your generous offer, Mr. DuBois."

"Wait! I'm not certain how Mr. Lytton feels about love scenes, but I'll soon find out."

"Is he here? Where is he?" Once again, Flo felt the color drain from her face. "Is he alone?"

Edward Lytton sat alone at the banquette table. Empty champagne goblets and hors d'oeuvre crusts embellished the tabletop, but his previous companions were traversing the room like a herd of omnivorous sheep. That left Edward free to blatantly stare at the beautiful girl who had posed for his paintings.

He pictured his deceased wife, Dolly, a tiny figure with finespun, flaxen hair. A dandelion puff compared to this incredible, full-blown rose.

Why had Jaygee concealed his model's identity? To protect her reputation or to keep her for himself? Edward understood both motives. Hadn't he hung his three paintings inside a private room, hidden from his cronies and Ned?

Edward longed for his lost youth. He had been told that his appearance belied his actual age of sixty-seven by ten years. His silver lion's mane of hair was still thick. A full mustache hid the grooves from his nose to his mouth. Sensible exercise fine-tuned his body.

Inside his body, his heart betrayed him. Every year it deteriorated faster, the rhythmic contractions growing more erratic as his arteries weakened. His doctor had given him a list of life-preserving rules. He could no longer smoke cigars. He couldn't overindulge with food or spirits. Moderate workouts were fine, but he dared not copulate.

"I'll be frank with you," his heart specialist had said. "Few realize the exertion sustained during sexual intercourse. It's more strenuous than riding, swimming or tennis. In your case, engaging in sexual activities would be suicide."

So be it. Edward could never bed that exquisite creature who had captured every glittering ray from the ballroom's crystal chandelier.

He began to rise from his chair. No. He didn't want to meet the young woman yet. He needed more information. There were only two times in his life when he had acted impulsively — his marriage proposal and welcoming his son back into the fold upon Ned's return from Cripple Creek.

Jaygee could provide a dossier, but Jaygee conversed with Speck Penrose. Interrupting them would be rude. Edward raised his hand and summoned Claude DuBois, then swallowed a grin as he watched a pair of polished boots scurry across the marbled floor. His decision to finance DuBois had been partially based on the director's subservience.

Claude nervously scraped his fingernails against his jodhpurs like a dog scratching fleas. "Are you enjoying the party, sir?"

"I've been admiring the view." Edward directed his gaze toward the group DuBois had just left.

"Would you like to meet my friends, Mr. Lytton? I've been discussing our venture with D.W. Griffith, Mary Pick—"

"Who is that young woman?"

"The girl in the yellow dress? Her name is Ruthie Adams."

"No. The purple gown."

"That's Flower Smith. I've decided to sign her as Dollyscope's first star, and with your permission, I'll call our western serial *The Foibles of Flower.*"

"Is she married? Where does she come from?"

"She's not married. She said the nugget ring she wears comes from Cripple Creek. Perhaps she does, too."

"You offered her the starring role in our

motion picture and you know nothing about her?"

"D.W. Griffith wanted her, so I decided you'd beat him to the punch."

"Very good, DuBois. If Griffith wants her, *we* want her. Don't just stand there. Sit down."

"Yes, sir. Thank you, Mr. Lytton." With an audible sigh, Claude sank onto a chair.

"Did she agree?"

"Agree?"

"Did Miss Smith say yes when you offered her the role?"

"Not exactly. First she wanted to know if there would be love scenes."

"She wanted love scenes?"

"No." Claude squirmed in his chair. "She said she didn't care to act out that emotion before a camera. She said the heroine should save the hero. Griffith said it was an interesting concept."

Interesting, indeed, thought Edward. Did Flower Smith indulge in "that emotion" off screen? Or was she too pure to play the siren? Probably the latter. Despite the subject matter, Jaygee's paintings had suggested a distinct purity.

Misunderstanding Edward's silence, Claude said, "We don't have to engage her, sir. Most women would give *anything* to appear in your serial. For example, Ruthie Adams, the yellow dress —"

"Miss Smith has a point. We don't want our motion pictures to be the same as all the others, do we?"

"No, sir."

"Did you mention a salary?"

"No, but we wouldn't have to pay her a great deal. She seems very talented and says she can ride a horse, but —"

"Dollyscope will not stint on salaries or production costs. I'll instruct Ned, but I want you to handle all the details. If we need to increase our budget, my accounting firm must be notified."

"Yes, sir."

"Enough of this lollygagging, DuBois. Your job is to circulate and spread the word about Dollyscope. I believe I see William S. Hart talking with our hostess, Julia Penrose. If we can steal Flower Smith from under D.W. Griffith's nose, perhaps we can lure Hart away from Thomas Ince."

Claude swallowed. "You know a lot about the movie business, Mr. Lytton."

"I make it my business to learn everything I can before investing. By the way, the next time you're invited to an important social gathering, wear proper evening attire."

"Yes, sir."

After watching the boots and jodhpurs scurry away, Edward stood. Then he strolled toward Jaygee. Flower Smith now stood by the artist's side.

"And he offered me the starring role," she said. "I couldn't accept, of course."

"Of course." Jack sighed audibly. "Hello, Edward."

"Good evening, Jaygee. Would you be kind enough to introduce me to your lovely companion?"

"Edward Lytton, this is Miss Smith. Honey, this is Edward Lytton, a patron of the arts."

Edward noted the omission of her first name. Shaking her hand, he felt her arm tremble. Was she embarrassed by the paintings? He should have arranged a more discreet introduction. Too late now. "I'm pleased to meet you, Miss Smith. Flower Smith, I believe."

"Flower is a *nom de theatre*, bestowed upon me by Mr. D.W. Griffith. My given name is Fools Gold. In French it would be *Folle d'or* and in Spanish . . . *Tonto de Oro*, I suppose. At least that would be a literal translation."

"You speak French and Spanish?"

"A little of both, Mr. Lytton. I have been educated as befits a Denver heiress." Flo

481

sneaked a peek at Jack, but he just stood there, his fingers cradling his chin.

"Denver heiress," Edward echoed. "I reside in Denver. Perhaps I've met your father."

"Perhaps."

"Who is your father?"

"His name is Edouard."

"French for Edward. And his last name?"

"Smith, of course. His mother, the daughter of a *Grand-duc,* was French. His father was an American from Colorado. My grandparents met in France. It was very romantic. They had many daughters, but Edouard was their only son."

"Does your father still live in Denver?"

For the briefest moment, Flo hesitated. "No, Mr. Lytton. Papa returned to France. He inherited the estates from his mother's father, the *Grand-duc.* My mother is deceased, so I decided to remain in Colorado under the supervision of my aunt, Sally Scott, and my Uncle Jack."

"And who, may I inquire, is your Uncle Jack?"

"You know him by his alias, Jaygee. Uncle Jack's deceased wife, Leah, was one of my grandparent's many daughters. Have I completely baffled you?"

"Yes," said Jack.

"I am intrigued rather than baffled," Edward said at the same time.

Now it all makes sense, he thought. *That's why Jaygee kept her identity a secret. He wouldn't want the world to know that his kin, the granddaughter of a French aristocrat no less, modeled nude. She sure had grit to pose that way.*

Jaygee's paintings didn't do her justice. They didn't quite capture the mischief in those dark-blue eyes. The girl was an aristocrat all right. It showed in every word, every royal gesture. But she was also pure Colorado, from her nugget ring to the golden hue of her complexion.

"I begged Papa to leave France," she said with a sob, "but he insisted on staying . . . fighting . . ."

"Please don't cry." Edward reached into his pocket for a handkerchief.

Flo accepted the monogrammed white linen and dabbed at her wet eyes. Mr. Griffith had asked if she could cry on command. She could. Bless "Uncle Jack" for not giving her away. She'd explain later. Perhaps, by then, she'd concoct a plausible explanation. Meanwhile, she must get rid of Jack. If she didn't, she could never successfully pull off this familial masquerade.

"I feel faint," she said.

483

Both men stepped forward.

"Jaygee, help me escort your niece from this stuffy room."

"Please, Mr. Lytton, Spencer Penrose is such an important patron. Uncle Jack must stay here. Perhaps some fresh air. I'm so ashamed."

"You need not feel ashamed. We were discussing a painful subject. Lean on me, Miss Smith. To others it will appear as though we are taking a stroll. Or would you prefer to sit?"

"Yes, honey, sit down."

Flo had a moment of sincere contrition at Jack's concerned expression. Didn't he realize she was playing a role? Sure he did. He knew she had no father fighting in France. Yet she had convinced him that she was upset. The art of acting wasn't difficult at all.

She stared into Jack's eyes. "I'm supposed to join Miss Pickford at the buffet table. Would you tell her I'll be delayed?"

At his nod, Flo squeezed out a strained smile. She watched him walk away then switched her focus to Edward, who immediately said, "May I fetch you a glass of wine, Miss Smith?"

"No, Mr. Lytton, thank you just the same. Please remove your arm from my waist.

People will gossip if you hold me in such a personal manner."

"Poppycock! I'm old enough to be your grandfather."

"Are you married, sir? Do you have children?"

"My wife is deceased. I have a son —"

"Is he here?" She felt her heart rise and beat against the base of her throat.

"No. Ned's in Denver."

"Your son was named for you. How proud you must be."

"Miss Smith, you appear flushed. Are you all right?"

"I'm still a bit woozy. Perhaps that breath of fresh air?"

"Let me escort you outside."

"Only if you call me Flo."

"I prefer Flower. When I first saw you, I compared you to a lovely rose."

"How sweet, Mr. Lytton."

"Please call me Edward."

"I have a confession to make, Edward." She looked down, hiding her eyes. "I feel . . . I honestly feel as if I've known you my whole life."

TWENTY-SIX

"I had to make up something on the spot," said Flo, "and I had to invent a story Mr. Lytton would find believable."

She sat on a Turkish rug in the middle of Jack's front parlor. Kittens roamed through the folds of her red skirt — Kathlyn's first litter. Flo's other pets had been set free or given away, but Kathlyn, or Kat, lived with Jack.

"I don't understand why you bothered," he grumbled, lighting his new pipe and drawing aromatic smoke through its stem.

Flo heaved an exasperated sigh. "Can you imagine the magazine articles? 'Flower Smith, bastard daughter of a Cripple Creek parlor girl, plays the virtuous heroine in Dollyscope's first motion picture.'"

"Before Lytton appeared, you were shrugging off DuBois's offer. One year ago you became frantic at the thought of starring in a movie."

"One year ago I became upset at the idea of performing love scenes. But Edward has accepted my concept of the heroine saving the hero. If Flower wants to initiate a tender moment —"

"Edward? What happened to Mr. Lytton?"

Flo placed the kittens close to Kat's belly. "Edward treats me with the utmost respect and seems impressed by my aristocratic background."

Jack towered above her, his pipe making exclamation points in the air. "Do you know anything at all about Edward Lytton? Do you know of his reputation as a womanizer? Are you aware that he always gets his own way? He even acquired my paintings, despite my sworn vow not to sell them."

"Are you fussed because of the paintings? Edward promised he'd return them to you, if that is my desire."

"He doesn't need my paintings when he has the flesh-and-blood model. Why can't you see that? He's biding his time, fishing, until he can lure you to his bed."

Rising, she faced Jack. "Edward can never 'lure me to his bed.' His heart is impaired, and making love would kill him. He confessed that fact two nights after the Penrose Ball, while we were dining at the Cheyenne Mountain Country Club."

"And you believed him?"

"Why would he lie? He even offered to introduce me to his younger associates, as if a lover was what I wanted."

"What *do* you want?"

What did she want? A fair question. Perhaps she wanted to exploit Edward's interest in a vague manner of revenge. Hadn't he held a financial whip over her father's head? A whip that had caused Ned to abandon Blueberry?

"I want to be a movie heroine," she said. "But I must be in control. If I control Edward, he'll control Claude DuBois."

"Lytton, like most men, is controlled by a certain portion of his anatomy."

Flo stepped forward and pressed her face against Jack's shirt. "Please don't be angry."

With an almost violent gesture, he pushed her away. Then he sat in his chair and fumbled for a match to relight his pipe.

She stumbled a few steps backwards, surprised. Why had Jack responded that way? Why were his eyes so cold?

"It was a mistake moving to Colorado Springs," he said. "You've learned how to use your beauty as a weapon. I never realized it until now, but you've absorbed more than French and Spanish from the inmates at Little Heaven."

"That's not fair!"

"Be careful, Flo. You have Lytton wound around your pretty finger, but weapons are dangerous. A gun can misfire, and a sword — no matter how blunted — can still slash."

She mumbled something about the water closet, and fled from the parlor. How dare Jack speak to her that way! For years she had cleaned his cabin, washed his clothes, cooked his meals, and posed for endless hours, expecting nothing in return. But she had forgotten that Jack was a man, and all men were the same. *Bulls is bulls.*

Entering the bathroom, she saw her face reflected in the mirror. She couldn't see any definitive resemblance to Edward Lytton, except perhaps the cleft in her chin, but she did see something else. Her complexion was unblemished, her nose and mouth well defined. Her eyes were very blue, framed by inky lashes. If her face had belonged to another woman, Flo would have thought: *How beautiful.*

Minta and Blueberry had used their beauty to gain advantages, but they hadn't aimed high enough. They had followed their hearts rather than their heads. No man would ever wield that kind of power over "Flower Smith."

She remembered her reunion with Cat

McDonald two years ago, and his words suddenly became crystal clear. A nighttime picnic. A new dress and hat. His voice syrupy, his demeanor decidedly *un*spiritual. Cat had been negotiating a fee. How could she have been so naive?

"I'll get Edward to borrow John Chinook from Triangle and costar him in one of Flower's movies," she told her reflection. "Our next meeting will be very different. I'll have Cat on his knees, begging for my favors, and he'll offer more than lemonade or a new hat."

What had Jack just said? Something about Edward fishing and luring her to his bed. Well, Flower Smith would do the fishing. She'd bait her hook, reel in her catch, and let Cat McDonald flop on the ground, gasping for air.

Edward's "sword" *was* blunted. He hadn't lied. After she had scorned his younger-associates offer, he'd remained in Colorado Springs, turning his Antlers suite into an office. They had supped together two evenings. As he escorted her through the plush dining rooms, Flo had sensed Edward's pride of ownership. Jack was mistaken. Control wasn't achieved by pandering to one portion of a man's anatomy. Edward's *ego* was Flo's advantage.

But Jack had an ego, too. Didn't all men? And Flo needed him to play the part of her uncle. Returning to the parlor, she saw that he still sat in his armchair, his mouth set in a sulk. He was no longer the amenable friend who protected her from thunderstorms and laughed with her over movie magazines. If she had changed, so had he. She had grown up and he didn't like it. Did he want her to remain frozen in one graven image, like Leah?

She took a few uncertain steps forward, planning to sit on Jack's lap and smooth the scowl from his brow. Then she remembered his violent gesture, pushing her away.

Thank God she had never told him the name of her real mother and father. Covering her face with her hands, she sobbed audibly.

"Flo?"

"Leave me alone."

"Don't cry, honey. I didn't mean what I said before. I was jealous of a man old enough to be your grandfather. Isn't that insane? Do you feel faint?"

"I never faint."

"And you rarely cry. I'm sorry."

"No, *I'm* sorry." She smiled through her tears, but her lower lip quivered anew.

"Here, have a caramel. There's a box of

candy somewhere in this clutter. I can't find my handkerchief. Wipe your face with the doily. We don't want your eyes all red and teary when the Scotts return from church."

"Edward is collecting me, not the Scotts. We've planned an outing, a ride on the Cog Railroad, straight up the mountains. Won't you join us?"

"No."

"Give Edward a chance, Jack. You'd like him."

"Why? Because we have so much in common?"

"Yes. Me. You have me in common."

Jack sucked at his pipe stem. "Sandy has arranged a gallery exhibit in New York City, and he wants me to be there for the opening. Would you like to tag along? We could stay at a grand hotel and go shopping on Fifth Avenue."

"I wish I could, Jack, but I can't leave right now."

I can't leave Edward, she thought.

"I can't leave Marylander," she said.

"Aunt Sally" allied herself with Flo and convinced Lorenzo to play along.

Opening her closet doors wide, she said, "The blue velvet is perfect for the Antlers' main dining room tonight. The Cheyenne

Mountain Club is less formal, so tomorrow night you'll wear my gray skirt and matching jacket, the one with mink trim. Fur at a woman's neckline makes a man itch to add a jewel. Don't forget to unbutton your jacket later in the evening. The blouse beneath is low-cut and very sheer. You must lean forward just so. You want to give Edward a taste, not the whole banquet."

If a man's wealth and power were aphrodisiacs, clothes were a woman's arsenal. The blue velvet gown dipped to Flo's waist in back, and this time she pinned her hair up. Edward's gift of a diamond pendant had to be a result of the blue velvet, since he presented her with the jewel during their next dinner date, before he had a chance to feast on fur.

Gazing down at the diamond, Flo experienced a moment of genuine guilt, but it swiftly vanished. Why shouldn't she receive an expensive gift from her grandfather? Didn't he owe her much more for his years of neglect?

She sighed and said, "This is lovely, Edward, but I can't accept it."

"Poppycock, Flower. It's a gesture made in friendship, nothing more."

"I know, but —"

"I realize this trinket is a mere trifle," he

said, his voice peevish. "Your grandmother probably owned a necklace handed down by Marie Antoinette."

"Have I ever worn any *trinket* except my nugget ring? The family heirlooms are in France. I would prefer Papa return to Colorado unscathed and leave all those baubles to rot."

"I'm sorry, dear girl. My remarks were uncalled for. I behaved like a churlish barbarian. Won't you accept this pendant as an apology?"

The next night he apologized with matching earrings.

Flo knew the first meeting with her father was imminent. She had prepared herself well and was determined to remain in control. She wanted to surround herself with other people, so she suggested a dinner party. Ned and his wife would travel, by train, from Denver; a suite was reserved for them at the Antlers. Engraved invitations were issued to Spencer and Julia Penrose, Lorenzo and Sally Scott, Claude DuBois and his protégé, Ruthie Adams.

To Flo's vast relief, Jack couldn't attend. He was in New York, hosting his art exhibit.

Accompanied by Sally and Lorenzo, Flo walked through the Antlers' lobby. Her peach velvet gown had been copied from a pen-and-ink illustration of a fourteenth-century English lady. Cut to fit closely over Flo's breasts and waist, the tight sleeves were wrist-length. White ermine surrounded a fairly low neckline. The skirt, a darker orange velvet, encircled Flo's hips with more ermine.

The white fur brought to mind Teddy and Alice, the bunnies she had long ago released to their natural habitat. If only she could be released to her natural habitat, entertain the Lytton family inside Jack's snug cabin. Flo straightened her shoulders and raised her chin. She must never forget that *she* was a Lytton.

Sally had suggested an intricate hairstyle, one that would complement the gown's elegance. Together, they had perused an illustrated history book.

"It must be English because your gown is English," Sally had said, turning pages. "Here's one associated with Queen Henrietta, wife of King Charles, but she was French. Not that it matters. After all," she said with a grin, "you're the daughter of French aristocracy."

"No, Sally. I'm the daughter of a *fille de joie,* plain and simple."

The hairstyle was neither plain nor simple.

First, Sally combed a short fringe across Flo's forehead. Then her skilled fingers drew Flo's hair into a coiled plait, worn high, decorated with tiny white silk flowers.

I'm all grown up and my hair never did turn yellow, Flo thought, admiring Sally's blonde chignon. *But at least I'm prepared to meet Nugget Ned Lytton.*

When she did, it was one of the biggest disappointments in her whole life.

Her father looked older than her grandfather!

The white shirt beneath Ned's suit jacket barely contained his stomach. Thin strands of hair had been combed forward, like a Roman Emperor, to hide his balding forehead. His cleft chin had blurred into a layered neck, where a bow tie wobbled precariously. His nose, cheeks and jowls were puffy. Reddish veins crisscrossed just below the skin's surface.

He kissed the back of Flo's right hand, and momentarily her heart skipped a beat. Would he recognize his nugget ring? Why hadn't she slipped it from her finger? Perhaps she had wanted to challenge his memory.

But he wasn't focusing on the ring. His lips were too busy devouring her knuckles. She drew back, resisting the urge to wipe her hands on her skirt.

Why had Blueberry loved this bloated rogue?

Standing amidst the green-and-ivory splendor of the Antlers' main dining room, Flo remembered Minta's words: "Nugget Ned would capture a woman's heart with a snap of his fingers, but he had a roving eye."

Now his roving eye lingered on the white fur at Flo's neckline. Repressing the impulse to slap his face, she turned toward Johanna, whose gown was hopelessly out of date, its heavy material adding to her considerable bulk. If Flo had dressed like a fourteenth-century English maiden, Johanna preferred America's Civil War era. Her full skirts were extended over layers of hoops and petticoats, and Flo wondered how she could stand so motionless without sinking to the floor in a puddle of gold brocade.

Perspiration beaded Johanna's brow while rivulets trickled through her gray-brown curls, bunched together at both sides of her full-moon face. She had small, pout-puckered lips beneath a thin line of facial hair. Her dark eyes were beautiful but soulful, like a basset hound puppy.

"Steven was so disappointed he had to stay at home," she said to Edward. "He misses his favorite grandfather."

"And I miss the lad. I'll make it up to him. Perhaps a new pony, eh?"

"Steven is your oldest child, Mrs. Lytton?"

"No, Miss Smith, my youngest. He was christened Edward Steven but we call him Steven. He's ten. Kate's around your age. Dorothy's nineteen. Dear me! Time passes so quickly, doesn't it? Only yesterday Kate and Dorothy played with dolls. Kate still plays with dolls . . ." As Johanna's voice trailed off, a crater-shaped crease dimpled her forehead.

Flo's mind raced. Kate was her age. So Ned had abandoned Blueberry to marry Johanna and make Kate legitimate. Dorothy, named for Dolly. Edward Steven, the heir. All tied up in one neat package.

Why had Ned looked so startled when Johanna mentioned Kate? His face had assumed an expression Flo couldn't decipher. He hadn't looked that way when Johanna talked about his other children.

Before she could evaluate Ned's reaction any further, Ruthie Adams arrived. Dressed in the same lemon-yellow gown she had worn at the Penrose Ball, she gushed and giggled over Edward. When he didn't respond, she shifted her attention to Ned.

A servile Claude DuBois ignored Ruthie's behavior and hovered by Edward's side.

498

Claude wore an oversized tuxedo, obviously rented. He'd rolled up the sleeves and pant legs but the white waistcoat sagged below his skinny flanks. Now Flo understood why the director preferred jodhpurs. They gave him thighs.

"You said to dress formal for social events, Mr. Lytton," Claude muttered, eyeballing the other men's dark suits.

Spencer and Julia Penrose had declined the invitation with regret — they had a previous engagement. Edward and his seven guests sat around the finely laid table. A waiter popped the cork on a bottle of champagne.

DuBois immediately rose from his chair. "Flower signed her contract today, so I want to propose a toast. Here's to Dollyscope Productions and our success with *Foibles*."

While Ned signaled a waiter and ordered whiskey, Edward lifted his crystal champagne goblet. "Here's to Flower Smith, the star who will ensure the success of our company."

Seated on his right, Flo inhaled fizzy bubbles.

Claude still stood. "Of course we must drink to Flower," he said. "We have our first script and I can't wait to begin. Flower can even use her own mare, though I suggested a name change. The audience wouldn't understand Dumas. They prefer simple names like Pinto Ben or Dorado or Tony. Maybe we should name Dumas for Flower's ring. Call her Nugget."

"They called me Nugget Ned when I dug for gold in Cripple Creek," slurred Ned from the foot of the table.

"Oh, you naughty boy. You're drinkin' whiskey. Can I have a taste?" Without waiting for a reply, Ruthie seized Ned's glass and drank, leaving lip-rouge smears on the crystal's rim.

Claude unclasped her fingers from the goblet. For a moment he seemed to contemplate pouring its contents into the centerpiece of roses and chrysanthemums. But he merely leaned across Ruthie and placed the glass at Ned's elbow.

Flo wondered why DuBois kept such a ninny under his wing. He wasn't attractive, yet his director's status should have warranted any number of women. Maybe Ruthie had a hold on him, something from his past. Was Cat the connection?

Edward summoned the waiter, nodded toward Ned's glass, raised two fingers. "If anyone else prefers a different beverage, please feel free to order at your convenience."

"I would enjoy a bottle of that medicinal mineral water from Manitou Springs, Edward." Johanna swiveled her face to the right. "I understand you make candy, Mr. Scott."

"Yes, Mrs. Lytton. In fact, I own a shop on Tejon Street, not far from the Antlers. If you visit my confectionery before your train leaves for Denver, I'll give you a gift selection."

Johanna licked her lips. "Perhaps a few treats for the children. Do you have children, Mr. Scott?"

From her seat on Edward's left, Sally said, "We have a little girl. Her name is Marylander. She's ten."

"The same age as Steven. I shall have to tell him all about her. Marylander's an uncommon name."

"It was my maiden name, Mrs. Lytton."

Flo dipped her spoon into her soup and looked toward the end of the table. "Did everybody in Cripple Creek call you Nugget Ned, Mr. Lytton?"

"Yes. Pseudonyms were an element of the time. I recall a man named Preacher and a woman named Leo the Lion. Maybe we should consider a lion for Dollyscope's logotype. It could roar before the movie begins."

Claude shook his head. "A lion might frighten people, especially children."

"Mr. Lytton, did you ever meet a lady named . . . Minta LaRue?" Flo had meant to say Blueberry, but while Ned might be dissipated, he wasn't dense. Surely he'd remember Blueberry.

"I don't recall the name LaRue, but I met many odd people. For example, Preacher wasn't a preacher and some professor fellow was illiterate."

The waiter collected the soup dishes, replacing them with small plates for salmon and boiled Philadelphia chicken in cream sauce.

"Minta's story is very sad," said Flo, ignoring the appetizer. "She fell in love, but her so-called gentleman abandoned her and she died in childbirth."

"Oh, that *is* a sad story." Johanna sniffled.

"Perhaps," said Flo, "we might script Minta's story for Dollyscope's first full-length motion picture."

"It would never work." Claude dabbed at his sleeve with a napkin, trying to remove a blob of cream sauce. "The public wants happy endings."

"What do you think, Mr. Lytton?"

"Please call me Ned, Miss Smith. I agree with DuBois. More to the point, who would

502

pay money to watch such a common theme?"

"I would," Johanna said. "Was Minta married, Miss Smith? Did her husband betray her?"

"Yes. He was able to pull the wool over her eyes because she loved him. I'm not sure they were legally wed, but I believe her gentleman swore fidelity."

"And she believed him?"

"Yes, Ned, she did."

"Then she was a stupid chit and could never be a Dollyscope heroine."

The waiter served the entrée — veal curry, peach fritters in wine sauce, stewed tomatoes and succotash. So far, Flo had not tasted one bite of her celebration dinner.

Edward didn't know the reason for her lack of appetite, but he thought it might be Ned's crude rebuttal. After all, Flower had eagerly offered her movie idea for Ned's consideration. Later, in private, Edward would chastise his son, insist Ned use more tact.

"I've heard that Sheena Owens wears false eyelashes for her role of Princess Beloved in D.W. Griffith's *Intolerance*," Sally said, in an obvious attempt to change the subject. "Is that true, Flower?"

"Yes. Sheena's lashes were created by a

wig maker who wove human hair through the warp of thin gauze. Every day two small pieces were cut from the end of a gauze strip and gummed to Sheena's eyelids. We shall have to try that trick, Edward."

"Poppycock! Your own lashes are so long and thick, they nearly hide the blue of your eyes."

"So what? Blue, brown, movies ain't made in color." Ruthie dropped her empty whiskey glass and hugged her stomach. "I don't feel good."

Sally stood up. "I need to powder my nose. Miss Adams, would you accompany me?"

"Where?"

"The water closet, you idiot." DuBois scowled. When the two women were out of earshot, he said, "I'm sorry, Mr. Lytton."

"Wait in the lobby, Claude. I prefer Miss Adams not grace our table again."

Ned jumped to his feet. "I'll escort Miss Adams to her room, Father."

"Sit down, Ned. I have an important announcement. On second thought, I shall state my intentions after Mrs. Scott returns, perhaps over dessert and brandy."

"Then I'll be here. I shouldn't be gone more than ten minutes." Ned walked swiftly through the dining room, toward the lobby.

"Maybe I should help," Johanna said. "I've watched Nanny nurse the children. Except for the whooping cough, Kate was never ill. Dorothy had migraines. Steven was a sickly child. Earaches."

"I believe Ned has the situation well in hand, my dear." Edward sounded composed, but when he raised his fluted goblet, Flo saw his fingers press hard against the glass.

"On second thought," Johanna said, "Miss Adams could be contagious and I wouldn't want to put myself at risk."

Contagious? Flo's eyes implored the ceiling. *Lord have mercy!*

Sally returned, and the rest of the meal continued, with inconsequential chatter about unusual movie techniques. Lorenzo said he'd make a taffy display for the premiere of the first Flower Smith serial.

Johanna placed her linen napkin over her empty plate. "Where's Ned? Why hasn't he come back yet?"

"Ned probably met a former business acquaintance and joined him for a drink," Edward said smoothly.

Flo suppressed the urge to shake Johanna. Was the woman really so dense? No. She played a role. By ignoring Ned's indiscretions, they didn't exist.

"Perhaps Ned had some difficulty with Miss Adams, Edward."

"Finish your mineral water, Johanna. I'm certain there's no cause for alarm. In fact, here he comes now."

Flo turned with the others to watch her father's approach. Johanna was all smiles. Didn't she notice the satisfied smirk on his face? Flo shuddered at the thought of Ruthie offering Ned her rouged nipples. How had Cat McDonald become involved with that blowsy actress? Except for Suzy and Swan, every single one of Little Heaven's Angels had possessed more breeding, more finesse, more downright good sense.

"Claude, I suspect you want to validate the condition of your protégé," Edward said.

"She's probably asleep."

"You'd better make sure."

"Yes, sir."

After the director had scurried away, Ned reached for a charlotte russe. "What's your important announcement, Father?"

"I plan to reopen Aguila del Oro."

"You can't be serious."

"I'm very serious."

"But it will cost a fortune."

"It's my fortune, Ned, not yours. I plan to sell some coal mining stocks."

"Those stocks are supposed to be held in

trust for Edward Steven, with me as executor."

"They are still *my* stocks. I'm not dead yet. Are you familiar with Aguila del Oro, Lorenzo?"

"Yes. Sally's upset over the grounds lying fallow and the stable going to waste. She'd like to find some more equine ruffians — untrained stallions and mares — but the barns at Turkey Creek are full-up."

"Your lovely wife is welcome to use my stables when repairs are completed. I hope she'll visit often." Edward swirled the brandy in his snifter. "Six architectural firms submitted plans. Yesterday I awarded the contract to Varian and Sterner. They're the ones who designed this hotel. So you see, we're celebrating more than one contract tonight."

"Do you plan to live there, Father?"

"Of course."

"Alone?"

"That is my concern and none of your business."

Seething, Ned glared at Flo. "My father will need someone to hostess his social events. Who better than the granddaughter of a duke? Did you think I wouldn't check you out, Flower Smith? Did you honestly believe I wouldn't hire detectives when my

507

father remained in Colorado Springs, waxing lyrical over your existence?"

"Ned, control yourself," Johanna gasped.

"For one thing, Sally Scott is not her aunt. Didn't you catch Sally's slip of the tongue, Father, when she said her maiden name was Marylander?"

"Of course. But only a rude, insufferable bore —"

"Wait! I'm not finished. Are you aware that Flower's given name is Fools Gold?"

"*Flower* told me during our introduction. Is there anything else you'd like to say?"

"I . . . no."

"Good. One more word and I would have severed your ties with Dollyscope and canceled your investment funds. Don't look so stricken, Johanna. I'd never neglect Kate's care, and you will always be welcome in my home. Flower, would you come with me, please?"

"Certainly, Edward." She accepted his extended arm and rose from her chair.

"I apologize for this trivial family spat," Edward said, looking toward the Scotts. "I don't believe Flower has seen Antlers Park in the moonlight, and I'd like to show her the plants my friend William Palmer transplanted here from Mexico. Would you care to join us?"

"No, thank you," Sally replied. "I hear the lobby orchestra playing a selection from Mr. Irving Berlin's syncopated musical show, *Watch Your Step.*" She slanted an angry glance toward Ned, her expression suggesting he watch his back as well as his step. "Lorenzo, would you escort me to a seat inside the lobby?"

"I would escort you to the ends of the earth, Sal my gal. In truth, I have consumed a great deal of champagne and brandy. You'll have to maneuver our Maxwell back to Turkey Creek."

"Why don't we register at the hotel, darling?"

"What a grand idea. Thanks for dinner, Edward."

"The mineral water has made me rather frisky," Johanna simpered, watching Lorenzo and Sally. "Will you escort me to our suite, Ned?"

"Why not? I'm feeling somewhat fatigued myself."

Flo's hand rested in the crook of Edward's elbow as she walked through the dining room and lobby. When they reached the park, she removed her hand and faced her grandfather. "You said you'd never neglect Kate's care. What has caused her illness?"

"Kate's twenty-one, but an . . . unpleasant

incident . . . left her incapacitated and she can't function beyond the age of a small child."

"Oh, I'm sorry."

"She's made good progress over the last three years, and we hope she'll recover completely. Pope put it well. 'Hope springs eternal in the human breast.' "

"Pope is correct, and so was Ned. Sally Scott is not my aunt."

"Is Jaygee your uncle?"

"No. My father disappeared before I was born. He said he was going into the mountains to find gold, but he never came back. When my mother died, Jack sheltered me. Our relationship has always been that of an uncle and niece. I'm sorry I lied."

"You made up your false background because you knew I owned the paintings. You figured I'd be less shocked if you were Jaygee's niece and the granddaughter of French aristocracy. We need not discuss this again."

"How kind you are, Edward. I, myself, could never sanction such deceit."

"Ned will keep his mouth shut. I've given him fair warning."

Enough of this charade, she thought. *It's time I told the truth.* She took a deep breath.

"Edward, please listen. I have a confession —"

"Hush. I heard your confession the first night we met, and now you must hear mine. I love you." He knelt. "I want you to be my wife and I won't take no for an answer."

"Edward, please stand up. I can never be your wife."

"I realize you deserve a young, healthy husband —"

"You're mistaken. I don't want any husband at all."

"Poppycock! Every woman wants a husband. However, since you do not care to wed another man, why not accept my proposal? Don't you love me a little?"

"I love you very much. But I love you as a —"

"Friend. Yes, I know. Our friendship can never lead to anything else. I value life too much, especially since I've met you. I'd never put my failing heart in jeopardy."

"If we cannot consummate the marriage, why do you want to marry me?"

Rising, he walked forward. "I enjoy the envy of my associates when you stand by my side. And you amuse me with your wit."

"There are many women who possess those qualities."

"I know none who possess your unique

511

blend of beauty and knowledge. If you marry me, you'll never want for anything."

"I have everything I want."

"After you accept my proposal, I shall change my will. You'll be my sole benefactor. I need you to protect my grandchildren. Ned lacks initiative, skill and luck. Also, he's involved with the Ku Klux Klan. Last year they established headquarters in Denver, and Ned aspires to be a force in that evil confederation. I cannot, in good conscience, leave my fortune to my son."

"Let me ask you a question, Edward. Remember the story I told at the dinner table, the one about Minta LaRue?"

"I have no objection if you wish to make a movie."

"That's not my question. Suppose your son was Minta's lover, but he was already married? If you knew your son had abandoned a pregnant woman, what would you do?"

"Did Ned abandon Minta?"

"No," she replied promptly, sincerely.

"Then I don't understand."

"Please answer honestly."

"If my son was already married, I'd make the woman financially comfortable and support the child."

"Would you acknowledge the child as a

Lytton?"

"I would educate him," Edward replied, sidestepping her question. "Now answer *my* question. Will you marry me?"

"First, there's something you should know about me. On my fourteenth birthday, a man tried to rape me. He was unsuccessful, but his attempt left its mark. I cannot tolerate being touched in any manner except friendship."

"No love scenes in your movies."

She nodded. "If we were to wed, you'd enjoy my loyalty and affection. But one intimate gesture from you and I'd leave straightaway."

"I'm sorry you had your horrible experience."

"Could you agree to my terms?"

"Of course."

"I'd have to retire from the movies."

"Why?"

"Wouldn't it bother you, having an actress for a wife?"

He glanced up at the starry sky. "Let's strike a bargain. Make your movies while I rebuild Aguila del Oro. Then we'll decide if you should retire."

Flo's thoughts scudded like windswept clouds. *All these years I've told myself Edward was responsible for Ned's betrayal of Blue-*

513

berry, and he wasn't.

If I married Edward, I'd love him like a grand-daughter. I'd make him happy. I'd inherit his fortune. I'd control Ned. What a perfect revenge.

She felt tears stain her lashes. *No. A thousand times no. I cannot wed my own grandfather.*

As if in a dream, she heard Edward repeat the words he'd said earlier. "I want you to be my wife, Flower, and I won't take no for an answer."

TWENTY-SEVEN

Colorado Springs: 1917
Edward Lytton heard his heart. Leaning back in his chair, he concentrated on every detail of the hotel's sun parlor — a trick his specialist has suggested — until his heart stopped pounding like a muted war drum.

The sun parlor was a glassed-in room with imported Indian rattan furniture. Sunbeams played follow-the-leader across potted palms, even though rain had been forecast. But sunshine and rain begat rainbows, and a pot of gold was said to be buried at the rainbow's foot. After years of cloudy aspirations, Edward had finally found his pot of gold, and it wasn't money or property or power.

It was happiness.

His young wife made him happy.

It was a pleasure just to look at her. He loved spoiling her with gowns and trinkets — a diamond here, a sapphire there. She never protested, accepting each expensive bauble with grateful enthusiasm. She refused to keep her jewels inside a vault and displayed them on every occasion. Only Flower could wear her nugget ring and a five-carat diamond that obscured her knuckle. Only Flower could wear emeralds at her throat, a silver, ruby-eyed lion brooch at her bodice. When she wore all those diverse gemstones, she reminded him of a peacock.

The best jewel of all was nearing completion. Aguila del Oro. Last week he'd ordered a bell cast by local craftsmen, to hang inside the new stone tower. Flower had called it "Bessie's Curfew Bell." Then she'd sung a funny song about a girl named Bessie, whose lover was doomed to die at curfew's knell. "You're supposed to weep," she had chided, which made him laugh even harder.

For Aguila del Oro's interior, he'd added an elevator, a telephone system, and ornamental stone for thirteen fireplaces. Jaygee helped him purchase a collection of canvasses that included works by artists named Cezanne, Gauguin and Picasso.

Billiard rooms and a wine cellar were under construction. Inside the library, workmen had added a movie screen and a high, extended projection room. Looking around, sniffing the fragrance of cedar sawdust, Flower had grinned impishly. "A long time ago I told someone I would buy a motion picture show. His name was Cat McDonald and he told me you don't buy them, you pay to watch. Cat was right about lots of things" — she patted her ebony braids — "but he was wrong about buying movies."

On the estate grounds, a swan-populated stream rippled through scrub oak, spruce trees and willows. There were cottages for the servants. An army of workers laid pipelines to provide water for the water closets, the kitchen, and three lily ponds.

Lichen-crusted blocks of Pikes Peak stone reinforced Aguila del Oro's crumbling walls. Weather permitting, the renovations would be completed by Thanksgiving.

Now Edward strolled through the Antlers until he entered his suite. He sank down onto a comfortable armchair, balancing *Motion Picture Magazine,* a newspaper, and *King Coal,* a new novel about Colorado coal mining by author Upton Sinclair.

Ignoring the printed matter, Edward thought about Claude's promotional scheme, what Flower had called a *coup d'etat.*

Last January Claude had arranged for a story to break in several national news-

517

papers, stating that popular screen star Flower Smith had been killed in a Colorado Springs streetcar accident. With the public's interest aroused, he then placed advertisements in the same papers:

"The blackest and at the same time silliest lie yet, circulated by enemies of DOLLYSCOPE PRODUCTIONS, was the story foisted on the people of America last week to the effect that FLOWER SMITH, known as The Brightest Bloom in Motion Pictures, had been killed by a streetcar. It was a cowardly black lie. Dollyscope's next film, THE FOIBLES OF FLOWER: COUNTESS OF THE CLIFFS, stars FLOWER SMITH and her famous horse ANGEL."

The public, which had greeted Dollyscope's first release with mild curiosity, flocked to the opening of *Countess*. A few theater owners canceled the longer movies scheduled to follow, playing the three-reel story over and over, collecting a new admission each time. In general, a reel was ten minutes long. Within the space of thirty minutes, Flower and Dumas — renamed Angel — had captured the passionate devotion of their audience. Fan clubs for the new actress sprang up in cities around the country.

"My fans grow like weeds," Flower had

said, her lovely mouth curved in an elfin grin.

Lytton didn't care for Claude DuBois personally, but he had to admit the ferret-faced director earned his inflated salary.

After the film's premiere, Edward had received a telegram from D.W. Griffith.

LYTTON: EXPECT THAT IN FIVE YEARS PICTURES WILL BE MADE AT A COST OF A MILLION DOLLARS. BIRTH OF A NATION COST HALF A MILLION. AND I EXPECT AUDIENCES WILL PAY NOT MERELY WHAT THEY ARE PAYING FOR A LEGITIMATE DRAMA TODAY BUT AS MUCH AS THEY PAY FOR GRAND OPERA. FIVE DOLLARS A SEAT. MANY HAPPY RETURNS ON YOUR INVESTMENT.

Griffith had been quoted as saying: "Good hair, good eyes, good teeth. These are essential for good movie actors."

Good hair. Since Flower usually wore a western hat for her role, she had created a new hairstyle. From a middle part, her long strands were plaited with intertwining ribbons. Then the braids were looped behind her ears and secured there with flower-decorated combs. Already women were placing their curling irons inside dressing-table drawers and adapting the new style.

Good eyes. Luckily, Flower's eyes were such a dark blue. Light eyes were seldom successful before the movie cameras because they photographed white, wild, or startled.

Good teeth. Flower's smile lit up the screen. Her mouth was perfect for kissing, yet no movie hero had achieved that goal. Sally Scott swore that women secretly applauded Flower's resistance to temptation and her control over her emotions.

Flower retained the services of haute couture designer Jeanne Lanvin. *Mademoiselle* Lanvin designed children's clothing, and Sally had discovered her while shopping for Marylander's wardrobe. Now, as a sideline, Lanvin originated the outfits worn on the screen by Flower Smith. Many were sewn from soft velvets or silks, and the feminine attire became a counterpoint to what DuBois still insisted was a backwards concept — the heroine rescuing the hero.

Backwards concept. Interesting concept. Flower's concept. Whatever one called it, Dollyscope Productions had become a financial success, and Flower Smith was a motion picture star. Right up there with Kathlyn Williams and Pearl White, who prided themselves on never using doubles for their thrilling stunts.

Edward's heart began its irritating drum-beat again, so he focused on the decor of his room. French doors led to a private balcony. The furniture was massive mahogany. Since he conducted business inside his suite, management had installed three telephones. From his window could be seen one of the city's most dramatic mountain views.

Flower's suite next door had the same view.

Despite the hotel's comforts, he looked forward to moving into Aguila del Oro. After all, he and Flower had lived at the Antlers for eight months.

The hotel was conducted upon the European plan. With the exception of serving table d'hotel dinner to those who requested it, all meals were served à la carte. Menus covered every delicacy and offered a variety of seafood, so it was easy to follow his doctor's instructions.

Entertainment furnished for the guests included tennis, golf, polo and dancing. During an outdoor tennis match, an associate of Edward's had watched Flower scamper back and forth, clothed in a white blouse and white skirt over knickerbockers. "Mrs. Lytton plays games like a delightful child," the associate said. "But when you talk to her, you discover that she is well versed on many subjects. Your wife is witty, sympathetic, and a marvelous listener."

Flower might be a marvelous listener, but Ned was not! Ignoring Edward's counsel, he'd installed Ruthie Adams in a boardinghouse. Johanna remained in Denver with Kate and the other children while Ned took up residence in Colorado Springs.

Ned had given Ruthie a small part in the first *Foibles* episode. She'd played an innocent victim, gunned down during a shoot-out, but the tart couldn't die properly. Lying on the ground, shot through the heart, she kept clutching her breast and giggling. After three takes, DuBois had called it quits.

Laying aside his reading material, Edward stood, stretched, and walked toward his desk. He glanced at a telephone. Should he call his Denver office manager and get a quote on cotton? Perhaps he should talk to his accountant. On March third, the damn-fool Congress had approved an "excess profits tax" to help pay for increased military spending.

Last month the Selective Service Act had passed, authorizing federal conscription for the armed forces, requiring registration of all males from twenty-one to thirty years of age. Edward's concern was for his grandson. But Steven had ten years to go before he reached the age of twenty-one, and Wilson's war would be over by then.

In ten years Edward would be seventy-eight. Still alive? He hoped so. Every moment with Flower was so much fun, he never wanted to die. He didn't fear death, but it would be damned inconvenient. He smiled, anticipating his wife's joy. He had reserved a private railway car for a trip to New York, where he and Flower would have box seats for the forty-ninth running of the Belmont Stakes. A few weeks ago they had watched the Kentucky Derby, and Flower had screamed with delight when her pick, Omar Khayyam, crossed the finish line first.

"You see, Edward, horses with an author's name are lucky, just like Dumas and your recent birthday gift of Hugo. Do you think the racehorse owner would be upset if I named my next horse Khayyam?"

"I have my eye on a chestnut mare, darling girl."

"Then we shall call her Rubaiyat."

Edward planned to buy "Rubaiyat" as soon as Aguila del Oro was inhabitable. Although she performed well in *Foibles*, Dumas was getting old. Hugo had a sense of mischief and sometimes refused to jump fences, so the new mare would be perfect for fox hunting, his wife's favorite sport.

"We don't actually chase foxes," she had said. "If we did, I'd align myself with the Humane Society and barricade the fences. Did you see Jaygee's latest painting, the one that celebrates the Colorado Springs Hunt?"

"Yes. It's a work of genius, darling girl, especially since every eye is drawn to your figure. There you are, riding on the plains east of town, your hair dripping flower petals."

After the hunt, Edward would join Flower, and they'd eat a breakfast that included bowls of steaming claret. Then they'd sing the traditional "Do Ye Ken John Peel" and "God Save The Queen." Even though the hunt participants were primarily British, the gathering always added "America the Beautiful" to their repertoire, since the anthem had been written by Katherine Lee Bates from her Antlers Hotel room, following a trip to the top of Pikes Peak.

Humming the tune, he thought about his other surprise for Flower. Shortly before their marriage she had suggested that Dollyscope hire Triangle's John Chinook to costar in one of her movies. She'd never mentioned it again, but Edward had recently undertaken secret negotiations with Chinook. Edward had also arranged to have a new script rendered — a script lengthy enough to fill eight reels.

The movie's plot would be based on Flower's dinner-party tale about the lovely betrayed woman, Minta LaRue. DuBois and Ned had thought the theme common, but common sense told Edward the theme was universal, although he had instructed the writer to alter the ending. After abandoning Minta, the hero would have a change of heart and return in time to save his beloved from flooding river waters, caused by an explosion set off by the wicked mine owner.

Titled *Heaven's Thunder,* the motion picture had every successful element. Danger. Greed. Romance. And it would be a tribute to Flower's acting abilities.

Edward only hoped she'd let her character accept a heroic rescue. John Chinook wouldn't perform the part if he didn't have equal responsibility for action scenes, and Edward knew the public would never accept the handsome actor in a subservient role. On the other hand, Flower would be playing Minta, not Flower.

"Hello, Edward. Are you awfully busy?"

"Not really. You look lovely, darling girl."

"Thank you." Flo tossed her braids. "I'm glad you don't object to a woman in blue jeans. They're so comfortable. I truly believe that one day a lady will be able to wear blue jeans out in the street and not draw raised eyebrows. In nineteen fourteen, when Dorothy Gish was sixteen, she wore blue jeans to the studio. Mr. Griffith wrote a stern message to her mother, and Dorothy never did it again."

"Since I am your producer, you needn't fear that will happen."

"I fear only for your health."

"Put your fears to rest, darling girl. I feel fine."

She tickled his chin with a braid and kissed his cheek. "Johanna is waiting downstairs."

"Johanna? Here?"

"Yes. With Steven. Oh, dear, did I forget to write it on your appointment calendar?" Flo glanced down at the open book on top of Edward's desk, where the only message read: JOHANNA AND STEVEN DUE AT NOON FOR PICNIC AT SALLY'S. Shutting the book, she said, "A carriage and driver have been hired. We've been invited to Turkey Creek for a picnic. It might rain, but Sally is so excited over Steven meeting Marylander, it doesn't matter. Can you get free?"

"I suppose I can take one afternoon off.

Will Ned be joining us?"

"No. I believe Ned's tied up in production all day. When are you going to tell me your big secret?"

"What secret?"

"The new script you've been working on."

"We must not keep Johanna waiting. I'll tell you all about it at Sally's picnic. By the way, did you read your newest fan letter?" He strolled over to his desk. "Here it is. 'Dear Miss Smith. You are my favorite motion picture actress. I would appreciate it so much if you would give me one of your old automobiles, any one, I don't care how small. If you can't, how about a horse?' "

Flo laughed. "Shall we send her a small automobile?"

"I'm sure you'd rather part with an automobile than one of your horses, darling girl."

This damn trail was built for horses, not automobiles.

With that thought Ned steered his canary-colored Lozier around a clump of brush, then navigated a deep rut in the road. He had purchased his vehicle after the Lozier stock car won the hundred-mile Los Angeles Motordrome race at an average speed of eighty miles an hour. Today he'd be lucky if the car managed eight miles an hour. Today he'd be lucky if Ruthie Adams managed eight minutes of coherency.

Should he leave her by the side of the road, fodder for the rattlesnakes that basked in the sun? What sun? The sodden air felt like molasses.

Ruthie had met him at the door, all dressed up. She said he'd promised to take her to the Cheyenne Mountain Club. Sweeping past him, she'd perched on the Lozier's front seat, but almost immediately she'd slumped sideways, eyes shut, painted lips snoring.

He'd been too drunk to carry her back inside.

Driving aimlessly, he'd found himself heading for the mountains.

The car hit a bump. Ruthie's body jerked and sagged against him. Ned shoved her away.

He shouldn't have consumed so much whiskey, but he had to match the scriptwriter drink for drink at their luncheon meeting. Without making the scriptwriter suspicious, he had to find out what his father was up to.

Why hadn't Ned been told about the new movie starring Flower and John Chinook? Eight reels! The scriptwriter had confessed all, just before he lurched toward the water closet. During his absence, Ned had left the restaurant. And the unpaid bill, as well.

Now he slanted a glance at Ruthie — his albatross.

In the beginning it had been a coup, stealing an attractive drinking partner away from Claude DuBois. Johanna consumed mineral water. Flower rarely drank more than one glass of wine.

Ned couldn't tolerate being in the same room with Flower. She looked so much like Katie, it wasn't fair. Flower would flash her smile and talk about severing diplomatic relations with Germany, and, in the same breath, bring up Sarah Bernhardt, the actress who toured the United States in Shakespeare's *Merchant of Venice* with an amputated leg. Flower was equally at ease chatting about the Kentucky Derby and last year's World Series, won by the Boston Red Sox or the Brooklyn Dodgers, Ned couldn't remember which, but Flower would tell him, along with the score.

She had even managed to get no-gumption Steven engrossed in baseball.

No, it wasn't fair. Flower thrived while Katie, who had once adored baseball, built walls with alphabet blocks, dug at the floorboards with a toy shovel, and drew pictures. "Look, Daddy," she'd once said. "I drawed a doggie on fire."

Ned scowled. With her golden complexion and black hair, he could easily believe Flower had a few drops of colored blood in her family tree. At least Ruthie Adams was one-hundred-percent white. However, after the disastrous *Foibles* episode, their relationship had changed. She'd still entertain him in bed, but now, more often than not, she was drunk when he arrived. The liquor consumption had increased her girth. Girth, hell! She was decidedly bay-windowed!

Today Ruthie wore the same yellow dress she'd worn the night they met, inappropriate for the Cheyenne Mountain Club. Didn't the chit know that? She said she was the daughter of a minister, for Christ's sake.

The Lozier swerved. Its front tire had sustained a blowout. Ned heard the *whoosh* of air from a second tire. Shit!

"Are we there, Neddy?"

"No, Ruthie. Go back to sleep."

"Thirsty."

"Too bad."

"Where the hell are we?"

"In the middle of nowhere with two blown tires."

"I'm thirsty."

"Ruthie, we're somewhere near Divide

and there's no saloon in sight."

"Divide . . . I've heard that name. Give over the flask."

"What flask?"

"The one you've got hid under the car blanket or the one inside your jacket pocket."

"Go to hell! If you hadn't slept in a drunken stupor for the last couple of hours, we wouldn't be in this pickle."

"Don't blame me, Ned. I didn't do anything. I'm hot and thirsty and if you don't give me a drink —"

"Okay, okay." To shut her up, he reached inside his pocket, handed her the silver flask, and watched her drain half its contents.

She wiped her mouth with the back of her hand. "What happened to the Cheyenne Mountain Club?"

"Unless Germany has declared war on *us,* I'd imagine it's still standing." Ned looked up at the sky, where storm clouds had gathered. A few raindrops spattered the Lozier's windshield. "It was such a *beautiful* day, I decided we'd drive to Divide."

"Divide? I've heard that name."

"You're so smart, Ruthie. A student of the theater *and* geography."

"Well, pardon me all to hell. I just happen

to have visited a ranch in Divide. The Mc-
Donald ranch, where they threw me a big
party and treated me like royalty."

"I don't believe that story for one moment."

"It's true." She pushed lanky strands of
hair away from her face. "I was once engaged to Tom Mix and Hartford Hoxie and
—"

"Hartford Hoxie? You're a damned liar!"

"Ask Claude. He directed me in a movie,
Mountain Gold. I played Myrtle Steadman's
best friend. Then John Chinook took me
with him to Divide."

"Shit! It's raining harder."

"Rained then, too. I think there's a miner's
shack nearby."

"Damned if you're not right, Ruthie. I see
a cabin of some sort on that rise."

"See? I'm no liar."

Ned squinted up at the sky then mopped
his face with a handkerchief. "Let's wait
inside your miner's shack until the rain
stops. Then you'll show me the way to the
McDonald ranch."

"Why?"

"So we can call a garage, you idiot."

"Neddy, wait! Get the blanket out and
help me."

"Help yourself." Retrieving the blanket

532

and flask, he raced toward the cabin.

Half the roof had fallen through. Raindrops spattered what was left of the rotting floor. A window had a broken pane. The room smelled of animal droppings, but someone had filled a crude shelf with canned goods.

Ruthie stumbled inside. "Shouldn't you make a fire?"

"*Me* make a fire? Are you crazy?"

"I want to die," she wailed. "I can't be in the movies and nobody cares. Why don't you kill me and bury me out back? They won't discover my body for a hundred years."

"That's a fine idea."

She looked at him through tear-drenched eyes. "Hand over the flask."

"No. You've had too much already."

"All right, be that way. You'll change your tune when I star in Dollyscope's first comedy."

"You're too fat to star in anything."

"I'm not fat. I've gained a few pounds 'cause I'm gonna have your baby."

"So what?" he said, his heart galloping. "It's happened before."

"Really, Ned? What did Johanna say?"

"Nothing. I sent the lady to Mexico at my expense and she got rid of it."

"I don't think I'd like Mexico."

"Listen, Ruthie, these things happen. I'll send you to Mexico and pay you a hundred dollars."

"No."

"How about five hundred?"

"No. I'll skip Johanna and go straight to the top."

"What do you mean?"

"Your father. He'll take care of me and his grandchild."

"You're really stupid if you believe that."

"I'll try anyway. What have I got to lose?"

Ned thought about the new script and his exclusion. "I can't marry you, Ruthie. If I divorce Johanna, I'll lose my father's support and we'll both be out of the movie business."

"I'm going to have this baby, Ned. It's the only thing that'll make you behave."

Time, he thought. *I need time to figure things out.*

"Look," he pleaded. "I'll pay —"

"Yes, you'll pay. I'm thirsty. Give over the flask."

"Sure, sweetheart. Are you cold? Here, wrap yourself in this fur blanket."

"I want a big house, like Pickfair."

"I'll try to find —"

"Wait, I'm not finished. I want my own

car and a chauffeur and pretty clothes and
—"

"Your own car?"

"I want everything *she* has."

"Mary Pickford?"

"No. Flower Smith. Wait a minute. She didn't say Flower. She said a different name. The girl in pink. She said she came from Cripple Creek. Not Flower Smith. Fools Gold Smith. A friend of Cat's."

Ned could feel the vein in his forehead throb. Soon it would explode and spatter his brains all over the rotting floorboards. Ruthie was babbling. He'd have to shut her up so he could think. He needed time to think.

There was only one way to shut Ruthie up. Ned seized the blanket from her shoulders, dropped it, and lowered her gown's bodice. He sucked at her breast while they sank to the floor.

She giggled.

I can handle Johanna, but if Ruthie tells Father —

"An' you'll put me in a comedy, Neddy, my very own movie. I'll show Cat Mc-Donald and his whore, Fools Gold Smith!"

Ned thought he heard a gasp from the direction of the open window. Maybe Ruthie had gasped. Maybe he himself had gasped.

He couldn't breathe. There had to be a solution. Edward must not know about her pregnancy.

"I'm gonna be a moo-vie star," she said in a singsong voice. "Put your hand between my legs. Oh, that feels good. Hey, what'cha' doin', Neddy?"

What was he doing? On their own volition, his fingers had traveled up her body and wound around her neck. His thumbs pressed the pulse at the base of her throat.

She struggled but she was whiskey-weak. Her eyes bulged, her mouth opened, her tongue fell out, and her body flopped like a grounded fish.

Ned pressed harder, until he thought he might puncture her damnfool throat. Then he buried her behind the shack, in a hole he dug with a rusty, abandoned shovel.

He heard the echo of her words: *Why don't you bury me out back? They won't discover my body for a hundred years.*

It was all her fault. She had put the idea in his head.

Twenty-three years ago he had dug a hole and found fool's gold. Today he had dug a hole and buried a fool.

TWENTY-EIGHT

The Antlers Hotel lobby usually bustled with activity, but today it was populated by the permanent orchestra, a solitary desk clerk, and a man who hadn't signed the register yet.

Everyone else was below, inside the billiard room or bowling alley, where telephones had been temporarily installed. Everyone else was following the progress of the World Series game between the Boston Red Sox and the Chicago Cubs.

Everyone but me, thought the disgruntled desk clerk.

He glanced down at the luggage stowed behind his counter. *Holy Grail!* Printed on the suitcase tag was the name John Chinook. Chinook was almost as famous as William S. Hart and Tom Mix, while Chinook's horse, Dorado, commanded the same respect as Hart's Pinto Ben or Mix's Tony. The desk clerk studied the luggage as if

Chinook's scruffy mongrel, Pistol, was packed inside. Then he shifted his gaze toward the actor.

Chinook didn't look like a movie star. There he sat, wearing faded Levi's and a white shirt. No ten-gallon hat. No spurs. No gun. No nothin'. And he read the newspaper just like any dime-a-dozen guy.

Cat gave the desk clerk an icy stare. Usually he shrugged off his fame but today he felt decidedly hostile. Why had he accepted Edward Lytton's offer to share star billing with Flower Smith, the brightest bloom in motion pictures?

Blighted bloom was more the case.

Twelve years ago, outside the bullfight arena, she had said that, when grown, she'd pleasure rich men. Lytton, rich as Midas, had even married the conniving parlor house girl.

Cat's sullen thoughts were interrupted by the subtle aroma of perfume. Laying aside his newspaper, he watched Fools Gold stride across the lobby's Oriental rugs.

She looked like a Russian peasant — a *wealthy* Russian peasant. She wore an embroidered white blouse beneath a red sleeveless jacket, a long gray skirt, white stockings, and a striped scarf. Over her arm she carried a wine-colored velvet coat with black-braid trim.

Rising from his chair, Cat heard the orchestra playing "I Wonder Who's Kissing Her Now."

"Hello, Fools Gold."

"My name is Mrs. Edward Lytton."

"That's not the right answer. You're supposed to say 'spit' or 'we meet in the strangest places.' "

"My husband will join us shortly."

"I look forward to meeting him, Mrs. Lytton."

Flo scrutinized the celebrated cowboy. Cat's lips twitched with amused bravado, but his leaf-green eyes appeared dog-tired. "Would you care to buy me a lemonade?" she asked softly, relenting.

"Sorry, I didn't hear you." He cocked his head. "I sustained a punctured eardrum from an accident with Romaine Fielding's motorbike."

"I wondered why you weren't in the armed services."

"I tried to enlist," he said, his voice bitter. "They turned me down. Seems Dame Fortune doesn't want me to die."

"Do you want to die, Cat?"

He glanced toward the orchestra. "It might be worthwhile getting laid to rest beneath the sod if Flower Smith Lytton fainted at my funeral."

"I never faint."

"Not even from ecstasy?"

Her cheeks turned one shade lighter than her jacket. "It would be a waste of ecstasy to faint. How could one enjoy ecstasy while unconscious?"

"Good point," he conceded. "However, I'd relish an opportunity to cause the fainting."

"That's an opportunity you'll never get."

"Are you sure?"

"Positive."

With a mournful flourish, the musicians finished "I Wonder Who's Kissing Her Now" and began playing Victor Herbert's score from *Naughty Marietta*.

"I'll wager my stallion against your mare that I'll have you swooning with rapture before we finish our movie."

"It's not *our* movie, Mr. Chinook. It's *my* movie."

"Is it a bet?"

"I wouldn't want to take your horse."

"Is it a bet?"

"Certainly. Shall I have Edward draw up the papers so you can't renege?"

"No. A handshake will suffice." Cat clasped her hand, bent forward, and traced the soft contours of her palm with his lips.

She snatched her hand away. "The stables at my husband's estate are very comfortable. Dorado should be happy playing the stud. After all, he's a McDonald."

Before Cat could reply, a boy wearing a hotel uniform approached. "I have a message for you, Mrs. Lytton. Mr. Lytton telephoned and said he'd be detained. He suggested you show your guest the park. He said he'd join you upon his return."

"Thank you, Martin." Flo drew a few coins from her reticule.

The lad negligently pocketed the gratuity, his gaze fixed on Cat. "You're John Chinook!"

"Yep."

"Gawd, I knew it! Did Pistol have her pups?"

"Pistol's a boy dog."

"Aw, Mr. Chinook, everybody knows Pistol's really a bitch, um, lady." Martin's freckles blurred into a blush. "Did she have her pups?"

"No. But she's due real soon."

"Could I buy one? I'll pay anything you ask."

"After the pups are born and weaned, I'll arrange to have one shipped to you at my expense."

"Thanks. Gawd, wait till I tell my sis that

I met John Chinook. She's gonna faint!"

Flo felt her cheeks flush at the sound of Cat's deep-throated chuckle. "What's the score, Martin?"

"Score, Mrs. Lytton?"

"The World Series."

"Don't know. Have you placed a wager, ma'am?"

"I only wager when the odds are in my favor." She thrust her arms inside the sleeves of her coat and walked through the lobby, toward the hotel exit. Cat followed by her side. "Have you seen *Tillie's Punctured Romance,* Mr. Chinook?" she asked. "It stars Marie Dressler and Charles Chaplin."

"Yes. Mack Sennett is brilliant. Have you enjoyed many punctured romances, honey?"

Seething, Flo ignored his question. A strong breeze whipped wisps of hair free from her neatly looped braids. The air was scented with the elusive odor of a crisp September day — ripe pumpkins, burning leaves, and smoke from the hotel's stoves.

"I hope the weather is warm for our river scenes," she said, glancing up at the cloud-crusted sky.

"Doesn't DuBois plan to use a stand-in?"

"Do you use a stand-in?"

"No, but —"

"Neither does Flower Smith. I've always

performed my own stunts."

"I know you ride well. Do you swim?"

She shook her head. "I've practiced in the hotel's pool, but I can't maneuver my legs with a steady kicking motion, so I tend to submerge. Women must wear such heavy bathing costumes. It's ridiculous, swimming in sleeves and a skirt. Did you know that Annette Kellerman, the Australian swimmer, was arrested on a beach in Boston for wearing a one-piece bathing costume in defiance of accepted convention?"

"Would you defy convention, Mrs. Lytton?"

"I defy it all the time. I wear blue jeans. I refuse to cover my head with a gaudy winged bonnet, even though convention insists that hats and gloves are *de rigeuer* for public appearances. In my movies, the heroine rescues the hero."

Cat grinned. "Not in our movie."

"*My* movie."

She tensed, waiting for his next innuendo. But he merely rolled his shirt sleeves up past his elbows, exposing sun-bronzed forearms. She had once admired his good bones, and now, eight years later, his body was even more substantial. Rough rawhide. No. Tempered steel. No. A drawn bow-string, ready to release sharp, risqué arrows.

Why had she mentioned wanting John Chinook for her costar? It had been an impulse brought on by her argument with Jack, and she had forgotten all about it. Edward hadn't. He was certain he'd pleased her, and she couldn't destroy his illusion.

Would Cat talk about Cripple Creek and Little Heaven? What if Ned heard and decided to dig deeper into her past? Flo knew she could have stopped her wedding with three words — you're my grandfather — but she'd gone too far in her masquerade, and the thought of Edward's repudiation had stilled her tongue. She loathed Ned but she loved Edward. What if he learned he'd married his own granddaughter? The shock might kill him.

She must control Cat. A man was controlled by a certain portion of his anatomy, Jack had said. If Flo made good her threat, if she hooked and landed a certain catfish, she'd have to walk a taut tightrope. She must display interest then have Cat repudiate *her*. For starters, she'd hire Jane Percival. Jane was young and beautiful. Jane would be the bait to lure Cat away from "Flower Smith."

Flo had adored Jane at first sight. A Divide rancher's daughter with golden-brown hair and eyes, she was a tiny slip of a girl who looked much younger than nineteen.

"I've lived on a ranch my whole life," she'd said, her voice wistful. "I can shoot, twirl a rope, and ride a horse better than Annie Oakley."

It would only be a matter of time before the young ingenue caught Cat's eye. But, for now, Flo had better walk that tightrope.

Despite the cool breeze, she shrugged off her coat, dropped it and sank to her knees. She let Cat help her rise, stumbled, and righted herself against his body. Then she walked a few steps backwards and lowered her lashes. "I want to make a confession, Cat."

"I'm all ears, Mrs. Lytton."

"Do you promise not to laugh?"

"I rarely make promises I can't keep."

Flo lifted her chin. "Then I shan't confess. Let's return to the lobby and wait for Edward there. Perhaps we might check the score of the baseball game."

"All right, you little devil, I won't laugh."

"Do you remember that day on Romaine Fielding's set? Oh, you've probably forgotten all about —"

"I remember."

"I said no to your picnic because I had other plans. Then Jack had to attend a silly business meeting and . . ."

"Go on."

"I walked to the Plaza Hotel. I couldn't wait to tell you I'd changed my mind. I kept hoping you hadn't changed yours —"

"Ruthie!"

"Miss Adams answered my knock. She invited me inside, offered me a drink, and told me about your engagement. She said she'd visited your ranch and met your mother."

"Ruthie visited the ranch but the engagement was a lie."

How easy it is to lie when one sticks to the truth. Flo looked down at the tips of her white shoes. "I felt terrible. We'd finally found each other after so many years. I turned to Edward for solace as a result of that afternoon."

Cat walked toward a Boston ivy. The scarlet foliage reminded him of blood, and blood reminded him of that long-ago day when he'd tarried with Fools Gold. He remembered stealing Romaine's motorbike and riding away from her, just as he had once ridden away from Madam Robin and Cripple Creek. But a motorbike wasn't Dorado. The bike had swerved and he'd been thrown from its seat.

What he didn't recall clearly was finding his way back to his hotel room and collapsing from a near-fatal head wound. Romaine's anger. A frightened Ruthie, promising she'd never touch a drop of liquor again, shouting it over and over because Cat was deaf in one ear.

They returned to California. Ruthie still wanted to be a movie star, and Cat couldn't help her. Maybe Claude DuBois could, she said, packing her bags and swinging her hips through his doorway for the last time. A shame the cactus nettle hadn't stuck a bit longer. Their parting had occurred just before the release of Hoxie's movie.

Now Cat stared at Fools Gold. Was she telling the truth? She had sounded sincere until that last part. "Are you telling me the truth, honey?"

"What do I have to gain by fibbing?"

"Look me in the eyes and repeat the part about turning to Lytton for comfort."

"Why don't you believe me? I swear I went to your room, and Miss Adams said you were betrothed. I swear it on my life."

"Flower! My God! Flower!"

Flo turned at the sound of Edward's call. Watching him walk swiftly down the path, she felt the color drain from her face. "What's wrong, Edward?"

"Darling girl, you're standing outside with

your coat off. Do you want to catch your death?"

"For heaven's sake, you *scared* me to death. I really believed there was cause for alarm. I'll put my coat back on since it bothers you so."

Edward grinned at Cat. "That thin garment doesn't do much good against the cold, does it? I've offered Flower every pelt in Colorado, but she always refuses. She says she doesn't want to be responsible for the slaughtering of animals."

"Yes, I know. I once had a rattler's vertebrae threaded with string and —"

"Speaking of snakes, Edward, didn't you just come from Aguila del Oro? Is the rattler problem truly solved?"

"I hope so. We've transported dozens of pigs so they can eat the snakes." He winked. "Now we have a pig problem."

"We haven't been formerly introduced, Mr. Lytton," said Cat. "I'm John Chinook."

"Yes. I could hardly fail to recognize you, even from a distance. I borrowed some of your oaters from Triangle after Flower expressed the desire to hire you as her costar."

"She requested me for her costar? I wasn't aware that Miss Smith . . . Mrs. Lytton . . ."

"Call me Flower, Mr. Chinook."

"Please call me John. In truth, it's my given name. I was named for my father. Surely you remember John McDon—"

"Edward, I believe I've caught a chill."

"My darling girl, you're shivering. A hot bath should thaw you out. Retire to our suites immediately. I'll entertain your new costar."

"Please, Edward, I want to hear about the latest progress on Aguila del Oro. Do you mind, Mr. Chinook?"

"Of course not. I'm sure there will be many opportunities to chat during the filming of *our* movie. We can start tonight."

"A hot bath should cure my shivers, but I believe I'll skip tonight's celebration."

"I'm sorry to hear that, Flower. I was hoping I might use the occasion to establish our newfound friendship."

"Thank you, John," she said, and Cat could have sworn she held back a sigh of relief. "If I cannot attend this evening, I'll send another actress in my stead. Her name is Jane and she's very pretty."

Not as pretty as you, my dove, thought Cat, watching the two figures stroll toward the hotel. *I wonder why Fools Gold shines brighter than real gold.*

I wonder why Lytton didn't wear the satis-fied smirk of a man who'd married the bright-

549

est bloom in motion pictures.

I wonder why he looked more like an elderly lion guarding his pride.

I wonder why he acts like a fond uncle, or a father, or a grandfather, rather than a husband.

I wonder if she ever tells him of me. I wonder who's kissing her now.

After Fools Gold and Edward Lytton had disappeared from sight, Cat walked aimlessly about the hotel. Eventually, he found himself in the sun parlor. A small form immediately launched herself into his arms.

"Cat! Oh, Cat, is it really you?"

"Dimity-Jane! What the hell are you doing here?"

"Well, that's a fine greeting, I must say. It's been years. Couldn't you fib and tell me how grown-up I look or how pretty I've become?"

Cat held his sister at arm's length. "It wouldn't be a fib. You're beautiful, Dimity-Jane."

"Thank you, but I'm not Dimity-Jane anymore. You used to call me Janey so I changed my name to Jane Percival. Why are you laughing?"

"Don't look so sorrowful. I didn't mean to hurt your feelings. I laughed because I once considered changing my last name to Percival, for Black Percy. Is that why you did it?"

She nodded.

"Come, give your favorite brother a big hug and kiss. Am I still your favorite brother?"

She burst into tears.

"What is it? My God, Janey, what did I say?" Stepping forward, Cat pressed her wet face against his chest. "Hush, baby. It can't be that bad. Whatever's wrong, I'll fix it."

"Sorry, Cat. I can't stop."

"All right, cry. We'll talk when you're finished."

"Is everybody looking at us?"

"We're the only ones in the room. In case you didn't notice, the sun parlor lacks sun."

She stepped away, smiled at his remark then burst into renewed tears. Cat scooped her up in his arms and sat on a cushioned rattan chair.

When her wild weeping had calmed, she dabbed at her eyes with her sleeve. "Hellfire, Cat, that felt good. So damn good."

"Don't you be airing your paunch at me, young lady. What would *Maman* say?"

"*Maman?*"

"Dimity. Our sainted mother."

"Luke said he wired you. We all wondered

why you didn't come . . . oh, God, you don't know."

"What don't I know?"

"*Maman* died last year."

Cat swallowed his first response. "How did she die?" he managed.

"It was cold and snowing, a blizzard. Papa was out on the range, looking for stray calves. Papa insisted Luke help. Luke wanted to stay inside the house by the fire — he's such a coward — but this time Papa stood firm. Everybody thought Mother was in her room, praying. She'd do that, stay in her room, on her knees, for hours and hours. It got worse after you left. Tonna . . . Rosita . . . we never thought to check . . ."

"She wasn't in her room."

"Tonna found her on the chapel steps, covered with snow, frozen to death. You weren't there when the chapel was built. It's near the house. Mother must have searched for Luke then tried to make her way back. Luke blames Papa. Luke was so nasty, Cat. 'If you hadn't made me come with you, *Maman* would still be alive,' he said over and over. Now Papa just sits in his chair all day, mumbling about the trail drive and the killing of baby calves."

"Who's running the ranch? Black Percy?"

"No. Luke."

"Luke doesn't know anything about ranching."

"He knows how to spend profits. Luke has his own automobile that he drives to Denver twice a week. He plays with investments, but I'm sure he gambles and loses more than he wins. He's joined the Ku Klux Klan. He has a woman but she's not the marrying kind, if you get my drift. Her name's Suzette, and here's the funny part. Luke has become friendly with Ned Lytton, whom he discovered at one of his Klan meetings. That's how I learned about Dollyscope's new movie. By the way, have you met Flower Smith?"

"Yes."

"Isn't she lovely? I adored her from the start, and she said she'd talk to the director and get me hired for a small role. She calls me by my first name . . . my new name . . . Jane."

"So you're the pretty actress I'm supposed to meet tonight. How are Tonna and Black Percy?"

"Tonna's the same. She never changes. I think they'd like to leave the ranch, but Percy frets over Papa and stays to care for him."

"Daniel?"

"He's taking instruction for the priesthood. A silent order."

"I'm not surprised. Do you have a steady fellow?"

"No. Do you have a steady lady friend? Whatever happened to the girl you brought to our ranch?"

"Ruthie Adams?" He shrugged. "She just . . . disappeared."

"Bridgida?"

Shifting Janey from his lap to the chair, Cat walked to the window-wall and stared out at the gray-tinged, bloated clouds. "Bridgida's dead."

"I'm sorry. You liked her a lot, didn't you? I'm sorry I cried just now, too. I couldn't cry at Mother's funeral, not one tear. It wasn't that she was cruel to me, but she had no love for any living person except Luke. She was so cold, Cat, even before she froze to death."

"What are your plans?" he asked, hoping to change the subject. Later he'd chew over Dimity's death.

"I thought I might stay at this hotel, but they're full-up. Then I thought about living at the ranch, traveling back and forth . . ." She paused, one eyebrow arched.

He could take a hint. "Would you like to stay here with me?"

"Could I really?" She jumped up, her

excitement palpable. "You wouldn't mind?"

"I insist."

"Might we pretend we're not related?"

"No. We'd be sharing a hotel suite and there'd be talk. Your reputation —"

"Hang my reputation! I want to make it in the movies as Jane Percival, not John Chinook's sister."

Cat walked toward her, admiring her honey-brown curls and dark-lashed, amber eyes. Maybe it was a good idea to install her inside his suite without revealing their kinship. Once the actors and crew took a good look at her, she'd be a baby lamb surrounded by hungry wolves. If they stayed together, Cat could protect her. When the others learned she'd hooked up with John Chinook, they'd leave her alone.

What about his damnfool wager? Fools Gold would not only *not* swoon with rapture, she'd beat a hasty retreat.

Fools Gold or Janey?

"Will you share my suite, Miss Percival?"

"I accept with pleasure, Mr. Chinook."

Cat had a sudden thought. "Luke!"

"Luke won't care, not so long as Tonna serves him a full dinner plate. Most of the time he ignores me."

"What if we run into him and he gives you away? You said he's established a friendship with Ned Lytton."

"I hadn't thought of that, but I'm not gonna fret. I'll just keep my eyes open. Right now I need to close my eyes and take a nap. I saw Flower before I found you, and she invited me to a party. She said I could borrow one of her gowns since my own clothes are still at the ranch. She insisted on sewing a hem because she's so much taller. Can you imagine? A famous movie star altering one of her beautiful gowns for a nobody?"

"You're not a nobody. You're Jane Percival." Cat tugged one glossy curl. "Maybe Flower remembers her own humble beginnings."

"Humble beginnings? She's the granddaughter of a French duke, isn't she?"

"So I've heard."

"I think she's wonderful, but I'm not sure about her husband's son. I need rest so I can be on my toes when I meet Ned Lytton tonight. I know it's not fair, but I have a feeling I won't like him. If Ned's a friend of Luke's, he must have flaws. Does that sound silly?"

"No, it sounds sensible. To be perfectly honest, I have the same damn feeling."

Ned Lytton met Lucas McDonald at a small Klan gathering. The introduction was made by Richard Reed, who had persuaded fifteen men to follow him to the summit of a boulder deep within the Rocky Mountains. There, they all knelt before an American flag and a burning cross and dedicated themselves to their Invisible Empire.

Ned wasn't impressed by the young man's appearance. His light-brown hair looked limp and greasy. His pale-blue eyes seemed lost between an expanse of balding forehead and fat cheeks. An enormous belly ended at heavy thighs. His shirt and trousers were stained with food.

His first words were polite but ominous. "Ned Lytton. I know all about *you.*"

"Lytton is a significant member of our Empire," Richard said judiciously.

Watching Richard walk away, attempting a superior smile, Ned turned toward Lucas. "Tell me about yourself, McDonald."

"That's not important, Ned. Can I call you Ned?"

Insolent puppy! "Of course, especially since we'll be working together as Kleagles."

"Kleagles?"

"Kleagles recruit new members."

"I'll enjoy working with you, Ned, yes indeed."

The words sounded right, but the boy's demeanor looked all wrong. "You've heard about the fees, Lucas?"

"Call me Luke. What fees?"

"Klectoken. Kleagles keep eight out of the ten-dollar membership fee."

"She was very pretty. I saw her when she visited my ranch. She was wet and she smelled awful and her face was sunburned, but she was pretty just the same."

"Who?"

"Ruthie Adams." Luke glanced around, lowered his voice. "Wasn't that her last name, Ned? Adams? I heard my mother say it. Ruthie Adams. My brother's whore."

Ned paced up and down Suzette Dorfman's bedroom. Suzette would return soon from a shopping expedition. Her present wardrobe was all wrong — a tart's wardrobe rather than a maid's wardrobe.

Ned's stomach churned as he thought about Lucas witnessing Ruthie's murder. Luke Lytton had been outside the miner's shack and spied through the broken window.

Luke didn't want money, thank God. Ned's funds were as shallow as the grave he'd dug for Ruthie. Luke wanted revenge. John Chinook was — in reality — Cat McDonald, Luke's brother. Luke had once overheard a conversation between his mother, now dead, and Chinook. Ned didn't have the vaguest idea what that conversation consisted of since Luke said he wouldn't spill his guts, even if tortured.

Ned would love to test *that* premise.

To his surprise, Luke also wanted to get his hands on Flower. He said his brother "owed" him Flower, in exchange for someone named Bridgida.

Flower's real name was Fools Gold, a fact Ned had already discovered. But he hadn't probed deep enough, hadn't learned that she was the daughter of a Cripple Creek parlor house girl. Luke had heard Ruthie say "Fools Gold" and had hired a retired Pinkerton to investigate.

Ned couldn't face his father with this new revelation. Edward had changed his will, leaving Flower his vast fortune. Ned wanted his father alive, at least for the moment, and the lowdown on his wife might shock him into a fatal heart attack.

Inheriting Father's estate was important, but Richard Reed said it was even more crucial that Ned gain control of Dollyscope. That way, the Ku Klux Klan could produce propaganda films. Look how *Birth of a Nation* had furthered their cause. Inspired by Thomas Dixon's novel, *The Clansman*, Griffith's movie had been responsible for a phenomenal increase in Klan membership.

If everything went as planned, Ned would soon run Dollyscope and select his own actors and scripts. Suzette insisted that all successful schemes took careful planning and patience.

Soon Flower would interview servants for Aguila del Oro's staff. Luke and Ned had decided to install Suzette inside the mansion. Edward would transfer his money, stocks, and the new will to Aguila del Oro's safe. Suzette would discover the whereabouts of that safe. Once the will was in Ned's hands, subject to alteration and a forged signature, Luke could have Flower. How Chinook figured in all this, Ned didn't know and Luke wouldn't say.

If Suzette wasn't clever enough to get hired, they'd have to think up another scheme. But Suzette *was* clever. She'd even managed to entertain both Ned and Luke with her incredibly talented body.

After the debacle with Ruthie, Suzette was the perfect companion. For starters, she had no interest in a movie career. She had beautiful hair, but her pale-blue eyes wouldn't photograph well and some of her teeth were missing.

Ned had privately hired a down-at-the-heels rodeo wrangler to rob Flower's suite. Johanna said Flower carelessly placed her valuable jewels inside a music box. Ned needed those jewels to replenish his funds. If the thief found Edward's will, so much the better.

TWENTY-NINE

Flo's scheme had worked perfectly. It was love at first sight, and Cat even shared his hotel suite with Jane Percival.

So why did she feel betrayed? Because she had underestimated Cat's charms and overestimated Jane's innocence?

Cat had taken to treating "Flower" like a rare orchid. At the same time, he was sarcastically deferential toward Claude DuBois.

Now Claude was calling his actors together, preparing to issue orders for the next scene.

They had been filming for three days. The weather was beautiful — Indian summer — and Claude had decided he'd shoot their last scenes first, including the flood episode where the hero rescued the heroine. Flo still seethed over the altered concept, even though she knew the public would never accept John Chinook in a subservient role.

The lion's share of the story took place during the winter, but Claude said they might as well take advantage of the fine weather and film their summer scenes straight away. Today's reel entailed the finding of gold by Minta and her fiancé, William. The discovery would turn out to be fool's gold, leading to William's reluctant abandonment of Minta. In the revised plot, Minta was the orphaned daughter of a minister.

Flo had argued over Minta's new status until she was blue in the face, but Edward agreed with Claude. A movie heroine must be pure. Only in books could she be naughty.

"Define pure, Claude," Flo had said during a luncheon meeting inside Edward's suite.

"Purity goes without saying, never referred to except by the color of the heroine's dress, white, or at the moment when her chastity is menaced. Define pure? That's easy. Mary Pickford, Blanche Sweet, Arlene Pretty, Louise Lovely."

"Define naughty."

"Theda Bara."

Flo had burst out laughing. "Theda Bara is an anagram for Arab Death. Did you know that her given name is Theodosia

Goodman and she hails from Ohio?"

Apparently, Claude hadn't known. Furious, he had shouted, "*Defloration!* That's how you define naughty."

Today they were filming in Cripple Creek, at the site of a deserted mine shaft. Claude carried a megaphone, but since the scene only involved John Chinook and Flower Smith, he didn't use it. "The cameras will focus on the mine entrance," he said. "When you emerge, Flower's hair must be mussed and her clothing in disarray."

Flo smiled. All their love scenes were directed that way. Except for a brief, chaste kiss before the final fade-out, Minta and William's frequent clinches occurred off-screen.

"Flower, you must show excitement at the thought of sighting gold because William will stay and you will become a rich lady."

She nodded.

"Any questions, Chinook?"

"Just one. Shouldn't William express his delight with a natural caress *outside* the cave?"

Flo's brow creased. "What do you consider natural?"

"A hug. Perhaps a fondling of your earlobe."

"Everybody knows what happened *inside*

the cave. We must trust our audience."

"Do you trust me?"

"What do you mean?"

"How do you know I won't caress your earlobe out of camera range?"

"The filming has just begun. If you caress any part of my body, I'll make certain Edward replaces you with a new costar. Read the morality clause in your contract, Mr. Chinook."

Cat's green eyes crinkled at the corners. "That so-called morality clause doesn't include an earlobe, but I'll play by the rules. Are you ready?"

"Yes. How many takes, Claude?"

"Three, possibly four. I want to shoot different angles, and there are shadows at the entrance. Ready? Action!"

When they emerged from the mine, Flo was momentarily blinded by sunlight.

"Cut!" Claude yelled. "I don't mean to complain, Flower, but you ruined Minta's close-up by blinking like a rabbit."

"I know. It's so dark inside. Wouldn't William carry a light? Perhaps a lantern?"

"How about a candle? We don't have a lantern and I'd rather not waste time sending for one."

"A candle's fine. What do you think, John?"

Cat stood at the mine's entrance. Ignoring Flo's question, he said, "Have you checked out the support timbers, DuBois? They seem unsteady."

"Of course I checked. Do you think I'd send Flower inside if the mine was unsafe?"

"All right, let's get this over with." Cat struck a match on his boot heel and lit the candle.

They entered. Almost immediately, Flo saw a brownish-gray mouse scurry across the dirt. Another lagged behind, dragging its foot. "Oh, look. The poor thing's wounded. Oh, the poor little mouse."

"Don't touch it, honey. It's probably covered with fleas."

Flo had begun bending, but Cat pushed her away. Off balance, she stumbled against the wall. She heard a creak like an old rocking chair, then the sound of a rushing waterfall.

No, more like thunder, she thought. *I hate thunder.*

Another rumble, and another, except there was no flash of lightning and the raindrops were pelting pebbles.

Squeezing her eyes shut, she pressed her hands against her ears and screamed, then screamed again when Cat pushed her to the ground and covered her body with his.

Opening her eyes, she inhaled dust. Cat was touching her all over. She pushed him off and staggered to her feet, her legs as shaky as a newborn calf. "What do you think you're doing, Cat McDonald?"

"Checking for broken bones. Are you all right, Fools Gold?"

"Yes. Are you?"

"Sure. During my rodeo days I jumped through hoops of fire and dogged bulls with my teeth. What's a mere cave-in?"

"Is that what happened? A cave-in?" She heard a scratchy sound and watched him hold a match to the wick of their candle. "Your face is covered with dirt, Cat. You look like a minstrel."

"You, too." With his free hand, he retrieved a handkerchief from his pocket and thrust it toward her. "Spit," he said.

Momentarily their eyes locked and they smiled, remembering.

"Mama Min hated that word," she said. "Never mind the rest of my face. Let's go."

"Go where?"

"Out."

"Are you ordering me to escort you outside?"

"Of course not. But you have the candle. You must lead the way."

"Don't you know what a cave-in means?

The walls came tumbling down, just like one of D.W. Griffith's biblical epics. There's no outside. There's no entrance or exit."

"But there must be. If we were trapped, the candle wouldn't burn."

"The candle is burning from oxygen already in this chamber. Look around. What do you see? Dirt walls. The ceiling's still there because the interior beams are stronger. The cave-in must have occurred at the mine's entrance. I hope your damn mice survived."

"Wait! I see a narrow cut in the wall. Perhaps it leads to an escape."

"I suspect it leads farther into the cave but I'll explore. Stay here. There might be bats."

Surrounded by darkness once again, Flo could hear time passing, measured by the pounding of her heart. She was breathing too fast, panting, and the walls were closing in on her. After what seemed an eternity, she saw the candle flicker as Cat wedged his broad shoulders through the small opening and shook off the dirt like a spaniel shaking off water.

"What did you find?"

"I'm sorry, Fools Gold."

"Nothing? No way out?"

"Relax. DuBois and the crew must be digging. They'll rescue us."

"How long will it take? How much air do we have left? When will the candle go out?"

"I don't know. I'm not a miner." Cat pressed her face against his chest.

"Are we going to die?" she murmured into his shirt.

"Are you afraid to die?"

"No."

"Liar," he said softly.

"Are you?"

"Since the age of seventeen, I've been afraid to live."

"Why?"

"I don't plan to relate the sad tale of —"

"Cat, the air's all gone. I can't breathe."

"Calm down." He released her, dripped wax over a rock, set the candle upright, and sat propped against the wall. Pulling her into his lap, he stroked her back. "The air isn't gone. If you don't get upset, it should last until we're found. Meanwhile, we can play earlobe."

"Don't tease. I can't even hear them digging. It's not that I'm afraid to die. It's just . . ."

"Just what?"

"I've never slept with a man," she blurted. "If I die I'll never feel passion or ecstasy. I'll never have a child. Dear God, I've never really been kissed."

"Liar!" This time the word was a shout.

"Why do you say I lie? What do you know about my life?"

"I know that you left Little Heaven for another parlor house. Madam Robin told me when I returned, six, maybe seven months after your birthday party. I had some boyhood notion about rescuing you from a life of degradation. Instead, you found your own protector. If you've never felt passion, you must have successfully feigned that emotion. Jack Gottlieb appeared satisfied."

"Are you insane? After the night of my party, I couldn't speak. Madam Robin had lost all her money. I tried to be a parlor girl, but I couldn't because a man's touch made me sick. So I rode to Jack's cabin, and he sheltered me, and I lived there, and he treated me like a daughter."

"The clothes. The hotel."

"I told you we had separate rooms."

"Hush. Don't cry. I'm sorry. I didn't understand."

Flo allowed him to press her face against his chest again then felt his shoulders stiffen.

"What a smooth actress you are," he said. "I suppose your marriage to Edward Lytton is a sham."

"Edward is my grandfather."

"What did you say?" Cat's voice betrayed his shock.

"You heard me. It makes no difference if I speak the truth when we're about to die. I've never shared my bed with Edward. I've never even shared one intimate caress."

"Does he know?"

"That he's my grandfather? Of course not. Do you think he'd have wed me if he knew?"

"Why did you wed him? His money?"

"In a way." Flo swiped at her tears with the back of her hand. "It's a long story."

"Tell me."

"My mother was a crib girl named Blueberry Smith. She fell in love with Ned Lytton. He abandoned her . . . and me, his bastard child. All my life I hated Ned, but I believed Edward had threatened him to make him obey. When I finally met Ned, I realized he rode away from Poverty Gulch without a second thought for Blueberry. If Edward had known about my mother, he would have provided her with a measure of financial security, and there's a good chance she wouldn't have died in childbirth."

"That's the truth, Fools Gold?"

"I swear. Edward proposed after a dinner party. That's where I met Ned. There's not enough air left in this death chamber to explain how I felt at that dinner. Edward has a weak heart. His doctor told him that sexual commerce would be suicide, so he offered marriage without consummation and he promised to make me his sole benefactor. Even so, I would have refused his proposal except he wouldn't take no for an answer."

Cat nodded. "I didn't want to costar with you in *Heaven's Thunder.* Somehow, before I knew what hit me, the deal was made and the contract signed. So, Ned Lytton is your father."

"Ned Lytton is *not* my father. I have no father. Why are you laughing?"

"Because I have no father, either, at least none I can brag about."

"But . . . but . . . John McDonald . . ."

"My father's name was Cherokee Bill. He was an outlaw, a murderer. He robbed banks, and he was hanged."

"That's impossible. Your mother . . ."

"I realize the girls at Little Heaven thought Dimity . . . priggish . . . but she did have an affair with an outlaw named Cherokee Bill and I'm the result. Don't you find that amusing?"

"No. Why do you?"

"Because we're both bastards. But an outlaw's blood taints my body, so if you want to faint —"

"I never faint. Anyway, a child can't inherit bad blood."

"You don't believe in bad blood, Fools Gold?"

"No. Do you have a tendency to pray a lot because you have Dimity's blood?"

"I inherited her temper and her spite."

"That's because she brought you up. If you had been raised by your father, you might have robbed banks. But you weren't, so you have no desire to rob banks. Do you?"

"In my movies I steal from the rich, like Robin Hood. And now that we've shared our most intimate secrets, it's time we escaped from this tomb."

She shook her head. "Why waste our last precious moments?"

"It's not a waste."

"No, Cat. I accept my fate."

"Fools Gold, please listen. We must —"

"I don't want to spend my last moments on earth searching for an impossible escape. If I'm to die, I want to learn passion from someone I love."

Precious minutes ticked away before he said, "Do you love me, Fools Gold?"

"I think I've always loved you. It started at the bullfight when you said I could puke into your bandanna."

"I loved you before that, when you said you'd make me puke up my teeth."

"During my birthday party, when I blew out my cake candles, I wished you'd suck my mouth the same way you were sucking a Coca-Cola bottle. Please, Cat, kiss me."

"I'll kiss you, but that's all."

"Why?"

"Because it's your first time and it will hurt."

"Will it stop hurting?" The candle's glow made Cat's grin appear wavy. "I know I sound naive but —"

"Your naiveté is sweet and I love you for it. Yes, it will stop hurting, if we have time."

"When time runs out, I'd rather die in your arms. I don't care if there's hurt as long as there's love."

Cat gently grasped her shoulders. "First we must unbutton your blouse and take it off. Now your boots, skirt and drawers. God, you're beautiful. Now my clothes. Do you like what you see? Was that a nod or a shiver?"

"Both."

"You can't possibly know how ironic it would be if DuBois dug through the entrance and found us like this."

"I don't hear picks and shovels. Please hurry."

"I won't perform this act of love in a hurry." He pulled her on top so that his own body sheltered her from the pebbly ground, then felt her unyielding lips bestow an eager kiss. "No, love, real men and women don't kiss like they do in the movies. Remember the Coca-Cola bottle? Open your mouth."

She obeyed, and gasped as he thrust his tongue beyond her teeth. Timidly, she returned the gesture with her own tongue, until, grinding his mouth hard against hers, he sucked all the breath from her body. At the same time, his hand stroked the inside of her legs.

"No, Cat! I thought I could but I can't."

"Am I hurting you?"

"No. But he did."

"Poor baby. The hurt was Minta's death. Don't you see how it's all mixed together? Peiffer's attack and Minta's murder? The hurt is Minta's death, not my hand caress-ing."

"I know, but I can't."

"All right, we'll stop."

"I can't die without knowing love," she said, her words the same but different.

"We don't have to do this to prove love."

"Yes, we do."

"Stay still." He extended his arms then moved them back and forth as if making angel wings in the snow.

"Why are you flapping your arms, Cat?"

"I'm not flapping. I'm trying to find our clothes. My trousers and your shirt will have to do." Cradling her back, he maneuvered her body so that she was on the bottom, somewhat protected by cotton and corduroy. "Stay still," he repeated, and kissed her eyes shut.

Flo waited but nothing happened. Had Cat run out of air?

No. His hands remained motionless but his lips moved as he kissed her nose, her chin, the hollow in her neck.

"I'm going to kiss your breasts now," he said. "Stop me if it hurts."

She felt his tongue lave her nipples, and, on their own volition, they hardened.

"Now I'm going to suck each lovely breast, one at a time. It won't hurt, I promise."

"You sound like a movie director," she murmured, then held her breath as she felt new, strange sensations spread throughout her body. Scared, she opened her eyes, planning to push him away. Instead, she pressed him closer.

"Ah, you like that," he said, raising his face. "Shall we try another take?"

"Yes."

She was nearly sobbing with desire when he relinquished her breasts.

"I'm going to kiss your belly, Fools Gold. It might tickle. Then I won't give directions because my mouth will be between your legs. It shouldn't hurt, especially if you relax and let me perform the scene. I won't use my hands. You fear my hands, not my mouth. When my tongue leaves your belly, you won't feel ticklish anymore. You might want to moan or scream. That's perfectly normal. Are you ready?"

"Yes." The candle's dim light was too nebulous to reveal shadows, but Flo imagined their forms silhouetted on the dirt wall's screen. Every portion of her body throbbed. Unflawed veins of melted ore were buried in the mine's concavity, buried beneath her skin.

"Don't squirm so, Fools Gold. Remain still until you can't any longer."

Trustingly, she followed his directions, and did feel ticklish when his tongue caressed her navel. His lips moved lower and she moaned, as he had warned. Twisting her fingers in his hair, she tensed then spread her thighs, pressing his face closer to the throb.

"Let go of my hair. Use your fingers to

spread . . . that's right. Good girl. Pretend you're a flower unfolding its petals. Inside is the sweetest bud." His tongue found her bud.

Consumed with spasm after spasm, she moaned a litany.

He changed their position so she lay on top again then caressed the debris from her back in soothing, circular motions.

"You're very wet now," he said. "My tongue has helped make you wet. But it's also your body reacting to my tongue's pleasure. Move your hand down and feel how wet you are. The wetness will make the hurt less. Now you must make me wet."

"Am I to take you into my mouth, Cat?"

"No, love, that's too hard . . ." He laughed. "Too *much* for the first lesson. You must spit on your palm and slide your hand over my . . . that's right. Don't be shy. Again. Good girl. Now shift your body quickly so your wetness meets mine. I'm already inside because we're both ready. I want you to ride me like you'd ride a horse. The hurt will come soon. If it's unbearable, lean back and I'll pull out. Now, spread your legs and move forward. My hands are holding you upright, but they will go no lower. You need not fear my hands. Now ride, my love, ride!"

Flo waited for the pain, but merely felt an exultation she had never imagined. She rocked back and forth, faster and faster, heard Cat groan.

"I'm sorry," he said. "Can't pull out now."

"No, don't." She felt his grip on her waist tighten. He moved slowly then increased his tempo until she matched her rhythm to his. His hands released her waist and she felt his fingers fondle the cleft in her buttocks. She caught her breath at this new, intimate invasion then forgot his fingers, overcome by her own sensations.

Bending forward again, she caressed his chin with her breasts. "All my life I've waited for this," she whispered, thrusting first one breast, then the other into his open mouth. As he sucked, she honestly believed she might faint from ecstasy.

I never faint, she thought incoherently, as her wet nipples touched his nipples. She traced the outline of his lips with her tongue. The prod of his sex penetrated so deeply, she was sure it would meet up with his fingers, still stroking her buttocks. She felt a series of renewed contractions and swallowed his deep kiss, along with her joyful whimpers.

He thrust again and again, spreading, stretching, possessing her. At long last, he released his own proof of desire. Incredibly, Cat's new wetness yielded a feeling of both power and submission, then a series of pulsating bursts, then a glittering rainbow that consumed her vision.

As he maneuvered them sideways, she said, "It didn't hurt."

"Is that a complaint?"

"No. Oh, my gosh! You said the first time would hurt and it didn't. I've never done this before, I swear. Do you believe me?"

"I believe you."

"When I was fourteen, after I moved into Jack's cabin, I was riding Dumas bareback and I sat her wrong when she jumped a fence. The pain was so intense I almost fell off. And I bled."

"That's what kept me from hurting you." Cat withdrew, grinning at her involuntary yelp of displeasure. "You did fine for a first lesson, but next time should be even better."

"There won't be a next time. The candle's nearly gone. Surely our air is used up."

"Get dressed, Fools Gold. We've tarried long enough and I want to leave before that idiot DuBois thinks to send a search party around to the back of the mine."

"What's the difference if I die naked as the day I was born? What do you mean, send a search party to the back of the mine?"

Cat clothed himself and cleansed away the moisture between her thighs with his hand-kerchief. "Where are your drawers? Never mind. Your skirt's sewn together like trousers. Slip your feet into your boots while I button your blouse." He finished buttoning and led her toward the cut in the wall. "Scurry like a good little mouse." He gave her rump a shove. "I'm right behind you."

She wriggled through the narrow slice and blinked at the dim light, shining from an exit farther down the tunnel. Turning her head, she stared into Cat's eyes. "You knew all the time we were safe! Why didn't you tell me? Why did you lie?"

"I didn't lie. I said DuBois and the crew were digging, and I'm sure they are. I even suggested we leave when you first begged me to make love to you."

"Begged? Oh! You should have been gelded at birth, Cat McDonald!"

"Would you have discovered rapture if you hadn't believed death imminent?"

"I hate you!"

"You said you loved me."

"I thought I was dying. I would have said I love you to any man. I would have spread my legs for any man. I fibbed to inflate your ego and make you strong."

"You inflated more than my ego. I didn't lie when I said I loved you, and if you let me direct you again, I'll cancel our wager."

"What wager?"

"I don't want to take your horse," he mimicked.

"Dumas! Oh, no!"

"Don't fret, Fools Gold. Since you believe your rapture the result of my duplicity, you may keep your mare."

THIRTY

"It will be better next time," Cat had said.

There will be no next time, Flo thought, saddling Dumas for a ride through the mountains.

No next time, she vowed, dismounting and racing toward Cat's waiting arms.

"No," she said, sinking onto a carpet of burnished leaves.

"Yes," he said. "I love you, Fools Gold."

"Love quickens all the senses," she said between kisses, "except common sense."

Every instinct screamed she must stay away, but she couldn't. Flower Smith, ice maiden, craved a man's touch.

Cat was both lover and friend. Flo told him about Jack and Sally and Marylander. She told him about Kate's illness; how she'd met Kate and immediately felt a connection, greater by far than she'd felt with Ned's other children. She told Cat about Steven, who'd shyly confessed that he liked

583

Auntie Flower better than Walter Johnson, a pitcher for the Washington Senators.

In turn, Cat told her about Jane and Ruthie and Bridgida. He talked about Percy and Tonna and his childhood. But he wouldn't discuss Cherokee Bill. That wound festered, and Flo couldn't hug the hurt away.

In Cat's arms, she reached the rapturous heights of passion. She fell from her tight-rope and sang her pleasure in a voice far sweeter than the one she had used to sing "The Bird on Nellie's Hat." There was no glass to shatter, but her cries of delight shattered the fragile cocoon she had wrapped around her emotions since the age of four-teen.

Colorado's capricious weather turned chilly, so Claude delayed filming the flood episode. Instead, he constructed an outdoor stage for the interior segments. A frost-nipped breeze ruffled the curtains on the window of their roofless cabin. Goosebumps pocked beneath her white heroine's dress, but Flo's heart was always warm.

She and Cat rehearsed their off-camera love scenes in their favorite mountain glen.

"You've taught me everything," she murmured, as his finger traced lazy figure-eights across her back and shoulders, "but I've never made love on a real bed."

"Repeat what you just said in my other ear. I couldn't hear you."

"Oh, I forgot," she said, then forgot anew when he caressed her into blissful oblivion.

It became difficult to remember the cameras, and only Claude's presence kept her from melting against "William" during a tender tableau. Cognizant of Cat's morality clause, they pretended to hate each other.

Flo postponed interviewing new servants for Aguila del Oro, dividing her free time between Edward, the Scott family and Cat.

Six weeks passed quickly. At long last, Chinook winds swept down from the mountains and the temperature hovered around seventy degrees. All interior reels had been completed, and Edward was pleased that the movie's premiere would coincide with the opening of Aguila del Oro. They hadn't discussed her retirement, but before Flo could bring it up, Edward said he planned to visit Denver. "I'll be gone three days. Claude has been told to wait for my return to film the flood. It's the last scene, and after that unnecessary cave-in, I want to be there."

Filming was tedious and taxed one's strength, so Flo said, "Why can't Ned observe?"

"Ned's scouting locations for the third *Foibles* episode. He's found a ranch in Divide, but the owner's son Rufus wants so much money —"

"Lucas, not Rufus. The JMD ranch."

"That's right. How'd you know?"

"I've never met Lucas, but I've met his father and brother . . . I mean, his sister."

"Take care of yourself, darling girl. Enjoy your brief holiday."

"Thank you, Edward."

As she packed his suitcase, she wondered if she'd get an opportunity to make love on a real bed.

The next day she and Cat consummated their mutual passions on their favorite leaf-strewn, pine-scented mattress.

Sitting up, she said, "I think I'm pregnant."

"You think?"

"I've never been late before."

"Are there any other signs?"

"What do I know about pregnancy? My cats looked like footballs. Then they'd expel tiny kittens that looked more like mice."

"Do you feel faint?"

"I never faint."

"Are you sick in the morning?"

"No."

"Are your breasts sore?"

"Yes."

"Are you crying?"

"A little. You sound so clinical. Don't you like babies?"

"Of course. I just wish we could hire a stand-in to carry yours."

"Flower Smith has never used a stand-in," she teased, her tears forgotten. Then she saw the frightened expression that clouded his green eyes. "Bridgida?"

"Yes. And my mother miscarried three times and swore she nearly died birthing me. I love you so much, Fools Gold. I can't lose you now."

"You won't. Surely God wouldn't separate us again. I'll give you a fine son, a fat Cat."

"I prefer a daughter."

"I want another John McDonald." She held her breath, hoping he wouldn't mention Cherokee Bill.

"John McDonald Lytton," he said.

"Oh, I'm not thinking clearly. I must ask Edward to release me from my vows."

"You'll have to give up your movie career."

"Do you think I care about that? Wait. Morality clause. The scandal. *Your* career."

"I can always play the rodeo circuit."

"No! The last time you joined a rodeo, you challenged death. This time —"

"Settle down. I was joking."

"I'm not serious, either. How can I ask Edward for a divorce? He's been so good to me."

"We'll face him together. He's a reasonable man. When her hears about the baby . . ." Cat's brow creased. "No matter what Edward says or does, I'll never let you go."

"Let me go!"

Ignoring Flo's shout, Lorenzo and Sally pulled her away from the hotel's entrance, away from the curious spectators and reporters. Forming a protective shield, they hustled her through a side door and made certain she reached her suite unmolested.

"Lorenzo, drive me to the hospital!"

"Sit down," Sally said. "Edward is fighting for his life. When you can control yourself, we'll drive —"

"Control myself? Whatever do you mean?"

"Confession may be good for the soul, Flo, but do you really think the reporters need to hear about how you were in the mountains with another man while your husband —"

"Oh, no! Did I say that?"

"Only Lorenzo and I heard, and it will go no further." Sally pressed a snifter of brandy against Flo's lips.

She sipped, choked, waved the glass away. "Tell me again what happened. I don't understand. Edward was supposed to be in Denver."

"Apparently the thief knew that, too. He'd already filched your jewelry and was rifling through Edward's papers when Edward entered his suite." Sally took a deep breath. "The thief was short and slight. He hit a young hotel employee over the head and donned his uniform. It was carefully planned. The thief didn't anticipate any interference. But when Edward arrived unexpectedly, the thief pulled a gun and —"

"Oh, my God! Edward was shot?"

"Calm down. Edward wasn't shot. His heart failed. Fortunately, he'd left the room's door ajar. The sound of his fall alerted a guest. The guest telephoned hotel security."

"I hope the damned thief hangs!"

"He won't hang, dear."

"He will if Edward . . ." Flo swallowed.

"He won't hang. He ran from the Antlers, followed by the police. He made it to Tejon Street before he was gunned down a few doors from Lorenzo's shop. I was at the shop. That's how I learned what happened."

"What about the thief?"

"Shot through the heart."

"But Edward's alive, isn't he? Tell me the truth."

"He was alive when he left for the hospital."

"I should have been here."

Lorenzo knelt by Flo's chair. "Nonsense. You didn't know this would happen. It's not your fault."

"Don't you see? If I hadn't left my jewelry lying around, if I hadn't been away from the hotel —"

"Then *you* might have been killed. I know it isn't much comfort, Flo, but Edward's heart attack saved his life. The thief would have fired if Edward hadn't fallen. Edward surprised the thief in his suite, not yours. It wasn't just your jewelry. The man was searching for something else. Money? Stocks? We'll never know. But blaming yourself won't make things turn out differently."

"May we go to the hospital now? Please?"

If Edward lives, thought Flo, *I shall never dishonor my marriage vows again. This I swear on the life of my unborn child.*

Thank God Father didn't die, Ned thought, sipping from his glass of whiskey. *Thank God that moronic rodeo wrangler was gunned down before he could talk.*

Ned poured himself another drink then whirled about at the sound of footsteps.

"You're as jumpy as a flea," lisped Suzette, kicking the door shut behind her. "Help me take off these damn clothes and change into something more comfortable. Come on, Ned, snap out of it. One would think you had suffered the heart attack, not your father. Besides, didn't part of your plan include Edward's demise?"

"Not yet, you idiot. Not until I get my hands on his will."

"Don't call me an idiot."

"How was your interview? Did Flower hire you?"

"Certainement, monsieur."

"You didn't talk French, did you? Your accent's atrocious."

"My accent's fine and she was taken in completely."

"Any problem over the references?"

"I shed a few tears and explained how my references were stolen. I even mentioned names, some from the finest families in Denver. Naturally Flower didn't know I'd never met their wives. Unfasten the back buttons, Ned. Why do servants have to wear such dull clothing?"

"You gave her names? Are you crazy?"

"Never mind the buttons. I've unfastened

591

them myself." Suzette wriggled free from the dark material and crawled toward Ned. "Remove the bobs from my hair," she lisped, tugging his trousers and underwear down about his ankles.

Ned felt her tongue caress. With a triumphant shriek of laughter, she took him into her mouth. When he had regained his sensibilities, he said, "If Flower checks out the names and decides not to hire you, I'll break your damn nose again."

"She won't check names. She hired me right away. You weren't there to see my performance. I had her completely fooled."

Flo ignored the sun parlor's sun. For twenty minutes she'd sat in the same position, her fingernails gashing her palms, her teeth clenched.

The woman hadn't fooled her at all.

Despite the blonde hair and false accent, it was Suzy. Little Heaven's Suzy. Minta's murderer.

More than eight years had passed, but Flo could never forget Suzy's eyes, nose and broken teeth. Suzy, who now called herself Suzette Dorfman.

Why did I hire her?

Flo's first inclination had been to scream, her second to send the woman far away.

Controlling both impulses, she had questioned Suzy carefully. Yes, she had served the finest families, said Suzy, and mentioned several names — a mind-boggling slipup on Suzy's part. Suppose Flo had decided to substantiate Suzy's credentials?

Why did I hire her?

Because, although she couldn't prove it, Flo knew that Suzy was responsible for Minta's death. With Suzy installed at Aguila del Oro, Flo could watch her closely and extract revenge. Somehow, some way, she'd even the score.

During their interview, Suzy hadn't conjoined Flo with the heavy parlor house waif. Flo wore a black peg-top skirt, full at the hips, diminishing in width toward the ankles. Over a high-collared red blouse, she sported a short bolero jacket, fashioned from black wool, with hand-sewn horizontal stripes of red and gold silk.

Suzy had merely said, "You look familiar, Mrs. Lytton. Have we met before?"

Before Flo could reply, the hateful woman had lisped, "Oh, how silly. I probably spotted you at one of the upper-crust homes where I worked as a housemaid."

Rather than focusing on Flo's telltale ebony hair, blue eyes, and cleft chin, Suzy's greedy eyes had been fixed on Flo's pink pearls and the jeweled combs that secured her braids.

With an effort, Flo unclenched her fingers. Sensing Cat's approach, she turned and watched him stride toward her.

"Hello, Fools Gold. Why won't you take my calls? Why won't you see me?"

"Go 'way, Cat. I'll see you on the movie set when Claude resumes filming tomorrow. I'll let you save me from the flood. Then you'll return to California. If you telephone, I'll hang up. If you send me letters, I'll burn them. Do you understand?"

"No." Glancing around the sun parlor, Cat saw several guests reading books, playing whist, or just gawking at John Chinook and Flower Smith. "Let's take a stroll through the park. We need to talk."

"Leave me alone."

"Not until we talk."

"All right. Talk."

"Not here."

"Yes, here. Or else we shan't talk at all."

He pulled a chair close to hers and sat on the edge of its cushion. "Edward is nearly recovered, isn't he?"

"Edward is better, but he shall never recover."

"That's not your fault or mine."

"I know."

594

"Then why do you refuse to see me?"

"Hush. This must be casual conversation."

Grasping her elbows, he pulled her from the chair. "Yes, it is a nice day for a stroll," he said, his voice loud.

"Damn your soul, Cat McDonald!" Flo stumbled to keep up as he led her swiftly through the lobby.

"How's Mr. Lytton, Mrs. Lytton?" A bandage covered the back of Martin's head, and the tunic buttons on his new uniform shined.

"Much better, thank you," Flo called over her shoulder.

"Mr. Chinook, you haven't forgotten about Pistol's pup, have you? You promised —"

Doors closed on the boy's words.

"That was cruel, Cat."

"I'll make it up to him. Hell, I'll send him the whole damn litter."

"Either slow down or release my elbow." Flo's steps, short and choppy, were constricted by the width of her skirt bottom. "Stop walking so fast, Cat, or I shall fall."

Dropping her arm, he turned abruptly. She stumbled forward. Her face landed in his shirt and she began to cry. Wordlessly, he stroked her back.

"I'm not pregnant after all," she said, stepping backwards.

"I don't believe you."

"Since there's no baby, I'll stay with Edward and manage his estate."

"I won't permit it."

"You can't stop me."

"Suppose I tell Edward he's your grand-father?"

"You won't do that."

"Why are you so sure?"

"Because you are the son of John Mc-Donald, not Cherokee Bill."

"I'll do anything to keep you, Fools Gold."

"If you think you can keep me by killing Edward, you're sadly mistaken."

"I thought you loved me."

"I do love you, and I'm grateful for the time we've had together. It's made me strong enough to end our affair."

"It was more than an affair and you know it. If Edward were to die, would you marry me?"

"No."

"Yes, you would. I'll wait. If necessary, I'll wait forever."

Flo stared up into Cat's anguished face. "Forever is a long, long time."

THIRTY-ONE

"I never realized that the Colorado was such a long river," said Jane, "or so wild. Are you sure you don't want me to stand in for you? I swim like a fish and they won't shoot any close-ups until after Cat, I mean John, has pulled you out."

"Claude wants to use a stand-in," Flo said, "but not a slip of a girl like you. He wants to dress a man in Minta's clothes."

"You refused, of course."

"I've been practicing my swimming, and Minta's calico weighs less than my bathing costume. A man, indeed!"

"You should join the suffragettes."

"I make statements for women with my movies. I hope you'll do the same when you take over my role."

"I still can't believe you want me to continue in your serial."

"Your serial. After this movie, Flower Smith will retire and Jane Percival will continue in *Janey's Journey.* I promised Claude I'd make one appearance, introduce you as my long-lost sister. When you have time, I hope you'll visit Aguila del Oro."

"Just try and keep me away. Oh, dear, Claude is gathering the troops. Soon I must beg my father, the evil mine owner, not to blast the river. I feel so silly, falling to my knees and wringing my hands. I wish motion pictures could talk."

"Someday movies will have sound, and your brother will play his guitar and sing 'The Western Home.' "

"Home, home, on the range, where the deer and the antelope play." Jane smiled ruefully. "Cat's the only member of my family who can sing. Daniel stutters and Lucas wouldn't recognize a song unless it was cooked inside a loaf of bread. Tonna says Cat was fathered by the Chinook wind. Maybe that's why his voice is so pure."

Flo glanced toward the eastern slopes of the Rocky Mountains. "I guess we'd better join the others. Claude wants to shoot this sequence before the sun sets."

Since there were quite a few players and four cameras, DuBois hefted his megaphone. "Qui-et, quiet everyone. Flower, we'll begin the scene with Minta kneeling by the river. Don't forget to wear the stuffed harness that makes you pregnant."

"For goodness sake, Claude, you needn't shout. I'm standing right in front of you."

He lowered his megaphone. "Minta washes her clothes. By mistake, she scoops up some sand. Surprise! Gold! Mouth the word, Flower. We'll flash the printed letters on the screen. Won't William be happy? Minta looks into the distance. Where's William? She drops her head into her hands and her shoulders shake. William isn't coming back. 'Woe is me.' "

"Woe is me?"

"Something like that."

"Nothing like that. The script reads 'I have faith. If William is alive, he'll return to me.' "

"What I want here is pathos."

"What we need here is faith."

"How do you show faith? Perhaps faithful pathos or pathetic trust."

"Perhaps."

"All right. We crosscut to the mine owner. Jane is begging him not to blast. He laughs and bears down on the handle." Pressing the megaphone against his lips, Claude shouted, "Are the dynamite sticks ready?"

"Ready, Mr. DuBois," called a man wearing denim overalls. "We set them upstream, round the bend in the river, so's nobody'll get hurt."

"There will be one take on the explosion."

"Yes, sir."

Claude lowered his megaphone. "All right. We cut to William. Where the bloody hell is William?"

"I'm here, DuBois."

Flo didn't turn around, but she sensed Cat standing behind her. In her mind's eye, he dwarfed the mountains.

"All right. William is riding back to Minta. We understand this because he says, 'I hope I'm not too late for the birth of my baby.' The words will be printed on the screen. William hears the explosion. Cup your ear, so the audience knows —"

"Which ear? My good ear or my deaf ear?"

"What's the difference? William kicks his horse . . . Chinook! You're not wearing spurs."

"I never wear spurs."

"I want your horse to go fast."

"He'll go fast."

"All right. We crosscut to the mine owner, killed in the explosion. Jane escapes by climbing over the rubble. May we have pathos here, Flower?"

"I believe the script calls for Jane to display courage."

"All right. We cut to Minta. She wades into the river because it's swollen from the explosion, and her poor dog is caught in the current. We'll film that later, after Pistol has her pups. Minta's trapped by the rushing waters. 'Help,' she screams. 'Help.' "

"No, Claude. Now we have your pathos. Minta simply says, 'I love you, William.' "

"Whatever. If the sun is still out, we'll film the rescue." Claude raised his megaphone. "Everybody ready? Remember, only one take on the explosion."

Flo attached her padded harness under her loose calico dress and knelt by the side of the river. She scooped up a handful of sand, discovered the shiny nuggets of fool's gold, and laughed at the irony. They couldn't use real gold since it didn't look real.

"That's good, Flower," DuBois yelled. "Minta's laughing with joy. She's going to be a rich lady. Now she remembers William's gone."

Soon Cat would be out of her life forever, thought Flo, and forever was a long, long time. Tears blurred her vision and she was only dimly aware of the camera moving in for a close-up. Lifting her chin, she said, "I have faith. If William is alive, he'll come back to me."

"Perfect, Flower! I'm not sure we'll print the words. Your expression says it all. You even convinced *me* you love Chinook, and I know how much you hate him."

Flo acknowledged Claude's compliment with a tight smile. She smelled wildflowers and decaying leaves. A swift breeze played with her braids and shifted the trail of tears on her face, but the river appeared calm since there was an earthen dam constructed farther upstream. The dam fed into a passageway that led toward a stock pond.

Claude was shouting orders for a second take on Jane's scene. Leaning over the bank, Flo dipped her hand into the water. It felt warm on top. Deeper, it felt icy.

"Please, God," she prayed, "don't let me catch a chill." Her hand strayed to her padded belly and she considered asking Claude for a stand-in, perhaps Janey. Before she could make a decision, she heard thunder.

No, not thunder. Claude was filming the explosion. She *felt* the sound reverberate, saw horned larks rise above the bordering pine trees. The ground beneath her shook, bucking like one of Sally's equine ruffians. Off balance from her bulky harness, Flo fell forward, into the river.

She tried to regain her footing but her drenched petticoats and padding kept her pinned to the bottom. On hands and knees she scuttled toward shore then realized she'd moved *away* from the muddy banks. Why hadn't Claude told her the bottom yielded a few feet from shore? Was it possible that, like the mine, he hadn't checked it out? Or had the dynamite charge broken the dam, causing a surge of water to swell the depths?

Cleaving the surface, she doggie-paddled. Why didn't somebody pull her free from this frigid shroud?

Because they hadn't noticed her distress. Everybody was farther up-river, watching the explosion from a safe distance. She could drown, and Claude would merely boom through his megaphone: "Where's Flower?"

"Here I am!" Swallowing water, Flo submerged.

I want a funeral like Mama Min's. A lavender casket and red roses dripping petals on my grave.

"Stop it," she admonished, after scissor-kicking her way to the surface again. "The current is carrying you downstream, toward the campsite. Someone will see you."

Rounding a bend, she groaned. The blast had dislodged tree roots, clumps of brush, and every loose branch in the vicinity. The sight of her bobbing head would be lost within the swirling debris.

Help, she thought. "I love you, Cat," she said.

"I love you, too."

Blinking moisture from her eyes, she watched Cat tread water. He looked like Neptune, his bare chest glistening in the bright sunlight. His dark hair was plastered to his skull and his jade eyes gleamed.

Was he real? Or was she dreaming?

"Help me, Cat. I'm drowning."

"I won't let you drown, Fools Gold."

His voice was real — Cat's voice.

"I'm so cold, Cat."

"Put your arms around my neck and ride piggyback while I swim to shore."

"Is Claude filming this?"

"Yes. Don't talk. Save your breath."

"Harness . . . heavy."

She felt his fingers unfasten the slippery knots. Nimble fingers. Experienced fingers. Fingers that had oft untangled corset strings.

The cameras wouldn't record the loss of her "pregnancy" — no more than her head and shoulders crested above the water. She shifted until she rode Cat's hips. With her last ounce of strength, she clasped her numb fingers across his chest.

"The crew is gathering ropes, just in case," he said. "Hang on. If we can make it to shore without ropes, we won't have to film another rescue sequence."

Impossible, she thought. They were so far away. "Are we going to die?" she asked.

He didn't answer. She'd whispered her question into his deaf ear. It didn't matter. Cat wouldn't let her die. He wouldn't let his baby die.

But she had told him there was no baby.

He didn't believe her. She was a competent actress but a dreadful liar.

Or was she? Jack believed her. Edward believed her. Claude believed her. Only Cat could see into her soul.

They reached the slippery bank, and Flo felt hands lift her. Still somewhat dazed, she saw a huge tree branch caught in the current.

"Cat! Look!"

"Janey!"

"What are you doing? You can't swim out again. It's too cold."

Cat ignored her.

She turned toward the cameramen. "Don't just stand there. Help him."

Nobody moved.

She watched Cat fight the strong current. He dove beneath the water, and it seemed an eternity until he emerged near Jane. Very quickly, he untangled her from the tree branch.

"Ride piggyback!" Flo shouted.

Jane's hands clutched Cat's neck and shoulders then fell, but he managed to hold her head above water until they reached the ropes. He tied one around her waist. After she'd been hauled to safety, he knotted another rope around his own waist.

Flo heaved a sigh of relief. Squeezing her sopping braids, she walked toward Jane.

Three crew members and Claude pulled on the rope with a steady motion. Cat waved reassuringly.

"Sorry," Jane huffed. "Saw you. Didn't think. Jumped in. Branch caught me."

"You were very brave," Flo said, still focused on Cat.

Wreckage from the explosion rushed downstream — tree branches, a miner's cap, several picks and shovels.

"What's taking them so long? Oh, no!" Flo raised her hands, as if to ward off disaster. Her throat clogged. For the second time in her life she couldn't scream.

The river had become a spinning vortex, and surging water created high peaks of foam. A pick rose above the foam and struck at Cat's face. The sharp points flashed then tumbled into the whirlpool. Cat floated, facedown. The men increased their pressure on the rope.

Flo forgot her exhaustion. She helped the others lift Cat's body and place him on the bank. His eyes were shut, his lids blue-tinged. Blood streamed down his face.

She knelt. "Claude, bring every blanket and jacket you can find. There's brandy inside the supply wagon. Someone heat water. Hurry!" As she spoke, she found a seam on her skirt and began tearing cloth. Her nails shredded along with the material. The wet calico was nearly unmanageable, but abject fear gave her an almost super-human strength.

Loose strips of skin showed a portion of Cat's cheekbone. His forehead and eyes seemed to have escaped the pick's attack. Thank God!

With a moan, he came to as she bathed his face. His eyes were a pale green. "The baby," he said hoarsely. "Is the baby all right?"

For a moment she just stared at him.

"He thinks he's William and you're Minta." Jane sat on her heels. "He thinks you're really pregnant."

Flo's blood-soaked fingers rested limply across her knees. She watched with detached interest as her hands began to tremble. All she could smell was blood.

Accepting the brandy flask from DuBois, she leaned over Cat. "The baby is fine," she said. "I feel no pain, none whatsoever."

"If it's a girl, name her Tonna. Promise."

"I promise." Flo tightened her grip on the flask. "I have to pour this over your face, Cat, to avoid infection. I don't want to hurt you. As God is my witness, I never wanted to hurt you."

He closed his eyes. She emptied the flask's contents and knew she'd dream about his agonized scream for the rest of her life.

"You can't die, Cat," she pleaded. "You've survived so much. The rodeo. Romaine's motorbike. The cave-in. You laughed at death then. You must laugh at death now."

She continued talking, needing her own voice to fight off the terror that coiled inside her belly like a snake.

Only after they had carried Cat away on a litter, did she slump prone on the ground. She heard the roar of the river. She felt pebbles caress her cheek. She smelled mud, tasted dirt.

"I never faint," she whispered, and fainted.

THIRTY-TWO

Colorado Springs: 1918

Confronting Cook in the kitchen, Flo said, "Food Administrator Herbert Hoover has called for one meatless day, two wheatless days, and two porkless days each week."

"Yes, ma'am." Ignoring Hoover — and Mrs. Flower — Cook prepared her own menus, which usually included one meat dish, one wheat dish, and one pork dish each day.

There was no fixed routine at Aguila del Oro. The maids, butlers and valets had a grand time.

"Mrs. Flower gave me her peg-top skirt." Daisy's snub nose quivered like a bunny's as she cut into her pork chop. "Mrs. Flower says it don't fit no more. Ain't she sweet?"

"She promised *me* a glad rag, too," Grace said, her glare insinuating that a certain peg-top skirt was the glad rag she'd hungered for.

"Lower your voices," Cook admonished, her plump cheeks apple-red. "As long as Mr. Edward's not bothered, Mrs. Flower treats us fair."

The downstairs maid, Suzette, agreed. In fact, Suzette was very agreeable. If there was an unfinished chore, she finished it, then shrugged off the gratitude of Daisy, who wanted to meet Harry down by the stream, or Cook, who'd been on her tootsies since sunrise and needed to prop her swollen feet atop a hassock.

The servants hummed about Suzette entertaining the master's son, who lived at the estate, but they didn't want it brought to Mrs. Flower's attention. Who'd finish up the dusting if Suzette was dismissed?

The Great War ended on the eleventh hour of the eleventh day of the eleventh month. Christmas followed, and Mr. Edward insisted on handing out the gifts personally. After pocketing their money packets, the servants joined hands around the wassail bowl and sang.

Mrs. Flower sang loudest of all. She was getting fat, said Cook, even though she didn't eat much. Daisy said the missus might be carrying a bun in her oven. Grace said she'd read about a hundred-year-old man who was still making babies.

But you could tell the master's health was failing, said Nomi, a French *femme de chambre* who brought Edward his dinner trays. Just look at the portrait above the fireplace. *Monsieur* didn't appear thin as tissue paper, or how-you-say? Saggy-faced.

"Didn't the missus take good care of the master?" Daisy said. Mrs. Flower was once a movie star. Now she hardly ever stepped out.

The missus took good care of the horses, too, said Little Toby. He had never worked for nobody who treated them horses like they was human. And now the master's son had told Old Bully-Ben there'd be a new horse coming. A chestnut mare with a posh name. Old Bully-Ben was surprised because he was in charge of the stables and he'd looked the mare over and told Mr. Edward that she was mean-tempered and skittish. But Mr. Ned told Bully-Ben to mind his own beeswax, and the mare Mrs. Flower called Ruby-yat would arrive next week.

"She's pregnant, Ned." Suzette stood before the bureau mirror, securing her ash-blonde strands with hairpins.

"Servant's gossip, my dear. It's impossible."

Suzette covered her elaborate coiffure with

a ruffled white servant's cap. "If your father's not responsible, some other man pierced her tender flesh, and I know who. John Chinook."

"You're crazy. Flower hates Chinook."

"Don't call me crazy. Watch their movie, especially their love scenes."

"There *are* no love scenes."

"Yes, there are. Watch the way Minta leans against William. Study her eyes. A woman can always tell."

"What do you know of love, Suzette? You honor your body, not your heart. That's why we get along so well. Just the same, it had to be somebody else who, as you so delicately put it, pierced her tender flesh. Edward's heart would have failed in the attempt."

"What a splendid way to die."

"Shut up, or you'll know how it feels. I'll wring your neck during a climactic moment."

"What do you know of climactic moments? Since you've taken over from Claude DuBois, your movies are a big joke. Jane Percival even signed with another studio."

"I've been trying to make a statement. It's not my fault if the public doesn't appreciate great art."

"Great art? Three reels of a man who

thinks he's a spider and chases a fly around the room?"

"The fly was symbolic, illustrating a moral principle."

"If you must show white people killing colored people, don't turn them into spiders and flies. In any case, Dollyscope hasn't had a hit movie since *Heaven's Thunder.*"

"Shut up!"

"Shut up yourself. Are you planning to wring my neck like a chicken and dig a shallow grave beneath your stepmother's roses? I'm not Ruthie Adams, and my cottage isn't some miner's shack stuck out in the middle of nowhere."

"How . . . how'd you know about Ruthie?"

"Luke told me. I don't care if you killed a whore, Ned. Whores die all the time." With a snaggle-toothed grin, she handed him a bottle of whiskey, stolen from Aguila del Oro's liquor cabinet.

"I'm glad you're not bothered by a little thing like murder, Suzette. I'll need your help."

"Luke will be furious if his Flower fades before he can have his way with her, so you'd better make it worth my while."

"You'll get Flower's diamonds. After my father dies, I'll hand over fifty thousand dollars. What can Luke offer to match that?"

"Nothing. His assets are frozen. When Chinook cut his handsome face to ribbons, he returned to the ranch and resurrected as Cat McDonald. Luke says he's gonna lie low a while and let Cat rebuild the family fortune. Then he'll strike."

"How?"

"I don't know. Wish I did. By the way, when do you plan to kill your stepmother?"

"That's a dilemma. Flower believes the wild mare a gift from Edward, but Old Bully-Ben and Little Toby know I bought her. I don't want to strike too quickly since I would surely be suspect, and yet I can't wait too long. If you're right and Flower is pregnant, she mustn't be allowed to whelp."

"Haven't you learned that I'm always right? Flower's blossoming, even though she tries to disguise it with loose peignoirs. I don't understand why she's hiding the blessed event, since your father, ill as he is, will hear the squalls of her brat once it's born."

"I should have killed Flower a long time ago. With Flower dead, I'd become Edward's heir again."

"Not if she has a child. If she gives your father a new heir and anything happens to her, the bulk of his fortune will be held in trust for the child."

"I wish I could determine how pregnant she is."

"The servants will know soon. I'll keep my ears open."

"And such lovely ears they are, Suzette. Won't they look even lovelier sporting Flower's diamonds?" Ned stomped to the window and stared out toward the stables. "I never should've bought the mare she calls Rubaiyat. When Edward learns his Flower was fertilized by another man, he'll send her packing."

Flo tied back the drapes, but the additional light showed just how wizened Edward had become. Only his blue eyes seemed alive.

She opened the window, hoping the March breeze would find its way inside and dissipate sickroom smells. Then she walked to the chiffonier and stropped a straight razor. "Take back your gold, for gold can never buy me," she sang, stirring lather with a brush. "Make me your wife, that's all I ask of you." Spreading the white lather beneath her nose, she sculpted a handlebar mustache.

"An apropos song," Edward grumbled. "I offered you a bribe to obtain your consent for our marriage, even though you are more nurse than wife."

"That's not true. I consented freely, without the offer of a bribe. In fact," she said with a smile, "I had no choice. You wouldn't take no for an answer."

She wiped the foam away with the sleeve of her gray velvet robe. "Remember when we watched the Kentucky Derby? I had such fun. I can't thank you enough for Hugo and Rubaiyat. I'm not dissatisfied with my life. Here, let me prop another pillow behind your shoulders so you can sit up more comfortably."

"When's the baby due, Flower?"

"What baby?"

"Did you honestly believe avoiding public appearances and clothing yourself in loose robes would hide your growing belly?"

"Edward, please don't get upset . . ." She paused when he realized he wasn't upset.

"Chinook's the father," he stated.

"Yes. How'd you know?"

"My heart is failing, darling girl, not my eyesight."

"Jack would say I had *chutzpah*. That's Jewish for brazenness." A new thought occurred. "Your Denver trip."

"I wanted you to have three days of perfect love without fear of discovery."

"But you came home early."

"I'm fallible. I began to wonder if I'd gone

616

too far and you'd leave me."

"How can I explain? I told you about the attempted rape. Cat . . . I mean John rescued me."

"I know Chinook is Cat McDonald. You mentioned living near the McDonald spread, so I contacted my retired Pinkerton. He's local, and it took him less than a day to ferret out Chinook's true identity. Was the cave-in the first time?"

"Yes. I thought about asking you for a divorce —"

"I wouldn't have agreed. I'm not that magnanimous."

"You want me to be your wife, even knowing that I carry his child?"

"Absolutely. I shall claim responsibility." A wicked gleam flickered in his eyes. "I plan to speed up my recovery, if only to enjoy the raised eyebrows. Please don't tell my pompous heart specialist the baby isn't mine. Perhaps he'll compose a paper for one of his medical journals." Edward sighed. "It's another bribe. Our son or daughter will never want for anything. He or she will be raised at Aguila del Oro and bear the Lytton name."

"Name! I promised . . . would you mind terribly if I named a girl Tonna?"

"That sounds Indian."

"Navaho. It means weaver-of-dreams."

"I won't object if you add my mother's name. Gay."

"Tonnagay. How beautiful."

"What about a boy? There are too many Edwards. Do you want to call him John?"

"And you said you weren't magnanimous," she chided. "No, although I do appreciate your generosity."

"We could call him Jaygee's funny Jewish word."

"Chutzpah Lytton?" She laughed. "Goodness, Edward, you sound much better."

"I feel much better. Would you do me a big favor? Forget about shaving this old face, and stitch up a pretty gown that shows your belly?"

"Thank you," she said, her throat clogged with tears.

"Poppycock! Assemble the servants. They are consumed with curiosity, and I shall bask in their satisfied smirks. Thank *you,* Flower."

Rising from his bed, Edward shifted his body into a wheelchair. He asked for his favorite hunting dog, Mercury, short for Mercurial, and trained the hound to heel beside the chair.

Edward shared Flo's dislike for smelly gas

automobiles. Just the same, he bought Jack's old Bearcat and hired a chauffeur named Karl.

"You've never seen Cave of the Winds," he said one day. "I'd like to see it again. Will you accompany me?"

"Of course," she replied.

"Let's take Mercury along. He can run for help if we get stuck at Fat Man's Misery. It's a narrow passageway, almost too narrow for an automobile. Damn, I wish we could ride."

"You'll ride, once you've regained your strength."

Edward leaned forward and stroked her belly. "I think Chutzpah just kicked."

When Ringling Brothers Circus came to town, camping near the Colorado Avenue viaduct, Edward bought tickets for himself, Flo, Steven and Marylander. He patiently explained every event to Marylander then led her through the grounds so she could "touch an elephant."

Marylander, now twelve and sightless, was still a spunky, stubborn, wild-natured girl. Steven adored her and told anybody who would listen that he planned to marry her.

"Edward, you're wonderful with children," Flo said.

"I didn't have time for my own. That's

probably why Ned turned out so poorly."

"Nonsense. Elizabeth fares very well. And Katie spruces up every time she sees you."

"I promise I shall live to see our baby born, Flower. Robert E. Lee once said the human spirit is equal to any calamity, and I believe a resolute mind can triumph over a useless body."

While Edward took his afternoon naps, Flo visited the stables, making Bully-Ben her reluctant accomplice. Edward had forbidden her to ride the horses until after "Chutzpah's" birth.

"I'm not *riding,*" she told Bully Ben with a smile, recalling Marylander's disobedience and subsequent justifications. "It's just that I have to take time by the forelock, or in this case fetlock, so that Rubaiyat will learn to trust me. Poor baby's been mistreated something awful."

"You've worked magic with Ruby, Missus Flower." Bully-Ben stood just inside the barn entrance, moving his head back and forth like a pendulum, looking out for a servant who might tattle. "None else but Little Toby can enter Ruby's stall."

Flo curried the mare's silky chestnut hide with a soft brush. "Stand still, my pretty red jewel. When you're a well-behaved lady, I'll introduce you to Khayyam and name your first colt Omar."

Bully-Ben's ruddy cheeks paled. "You'd better hide. Master Ned's comin' this way."

Flo ducked inside the tack room but peered through a crack in the door. Rubaiyat pounded her hooves and gave a shrill whinny when she caught Ned's scent.

Good judge of character, thought Flo.

"How's the mare today, Bully-Ben?"

"You can see for yourself, Mr. Ned."

"Her disposition hasn't improved?"

"Does she look like she's improved?"

"The mare will behave once Mrs. Flower has time to gentle her. By the way, Cook's been grousing that you ain't paid her a visit of late."

Bully-Ben fumbled for his corncob pipe, then seemed to remember he was in the barn and couldn't light it.

Ned nudged the stable hand with an elbow. "I promised I'd talk you into joining her tonight, after everyone's gone to bed. She's already baking up apple fritters."

Bully-Ben licked his lips.

"And now I'll be on my way. I've a business meeting in Divide, but I'll visit the mare again tomorrow. Perhaps she should be shipped back to her previous owner."

"I told Mr. Edward that Ruby was skittish."

"I hope Mrs. Flower doesn't try to tame her. Mrs. Flower is eight months pregnant, and yet a servant saw her headed for the barn around midnight. More than once, I might add."

That's a lie, thought Flo. She visited the stables during the afternoon, never at night.

A perfect night for a murder, thought Ned.

He glanced at the clock above the sideboard, then the men sitting around the dining room table. As host, Luke kept offering barbecued beef sandwiches, but he was the only one who ate them. Richard Reed was a vegetarian. Randolph Tassler puffed a fat cigar. Alan Tassler, who'd matched Ned drink for drink, now slumped in his chair with his eyes shut, his mouth open. Ever since Katie's accident —

"Is it safe to talk?" Richard ran his hand through his hair.

"I've given the servants the night off," Luke said between bites of thick-baked bread and savory beef. "My father's upstairs, asleep. My brother lives at the ranch, but avoids contact with outsiders. He's terribly scarred, you know."

"Lytton, check out the kitchen," Richard ordered.

Ned lurched to his feet. Ignoring the

kitchen at the end of the hallway, he leaned into the front hall banister. Richard must never guess how much whiskey he'd had before the meeting. Richard wouldn't approve. Richard purged his body daily with a rectal enema.

Was Suzette gearing herself up for Flower's murder? Ned pictured Aguila del Oro. Soon Little Toby would go to bed inside the cottage he shared with the chauffer, Karl. Old Bully-Ben would wait until Little Toby hit the sack before sampling Cook's fritters, and whatever else she had to offer, leaving the stables unguarded.

The dilemma had been how to get Flower inside the barn. Ned had suggested Suzette whip Rubaiyat, trusting the mare's shrill cries would bring Flower running.

"Ruby's screams might wake others," Suzette had argued.

"I suppose you have a better plan."

"Nothing's more valuable than a workable plan. Listen closely, Ned, because the best way to put an idea across is to wrap it up in a person."

"What does that mean? I'm sick of your axioms, Suzette."

"Flower gives your father his medicine at midnight. While she's gone from her room, I'll slip a note under her door."

"You'll send her an invitation?"

"The note will be a forgery, signed by Cat McDonald."

"What if you're wrong and Chinook's not the one?"

"I'm never wrong. But I'll word the note so it sounds more like a plea than an assignation."

"I suppose you have that figured out, too."

"Certainly. The note will beg Flower to meet him in the barn because he wants darkness to hide his scars. How can she refuse? Even if Cat wasn't her lover, he saved her life."

"How will you get Rubaiyat to attack?"

"I'll wait until Flower is at the barn entrance, *then* whip the mare into a frenzy. By the time others arrive, she'll be dead and I can intermingle. I'll wear nightclothes."

Ned had decided that tonight was the perfect occasion since he'd be at a Klan meeting. Suzette had agreed, eager to perform the deed and reap the rewards. Brainless idiot! She didn't realize he planned to kill her, too. He didn't know how yet, but he'd find a way. After all, nothing was more valuable than a workable plan, he thought, returning to the dining room and glancing at the clock.

Luke wiped his mouth on his sleeve. "Why

do you keep looking at the clock, Lytton?"

"Because shortly after midnight I'll control my father's assets."

"What do you mean? We don't want trouble with the law," Richard said.

"I'm in Divide!" Ned shouted. "If Flower's dead, I'm not accountable. The shock might even kill Edward. Suzette would say something about killing two birds with one stone. I'll wager my inheritance that's just what she'd say."

Flo read the short letter for the third time. Then she ripped the paper into shreds. Even so, the words remained indelibly etched on her mind.

Why did Cat want to see her?

If his note had mentioned their affair, she'd have ignored it. But he'd pleaded for understanding, and she had no right to refuse. After all, he had saved her life.

He had battled to live, and how had God rewarded him? When his bandages were taken off, the left side of his face, from cheekbone to chin, was a mass of scars. He'd even lost most of his ear.

"That was my deaf ear," he had murmured from his hospital bed. "Too bad they never recovered the raggedy piece. You could have worn it inside a locket."

She had turned away to hide her tears.

After that one visit, Cat refused to see her again.

Why had he changed his mind tonight? How had he delivered his note? By greasing a servant's palm, of course. Which servant? Did it matter?

With a sigh, Flo donned the extra-large pair of blue jeans Edward had insisted on buying for her. Then she added a cable-stitched, oversized white sweater. Twisting her braids into a coronet, she glimpsed her reflection.

If Cat had any romantic notions, the sight of her belly would dissuade him. Her mirror revealed an ashen face. Smudges of fatigue shadowed eyes that bore an expression of fearful anxiety. And if that wasn't enough, her body resembled a goose. A goose wearing blue jeans. An enormous gestational goose.

Shielded by her ungainly bulk, Flo left the house and walked toward the barn.

Grateful for the darkness, Cat McDonald crept through the grounds of Aguila del Oro. He felt like Don Quixote. He remembered Titanic the bull. Canon City didn't have icebergs, and Aguila del Oro didn't have windmills — just trees and pastures and lily ponds.

Craving a slice of Tonna's rhubarb pie, Cat had walked into the kitchen and over-heard Ned Lytton's drunken boast.

Luke's Buick Speedster had been close at hand.

By Cat's reckoning, it was just past midnight. He stared at the house with its gables and bell tower. It loomed majestically, a solemn, brooding storybook castle. Suppose he guessed which room belonged to Fools Gold? How would he get inside? Storm the castle? Scale the walls? Damn! The image of John Chinook, quixotic hero, refused to die.

He pictured himself entering her room. He'd bend over the bed. Her inky lashes would flutter open. She'd scream.

With a self-mocking grin, he adjusted his Stetson's brim, shading the left side of his face. Then he laughed. Who was he hiding from? The man in the moon?

"Do a few scratches on your face make your arms and legs weak?" Tonna had asked. "Do your eyes not see? Does your voice not sing? Answer me, Cat."

"A few scratches? My face looks like a patchwork quilt."

"Does Dorado trot away at the sight of your scars? Do the birds spread their wings in frightened flight? Does the Chinook wind change direction or the mountain lion retreat?"

"Of course not, Tonna. Birds don't care. Animals have hearts and souls. It's the men who have no souls."

He had been quoting Fools Gold, yet even she had turned away, unable to stomach the sight of his mutilated face.

Tonna had numbed his pain with medicinal herbs, and, in due course, the purple-bruised, red-puckered skin faded. But Tonna couldn't work miracles.

Cat had always scoffed at movie-magazine stories, especially the critic who'd described John Chinook as "a handsome drifter."

Handsome drifter? Not hardly. How about scar-faced nomad?

Even Fools Gold couldn't face his face.

After their first flinch, the hands grew accustomed to Cat's altered appearance. Several had left when Luke took over, but a few wandered back to obey Cat's firm commands and the ranch throbbed with productivity once again.

Cat had anticipated battling his brother for control. However, Luke made a clean breast of his negligence, even apologized for the angry words flung at Papa following Dimity's death.

But that came too late. John McDonald

was now a grizzled old man who sat on the front porch, rocking back and forth in his chair. His watery eyes gazed into the distance and he rubbed an emerald necklace between his fingers as if it were a rosary. In the beginning, before her heart and body turned so cold, Papa must have truly loved Dimity.

Was it true love that had brought Cat here tonight? Or was he still playing hero?

As Flo navigated the path to the stables, her whole body trembled. Suppose Cat had used the plea in his note to trick her? What if he wanted the baby? What if he threatened, once again, to confront Edward?

She pictured Claude DuBois pressing a megaphone against his lips. She knew exactly what he'd say. "All right, Flower. You are no longer Fools Gold Smith, the parlor house waif. You are Mrs. Edward Lytton, lady of the manor. We don't want faith. We don't want pathos."

"What do we want, Claude?"

"Gumption."

Squaring her shoulders, she walked toward the barn, and was almost at the entrance when she heard her mare scream. Without delay, she ran inside.

From a middle aisle, box stalls stretched

on each side, ending with a large breeding enclosure on the right and a tack room on the left. Every alcove had a Dutch-style door, barred by a half-gate. Except for Rubaiyat, the horses were out to pasture. The tack room's light encompassed Rubaiyat's stall.

Flo saw the mare flail with her hooves. Blood streamed down her flanks, and welts crisscrossed her haunches.

Standing just outside the stall, Suzette wore a black silk kimono with embroidered red roses. She held a bloodied leather whip. Spying Flo, she pulled a roped handle, swung open Rubaiyat's gate, and cowered behind the gate's slats.

Rubaiyat's ears lay flat against her head. Her lips were drawn back over her teeth. She screamed again, first in pain, then with triumph, as her wild eyes focused on the open space that led to freedom. Darting into the middle of the barn, she skidded to a halt when she saw Flo, who blocked the exit.

With sudden insight, Flo remembered the lie Ned had told Bully-Ben. Tomorrow morning, when Edward found her body, he'd think she had paid Rubaiyat a night-time visit. Nobody would believe she'd whip an animal, but Ned would have an explanation for that too. Flower was eight months pregnant. Her temper had frayed. Her judgment had become impaired.

Edward would blame himself for purchasing Rubaiyat. The shock might even kill him.

Clutching her belly, Flo careened toward the exit.

"Oh, no you don't!" Suzette ran forward, skirting the mare, and pushed roughly at Flo with both hands.

Flo stumbled, fell, scrambled to her knees. Suzette lashed out with her feet. Flo crawled toward the barn door. She must protect the baby. She must protect Edward.

Suzette laughed. "Look at Flower Smith on her knees. That's a sight I'll enjoy for the rest of my life."

The rest of her life was brief. Ignoring Flo, who had never shown her anything but kindness, the mare, a blur of red fire, reared up and struck at Suzette. Rubaiyat's front legs thrashed in a mesmerizing rhythm of continuity as she issued forth a series of shrill whinnies.

Sarah Ann Dusseldorf, also known as Suzy, masquerading as Suzette Dorfman, slid to the floor, her shrieks of terror echoing throughout the barn's raftered roof.

At long last Rubaiyat stood motionless. Despite the pain coursing through her body, Flo managed to rise and maintain her balance while she walked toward the quivering mare. "There, there, my pretty jewel," she crooned. "It's all over. We're both safe now." Twisting her fingers in Rubaiyat's mane, she led the mare inside an empty stall and closed the gate.

Suzy lay in a puddle of blood. Rubaiyat's hooves had crushed her skull. Straw stuck to her body wounds and she looked like a crimson-painted scarecrow. Her left arm was nearly severed from her shoulder.

Controlling the urge to vomit, Flo knelt and captured Suzy's wrist, trying to find a pulse. There wasn't any. How could there be?

She heard footsteps. Still on her knees, she slanted a glance toward the barn's entrance. A tall figure stepped aside and melded into shadows, allowing the emergence of several servants. Karl pushed Edward's wheelchair. As if from a distance, Flo watched everybody freeze in various postures of horrified fascination.

Aggravated by new scents, Rubaiyat struck at the boards of her stall. The servants' deep silence magnified the loud thud of the mare's flailing hooves.

Edward wheeled his chair closer, saw the stained whip, saw Flo's sweater and jeans, crusted with blood. Clutching at his chest, he began to rise.

"What are you doing?" Flo shouted. "Sit down! Do you want to kill yourself? Karl, wheel Mr. Edward back to the house."

"Stay right here, Karl. Is the blood on your clothes from the whip's lash, Flower?"

"No. From Suzy . . . Suzette. From her wounds."

"What happened to Suzette?"

"The mare attacked."

"Which mare?"

"Rubaiyat. She was once called Red Lady. I changed her name when —"

"I gave strict instructions not to purchase Red Lady."

Flo took a deep breath and almost cried aloud from the pain of her bruised ribs. "Ned wanted to get rid of me and blame it on my mare. He didn't know that, against your orders, I frequently visited the stables. Suzette brutally whipped Ruby and . . . is Little Toby here?"

"Yes, Missus."

"Bully-Ben says Ruby will let you enter her stall. Please cleanse her cuts and apply salve."

"Yes, Missus."

Flo bit her lip hard, but she couldn't control the whimper that pushed its way up her throat.

"What's wrong?" Edward's face blanched.

"The baby. Oh!" Flo felt her back explode. She bent over double.

"If that mare harmed you, I'll have her shot."

"Please, Edward, it's the baby. Suzette kicked my ribs and belly. Rubaiyat saved my life. Oh, God, I hurt."

Edward turned toward the servants, who were still assembled in a tableau of mute bewilderment. "Carry Mrs. Flower inside the house, Karl."

"No, too late." Flo rocked back and forth on her heels. "Carry Suzette away. Leave me in peace."

"Karl, take Mrs. Flower's head. Bully-Ben, her feet."

Flo felt her body lifted.

Rubaiyat whinnied.

"Put me down," Flo pleaded. "Suzette kicked my ribs. They're bruised, perhaps broken. Don't carry me to the house. You could do more harm than good."

Edward's face was now the color of parchment, but he calmly said, "Harry, get rid of Suzette's body. Lift it or drag it from the barn. Grace, fetch clean towels. Cook, go with her and boil some water. Daisy, collect all the horse and buggy blankets and make a pallet inside the breeding stall. Bully-Ben,

Karl, place Mrs. Flower very carefully on the pallet."

The servants hastened to obey.

"Little Toby, how's the mare?" Edward asked.

"She's hurting, sir, but nothing's broke."

"Good. Find some feed bags for Mrs. Flower's head and legs. Karl, fetch the doctor."

Within the confines of the breeding stall, Flo gratefully breathed the familiar stable odors she had always loved. She felt Daisy remove her blue jeans and panties, then cover her lower body with a scratchy horse blanket.

When Edward wheeled his chair to the stall's entrance, Flo subdued her agony. His trepidation was palpable and she wouldn't be the cause of his heart's final convulsion.

"A first baby takes a while, doesn't it?" Edward's voice betrayed his agitation. "I must be losing my mind, sending Karl for the doctor. We have telephones. Is it all right if Little Toby wheels me to the house? Or would you prefer I stay?"

She forced her mouth into the semblance of a smile. "There's nothing you can do here, Edward, and if I don't have to worry about you, I can concentrate on the birth of our child."

"Don't forget the words of Robert E. Lee. The human spirit is equal to any calamity."

But Lee lost the war, she thought, as another wave of pain swept through her. Damn Suzy! Damn Cat McDonald!

How did Cat fit into all this? Hellfire! Cat's note was a forgery! Clever Suzy.

Why hadn't she watched Suzy more carefully? Because "Flower Lytton" had grown complacent, lulled by her pregnancy, forgetting her sworn revenge on the woman.

Flo seemed to be floating above her pain now. Several of the servants had left the barn. A few remained, frightened and useless, but they didn't exist. She didn't exist. Only the wild duck was real. Soft feathers folded around her body and carried her up past the barn's rafters.

What a beautiful duck.

I'm dying. That's why the pain is gone.

Poor Edward. Tonight he'd lose both his wife, Flower, and his granddaughter, Fools Gold.

Faceless multitudes would mourn the passing of motion picture actress Flower Smith, but there'd be another star to take her place. Would Flower's movies survive? Probably not. After all, movies were merely dreams that pierced the darkness.

Did heaven exist? If it did, Blueberry

would be waiting there. Minta and Robin, too. Wouldn't it be nice to see their faces and bury herself in their loving arms?

Flower Lytton lay on the stable floor, writhing with unbearable pain. Fools Gold Smith floated above her, and all she had to do was close her eyes and let the beautiful wild duck carry her up to heaven.

Horrified, she watched her duck merge into a carnivorous shrike. This new bird would surely impale her on his talons. She fought against the talons. With profound relief, she felt the hard stable floor beneath her bed of blankets. The pain went away and so did the shrike. She had fought hard and she was exhausted. When the wild duck lifted her, she snuggled against its soft plumage.

Somebody called her name. She didn't want to answer.

"Hello, Fools Gold," the man's voice repeated. A familiar voice.

Though her eyes stung with tears, she saw a shape kneel by the pallet. Hands shifted the grain sack from beneath her ankles so that her knees were bent across the burlap. "Hello, Cat," she whispered. "Are you really here? This isn't a dream?"

"I'm really here."

"Why can't I see your face?"

"Because the light is dim and a hat hides my eyes. Do you feel my hand holding yours?"

"Yes. Why are you pressing my fingers so hard?"

"I want you to feel your pain. Remember what I told you about Dimity? She let the snow cover her body and lull her to sleep. I want you to stay awake."

"I was riding a duck . . . a wild duck. I almost recited that poem at the Penrose Ball. It mentions gold and flowers and . . . I'm so tired, Cat. Please let me ride the wild duck."

"Ride your pain, Fools Gold, not the duck."

Lost within his hand's grip, she said, "Look how beautiful he is . . . he is bound for the hilltops . . . the gold hilltops . . ."

"Rest later, my love. Someday we will ride through the gold hilltops, I promise. Now you must ride your pain."

"Happy wild duck."

Cat's breath caught in his throat. How could he reach her?

"Poor little wild duck."

Cat groaned. There had to be a way to reach her. Frantic, he said, "You cannot die with your baby trapped inside your body."

"Oh, I forgot about the baby. Poor little

wild baby."

"When you feel the pain return, squeeze my hand."

"I feel it. But . . . I . . . cannot . . . bear it."

"Squeeze harder," Cat said, and felt her fingernails gash his palm. "That's my good girl. Now, take a deep breath."

"I can't. My ribs hurt. Suzette kicked me. My fault. I hired her. If the baby dies —"

"The baby won't die. I won't let it die."

Cat lost all track of time. The servants must have wondered who he was, but they seemed grateful for his presence. Keeping away from the enclosure, they whispered among themselves or wrung their hands.

Fools Gold smelled hot and sick. Cat bathed her brow and kneaded her belly and listened to her moans become whimpers.

Where was her damned doctor? Forget the doctor. Her contractions were arriving one after the other, nary a pause. If he didn't do something quick, she would die. Pivoting on his knees, he stared at one of the servants, huddled near the tack. "You!" he shouted. "Fetch hot water, strong soap, and the oil that anoints the newborn colts. Hurry!"

The window above allowed dawn's inception to permeate the stall. Fools Gold's strength was waning fast. Cat could see it in her glazed eyes, now purple-black with exhaustion, and in the ashy hue of her face.

He washed his hands, covered them with oil, waited until the next contraction had passed, then thrust his fingers inside her tight passage. He'd done this before with the livestock on his ranch, but never a woman. His groping fingers felt the baby's head. Perspiration poured into his eyes and down his scarred cheek as he guided the baby's head toward the birth canal.

Hugging her bruised ribs, Fools Gold gave one last scream. Then she bore down to dislodge her child.

Cat gazed with wonder at ten perfect fingers and toes. "It's a girl," he said, tears flooding his voice.

"Tonna . . . Tonnagay. Is she alive?"

"Yes. She's very tiny, but she looks strong."

"Like you."

"No, my love. You."

Flo heard the sound of Edward's wheel-chair and the voice of her doctor: "A felled tree blocked the road. Thank God for your chauffer . . ."

Cat placed the baby on her belly. "Do you still see the wild duck, Fools Gold?"

"No. The duck's gone."

"Then I'll be gone, too." With a nimbleness that belied his size, he hoisted himself up and out through the window.

Cat, don't go. Cat, I love you.

Shifting her gaze toward the wheelchair, Flo said, "You have a new daughter, Edward. Now you must stay alive for a long, long time. Now you must watch her grow."

THIRTY-THREE

By 1920 Colorado Springs was overwhelmingly white and Protestant, counting only 500 Jews, 2,965 Catholics, slightly more than 1,000 Negroes, and 2,600 foreign-born immigrants among its 30,605 inhabitants. Unlike Denver, Colorado Springs had no ethnic neighborhoods.

As recruiting Kleagles, Ned Lytton and Lucas McDonald were failing miserably. Luke tried to manipulate the Catholic menace, repeating the usual refrains concerning priestly corruption, but those allegations collapsed in the wake of intelligent Catholic passivity. Ned had only slightly more success with parental concerns regarding suggestive forms of dancing and adolescent petting parties. He and Luke secured most of their small Klan membership from the city's rough, bigoted working-class men, who commanded little influence or respect.

Ned wished he still lived in Denver where

the Klan thrived, where Klansmen successfully vied for power and became the arbiters of community policy, but he stayed on at Aguila del Oro, waiting for Edward to die.

"Father will outlive us all," Ned said to his grandfather's portrait, and could have sworn the benign gent bobbed his head. "Father will outlive Flower, damn her grit."

Following Tonnagay's birth, there had been no obvious repercussions. Ned had professed innocence. Yes, he had purchased Rubaiyat, misunderstanding his father's apprehensions. But he had no idea Suzette planned to kill Flower. Hadn't he told Old Bully-Ben that Rubaiyat should be shipped back to her previous owner?

Flower, perhaps unwilling to distress Edward further, implied that Suzette was insane with envy. But somehow Flower knew about Ned's part in the plot. When they were together, her blue eyes glittered with undisguised hatred.

It might be prudent to lie low a while, Ned mused, slurping whiskey from a wine glass.

Why hadn't Flower died in childbirth?

Admittedly, one-year-old Tonnagay was an enchanting child. With her porcupine-quill hair, blue-green eyes, and miniature chin-crease, she looked a lot like his beloved Katie. Suzette had been wrong about John

Chinook — dead wrong. Tonnagay looked like a Lytton!

Three weeks ago, following his sister Dorothy's marriage to Alan Tassler, Father had moved the whole family to Aguila del Oro. Kate's condition had improved moderately. She could dress and feed herself, and sometimes she talked a blue streak, but her mind still functioned like a child's. Her doctor had very nearly persuaded Johanna to have Kate placed in a private institution, insisting that qualified personnel might restore Kate's memory. Ned had fired the doctor and hired another. His darling Katie was ill, not crazy.

Dollyscope was no longer a Lytton enterprise. Its assets had been gobbled up by another film company. Just like Dolly, Dollyscope had died from acute inflammation of the gut, or at least that's what everybody whispered loudly behind Ned's back.

So be it. He had become bored with the motion picture business. In fact, until recently, he couldn't summon enthusiasm for anything.

Now Ned refilled his glass, tilting the crystal decanter that perched atop the music room's Chippendale table. Soon he'd leave for a Konclave to be held in a field fifteen miles east of Colorado Springs. In the meantime, Luke would have arranged for the abduction of Cat McDonald.

Ned had resented Chinook's superior attitude during the filming of *Heaven's Thunder,* and was well pleased when the handsome actor's face got scarred. Handsome is as handsome does, Suzette would have said. As it turned out, Chinook was part Mex, part Injun, part Negro.

Luke had finally blurted out the truth about his brother's mixed heritage. He'd kept it under wraps, unwilling to sully his mother's reputation, but Cat's control over the JMD ranch, at first welcomed, had become an irritant. In any case, Luke had overheard his mother tearfully confess that she'd been raped by an outlaw who was part Mex, part Injun, part Negro, and Cat was his son.

"John Chinook's a tar baby," Ned chanted, just before he tainted the air with a belch. He planned to star the former actor in tonight's performance. Cowardly Luke had chosen to shun the Konclave. Tonight's script called for several Klansmen to frighten Cat so badly that the scar-faced bastard would flee Colorado. Ned had already stored the tar and feathers inside the trunk of his Rolls-Royce.

Following Cat's punishment, a letter

would be delivered to a ranch hand named Black Percy, warning that a similar fate was in store for him if he didn't leave the state.

A thrill coursed through Ned's body. Tonight's Konclave would be rollicking good fun.

Kate stared into Mummy's dressing-table mirror. Mummy's mirror was so much prettier than the tent mirror. The tent mirror had been shot, broken.

I look like a grown-up lady, Kate thought as she dipped her fingers through the top layer of Mummy's rouge pot and smeared carmine across her cheeks. She had tied back her long black hair with a yellow ribbon and a string of Mummy's pearls, but Kate hated her body. Her body had two big bumps on top with two bitty bumps on the end of the big bumps.

"Breasts and nipples," said Mummy.

There was fuzz between Kate's legs, dark furry hair, darker than her teddy bear, who was named for a president. Beneath the fur, her legs made her taller than Mummy and Dorothy, taller than her brother Steven. For her last birthday, she had blown out twenty-five candles on Cook's cake, anxious to blow away the fire.

"I like white cake," she'd said, after blowing out the flames on the candle stars. Her daddy had laughed and said white was good and K-K-Katie was a good girl.

Now Kate looked around for a towel. There was no towel, so she wiped her red face and red fingers on her nightie's hem. Oh, no. She'd messed the white nightie, and Nurse would be mad. Nurse was always mad. She didn't like moving into this new house away from all her "Denver-kin." Nurse said she needed the salad . . . no, *sal-ree.*

Kate didn't like the new house, either. It was hard to find the rooms. Her room looked the same. Same bed and chair and coloring books and building blocks. Mummy's room looked the same. Same bed and dressing table and cushion-baskets for the doggies. But the other rooms looked different. Scary.

Nurse would be mad at the dirty white nightie, so Kate had better change her clothes. But if she went to her own room, wherever it was, she'd be caught and she couldn't come back and play with Mummy's rouge pot.

Maybe she could borrow one of Mummy's dresses from the big closet. Mummy was fat and the dress would be fat, but that was okay because the fat dress would hide

Kate's hateful breasts and nipples.

She opened the closet door. A pink-and-white hatbox caught her eye. Pretty box. She placed it on the bed, opened it, and gasped with pleasure at the sight of the fruit on the straw hat. Yanking a green grape free, she bit and spit. It wasn't a real grape.

Disappointed, she hurled the hat across the room. Then she peered into the box again. Nestled in tissue paper was a ladies' revolver with a white mother-of-pearl handle. Pretty gun.

So different than the strikers' guns.

What's a striker?

Kate looked out the window. In the distance, shadows played hide-and-seek. No sun. No moon. No candle stars. She could see grass and flowers and trees. The stables and horses were too far away, but she could see the path from the garage where the cars lived. On the wall, clock fingers pointed to the numbers seven and one, and Kate thought that meant night, but the sky wasn't black yet.

Daddy was driving a car he called an Alpine Eagle down the path from the garage to the house. He stopped, got out, and walked away. Kate could hear the car go chug-chug-chug. She hated Daddy's car. It smelled like fire.

Was Daddy planning to leave? When Nurse was mad, Daddy would say that's-all-right-leave-my-girl-alone. Kate forgot why Nurse was mad tonight, but Daddy was leaving her alone with Nurse. Maybe she could bully Nurse with Mummy's revolver.

Steven had a gun with paper bullets that sounded like snapping fingers when he pulled the trigger. Then he'd blow on the front end and put the gun in his pocket. No, not his pocket. His hole-stir.

She didn't have a hole-stir, so she lifted her nightie and tucked the pretty little gun underneath the elastic of her panties. It felt cold. Then she scurried from Mummy's room, ran down the long staircase, and out the front door. She turned a corner and saw the Alpine Eagle.

Daddy hadn't come back yet. The Eagle's top was down and Kate glimpsed a fur-lined car rug on the backseat, so she curled herself into a ball and hid underneath the rug, like the children who'd once hid in the holes she dug underneath the tents. The fur made her want to sneeze, but if she did the soldiers would find her, so she held her breath until the sneeze went away. The gun pressed against her belly.

Oh, no. If Karl drove, Daddy would sit in back and squish her.

But Daddy sat on the front seat. Kate heard him say, "Almost forgot my robe and hood."

The car went chug-chug-chug and she fell asleep.

Cat strummed his mandolinetto with a tortoiseshell pick. The mandolinetto looked like a guitar but sounded like a mandolin, and Janey had sent it all the way from California.

"The day has passed and gone, the evening shades appear," he sang. "Oh may we all remember well, the night of death draws near."

"No, *Gato,* sing a happy song." Maria stamped her foot. "Sing a song of love, and I shall reward you well."

"I'm honored, *querida,* but you would not enjoy sharing the loft with a devil."

"If you are truly *el diablo, Gato,* I would enjoy sharing a bed *de cacto.*" With a wicked grin, she stretched the neck of her blouse so that it dipped below her breasts.

Cat felt a stirring beneath his belt. How long had it been since he'd had a woman?

When time allowed, he'd drive to the red-light districts in Colorado Springs or Denver. After their first startled wince at the sight of his face, the parlor girls performed with gusto. A paid whore didn't make promises she couldn't keep. A paid whore didn't talk of love then turn away.

Maria had noted the bulge in his trousers. With another grin, she snuggled her pliant body against his. "My husband Rodolfo snores in the big chair," she said, "and fills the room with loud odors from his dinner of *torrijas* . . ." Her voice faltered. Her dark eyes widened. She screamed.

Cat whirled about.

The moon shone down upon eight white-robed, hooded figures with conical hats. In the distance, parked close to a grove of spruce, were two Model-T Fords.

One Klansman pointed a double-barreled shotgun, one a Colt .38-caliber pistol, a third stood leaning against a fence post. "On-ward Chris-chun sol-jurs," he sang in a high, squeaky voice.

"Here, take this." Cat held out his mandolinetto with both hands. The man with the Colt reached for it. Cat swung, and heard a roar of pain as the man dropped his gun and clutched at his face. With regret, Cat glanced down at his splintered mandolinetto.

Before he could retrieve the fallen pistol, he felt a gun's barrel against his belly. "Move again and I'll shoot," said the man who held the shotgun.

"Shoot 'im now," whined the Klansman who'd been struck, who still held his face as though nursing a bad toothache.

"We're supposed to bring him alive to be tarred and feathered," said Shotgun. He looked at Maria. "Git along, Sen-whore-rita. If you warn the hands, we'll come back for ya."

"Gato?"

"Go, sweetheart, and keep your mouth shut."

After Maria was safely out of sight, Cat decided what the hell and stepped back a few paces. Clasping his fingers together, he swung and heard bones crunch. *A nose,* he thought happily, as Shotgun gave a painful yelp and dropped his weapon.

Immediately, Cat felt several pairs of restraining hands. One man spat on the blade of a knife, brandished it in front of Cat's face, and severed Cat's shirt until it hung in tatters.

"You just made a big mistake, nigra," Knife growled.

Cat saw the blackjacks before they landed. The thudding sounds reminded him of Tonna beating a carpet. The moon spun and he shut his eyes, still hearing, as if from a far distance, the strange soprano-voiced

Klansman singing, "On-ward, Chris-chun sol-jurs, march-ing off to . . ."

Hell, thought Kate, peeking over the side of the car.

Nurse said how bad people went to hell. Nurse said Kate was bad when she got her clothes dirty. Oh, no! Kate went and got her nightie dirty so now she was in hell.

Hell had a moon and candle stars. Hell had a twisting trail that led toward a high ridge. Kate looked east and saw evergreens, brush, briars and ghosts.

The ghosts were missing mouths, and on their faces where they should have had eyes and noses there were black holes. Holes, not hole-stirs. Kate remembered the revolver and drew it out from under her nightie.

The sky was black, except for the moon and candle stars. She closed her eyes. When she opened them again, the ghosts were still there. She started crying and tried to stop, knowing the ghosts might hear her tears and find her in the car. But she couldn't stop. She didn't like hell and wanted to go home. Daddy would drive her home. Where was Daddy?

Flinging her leg over the Alpine Eagle's side, she waited for Mike to lift her across

Rosalind Tassler's window sill.

Mike? Mike who? Silly Kate. She needed to find her daddy, not a man named Mike. She slid down the side of the car and felt pebbles through the soles of her slippers. The ghosts hadn't noticed her yet, probably because she was dressed in white, too.

She had never been so scared in her life, not even when the dynamite went boom and the ground shook, not even when Pearl Jolly said to collect the women and children and run for the ranch, ignoring the soldiers' guns.

Confused, Kate stood by the Alpine Eagle, her thoughts twisting and turning, making no sense. Her daddy would tell her who Mike was — and now this new name, Pearl Jolly — if she could only find him.

Two ghosts moved sideways and Kate saw a man on the ground. Was *he* Mike? Had the ghosts killed him? He looked dead but Kate saw him raise his face a little, glance around, then close his eyes again. Mike was *pretending* to be dead.

"You can have the honor, Lytton," said a man's voice, and Kate saw a piece of fire being passed along until it stopped and glowed brightly. Would they throw the stick of fire so that Mrs. Bebout's Saint Bernard could chase it?

Who's Mrs. Bebout? What's a Saint Bernard?

"Don't use my name, you idiot," yelled the angry voice of her daddy.

Thank God. Daddy was here in hell and could take her home. He'd tell her 'bout Mike and Pearl and the Saint Bernard who chased fire-sticks.

Kate tiptoed forward and aimed her pretty gun at the ghosts, even though she was fairly certain you couldn't kill a ghost. As she pulled back on what Steven called the hammer, she caught sight of a ghost standing next to a big wooden cross.

The ghost raised a flaming torch and she smelled fire.

Tents! Dug holes! Children hiding! Soldiers! Smoke! Fire!

Kate's mind cleared. Years of cloudy images vanished. She focused on the white-robed man with the torch, and saw a soldier igniting the side of a canvas tent.

Ludlow! The strikers' colony! Kate could hear the roar of flames, the shrieks and sobs from the wounded. She pictured a band tied round her arm — a white band with a red cross. *Red cross! Cross fire!* Soon they'd be caught in the cross fire.

"You bastard!" Kate raced toward the white-hooded figure who'd lit the cross, the soldier who'd flamed the tent. She was only a few feet away when she pulled her revolver's trigger.

She'd aimed too low. She saw blood stain the hem of the soldier's white robe. The soldier screamed and fell to his knees. She shot again. This time a hole appeared in the soldier's hood — a smoking red mouth, not far from where his mouth should have been anyway.

Kate laughed and shot her pretty revolver until it clicked.

Horror-struck, Cat watched, along with Shotgun, Knife, and the other Klansmen.

Cat staggered to his feet, sprinted toward the girl, scooped her up in his arms, turned east, and zigzagged through the densely shadowed evergreens. The girl twisted away from his chest, aimed over his shoulder, and shot her empty gun toward the spot where Ned Lytton lay in a heap.

It had to be Lytton. Cat had heard somebody shout for Lytton to light the cross.

As he ran, Cat broke out in a cold sweat, even though he had a feeling there wouldn't be any pursuit. Despite the yellow ribbon and pearls encircling her lustrous dark hair, the girl in his arms had looked like an avenging angel, her white nightgown sustaining that illusion. The superstitious, cowardly Klansmen wouldn't give chase.

Cat's bruised body was sending signals to every portion of his brain. His calves and thighs felt hot with pain. He stopped and eased the girl to the ground. Breath raspy, he said, "What's your name, my brave little friend?"

"Kate Loutra."

Once again, Cat felt cold sweat bathe his body. Hadn't Fools Gold mentioned Ned Lytton's eldest daughter, Kate? Hadn't Kate married a man named Mike Loutra?

Cat had seen three bullets — maybe more — shatter Ned Lytton's ankle, face and chest. This beautiful young woman had just killed her own father.

THIRTY-FOUR

"Rain, rain, go away," Flo crooned to her daughter. "Come again some other day. Tonnagay Lytton wants to play."

It was June second, 1922, and the gray sky looked like a piece of blotting paper.

The constant pitter-pat of raindrops had lulled Tonnagay into a late-afternoon nap. Flo covered her daughter with a light blanket then sat in front of the nursery's window. The sky's color reflected her mood, and she'd heard that the Arkansas River was overflowing its banks, menacing the nearby city of Pueblo.

Pueblo was only a few miles from Trinidad and Ludlow.

Eight years ago the Ludlow strikers had given up their fight. Eighteen months after the fire and massacre, John D. Rockefeller Jr. had toured his Colorado mines. "These beans are bully," he'd said, eating a meal at a company boardinghouse. He danced "The

Hesitation Waltz" with a miner's wife, fretted over a mule's harness gall, put on a suit of overalls, descended into a mine, and hacked away at a coal seam for ten minutes.

"We are partners," he told the miners.

Although these events had happened long ago, they were all new to Kate.

Upon regaining her memory, her first tearful question had been, "Where's Mike?"

It took Edward three days to discover Mike Loutra's whereabouts and secure his release.

Mike wouldn't accept "Lytton money," even as recompense, so Flo proposed that Edward buy Mike and Kate a house — a belated wedding gift.

Now Flo reached out and retrieved the letter that lay on top of Tonnagay's bureau. Kate's neat script filled two pages of pink stationary. Mike still crabbed about Grandfather's payoff, Kate wrote, but she, for one, was incredibly grateful for the house on Long Island, so close to New York City and Mike's work. She had bought a Saint Bernard puppy and named it Cat, after Cat McDonald, who had saved her from the "ghosts." And Flower should tell Grandfather that "Chutzpah Loutra" was doing that new dance, the soft-shoe, inside Kate's belly.

Aunt Elizabeth had taken her to see *The Emperor Jones* — a Broadway play that used eight scenes to explore themes of justice and retribution.

Mike had written a book about convict labor gangs, to be published by Doubleday, and he took great pleasure in Kate's home-cooked meals. Right now he was away from home, campaigning for Samuel Gompers to beat John L. Lewis in the June election. Four or five years ago — she still had trouble with dates — Lewis had traveled to Colorado, declared the union bankrupt, and purged it of its militants. Mike loathed Lewis.

Had Flo read *The Sheik* by Edith Hull? Its story told of a beautiful girl carried off into the desert by an Arab chief.

"It reminds me of Mike," Kate wrote, "even though Mike didn't carry me into our Ludlow tent. I practically carried him. Daddy never really knew Mike."

Here, Kate had written a few lines and scratched through them.

Her doctor wore a goatee and felt Kate's mental health improved daily. "Dr. Rubenstein says Daddy's death was justice and retribution," Kate wrote, "just like Eugene O'Neill's play. I wish I could believe that."

Believe it, dearest sister, Flo thought. *Jus-*

tice for Ned's part in your illness, retribution for Blueberry's abandonment.

Flo had searched her heart, but could feel nothing except relief over Ned's death. She was only sorry that she and Ned had never performed the final confrontation reel.

With a tight smile, she pictured Claude DuBois raising his megaphone. "This scene is filled with pathos, Flower. Your father is dying. Fall to your knees and clutch his hand. Your tears purify his wounds."

"No, Claude, my tears cauterize his soul."

The Klansmen insisted an Angel of Death had "come out of nowhere" and shot Ned. The authorities couldn't find the murder weapon — now safely back in Johanna's hatbox — or even a suspect, but Flo maintained they ditched the investigation because they couldn't depict an Angel of Death on a Wanted poster.

Putting Kate's letter aside, she peered through the rain-streaked window at the rolling lawn, blooming plants, and fat, sassy livestock. The estate thrived, despite Edward's illness. Bedridden once again, he had accepted Ned's death stoically, even agreed to the Denver Klan's request to bury Ned in their own cemetery.

"Are you sure you don't want Ned buried in the family plot?" she had asked.

"My heart is failing, darling girl, not my ears. I heard your words inside the barn. You've been watched and protected ever since Tonnagay's birth."

Edward never mentioned his son's name again.

On Tonnagay's third birthday, Edward died in his sleep. He had requested that his body be cremated. Flo saddled Rubaiyat, rode through the Garden of the Gods, and climbed to the top of a red boulder.

Edward adored high places, she thought, remembering their drive through Fat Man's Misery. Edward would enjoy his ride atop the wild duck.

The sky was a blaze of twilight colors as she flung his ashes into the breeze. "I love you, Grandfather," she whispered.

A few days later, she dispatched a brief note to Cat, inviting him to Edward's memorial service. Although Cat sent back an equally brief letter of sympathy, he didn't appear. She heard the echo of his words: *I'll wait forever.*

She'd half expected him to visit the ranch, sweep her up into his arms, and gallop toward the gold hilltops. Why didn't he? The answer was simple. His love had waned. Forever wasn't such a long time, after all.

Naturally, she learned all about him during Jane's frequent visits.

Jane's innocence had disappeared along with her curls. She played the part of the vamp in her popular films, wore daringly short skirts, and rolled her stockings below her dimpled knees. Her hair was bobbed, her eyebrows plucked thin, her amber eyes enhanced with black kohl.

Today, July fourth, 1923, Flo sat back in her chair and tugged at the hem of her own short red skirt. "Remember how you once begged for sound in motion pictures, Janey? A man named De Forest has demonstrated sound. He even included a performance by an orchestra."

"Yes, I know."

"Janey, are you all right?"

"Please understand that the newspaper and magazine stories about wild parties and my broken engagements are merely studio publicity."

"Of course. May I assume, then, that you have no special fellow?"

"You sound like Cat." With a smile Jane withdrew a flask of bootleg whiskey from her beaded purse and added the contents to her glass of lemonade.

"How *is* Cat?"

"I wondered when you'd finally get

around to asking about my mule-headed brother."

"Mule-headed?"

"Yes. He's been learning how to fly."

"Airplanes?"

"Yes. Did you think I meant flapping his arms like a bird? Ever since they inaugurated the municipal airport in Tucson, Cat talks of nothing else. I keep remembering Vernon Castle's air accident, and Vernon even served with the Royal Flying Corps in Europe."

"Cat's outsmarted death before. He'll be fine."

"Then why did your face turn pale when I mentioned flying?"

Ignoring Jane's query, Flo sipped from her glass of unaltered lemonade. "How's the ranch?"

"Better. Luke laughed at Cat's idea to raise hogs. Luke would, since he so closely resembles the swine. But in his last letter, Cat wrote that hogs on the hoof were bringing the highest price ever." She sighed. "Luke's causing trouble again. His slimy Klan friends have convinced him that the JMD would make an excellent resort, but I'm sure they plan to serve up more than fine cuisine and horseback rides. Frankly, I'm scared for Tonna and Black Percy."

"Luke can't do that. When your father died, Cat inherited the ranch, and it's only Cat's incredible generosity that allows Luke to remain there at all."

"Incredible stupidity, you mean. I think my gorbellied slug of a brother plans to fight Cat for control of — hey, look! Who's cutting across your pasture?"

"I've no idea." Flo stood, shading her eyes from the sun's glare with her hand. "Most of my guests chug up to the gate in their smelly automobiles. It's been a while since I had a visitor on horseback."

"Why, it's Black Percy." Jane pushed back her chair and stood next to Flo. "He's riding Avalanche. I hope nothing's wrong at the ranch. They know I'm here because I planned to visit after tonight's party."

Flo watched the tall man dismount and walk toward them. Jane stepped forward and greeted him with a hug. "Is everything all right at home, Percy?"

"As right as it was last time you come. Dang, it's hotter than the trail along the Pecos."

"Why didn't you drive one of Luke's automobiles?"

"On a day like this I'd have to stop every few feet and fill the radiator, probably burn my hands to cinders in the bargain. You look fit, but skinny as a newborn eaglet. Tonna will tan your hide before she stuffs you with strawberry muffins."

Flo nodded toward a pitcher. "Would you care for some lemonade, Mr. Percival?"

"Thank you kindly, Mrs. Lytton."

"Have you ever met Black Percy, Flo?"

"Once, Janey, a long time ago. He kept me from fainting in the aisle at a bullfight, and seemed to understand my pain at the brutality of the event."

"Don't cotton to the torture of animals. People, neither. The hands keep watch day and night to prevent that very thing from happening again. Can I talk to you a short spell, Mrs. Lytton?"

"Only if you call me Flo."

"Why don't I water Avalanche?" Jane grasped the gelding's reins.

"Please sit down, Mr. Percival," said Flo, after Jane had kicked off her heeled pumps, removed her stockings, and dashed barefoot toward a lily pond.

"You talkin' to me or someone named Mister Percival?"

With a grin, Flo indicated the rattan chairs, copied from the furniture that decorated the Antlers Hotel's sun parlor. "Won't you please set, Percy?"

"Thank you kindly. These old bones don't

have the strength they used to. A dang steer could bulldog me."

"Did Cat send you?"

"I like a gal who gets straight to the mountain without twistin' off the trail. No, Cat didn't send me. But he's the reason I rode here."

"Anything wrong?"

"There's lots wrong, but that ain't why I'm here. My wife Tonna pestered me till I thought her words would go clear through to the other side of my head. Let me ask you one question. Dimity-Jane says you have a child you call Tonnagay. Is she Cat's little girl?"

"Yes."

"We reckoned so. Couldn't figure why you'd choose Tonna's name otherwise."

"I promised Cat during the river accident, but I've always thought the name beautiful."

"Your husband died last year?"

"Yes."

"Then why ain't you rode to the ranch and paid Cat a call?"

"You've asked me three questions, Percy." When he didn't reply, she forced a swallow of lemonade down her throat. "I figured Cat didn't want to see me. I assumed he didn't love me anymore. Why are you smiling?"

"Because Tonna said that's what you'd say. It ain't true, 'specially the last part. I believe Cat loves you greatly. He just don't want you to see him."

"Why? His scarred face?"

"Ain't so terrible to look at no more. It's been medicined, and the sun's tanned it good."

"Then I don't understand —"

"Luke. He's got a wicked tongue. Lit into my friend Mac with that tongue after Dimity's death till Mac couldn't think clear. Now Luke's pullin' the same stunt on Cat. Luke's like a bloodsuckin' tick 'neath a pup's skin. No matter how hard puppy scratches, the tick burrows deeper. Every day Luke tells Cat how much better he looks, which ain't no lie. But Luke says it in a voice that's too slick. Cat won't have mirrors in the house, so he don't know the truth."

"I didn't realize . . . Jane never said . . . I don't care how Cat looks!"

"Somehow Luke's learned 'bout Cat lovin' you, and he tells Cat you're seein' this man or that man and watchin' polo or dancin' till dawn at the Antlers."

"And Cat believed those lies? Of course he did. I have to see him, convince him Luke's wrong."

"Tonna and me was hopin' you'd say that.

Will you come callin' real soon?"

"Not soon. Today. I hate automobiles as much as you do, but I want to get there before darkness, so I'll have my chauffeur saddle up our new Cadillac. Please come with me. Janey can hostess my Fourth of July party. Tomorrow she can return Avalanche. I think she'd purely enjoy a horseback ride."

"Cat's mule-headed," Percy warned. "It won't be easy."

"Sure it will. I'll just tell him the truth."

It wasn't easy at all.

When Flo arrived at the ranch, it was late afternoon. Luke offered an effusive greeting, which Flo cut short by saying, "Where's Cat?"

Small eyes glittered from the expanse of Luke's bloated face. His nose was flat and wide, he weighed at least three hundred pounds, and she understood why Janey had compared him to a hog.

"My brother's mending fences out on the range, Mrs. Lytton," he said. "Or can I call you Flower?"

"May I borrow a horse, Mr. McDonald, and would you be kind enough to point me in the right direction?"

"Follow our pastures west toward the

mountains. Percy'll saddle up one of my prize palomino mares."

Cat's prize palomino mares, you slug! Turning on her heels, Flo followed Percy, who walked toward the barn. Thank goodness she'd changed into blue jeans and boots.

It took another hour before Flo's dainty mare whinnied and Flo heard a response from a great golden stallion. Cat whirled about in his saddle. Watching her approach, he said, "What the hell are you doing here?"

"Hello, Cat McDonald."

"Get off my ranch!" he shouted, adjusting his Stetson's brim so that it shadowed more of his face.

"Why are you so angry?"

"Because you rode here uninvited."

"If I remember rightly, the last time you visited me it was without an invitation, thank God." She dismounted. "Would you like to know how your daughter fares?"

"No. Yes."

"Get down off your high horse, Cat. I don't cotton to shout at the sky."

"Cotton? Mighty plain talk for a rich lady, Mrs. Lytton."

"Mighty plain talk for a parlor house girl, too."

"What's that supposed to mean?"

670

"For years you believed I was a *fille de joie.*"

"Are you saying you're not a rich widow?"

"Certainly I'm wealthy. Is that a sin? I'm also very lonely."

"Tell me about my daughter," he said, dismounting.

"Tonnagay is very beautiful and very spoiled." Flo leaned against her saddle. "Are you pretending not to hear me? I said I was lonely."

"I suppose it gets downright lonesome to watch polo during the day, then drink and dance all night."

"I've never done those things, no matter what Luke says."

"How the hell do you know about Luke?"

"Percy."

"He has no right."

"He has every right, especially since he loves you too."

Cat picked a handful of grass and sifted it through his fingers. "Are you saying you love me, Fools Gold?"

"With all my heart."

"You have a strange way of showing it."

"I've never denied my love for you, Cat, not since the cave-in."

"You gave my child to another man!"

"I've made many mistakes, but regarding

Tonnagay, I had no choice." When he didn't reply, she placed her foot in the stirrup. "Well, I've said my piece." The mare pranced away. "Please help me up into the saddle. Why won't you come closer? Your scars?"

He spun around, facing the mountains. "I don't want to see your love become disgust."

She stared at his straight back and broad shoulders. "You can't possibly believe that. Do you think so little of me? Do you honestly think I fell in love with your face? Would you love me less if it were the other way around? Would you feel repelled if my ear was raggedy or my cheek scarred?"

"You turned away at the hospital. Even you couldn't look at —"

"Spit!"

"Spit?"

She heard the semblance of a smile in his voice. "Yes, spit. You were hurting and your hurt was my hurt. I turned away to hide my tears. I didn't want you to think I felt sorry for you. Look at me, Cat. If you see one flicker of disgust in my eyes, I'll ride away and leave you alone forever."

"Forever is a long, long time," he said, making an about-face.

The setting sun blinded her. She took a few steps forward until Cat's body tucked the sun out of sight. With a sigh, she took off his hat and tossed it aside.

Thick dark hair. Eyes the color of a summer leaf.

"Are you going to faint, Fools Gold?"

"I never faint . . . hardly ever . . . once."

On tiptoe, she caressed his face with her fingertips, ran her lips over his left cheek and chin, kissed each ridged scar, every white line of damaged tissue, until she found his mouth. Pulling away, she gasped for breath. "My legs don't have any strength, Cat. Oh, God, I want you so badly."

He swept her up into his arms. "Have you no shame, Fools Gold?"

"None. We've never loved on a bed before. Why should this time be different?"

"I'll make a bed for you." He walked toward a copse of trees, stopping every few steps to find her mouth and take her breath away.

"Hurry, Cat! No. Kiss me again. I can't wait to feel you inside me. I hope you can't wait, either."

But when he placed her on the thick bed of leaves, their haste diminished. Slowly, they removed every stitch of clothing. This time there would be no barriers between them, not even cotton, denim and leather.

He traced her soft curves while she tracked

his hard muscles. He caressed urgently, a Chinook wind. She responded fiercely, a mountain lion clawing at his back and shoulders.

When he would have waited, she incited his entry, arching her body to meet his. When he would have withdrawn, she twined her long legs about his waist, capturing him inside until his hot need began to build again.

"You little devil," he said, after she'd allowed him release.

"I'm only half alive without you, Cat. Without you, the world is a black-and-white movie, no color at all. Why does the darkness seem so much brighter now?"

"Darkness . . . night . . . we've lost the sun."

"No, my love, we've found it again."

Cat and Flo were married at Aguila del Oro. In attendance were Johanna and Steven Lytton, Alan and Dorothy Tassler, Jane Percival, Tonna, Percy, Sally, Lorenzo, Marylander and Jack. Cat's brother Daniel was in Rome and Mike wouldn't allow his newly pregnant Katie to travel the long distance. Lucas was not invited.

As Flo walked down the living-room aisle, she saw the right side of Cat's face, his flawless profile. *I prefer the left side,* she thought.

In a strange way, his scars were a cynosure that attracted rather than repelled. If Cat's face graced movie screens again, the two ladies in Cincinnati would probably faint from love, not fear.

Flo spoke her vows, thinking how most people spent their entire lives searching for gold, believing the discovery of the precious ore would buy happiness or health or harmony. Some took time to enjoy their dreams, like Kate and Mike, Jack, Lorenzo and Sally, and, at the end of his life, Edward. But some, like Ned and Suzy, kept searching, never content, never at peace.

During the reception that followed, while Cat danced with Marylander, Flo beckoned to Tonna and led her toward a newly constructed cottage.

Tonna smiled when she reached the bedroom. Spread across a white bedspread were fresh flowers: red roses, snapdragons, lilies and daisies. A wall mirror reflected the blooms.

"This is the house for your wedding journey?"

Flo felt her cheeks flush. "Cat and I plan to honeymoon in New York, visit Kate and Mike. Then we'll satisfy a promise Cat made and ride to the gold hilltops. I had this cottage furnished for you and Percy. When Cat agreed to live at Aguila del Oro, I thought you might be in danger. Lucas and his damned Ku Klux Klan. Cat loves you both so much, and so do I . . ." She paused, searching for the right words. "Would you prefer to live in the main house?"

Tonna walked to the bed, scooped up an armful of flowers, and hid her face within the exquisite blooms.

Flo wished Jack stood beside her. He'd want to memorize Tonna's beaded braids and dark eyes — oh, no! Tonna's eyes were filled with tears. Flo hugged her, crushing the flowers. "Why are you crying? I swear these aren't servants' quarters. Cat regards you and Percy as his parents. We have room for Percy's white horses and John McDonald's palominos, not to mention those stupid hogs. Cat will transfer the stock, despite Luke's threats, and we want Percy to be in charge. Won't you please think about it? I need you."

"The spirits did not bless me with children." Tears coursed, unheeded, down Tonna's smooth cheeks. "I've always felt Cat was my son. Dimity did not want him, was blind to the goodness of his soul. Now you offer me a chance to live next to my son. I do not know what to say."

"Say yes."

"My heart sings."

"Mine, too." Flo felt limp with relief. "Together we must banish the demons from Cat's mind. For starters, I've placed mirrors in every room. I have a feeling he thinks he married a very vain woman, but I don't care. We must exorcise Cherokee Bill's ghost."

Tonna stared directly at Flo. "Do you believe Cat the son of an outlaw?"

"I don't give a damn if he is or isn't, and I've told him so. Anyway, in the eyes of the law Cat's legitimate. He was born of legally married parents. Luke doesn't have a case, even though he claims to have found a new will. I believe it's a forgery and we'll prove it in court. I just don't want Cat waging war until he's secure about his appearance."

"Cat is as stubborn as the Chinook wind that fathered him. It will not be easy."

This time Flo didn't say "sure it will."

Tonna said, "May it be delightful, my house. From my head may it be delightful. To my feet may it be delightful. Where I lie may it be delightful. All above me may it be delightful. All around me may it be delightful."

"How beautiful," Flo breathed, awed.

"In the old days the Navajo would have a

celebration to bless their *hogan*. This cer-emony is known as the *gogan aiilan*. If not done, dreams plague the dwellers, tooth-aches visit, flocks dwindle, and the house will be *basic*."

"Taboo?"

"Yes." Tonna walked outside. "For a house blessing, friends gather to feast and smoke. The shaman warns the evil spirits away. There are many words, but my husband must share in the blessing and sprinkle corn meal."

"Will you teach me the words? I want to bless the house I now share with Cat."

"I will teach you the words tomorrow. I do not believe the spirits require you to play shaman on your wedding night."

Hours later, Flo climbed the staircase, entered the bedroom, and stared at the new four-poster. "Would you do me a great favor, Cat?"

"Sure."

"Grab the quilt from our bed and join me outside. There's a place near the stream, filled with wild flowers, protected by tall trees."

"You *cotton* to spend the nights of our marriage outdoors? I must warn you that a certain portion of my anatomy might freeze during the winter months."

"Just tonight, Cat. Please? I want to bless this house with Tonna's words before we bless our union inside. At any rate, we've never made love on a real bed." She grinned. "I'm not sure I know how."

Hand in hand, they stood in the hallway and listened for the sounds of silence. Like two errant children, they tiptoed downstairs and out the door and sprinted toward the woods.

The air smelled of spruce.

They gathered leaves, moss, grass, and, as one, sank down onto the spongy ground. Cat removed their clothes, wrapped the quilt loosely around their bodies, and ran his fingers over the swell of Flo's breasts.

"From your head may it be delightful," she murmured, returning his touch. "From your feet may it be delightful. Where we lie may it be delightful."

He penetrated and she reached toward the sky with both hands, as if she might capture a star. "Oh, Cat, my love, my life," she cried. "Delightful man."

AUTHOR POSTSCRIPT

My determination to present authentic history has necessitated a scrupulous adherence to the findings of research, but all names, characters and incidents are either products of my imagination or are used fictitiously. Based upon a solid framework of fact, I have never knowingly changed a date or circumstance, except for the date of the Gillette bullfight.

Although many historians seem to imply that filmmaking took a widespread leap from New Jersey to Hollywood, there were years in between when filmmakers were looking for the right scenery and lots of sunshine. H.H. "Buck" Buckwalter, an agent for the Selig-Polyscope Company of Chicago, made short films in Colorado from 1904 to 1909. Colonel Selig, himself, arrived in 1911 with cowboy star Tom Mix. Stories have been passed down about how Mix and his buddies would shoot lemons off the glasses in the local bar.

The most intriguing gamble of all was the creation of the Colorado Motion Picture Company. A tragic event in that company's brief history involved the drowning deaths of star Grace McHugh and cameraman Owen Carter during a river-crossing scene in the silent film, *Across the Border.* After reading about that incident, I began the intensive research that would lead to my writing of *Heaven's Thunder.*

ABOUT THE AUTHOR

Mary Ellen Dennis is the author of. *The Landlord's Black-Eyed Daughter* and *Stars of Fire.* When she was very young she developed a love for Alfred Noyes's poem, *The Highwayman,* and the *Angélique* series by Sergeanne Golon. Mary Ellen's fifth-grade teacher was gobsmacked to hear her rambunctious student state that someday she'd write novels inspired by her favorite poem and favorite series. It has taken years to achieve her goal, but Mary Ellen says, "If you drop a dream, it breaks" (a saying coined by author Denise Dietz). Mary Ellen, who lives on Vancouver Island with her chocolate Labrador retriever Magic, likes to hear from readers. Her e-mail address is maryellendennis@shaw.ca.